THE HERETIC LAND

Crewmen shouted, waves thudded into the ship as they swung booms and changed direction, harpoons hissed and whistled as they were fired, and three times something immense struck the vessel, impacts knocking Bon and the others down, wood creaking and metal bracings shrieking. The attack did not last for long, but Bon was far more afraid than he had expected. He was thinking of Leki in the neighbouring hold, and when after the second impact someone shouted that they'd been breached, he heard water hissing in and the cries of those drowning, and Bon dashed across to the separating wall. Banging on the wood, he shouted her name. Screamed it. It was only as an old man grabbed his arm to quieten him, and he pressed his ear to the wall, that he realised the hull had not been compromised at all.

Later, a guard opened the hatch and threw down several bags.

'What happened?' someone asked. 'Did they kill the spineback?'

'Kill it?' the guard scoffed. He slammed the hatch, laughing.

BY TIM LEBBON

Echo City
The Heretic Land

PO

THE HERETIC LAND

TIM LEBBON

www.orbitbooks.net

ORBIT

First published in Great Britain in 2012 by Orbit

A CIP catalogue record for this book
is available from the British Library.

ISBN 978-1-84149-938-3

Typeset in Times by
Palimpsest Book Production Limited, Falkirk, Stirlingshire

Printed and bound by CPI Group (UK) Ltd, Croydon, CR0 4YY

Papers used by Orbit are from well-managed forests
and other responsible sources.

 MIX
Paper from
responsible sources
FSC
www.fsc.org   FSC® C104740

Orbit
An imprint of
Little, Brown Book Group
100 Victoria Embankment
London EC4Y 0DY

An Hachette UK Company
www.hachette.co.uk

www.orbitbooks.net

'All the ancient histories . . . are just fables that have been agreed upon'

VOLTAIRE

PART ONE

RISE

Chapter 1

betrayals

After six days at sea, following a storm that almost swamped the ship, a waterspout that toyed with them for half a day, and an attack by sea scorps that left three crewmen swelling until their skin split and bones ruptured, it was the food that almost killed Bon Ugane.

'I mean it,' the woman said. He'd noticed her before, emerging from the second hold with other prisoners and walking the deck during exercise periods. He could hardly *not* notice her. But they had not spoken until now. 'Don't eat it. I've cooked flatfish all my life, and that one is diseased. The colour of the flesh, the texture . . .' She shrugged.

'There'll be nothing else from them today,' Bon said. His stomach was rumbling, and he'd already lost weight from hunger and sea sickness.

'So go hungry.'

He looked down at the meagre meal their guards had presented him with, watched and listened to the other prisoners chomping down on their fish, lifted it close to his nose to take a sniff, then tipped it over the railing.

3

'Here,' the woman said. She held out her plate to him. She'd already eaten most of the good meat. 'Go on.'

Bon scooped up the thin fins in one hand and stared at them. The woman paused in her chewing, offended. Bon smiled and ate, nodding his thanks as the stringy, spiky fins came apart in his mouth.

They'd been allowed up out of the holds to eat today. The sea rolled as waves clashed from two directions, colliding with thunderous impacts, flinging spray skyward to be caught by the easterly wind and blown stinging across the ship's deck. Wave tops rolled white, and flying fish drifted through the spray as they hunted unsuspecting prey. The sky was a deep, threatening grey, and far to the west the clouds had burst, rain falling in silent sheets. They'd only seen one spineback today, and rumour had it the last reported sighting of a deep pirate was a hundred miles east of here. This was as calm and safe as the Forsaken Sea ever was, and the crew's good cheer had filtered across to the usually gruff, hard guards.

The dozen guards leaned against the railing or strolled the deck in pairs, casual, chatting, weapons sheathed. They were recruited from the Steppe clans that lived across Alderia's central regions, where the Harcrassyan Mountains and Chasm Cliffs ravaged the landscape and effectively divided the continent in two. The tallest, strongest people on Alderia – with stocky limbs for negotiating slopes, and vicious teeth for catching prey whilst clinging to rock faces – through the years those generations that left their challenging hunting heritage behind had naturally found their way into the military. Most worked for regional armies or the prison ships, and those few that excelled might even find their way into the Spike, the Ald's own expansive personal defence force. Bon had always found an irony in Alderia's ruling elite requiring their own guard, when they professed to encourage freedom and peace for all.

'What's your name?' he asked after he'd managed to swallow the remains of the fins.

'Name?' the woman asked. 'Oh, so we're straight onto the formalities. Name, where am I from, what did I do that put me on this ship? Life fucking story. But I left all that behind. We're all heading for a new life.'

Perhaps she saw Bon's face drop a little, because her rant faded almost as soon as it had begun.

'My life's been this shit for years,' he said. He smiled, not to show that he was joking, but that he could live with it.

The woman smiled back. 'Lucky you. Head start.'

'And I know where you're from,' Bon said.

'Is it so obvious?' She held up one splayed hand, the thin webs between her long fingers almost transparent.

'I thought your sort might just jump overboard and escape.'

She looked at him for some time, expressionless, eyes never leaving his face. He glanced away first, and when he looked back she was still staring.

'My sort?' she asked at last.

'Amphys,' Bon said.

'Well, at least you use the polite name. Most just call us floaters.' She glanced around at the other prisoners sat across the deck – one woman had tried standing when they'd first been brought up, and had been kicked back down by a guard – and she and Bon shared a silent moment. It was strange. He had not felt truly comfortable in a woman's presence since his wife's death, and now he was sitting with this amphy stranger and feeling more settled than he had since they'd left Alderia's coast on their journey north towards banishment. Maybe it was her straightforward manner, her easy way of talking. Or perhaps it was the hint of exoticism that all amphys held for him, and had done ever since his parents had first welcomed an amphy friend into their home thirty years before. Many people hated them because they were different, or more graceful than most, or often simply because hating came easy to some.

'Lechmy Borle,' she said, holding out her hand palm up. 'Leki to my friends. Haven't got many of those on board, that's for sure.'

'Bon Ugane,' Bon said. He pressed his hand to hers, and they pushed against each other. It was a formal greeting, but their smiles diluted some of the formality.

'I can't just jump and swim,' Leki said. 'A distant cousin of mine was arrested and deported seven years ago. He jumped ship a day out and was never seen again.'

'Maybe he swam along the coast, made a new life for himself?'

'He's dead. The bone sharks got him, or some other wild-life. Or the deep pirates. They come that far south, sometimes, if pickings are thin to the north. Or more likely he drowned.'

'Drowned?'

'We're good swimmers,' Leki said. 'I can hold my breath for a lot longer than you. But we're not fucking fish.'

Bon chuckled. It felt good, and he thought it was simply because he was talking to someone like a person for the first time in days. Other prisoners had engaged him in conversation, but it was always light, and rarely developed into anything more than cautious platitudes. The disgraced Fade priest in his hold seemed immune to anyone's efforts to enter into conversation. Bon wondered what the priest had done to deserve this, and how he had offended Alderia's official Fade religion. But when Bon had approached, he had not even lifted his eyes. The guards spoke sometimes. But even those who were more fair and reasonable would not grow familiar with the prisoners, because they knew what was to become of them.

'They say it's two more days to Skythe,' Bon said.

'And the worst of the storms are always closer to the Duntang Archipelago.'

'Great. I think I've already vomited everything that's not tied down.'

Leki laughed silently. He watched her as she glanced away, eyeing her up and down. The amphys had always fascinated him, and it went way beyond their webbed hands and feet, and their wider chests that contained the larger lungs. It was the less obvious differences that he found more compelling. They were all blue-eyed, a trait unique to them. They were usually taller than the northern Alderians, and though their limbs were streamlined, they were much stronger. They wore clothing only out of water, and they were always loose and flowing, their natural grace matching the swish of cloth. Their favoured material was sea-spider silk, shimmering with a rainbow of colours from the natural oils. Waterproof, strong and light, their clothing was one of the amphys' main exports from Alderia's three southern states.

Leki was dressed in a dirty, shapeless jacket and trousers, with a heavy belt and clumsily stitched leather boots. She'd probably lost her own clothes the moment she was arrested.

Bon was intrigued, but he had no wish to be pushy. If her story came naturally, he would be interested to hear. If not, it made little difference. He was simply grateful that she had spoken to him at all. It almost made him believe he had a future.

'They'll be putting put us back in the holds soon,' Bon said. 'Maybe we should try—'

'Spineback,' Leki said softly.

'Where?'

'About three miles to port.'

'Must be big if you can see it that far out.' He stretched up to see past Leki, out over the port railings and across the angry grey ocean. He spied nothing, and feared she was teasing. He didn't know her.

Then one of the three lookouts up in the skynests sounded his horn twice, and the deck erupted into chaos. Crewmen dashed back and forth, and the guards started urging the prisoners back towards the two ladders leading down into the holds.

'It *is* a big one,' Leki said as she and Bon stood together. 'But don't worry.'

As they were parted and shoved towards different ladders, Bon turned to look past his fellow prisoners and their animated guards. He spotted the shimmer of weak sunlight on a spine-back's slick skin, and seeing the upright spikes along its back from this distance meant they must be taller than a man. The huge beast was cutting through the waves towards them, and occasionally it reared up, revealing a wide head and heavily toothed mouth. *How can she tell me not to worry?* he thought.

'Get a shift on!' a guard growled, and Bon obeyed. The fear was palpable – prisoners hurried, guards shouted, and the activity across and above the ship's deck was frantic. Harpoon guns were uncovered, and heavy, glass-tipped harpoons were loaded, the guns' steam mechanisms pumped and primed. Sails billowed, booms swung, rigging creaked and whipped as the ship turned to face the threat, offering a narrower target for the spineback to tear through. The crew started singing a strange song in their own seafaring language, a bastardisation of Alderian blended with the ancient languages found written in western coastal caves. The song beseeched Venthia, the Fade god of water, to help them. Bon did not believe in Alderia's Fade religion and its seven deities, and yet he found great irony in this – the crew prayed to a god which even devout Faders contended had vanished from the Forsaken Sea at the time of the Skythian War six centuries before. Sending criminals across such godless waters was the Ald's favourite way of getting rid of them.

Silent, resigned, Bon caught one last glimpse of Leki as she was ushered down into the second hold. She was not looking his way. That gave him a surprising stab of loss, and his heart was in confusion. On the ship until now, he had given no thought to his fate. Life for him was over.

The hold grating slammed shut, locking them inside. Excited, frightened chatter filled the shadows. The roar of the approaching giant sent shockwaves through the sea and against the prison ship's hull. The Fade priest sat silent and motionless. And as he waited for the end, all Bon could think was, *I want to see her again.*

Bon's hold was not completely dark. Many of the prisoners had brought candles, and the fifteen other deportees down there with him listened to the chaos with flickering flames reflected in their wide, frightened eyes.

Crewmen shouted, waves thudded into the ship as they swung booms and changed direction, harpoons hissed and whistled as they were fired, and three times something immense struck the vessel, impacts knocking Bon and the others down, wood creaking and metal bracings shrieking. The attack did not last for long, but Bon was far more afraid than he had expected. He was thinking of Leki in the neighbouring hold, and when after the second impact someone shouted that they'd been breached, he heard water hissing in and the cries of those drowning, and Bon dashed across to the separating wall. Banging on the wood, he shouted her name. Screamed it. It was only as an old man grabbed his arm to quieten him, and he pressed his ear to the wall, that he realised the hull had not been compromised at all.

Later, a guard opened the hatch and threw down several bags.

'What happened?' someone asked. 'Did they kill the spineback?'

'Kill it?' the guard scoffed. He slammed the hatch, laughing, and the prisoners went about sharing out the food.

As Bon ate he looked around at the others. Before today he'd had little interest in them. But the closer they drew to the huge island of Skythe – a hundred miles from east to west, and its northern limits unknown – the more he began to wonder. Some would be political dissidents like him, banished by Alderia's rulers, the Ald, for questioning their word and the tenets of their rule. Others could be religious exiles sent away for being too vocal in their own beliefs; some fringe religions were allowed, but if they actively challenged belief in the Fade they had gone too far. Perhaps there were murderers, rapists, or terrorists. He would not ask, and few people seemed willing to betray their crimes. They might all be classed as criminals by the Ald, but in many cases that would be all they had in common.

In one corner he saw several people praying to the seven Fade gods, changing position, prayers and tone for each deity. Bon felt what he always felt when confronted with such a scene – a faintly painful nostalgia for his childhood years when his parents had made him pray, and a vague sense of disgust. He knew things that, if proven, would expose the Fade for the lie it was. *Many* people knew. His crime was in believing them.

He glanced again at the Fade priest, hunkered beneath dark robes and staring down at the deck between his knees. The man was quite young, handsome, but his face was etched with bitterness. One side of it was bruised, his lips split and scabbed. He rested his hands on his bent knees, and the finger on his right hand that should have borne a priest's Fade ring was missing. The stump was roughly bandaged. The wound was recent.

Bon crawled across closer to the priest. Even as he moved he berated himself, because he had no wish to become involved with anyone down here. *Except Leki*, he thought.

'Fuck off,' the priest said. Bon paused and sat back against a heavy timber brace.

'Not a typical greeting from a priest,' Bon said. He sighed and leaned his head back against the bracing. He could feel the impact of sea against hull transmitted through his skull, and each shiver or thud brought Skythe close.

'I used to believe,' Bon said, softly, quietly. The priest did not respond, and Bon felt that he was talking to himself. 'It's traditional. You're brought up that way, and my parents never gave me any cause to doubt. Seven gods of the Fade, each of them watching over us, demanding prayer and fealty in return for wellbeing . . . it sounds so attractive. So comforting. I had no reason *not* to believe.' He snorted. 'How stupid. I'm so glad I saw the light.'

'And in that light, darkness,' the priest said. His voice was gravelly, older than his years.

'No,' Bon said. 'Enlightenment.'

'The Fade provides,' the priest said, intoning a familiar prayer. 'From before time, the Fade has watched the world for us, and now watches over us. All hail the seven gods.' He lifted his hand and kissed the space between fingers where the missing digit had once resided, his eyes closed and his face almost serene.

'But you're here,' Bon said.

'You think because I'm a priest I must have been banished

for betraying my faith. Which means you're as much a fool as anyone else on this damned vessel.'

'Then why are you—?'

'Every moment, I pray to the Fade to send a deep pirate to take us down and consume us all,' the priest said.

'You must have done something terrible,' Bon whispered, staring at the man's mutilated hand.

'Fuck off,' the priest said again. 'Take your heathen heart away from me.'

Bon wanted to protest, and argue, and tell the priest what a fool he must be for still believing in a religion that had done nothing to save him. But the priest closed his eyes and breathed in deeply, praying and finding comfort. Alone, Bon crawled away and sat in the shadows. He had only his own company for the rest of that night, and as usual he found it wanting.

They were not let out for another exercise session that evening. They could hear some pained crying from far away, and Bon guessed that some of the crew or guards had been injured in the spineback attack. It was said that the creatures were infected with poisonous, fist-sized parasites, which were known to infect some of those vessels they came into contact with. As darkness fell outside, occasional shouts, running footsteps, and the sound of crossbows firing seemed to bear out that tale.

Bon bedded down. All but one candle was blown out, and in the darkness he heard the sound of a couple rutting, and someone else muttering insane words as the Forsaken Sea rocked them into sleep.

The silent priest was comforted by his gods.

Bon was already leaning on the starboard railing and silently observing the damage to the ship when Leki's hold was opened the following morning. Crew members worked to fix several shattered lengths of the port railing, and two of the smallest sailors were being lowered down against the ship's hull to effect repairs. There was hammering and shouting, but none of the singing of the previous afternoon. There were now six lookouts in the skynests, and two extra harpoons had been rigged alongside the four already there.

The ship's sails were full, and the rolling sea seemed for once to be accommodating their direction. North was grey and obscured by mist, and somewhere beyond that mist lay the forbidding island of Skythe.

The guards unbolted the second hold, and Leki was the fifth person out. She squinted against the dazzling light, looking around the ship until she saw Bon. Then she smiled.

At me, Bon thought as she walked slowly towards him. The prisoners already knew that sudden movements were ill-advised. Escape was impossible, and the guards might appear relaxed, but they were always ready for an attack.

'I'm famished,' he said.

'Good. A woman in my hold has been stinking the place out all night. Bad flatfish. She might survive, but . . .' Leki shrugged. It set her hair moving, and Bon found that he liked that. She rubbed her eyes and yawned, stretched, pulling her clothing tight across her wide shoulders.

'I've heard about spinebacks, but never thought I'd see one. Never thought we'd be *attacked* by one.'

'The Forsaken Sea is full of monsters,' Leki said. 'They made it that way.' She leaned on the railing beside Bon looking out, and he turned so that they faced the same way.

'You mean the Skythians?' he asked softly. 'Do you really believe they corrupted their own sea?'

'Don't you?' Leki glanced sidelong at him, smiling. This was heretical talk.

'It's what we're told,' he said, uncertain how much he could trust her. It could be that, like the priest, she was a devout Fader, sent here for crimes completely different from his. Discussing his beliefs less than a day after meeting her might not be the best start to a friendship. Wearing his own beliefs on his sleeve, blasphemous and seditious as they were, might get him killed. And though there was a time when he would not have minded that, it was, ironically, since boarding this ship and meeting this woman that his mind had begun to change.

'Whoever did it, it was a long time ago,' she said, dismissing questions of gods and beliefs, tradition and society, with one wave of her webbed hand. 'There are whirlpools that have lasted for centuries, mists that melt flesh from bone, flying fish with two mouths and no brains. The bone sharks are just that – sharks made of bone and cartilage – and they shouldn't live and swim, but do. Knowing who did all that wouldn't change the fact that this sea *is* corrupted. And Venthia hasn't made it her home for centuries.' She shrugged, smiled at him, then turned and walked across the deck towards where a breakfast of bread and smoked fish was being handed out.

She believes in Venthia? Bon wondered. But not only was he unsure, he also didn't think it mattered. Many of his best friends had been devout, believing in things he found bemusing. While he had kept his own frowned-upon beliefs quiet, some of them had sensed his doubts, but their friendships had mostly remained. Mostly.

He followed her and they ate breakfast together. Though sentenced by their homeland to a life of banishment upon a dying island, for that short time they were content in each other's company. The constant rolling sea had settled in Bon's guts, and he was sure it would take many days of shore time for it to settle. But he was no longer throwing up everything he ate. He was already adapting to life beyond Alderia.

14

Bon and Leki found a spot by the railing where they sat and talked as other prisoners were allowed to stroll around the deck. They exercised their minds while others exercised their limbs and bodies, and when the time came for them to be locked up again, the guards did not seem to notice that they descended into the same hold.

There they sat, talking quietly in the subdued lighting, their voices a murmur against the constant pounding of waves against the hull, other prisoners' talk and sometimes shouts, and the footsteps of their guards overhead. Destined to deportation, locked away, Bon thought it was some time since he had felt so free. He told Leki about his beautiful wife falling from a tower to her death, and how her passing had seemed to darken his skies and blur his horizons. He told her about his son, Venden, and the boy's fascination with Skythe – its history, the old war, and what had become of that once-proud island state afterwards – and how Bon's own studies of Skythe had become an obsession following Venden's death.

'He was taken and murdered,' Bon said.

'The Ald deport, they don't murder.'

'I didn't say it was the Ald.' Bon sighed. He frequently relived his losses – staring into an unknown distance whilst awake, and trying to catch his falling wife and rescue his vanished son as he slept.

'Then who?' Leki asked.

'Venden was a . . . genius, I suppose. Our only child. He developed very quickly, could read by the time he was four. My wife wanted to send him south to Lakeside for schooling, but I wanted him home with us, and he went to dayschool in Gakota. I walked him there every morning, and collected him every evening.' Bon drifted for a while, remembering those walks out from their village of Sefton Breaks along the

Ton River, Venden asking questions all the time and stopping to examine plants and insects, always delicate, careful not to hurt them. Then on the way home he would relate what he had learned that day, and it wasn't long past his sixth birthday that he would start questioning some of the things he had been taught. Bon had been surprised at first, and then calmly approving. *A priest came in today*, Venden said once, skimming stones across the river. Bon had nodded, letting his son find his own time to continue. *He said that there are gods in the water and the air, and in fire, and in rock and the mind. But . . . what about in my hair? And in river mud? And the clouds in the air, and a bird's feathers? There can't be a god in* everything*, can there, Daddy?*

The seven gods of the Fade, Bon had replied, and fear drove a spike into him, because he was simply repeating all the things he had been taught. It was a painful sensation, answering his own unspoken doubt. Venden had stared at him expecting more, and Bon could identify that moment as when he knew that his son was different. *He'll find his own way*, he thought. *Whatever I tell him, whatever I say now or later, his mind is his own to make up.* That had made him proud, and a little afraid.

'He was marked for special schooling very early on, and at first I was resistant. I didn't want to hold him back, but I was also . . . mistrustful of some of those wanting to school him. I know what sometimes happens to people like him, and I was afraid. Of course I was. I'm his father.'

'What sometimes happens?' Leki asked, and she sounded so innocent.

Bon looked at her in the faint light, but it was difficult to make out her expression. Besides, he did not know her at all, and doubted he could read her. 'Have you never been to New Kotrugam?'

16

Leki laughed, and a few pale faces turned her way. There was not much laughter in the holds.

'Only for my sentencing,' she said. 'And then I was blind-folded and carried inside a prison wagon. No windows, no air. I saw nothing but the inside of a prison and a courtroom.'

'An amazing city,' Bon said. 'I'll tell you all about it one day.'

'No need,' Leki said lightly. 'It's in the past now. So, what were you afraid of for Venden?'

'I was afraid they'd send him down into the depths,' Bon said. 'You do know the story of why New Kotrugam is new?'

'Of course. The fireball from the gods. Shore and Flaze combining to punish Kotrugam for its sins, wiping it from the world, seeding New Kotrugam as a perfected model of the old, tainted city.'

'Yeah, the gods,' Bon said. He watched Leki as he did so, but there was no reaction. 'Something fell from the sky, from the space beyond the world, and wiped out the ancient city. You can see evidence all over. What do you think the city walls are? Why is New Kotrugam so much lower than the surrounding landscape?'

Leki only shrugged.

'The city lies in an impact crater,' Bon said, and verbalising the forbidden story gave him a thrill. He glanced at the priest across the hold, head bowed, apparently sleeping. Another man leaned close to listen, and Bon no longer cared. They were all criminals here. 'The city walls are where the ground was rippled from the blast, rocks and dust and the smashed remains of Old Kotrugam thrown up and landing in concentric rings around the hole it made in the world. I'm certain that's the truth, though it's hidden. That's what happened, though it denies the Fade. So people are scared of the truth.'

'You're talking very loudly,' Leki said.

'Does that scare you?' Bon asked. He leaned in close enough to smell her for the first time.

'Where were you afraid that they would send your son?' she asked quietly.

'Down. Beneath the city, into the catacombs. It's said that whatever annihilated Old Kotrugam is buried down there still, and sometimes senior Fade priests choose an exceptional child from outlying communities to venture down and commune with it. The story they reveal is that they're communicating with the gods. But they know.'

'You're suggesting that they lie,' Leki said.

'Of *course* they lie, about everything! Isn't that why you're here? Because you doubt the lie?'

Leki blinked slowly. 'You feared for Venden,' she prompted.

'They send them down, and when these people finally surface again they're dying, skin boiling, flesh melting. The priests write down all their mad ravings and translate them as messages from the Fade. And I thought . . . I thought Venden might be chosen.'

'But he wasn't,' Leki said. 'So what *did* happen to him?'

'He was accepted into the Guild of Inventors,' Bon said.

'Even *I've* heard of them.' Leki sounded impressed, but her voice remained uncertain, balanced. She already knew that this tale did not end well.

'He was as pleased as me. He was still a child really, even at thirteen, because he spent more time inside his own head than outside with friends or girls. A tutor was assigned him, and once every moon this man made the trip from New Kotrugam to Venden's school in Gakota. He set Venden tasks, which he completed easily. He asked him for research contemplations on some of the constructs and devices being investigated by the Guild, and more than once the tutor told me some of Venden's ideas had been incorporated. But all the while, his true interest lay elsewhere. He didn't want to invent, he wanted to investigate. And he did, every chance he had. Investigating Skythe, and the Skythian War, and he believed *nothing* he was being told.'

'Strange, a boy so young interested in something so old.'

'Perhaps,' Bon said. He fell silent, closing his eyes and remembering one of the last times he'd set eyes on his son. Venden had been sitting at the table in their small kitchen, a construct in pieces before him. He was placing each piece precisely in size order, from the smallest washers, to gasp valves, to steam cells and stark gills, concentrating so hard that he had not noticed his father watching. And beside the deconstructed device – Bon never had known its intent, and had never seen it remade – was a single, old parchment, little wider than Venden's hand. The designs were a mystery to Bon, but Venden moved his finger just above the parchment and whispered unknown words. He was not translating, but reading. Bon coughed. Venden stood and knocked the chair over, and snatched the parchment from the table. Even when he saw that it was his father, he hid the thing behind his back.

'The Guild found out,' Leki said.

'The next day Venden walked to school on his own, without even saying goodbye. I'd missed those morning walks along the river with him, but he was growing older, and . . . and a boy and his father, they drift apart. You understand? Independence is a lonely thing.

'I know from his few friends that he reached the school. And after that, I know nothing. Venden vanished. The school could tell me nothing, other than he'd been growing more distant and difficult to communicate with. His teacher told me she'd put that down to his Guild involvement.'

'And the Guild?'

'I wrote to them many times. No reply. I made three journeys to New Kotrugam to visit them. Each time it was the same – two days riding there, two days waiting in one of the Guild's contact offices with no result, two days back. They never even acknowledged to me that Venden had been one of their students. I was invisible to them.' Bon shook his head and leaned back against the bulkhead.

'You never found . . .?'

'His body? No. But the Guild would have disposed of him well.'

'And since then you've been following his research.'

'I found a box in the wall of his room. It was filled with books, parchments, maps and testaments. And other things, dangerous and rare. There was even . . .' He trailed off, shaking his head gently. The ship jarred as a heavy wave struck, and people around them cried out in fear. But this was only the sea.

'You can trust me,' Leki said.

'Like I trusted my friends?'

'You were betrayed?'

Bon nodded and sighed. 'As a young man, I was a bookbinder, but I've been interested in history, too. Skythe's especially. The histories we're told, and those that others claim to be true. They fascinated me. And so following what Venden had been researching felt like the right thing to do. A way to honour him. Everything I did was dedicated to him, and I continued his notes from where he'd left them, transcribing accounts in the old Skythian tongue, analysing stolen secrets that smelled old but still persisted. I was never . . .' He waved a hand dismissively. 'Never quite as dedicated as him, perhaps. I would go through phases of study, and longer periods when the box was shut away again and I barely even existed.' His voice had grown weak, swallowed by those dark, lethargic times.

'And then?'

'A stupid mistake. I left the box open and its contents spread to view. I received a visit from a volunteer for the local Fade church. I'd never seen her before; just bad luck. She was knocking on doors. *Do you believe enough? Do you pay homage as you should?*' He trailed off again, anger stealing his voice.

'She saw something she shouldn't have.'

The story needed no ending, and Bon felt sick from the recollections. He wished the sea would whip into a storm and make him vomit. Wished the spineback would return and carve the ship in two, giving him a reason for his sadness, his hopelessness. They were familiar wishes. Often, he contemplated his own death with nothing but relief.

'You're not convinced he's dead, are you?' she asked.

'Of course not,' Bon whispered. 'What sort of a father would I be if I just gave up?'

Leki placed her hand on his leg and squeezed, and her warmth was a shock to him. It was a tender contact, friendly, not sexual. He took great comfort from it.

'So what about you?' he asked.

Leki's eyes glimmered in the candlelight. But she did not reply.

'Leki?'

She leaned her head on his shoulder, hand still resting on his. Her warmth bled into him.

'My story is complicated, and for another time,' she said. 'For now, we have a harsh night ahead of us.'

What do you mean? Bon thought, but he did not ask. He had no wish to discuss with her what harshness might come. Right then, he was living the closest thing to a calm, perfect moment that he had experienced for years.

He closed his eyes and relished the time.

*   *   *

All through that terrible night, Bon Ugane wondered just how Leki had known.

The seas rose, hurling the ship into the valleys between waves, crashing down upon it, water pouring into the holds through deck gratings. With the water came stinging things, hand-sized crustaceans bearing whip-claws that scuttled across the floor, clicking and hissing. One old man was stung on the foot and he started screaming, hacking at his appendage with a knife in an attempt to open it up and let out the scorching pain. The prisoners started a stomping dance. Shells crunched. The screaming continued until the man fainted away, and another man started tending his wounds.

On deck, there was more screaming as the crew and guards tackled the results of wave after wave. Candles were extinguished. The ship rolled, and in the darkness more people were stung.

Bon and Leki stayed closed, pressed together when they could, trying to hold hands if they were flung from their seats. They did not talk for most of the night, because the sea's roaring was too loud, and the need to speak too slight. Touch was communication enough.

Other things boarded the ship. Bon heard them against the sides of the hull, a thud followed by the splintering of wood as they climbed from the sea up onto deck. Shouts, running, scampering, fighting, it soon became impossible to distinguish one noise from another. And all the while the sea roared against the hull from all sides, its endless noise bearing witness to events no one could see.

In the darkest part of the night, when clouds blocked the pale moonlight and the ship dropped from wave to wave, something caressed the back of Bon's hand. He thought it was Leki, so he reached out. He touched something wet and hard, and then a piercing pain erupted in the fleshy part of his thumb.

Bon screamed as his vision turned white with agony. He reached for his knife, because to remove his hand was the only escape from this pain, surely, the only way to remove the fire?

Something knocked him sideways. He fell from consciousness, and the ship faded away.

In Bon's dreams, his son Venden – older now, almost an adult – waited with a giant, unnatural shadow at his back.

'Bon,' the voice said, and it was calm and confident. 'Bon, we're almost there, and if they fling you into the sea like this, you'll drown.' He kept his eyes closed for a little while longer, enjoying the darkness that hid away everything that might have happened.

Then the pain in his hand kicked in, and he had to open his eyes.

'That hurts so much I think I'm going to puke.'

'Puke now, then. Get it all up. We've got a long swim ahead.'

'Swim?' He looked up at Leki where she must have been sitting beside him ever since he'd passed out. Then he glanced around the hold at the other prisoners. They were afraid, expectant, alert, their eyes wide and heavier clothing tied into clumps at their feet. All but the priest, who remained in the same place and pose as before. 'Swim?' he asked again.

'You think they land us on the island?' a young man close to the hatch said. 'I'm amazed they've gone in this far. Lillium's tits, half of us won't make it to the beach.' Someone in the shadows gasped, though at the man's blasphemy or his prediction, Bon could not tell.

'Come on,' Leki said. 'They've got to deal with the other hold first.'

'What about the other hold?'

Leki helped him to his feet without answering, examining his hand, then tugging at his heavy jacket. The less they wore, the easier it would be to swim. Several had stripped completely, and they stood pale and vulnerable in the weak light.

'Something got in,' the young man said when no one else answered. 'We heard it. Heard *them*.' He shook his head and reached up for the hatch, rattling it in its frame. Eager to get out, move on.

Bon caught Leki's eye, and she looked grim.

His hand was bound tightly in a soft white cloth, wound several times then tied in a knot. It throbbed beneath the binding, sending warm waves of pain up his arm to nestle in his shoulder.

'Sorry I hit you,' Leki said.

The hatch rattled open, and Bon grabbed his loose jacket and boots. She'd knocked him out to stop him cutting off his own hand. Then she'd sat and tended him. As the guard shouted down at them – *Up you come, bastards, paradise awaits!* – he could not help but wonder why.

There was a pile of corpses on deck. The surviving prisoners from the other hold stood at the railing, huddled close together and shivering in their nakedness. There were only six of them left. The corpses were swollen and blackened with poison, and some of them showed evidence of something having chewed at them. Above the corpses, three spiky shapes hung from the rigging. The killers, Bon guessed. Sea creatures as large as a man, with sharp limbs and stinging things, liquid eyes and mandibles still caked with the dried blood and flesh of their victims.

'Over there!' one of the guards shouted, pointing at the prisoners at the railing. 'Get them off! What are you waiting for, the Fade's blessing? Get them *off* there!'

North of the anchored ship, waves broke against a rocky

shore. It was a rugged, seemingly uninhabited coastline, stark and windswept, and the few trees Bon could see were skeletal and tall, their branches whipping the air with long spiked leaves. Two dark shapes moved back and forth across the beach, but from this distance he could not tell whether they were human. Behind the beach the land rose steadily inland, and a veil of mist hid whatever lay beyond.

Two guards edged closer to the huddled prisoners, swords drawn, and started nudging them over the side.

Bon gasped, and a chill went through him. A woman shouted an objection, and the guard in charge stormed forward, leaning down to press his face close to hers, forcing her back against the cabin wall. 'You swim with all your limbs, or we hold you down and cut one off, and *then* you swim. You decide.'

He's done that before, Bon thought, and the chill settled in him. He could smell the dead bodies – blood, insides, shit, and the acid stench of something that might have been the poison that had killed them.

'You and you,' the guard said, pointing to the angry young man and an older, stooped man. 'The bodies go over the side. Don't touch the bites.' He laughed, surprisingly high and light. 'Wouldn't want you hurting yourselves.'

As the two men approached the dead prisoners, Bon and the others were edged towards the railing. The naked prisoners were already swimming for shore, two of them striking out confidently for the rocky, violent coast, the others struggling in the surf. They thrashed against the water and went under when the large waves broke over them, just gathering themselves in time for the next wave.

Something bobbed on the waves closer to the beach.

'Don't let go of me,' Leki said, 'and try not to swallow any water.'

Bon nodded. They held hands. He only hoped the guards did not decide to cut off one of her limbs anyway, to try and disadvantage her.

As they reached the railing, Bon glanced back. The guards were gathered behind them, smiling, unconcerned. The crew went about their business as if nothing was happening, but a couple glanced their way, faces drawn. Whether they were saddened at what they saw, or concerned that they needed to be underway, Bon would never know.

The priest was also there. He stood at the back of the grouped prisoners, staring out past Bon at Skythe's coast. His expression was unreadable. Bon wondered what he had done, or what beliefs or opinions had led to this, and suddenly he wanted to know more than anything. He tried to catch the priest's eye. But the younger man seemed to see nothing.

Nudged forward to climb the railing, he turned to look towards Skythe. Here was the island he had never thought he would see; the place that had fascinated Venden, and which had then become Bon's curse. A land where a great civilisation had lived and died, and the disputed cause of its demise six centuries before was the reason he was here now. The Ald maintained that Skythe had launched an unprovoked attack south against Alderia, seeking dominance over that continent in the name of their heathen god Aeon. When their attack was countered by Alderian opposition, the Skythians unveiled their ultimate weapon – a plague, cultured from a distant Outer island and intended solely for war. It backfired, infecting tens of thousands of Skythians, driving them to a murderous frenzy. The Alderian story called these infected people Kolts, and they had destroyed their civilisation as the plague polluted their island and its surrounding waters. Alderia only survived because of the ocean between them – the Kolts were mindless with rage, and could not sail or swim.

That was the official story, at least.

And yet Bon had seen the evidence that refuted this account. Evidence that spoke of the Ald's ancestors actually being the aggressors, attacking Skythe because of the physical manifestation of Skythe's god, and destroying Aeon with forbidden magic. The Ald could not accept that their entire Fade religion was built upon falsehood, and so they set out to destroy the very thing that brought doubts upon it. Aeon died, and the murderous Kolts were the result.

There was so much fear, rumour and obfuscation over that ancient war that Bon could not understand why more people did not question it. But he supposed fear itself was a great motivator.

Leki touched his hand, and her skin was still warm. 'We'll go under,' she said. 'Hold your breath, exhale slowly through your nose. Don't thrash or panic. It'll be easier for me to swim underwater and pull you along.'

'But the things in the water . . .'

'We're quite close to shore,' she said uncertainly. 'Quite.'

'Just don't forget I can't hold my breath as long as you,' Bon said.

Leki kept her eyes on him as she dropped her trousers, and in one fluid motion lifted the jacket up and over her shoulders, leaving only her undergarments. He tried not to, but he could not help glancing at her heavy breasts, her flat stomach. His sudden thrill of desire was so out of place that he chuckled.

'Welcome to Skythe,' the lead guard said, and Bon felt a meaty hand strike him between the shoulders.

They fell towards the angry Forsaken Sea, and as he struck the surface he squeezed Leki's hand. The water closed over his head, flooding his mouth and nose and ears, stinging his eyes, the cold snatching his breath away, and he thought of all the stories he had heard of this dreaded ocean. None of them were good, and most involved biting things.

Leki's fingers were long and tight, seeming to envelop his hand entirely, and when Bon opened his eyes she was a pale blur beside him. Above, poor light lit the sea's violent surface, and below and around him clouds of sand and sediment swirled to the sea's pulse. He breathed out gently through his nose, and the bubbles seemed to fall rather than rise. He gasped more bubbles of surprise, then saw that down was up, and the faint light was actually splayed across the ocean's uneven bed. Thousands of fish sparkled with throbbing light, creating a display that was both beautiful and hypnotic.

Leki tugged at his hand and started swimming for shore. Bon kicked, trying to help, but it was her own sinuous movements – body flexing, feet kicking, spare hand sweeping water behind her – that powered them through the water.

Bon started to struggle. His vision darkened, and Leki lifted them up to break the surface. The sudden roar and violence of the sea was shocking, and people shouted for help, and behind it all there was a voice calling—

Leki took him down and started swimming again.

A shape waved through the sea towards them. It was a silhouette with fine fins, twisting like a snake and always seeming to dance just out of Bon's view. It might have been as long as his hand or the length of the ship, and then he felt a dull stab on his ankle and the thing was flitting away again.

Leki paused and turned before him, floating effortlessly in the water. She leaned forward and touched his leg, and then Bon noticed the cloud of blood pulsing from the bite. Like shadows cast by the spreading cloud, more snake-creatures were arcing in towards him.

Leki flicked out a hand and caught a creature, and even as it whipped itself around her hand, head thrashing and pale

28

teeth exposed, she bit it in half and shook its spasming parts away from her. She let go of Bon and pushed him back from her, snatching at shapes as silent waves broke above their heads. She kicked as well, each movement shifting her in the water so that she performed a graceful dance as she fought the biting things.

Bon let himself rise, needing to breathe again. Through his blurred vision he could see the roaring waves smashing overhead, carrying vague shapes that might or might not have been his fellow prisoners. And just for a moment he held back, not wishing to subject himself to the violence up there again.

But then Leki was with him once more, grasping his belt and hauling him after her as she surfaced.

Bon gasped in several deep breaths. They were closer to the rocky beach than the ship now, and the vessel was already making sail. A wave smashed over them, Bon spluttered and spat water from his mouth, and a body was rolled past them in the sea's embrace. It was a woman, her dark flowing hair mimicking the blood staining the water around her. Her body was battered, head caved in from some impact. And there were bites.

Leki pulled him down again. As they dived, Bon caught one last glimpse of the waves breaking onto the rocky shore, and the beach beyond. There were prisoners in the waves, some clambering across the rocks towards the beach, a few seemingly as looselimbed as the dead woman. One of them reached shore and staggered up the beach, passing the two large, dark shapes seeming to stand guard. They were human-shaped, but something about the way they stood was very wrong. They held long objects, and at the feet of one lay a huddled form. As seawater stole Bon's vision again, he was certain he saw blood darkening the pale sand.

'Bon—' a voice seemed to call, and then Bon's hearing was taken also.

Leki dragged him down and swam again, hauling him against the surge and pull of the undertow. Bon's eyes must have become more used to the saltwater – either that or the light here was different, the water kept clear by back-surge from the land – because he could make out more detail. Seaweed waved feathery fronds, some of them twice his height, and forms scampered within shadows. Corals rose from the seabed in elaborate shapes, beautiful echoes of history building upon the dead past and reaching towards unknown futures. Bon had a sudden, overpowering urge to search for evidence of the Skythian War buried deep; perhaps the remnants of an Engine, a mythical tool used by the Ald to conjure magic. Larger creatures haunted the extremes of his vision – swimming, floating, scampering, crawling. One of them rolled across the seabed, and then he recognised the priest, limbs flailing to the sea's urges as his sodden robe and boots held him down, drowned. As Leki took Bon upwards once again, he saw more of those shadowy snake shapes darting in to bite the priest's pale skin. Easy pickings.

They broke surface, and someone shouted almost in his ear.

'—Ugane! Bon Ugane! Does anyone know—?'

'Here!' Bon shouted. Leki glared at him, a transparent film passing across her wide eyes. A wave shoved them forward and broke over them, and Leki's hand slipped from his grasp. Bon panicked for a moment as the sea drove him down, and when something grabbed his leg and pulled he kicked out, mouth opening and bubbles rushing past his chest and stomach for the surface.

He breathed in air again and Leki pulled him close. For the first time he saw a flicker of panic in her eyes, and glancing back he saw the looming rocks. Waves smashed across them, and a dead man had been forced into a crevasse by the water. He was facing in, but would never see land.

'There he is. Come on!' Leki said, and she kicked against the draw of the tide.

'Where?'

'Bon Ugane!' a voice called again, and then Bon saw the boat riding the waves a few lengths back out to sea. With three great kicks Leki pulled them there, and Bon squeezed his eyes closed against the next wave. Once it had passed over them, Leki grabbed him beneath the arms and lifted. Her strength was immense. He rose from the sea as if he were kicking against rock, and the man in the boat dropped oars and reached for him. He clasped Bon by his torn shirt and fell back into the boat.

Bon landed hard atop the man, and the man gasped, winded. The cigar he'd been smoking fell from his mouth and rolled across his shoulder, leaving a trail of sparkling, smoking tobacco that held Bon's bemused attention.

'Up and off me, for the Fade's fucking sake!' the man said, galvanising Bon into motion. He rolled off and sat up, reaching over the side of the boat for Leki. But she did not need his help. She kicked herself aboard, lifting into the boat with minimal effort, and then she crouched down and stared at the boatman. Water beaded and dripped from her skin, and a tracework of fine bites bled across her left shoulder.

'No need to stare at me like that, water lady,' the man said. He took up his oars and started rowing, cigar clamped firmly between his teeth once more. The smoke seemed to dance around his head in defiance of the strong sea breeze. 'I'm no harm, and if I was I'd have not hauled you from the sea, and if you are going to attack me can you do it now instead of later when I've saved your skins, save me the effort, save us

31

all the effort.' He glanced Leki up and down. 'Nice teats. There's a coat behind you if you want to cover yourself.' Still rowing, he looked ashore, past the cruel rocks at the relatively calm beach. 'You should see what I'm seeing, then we'll talk.' He spoke quieter now, and Bon turned to see.

Though the boat rocked and the sea spray obscured his view, the violence taking place on the beach was obvious. One of the tall, heavy shapes held a naked prisoner with one huge hand, and with the other it was gutting the man, hacking at his torso with a knife, sawing, then slashing at the guts as they spilled to the sand. The man must have been screaming – *must* have – but the sea stole his voice. Once the man's guts stopped spooling from the wound across his stomach, the long-haired guard moved the knife up to his throat, transferring its grip to its victim's hair. The man's arms waved feebly as the guard slashed at his neck, and as his body fell away from his severed head, hands seemed to clasp at the air to hold himself upright.

Bon turned away and leaned forward, trying not to puke.

'Slayers get certain names, the names get executed,' the man said.

'Saves the Ald bloodying their hands on Alderia,' Leki said.

'Oh, the Ald's hands are bloodied,' the man said. He had never stopped rowing, but he turned now to look down at Bon. 'You going to puke in my boat?'

'You were calling my name,' Bon said.

'Your name,' the man said. He turned and put more effort into rowing, and Bon saw big muscles flexing beneath the loose clothing. His hat was made of some red-furred creature. He wore three white metal rings on each thumb. Rough and refined – his voice holding a taint of both – the man was an enigma.

32

'The slayers were ready to kill Bon?' Leki said.

'They were.' The man still rowed hard, glancing back only to steer their way. 'Still are. This is where you two need to trust me.' He glanced across at the beach. The second slayer was keeping pace with them, staring through the spray, and its long spear was now held across its shoulder.

'Why would they want to—?' Bon asked, and then the man dropped his oars.

'Into the water,' he said.

Something on the beach flashed, and a roar louder than the sea swallowed Bon's voice when he screamed. Leki grabbed his hand, the boat tipped, and they were sinking once again.

Maybe this will be the one, Juda thought as he pulled himself down the anchored rope, hand over hand, towards the cave mouth. But even if Bon Ugane wasn't the one, this would be the last time he ever used this route past the slayers. They weren't stupid, and they might have seen him disappearing out here before.

Juda couldn't afford to be clumsy. He was too close for that. To come all this way, wait all this time, to have it undone by clumsiness would be . . .

Idiot, he tried to say, but the sea rushed into his mouth and he gagged, coughing and spluttering as he pulled himself towards the underwater cave.

He had to assume the man and woman were following. Once the slayer had started shooting at them with its pike, there was no way he'd have stayed in the boat, sitting there and waiting to be fried by shellspot poison. He had pulled them out of the water, and only hoped they'd had the sense to go back in, especially after seeing what had happened on the beach. The man – Bon Ugane, the one marked for death – had seemed sickened by that. The amphy accompanying him hadn't. She must have already witnessed some bad things in her life, and Juda wondered whether it was something that would be of interest to him, and his quest. As he pulled himself through the tunnel and up towards the light, he was already thinking that he might have struck it lucky.

Juda crawled quickly from the water and scanned the small cave. It was empty and, for now, safe. The oil lamp he'd lit the previous night still burned, and the food and drink he'd stored was undisturbed. He'd worried that sea things might have come in during the night and eaten it, as had happened before. But fate had smiled upon him.

He picked up the small pistol beside the oil lamp, checked that the steam valve still showed full, and turned around to face the splashing pair.

The amphy came first, pulling Bon Ugane. Her eyes flickered with the clear film that protected them whilst swimming, and it cast a strange reflection from the oil lamp. She took everything in with a glance and stopped, up to her waist in water. The coat she'd tied on at his invitation drooped heavily. Behind her, Ugane wiped water from his eyes and gasped in several deep breaths. Then he saw what Juda was holding and froze.

'Oh, that's nice,' Ugane said.

'Two of us, one shot,' the amphy said.

Juda shook his head, laughing softly. 'The last thing I want right now is to shoot either of you, believe me. But on Skythe, the last thing you want is usually just around the corner.' He waved the pistol slightly, indicating that they should emerge from the water. It brought them close to him – close enough to make a move for the weapon, if they so desired – but Juda thought it inspired trust. And he knew how cold the water was.

'So,' the amphy said.

'So,' Juda said. 'I know Bon Ugane, but what's your name?'

'Lechmy Borle.'

'And I'm Juda.'

'Why rescue us to point a pistol at us?' Bon asked, and Juda could see from his expression that he hadn't seen many guns. Eyes wide, Bon had the face of the eternally curious.

'For all the fucking Fade gods, can I just sit down?' Lechmy Borle asked.

Juda smiled. 'You don't look tired.' He looked her up and down. She was strong and wiry like most amphys, wide chest, webbed feet and hands. He'd always found amphy women incredibly attractive, and this one was no exception.

'I'm good at hiding it.' Without his permission she sat, leaning back against the wall and groaning softly.

'So you're our welcome to Skythe?' Bon asked. He went slowly to his knees, sighing as his joints clicked. *Not used to exercise*, Juda thought. That would have to change if he wanted to stay alive.

'Your unofficial welcome,' Juda said. He nodded up at the cave's ceiling. 'And better than the alternative. I don't have the strength or inclination to gut you both. So what are you here for, Bon Ugane and Lechmy Borle?'

'Sedition,' Bon said.

'Call me Leki. And yes, me too.' Juda noticed Bon glancing at the woman. Perhaps it was his first time hearing why she was being deported. 'Shoot us now if you have to,' Leki continued. 'And if you don't have to, are you going to share that food?'

Juda hesitated for only a moment before lowering the pistol. He unscrewed the steam valve and pocketed it, then dropped the weapon into the bag he'd left there the previous night. He'd only once had to use it in this place, and that was something he did not like to remember.

35

He plucked a metal case from his jacket's inner pocket, opened it, took out a cigar, and lit it from the oil lamp. Inhaling the smoke, he felt his blood absorbing the drug and smoothing it through his body, and the pressures of darkness receding for a time. But soon even the scamp smoke would not keep his familiar nightmares at bay.

'What are those things on the beach?' Bon asked. 'And why were you calling my name?'

Juda reached over for the food, keeping his head down. The cave was small, and often flooded during high tides or when the Forsaken Sea developed one of its irregular surges. With the three of them inside, it already felt crowded.

'There are plenty of questions,' Juda said. 'But now isn't the time. If you're hungry, eat. If you're thirsty, drink. Scratch your arses if you have to. Then we have to leave.'

'Back through there?' Bon said, nodding at the dark water.

'Trust me,' Juda said.

Bon glanced at the bag containing the pistol. Leki raised an eyebrow.

'The slayers were waiting for you,' Juda said.

'Slayers. Nice name,' Bon said.

'Sums them up. And if I hadn't been here today, you'd have met the same fate as the man you saw on the beach.'

'That wasn't just an execution,' Leki said.

'Of course not. It was fun. The slayers are bred violent, have been for decades. The Spike nurture them to serve the Ald. Big, mindless things, they like killing, and that's why they're here.' He handed a small loaf of bread and a chunk of meat to each of them, but took none for himself. Juda had been on Skythe long enough to know how to eat well.

He closed his eyes as they chewed, the clicking of their teeth and their grateful gulping echoing around the small cave. He tried to remember the way up out of the cave, following the route through memory, and frowned as one junction gave him multiple opportunities. Each dark tunnel mouth – wide, narrow, low, or high up on the uneven cave wall – offered nothing familiar. He'd been this way ten times before, in and out, but that part of the tunnels . . .

'What is it?' Leki asked. Juda opened his eyes and saw his hands raised before his face, trying to feel this way or that.

'Nothing,' he said. 'Stretching.' But he saw the glance between Leki and Bon, and knew that they would be on their guard.

That was fine. He didn't yet mean them any harm.

'We should go,' he said. 'Once a slayer has a name, they won't rest until they've spilled its owner's guts.'

'Great,' Bon said, spitting breadcrumbs.

'You'll be safe with me,' Juda said.

'Great.' Bon took another mouthful of bread.

Juda picked up the oil lamp and turned towards the rear of the cave. Now he only had to hope that the slayers had not discovered the cave entrance. If they met one in these tunnels . . .

'Hurry,' he said. 'Shake your bits and get a fucking move on. I've been awake since dawn.'

'And what does that mean?' Leki asked, behind him.

You don't want to know, Juda thought. But he said nothing, and as he crawled into the first of the low tunnels leading inland, he heard Bon and Leki scrambling to keep up.

Chapter 2
shards

Sometimes, Milian Mu opens her eyes. Nothing is revealed in the endless darkness, but the action inspires an awareness that is otherwise absent or confused. As part of this awareness, she can sense the incredible time that has passed – centuries, perhaps – and feel the weight of rock encasing her in a womb-like cave. With her eyes open, she feels more *there* than she has been for a long, long time.

But that barely-there existence is preferable to the memories.

Those ancient, terrible memories . . .

As Milian sprinted downhill towards the collection of angular stone buildings, a hail of rockbill feathers came at her from the shattered windows to the left of the main entrance. They whistled as they twisted through the air, flights slicked with oil to give them direction, tips glinting with the poison ever-present in their quills. She roared, the air before her blasting with an intense heat haze, and the poisonous feathers – a favoured weapon of the military of her homeland of Skythe – were diverted left and right, or snapped and shredded before her as they fell to the blood-muddied ground. There they merged with a mess of bodies and insides that still steamed in the morning sun. Not everyone had made it to cover, and Milian splashed through the gory mess.

She had been running since early evening, when the strange explosion had rippled across the landscape and freed her from the weak thing she had been. She'd felt the *thing* worming into her, a terrible intrusion, and for an instant she had been terrified. *Daemon within me, I feel its heat, I taste its fury!* Then the presence had surged to the fore. It had *become* her, shredding all but her most basic perceptions and memories. Milian Mu – the holy woman, the wife, the mother – had become a thing meant only for killing.

She dripped with fresh blood, and crackled with blood already dried. Some of it was hers. Her fingernails were torn away, fingers slashed, hands clawed, and there were several deep gashes across her palms where some had tried defending themselves. None of them had succeeded. She and the many others like her killed them all, and seeing herself reflected in her victims' eyes – a similar face, the same pale skin – did nothing to lessen her viciousness.

Milian ran through the next hail of rockbill feathers and knocked some aside, others slipping past her as though the air around her had curved, steering them away. She heard the cries and smelled the fear of those inside, and that drew her on like a fly to raw meat. Inside, a heavy sword swung at her from shadows to the left of the entrance. The weapon was wielded by a tall, terrified man. She grabbed and broke both, merging them together in a wet sculpture of metal and flesh. A flurry of movement in the shadows, a startling illumination, and three burning hay bales came at her. She kicked them back where they had come from, and the stench of burning hair filled the farmhouse.

'Aeon save us, Aeon help us!' someone pleaded to Skythe's known and loving god, and though Milian could hear the words she did not know them. Her mind was fried and detached. She ran through the smoke and flames and stomped on the burning woman, crushing her skull, taking pleasure from killing the wretch beneath her feet rather than from putting her out of her misery.

Misery was *her* currency, and madness her means of delivery.

There were seven of them hidden in three rooms, and Milian took them all apart. Blades came at her and she broke or dodged them, thrown punches were caught and fists crushed, a haze of poison spray swept across her eyes and was blinked away by the mad daemon inside her. It took heartbeats, and then the screaming ended and she could feed again. She dug for the livers, because she liked them best.

Afterwards, she left the farmstead and ran on, down towards the sea fifty miles distant where fishing villages would provide more game. Instinct urged her this way. The need to kill, and feed. The daemon that had entered her was stronger than ever now, and becoming used to the fit of her body. It had its own agenda. It *revelled* in this newfound freedom.

To her left and right she saw occasional shapes bounding across the moonlit landscape. Blood hazed the air behind them. They were like her, Skythians giving home to daemons, and the only things she was not driven to kill.

She had murdered more than thirty people since dusk, and the night had only just begun.

Later, standing on the shore with the village ablaze behind her, still her hunger was not sated. Her stomach was distended with all she had eaten; liver, so rich. Her teeth were clotted with the flesh of many bodies, and the daemon inside her thrummed in its eagerness for more.

Wet cold dark alone, she thought, and a wave crashed in around her feet. Several sand runners came in with it, claws held high as they surfed the water and then started busily scouring the sand for burrowing, fleshy things to eat. In their enthusiasm they brushed against her bare legs, shrivelled, and died.

Further along the coast she smelled people still living, and she turned that way.

The blazing village cast her shadow across the sea, and more of her kind – normal, loving Skythians changed by events into killing things – trailed after her. Some of them were burning. These walked until they fell, and even then she could feel their daemons raging on, darkening the land without shadow.

From the ridge of the next spur of land protruding into the sea, on a scree of fallen rocks at the foot of the cliff, she saw one of the fabled Engines set into the land. She had heard the rumours about Alderians sailing towards some of the more remote southern beaches. She had heard whispers of the Engines, Alderian constructs supposedly sent to destroy the Skythian god Aeon. No one had believed that the Engines could be real. *Alderia is our friend*, people had said of the continent four hundred miles to the south, and that had been true for so long. *Why would they turn against us and the truth of Aeon? Would they* truly *be foolish enough to build Engines that could conjure* magic?

But that had been before Aeon's manifestation into a physical presence. The Alderia's Fade religion could not be touched. Perhaps they feared Aeon, which could.

The thing within Milian raged, damping down such sane contemplations. Her hunger burned.

The sand and rock around the Engine were melted into shapes that mimicked the living. Its curved metal casings glimmered with moisture. Long limbs arced from the construct and into the beach, and it looked like an exposed organ from within some gigantic living thing. *The land has been ripped open*, Milian thought, and the idea suited the red-tinted rage of her daemon.

Around the Engine fussed busy, frightened people in clothing she recognised as Alderian. She had seen them before on trade and cultural visits, but now they were the invaders, the aggressors. These were the real targets for her newfound rage.

She opened her mouth, and her daemon roared.

Those terrible memories haunting her, Milian has begun slowly flexing her limbs. Muscles in her thighs perform involuntary jumps, and her arms shift. They make a sound. It is like rock grinding against rock, and she wonders if she has been in this cave for so long that she has become a fossil. She saw fossils once when she was a child, excavating a hillside thirty miles north of her village with her school class. Her teacher showed her how to hold a trowel and explained why she must be so sensitive when she found a protruding fossil, brushing at it gently so as not to damage it. She had learned that old things demand reverence. She had still believed that when she became a holy woman, revering Aeon.

I'm an old thing now, she thinks, and she moves her arms again. They scrape across something until they press against the sides of her body. She might have been here for hundreds of years. The air around her has grown old and stale, like her mind.

She wonders how she is still alive, and such musings bring the taste of brine and a chilling coolness closing all around her. She is certain that her daemon is gone, and that she is waking. But in doing so, her memories seem to come even richer, and more horribly detailed than ever.

She scrambled down the cliff face with three others like her – Skythians made furious, overflowing with daemon. Their rage was a physical thing, heating the air around them, cliffs echoing with their cries. The fear she saw in the Alderians around the Engine drew her on. The anticipation was delicious.

One of the others slipped and fell, bouncing from outcroppings and dashing himself to pieces on the rocky beach below. She heard the impact and saw the splash of blood, and then he hauled himself upright and started across the sands. His left leg was broken and dragging, and a spew of blood and brains stained the back of his ragged shirt. She could hear him panting and groaning as he made for the Engine, and the daemon within him was struggling loose now, bursting from his open wounds like rats fleeing a sinking ship. Its disparate parts danced around his head like cold blue fire, whipping at the air and setting it alight. His hair burned. He rushed on, faster, and then the strangers around the Engine started firing crossbow bolts his way.

They had come to destroy the Skythian god Aeon, but now had no idea what they faced.

The man's damage was great, and the bolts hit home. By the time she and the two others reached the bottom of the cliff, he was crawling across the sand with a dozen bolts embedded in his face and the lashing flames faded almost to nothing.

Milian ran, and when she came within range of their weapons she roared, and they veered away and broke. Her daemon scream and rage held such power and strength. Feet pounded sand, blood splashed her body from the wounds she had already received, and she could see the terror etched on the faces of the strange people around the Engine. Three of them worked on it, eight others tried to protect them.

She was anticipating the feel of flesh parting between her hands once again when—

The world lit up. The Engine howled like an impossible beast in pain, its limbs flexing and then rising, issuing a terrible glow that grew brighter and brighter. The ground shook. Sand made fluid by the movement rippled like water away from the Engine, and Milian felt her daemon shiver with something that might have been fear.

The enemy dropped their weapons and took several steps back towards the sea, an unconscious retreat towards their homeland across the water. Their eyes went wide in fright . . . and then awful acceptance.

Milian pursued them, and then the Engine exploded. The blast threw her far out past the beach and over the water, and behind her the land had come alight. The whole stretch of coast she could see had blossomed into bright white flame, the fires blasting way above the cliffs, spiralling up and out from the Engine on the beach and splashing across the land. Molten rock flowed, trees exploded, and the atmosphere itself thudded with shock after shock. As she dropped, another body fell with her, and they both flitted through the air as if carried by giant hands. Just before she splashed down she saw the ruin of the man it had once been. His body was split by some vast impact, his head a dangling mess pinned with crossbow bolts, and the dregs of his daemon hissed away to the air.

She thought, *How much of that is in me?* Then, moments before she struck the water, something struck her.

The touch of Aeon was unmistakeable. As a holy woman she had imagined its touch, but actually experiencing it was undeniable, and shattering. It scorched the daemon within her to nothing, instantly ridding her of the thing that had turned her, for a time, into a beast. A moment of joy followed, quickly subsumed by sadness because—

She hit the violent surface of the sea, but hardly noticed.

—Aeon was no more. Object of Skythian worship for millennia, a passive god that observed but did not intrude, exuded power but did not demand fealty and fear, she sensed its passing as surely as she felt this single shard of it passing into her. It parted her soul and settled inside, and the shard became the centre of her perception.

They killed it! she thought, hardly believing. *They murdered Aeon!* With the cataclysmic power that had just blasted from the Engine on the beach, what was left of Skythe now? What was left of anything?

There is always something left, a voice had said, and Milian opened her mouth to gasp. Water flooded in, but she did not drown. *I have you*, the voice continued. The voice of her god. *And you have me. This shard is a part of me, and will become a seed. But it will take time. The material part of Aeon is ruined. But . . . will you carry this shard of me?*

Milian could not believe that Aeon was asking her permission. But she agreed silently, and felt her god acknowledge.

What was the daemon? she thought. *Was that born of the Alderian Engines?*

I must rest, Aeon said. It sounded pained, and shocked, and its voice was growing more and more distant. *I must . . . recuperate . . .*

And me?

South, away from Alderia, Aeon said. *And when you reach land, you must rest also.*

For how long?

Until I am ready to wake.

They destroyed you, Milian thought, and her tears mixing with vast seas could have been endless.

Nothing is for ever, Aeon said, *death least of all.*

With her land aflame behind her, Milian sank into the water until darkness flooded her.

In the cave, back in the present and away from those distant memories for a while, Milian blinks sore eyes. Pain is better than no feeling at all, so she blinks again. Sand in her eyes, or salt, and she goes to lift her hand and rub them. Her hand refuses to move, but there is pressure in her shoulder. Her stomach muscles flex. She is coming alive again, but . . .

No sign of the shard. No sense of Aeon.

Perhaps I am *dead. Landed in the sea after the Engine erupted, sank, settled on the seabed and dreamed of Aeon. And the movements I feel are the sea creatures of the Duntang Archipelago tasting my eyes and tongue, my skin, rooting in the wounded flesh across my chest and stomach and hips . . .*

This is real, however, and the movements she feels are her own. These thoughts are level and unpanicked, not the drone-like ravings of the murderous thing she had once been. And the old memories carry a story that is not yet finished.

As she sank into the sea, saltwater soothed her wounds. She only noticed them as the pain receded, and awareness returned to her as her senses became more deprived – sight limited by darkness, hearing by the pressures of depth. Above her she saw the remains of the ruined man drifting down towards her. A cloud of blood softened his outline, and past him the sea's surface shone and glimmered with an unknowable light-show. It looked both beautiful and deadly.

A large shadow flitted quickly through the water, stream-lined and sharp, and snatched the man's remains from within the spreading cloud. The shadow disappeared as quickly as it had arrived, leaving only an echo of the dead man's presence slowly dispersing into the water.

Am I bleeding too? she wondered. It seemed an age since she had thought of herself, though she knew it had only been hours since the daemon had come – those shockwaves that had seemed to thump through the air, the land, the rock of the world itself, and then the thing ripping into her, fixing against her soul with barbed tenacity.

She opened her mouth to cry out at the horror of what she had done, but the last of her air had already escaped her lungs. She sank deeper, coming to rest on the ocean floor. Something large and flat moved beneath her feet, and in the faint light she saw only a hint of the wide, circular creature as it glided gracefully into the obscure distance.

I should be dead! she thought, and a wave of heat closed around her from the direction of the land. Whatever was happening back there was also forcing heat into the endless sea. She turned slowly, raising her hands to protect her eyes and face from the swarm of creatures fleeing away from the land and towards her. Jellyfish slicked by, trailing tentacles that set fire to her skin wherever they touched. Tiny fish nibbled at her eyes and lips. Things with shells almost as large as her sprung along the seabed, landing around and upon her and leaping again, their spiked feet piercing her thighs and ankles. Sharks arrowed by, a sea snake curled around her flailing arm, fishes nibbled at her bleeding flesh. There was no pain from the bites, though the jellyfish caresses burned so much she was amazed her skin was not aflame.

Something inside hurt worst of all. The shard – silent now, and buried deep – reminded her of madness and the things she had done, and then it prodded home again, a terribly sentient pain that seemed to speak to her and guide her, demanding something she barely understood.

She tried to breathe, but water filled her lungs. Death surely circled her but, like the dozens of arm-sized bone sharks that formed a dark cloud above her head, it did not close in entirely. The shard of Aeon warded it and them away, and she felt it urging her onward. Away from the land. Out across the ocean floor. *South*, it had said. *And when you reach land, you must rest also*. Hundreds of miles south was Alderia. All that was left of Aeon wanted to hide under its enemy's nose.

Her body leaking blood and tears, senses all but useless the steeper the seabed sloped down, creatures investigating this intruder in their midst, Milian followed the shard's bidding.

She walked across the seabed, leaving both madness and sanity behind. In their place settled a curious, distant calmness, as though both fear and normality were being crushed from her by immense pressures. Soon, the glare of fires was lost above and behind her. The darkness welcomed her in and down.

Great things moved in the waters around her, and in the ocean floor beneath. Eyes sought, nostrils flared, other organs sensed her heat and electrical charge, her womanhood and the memory of the songs her mother sang, echoes of her past drawing giant star-nosed slugs that fed on pain. But these things would mostly move aside as she approached, or fade back to their own nebulous pasts at the last moment. They were confused, and then forgetful. She was there, and then she was not. The shard of the dead god within was protecting her.

She fell into chasms and was lifted by warm tides. She passed the rearing edifices of the islands of Duntang Archipelago, and avoided their rise towards land. She stumbled through seaweed forests for days, avoided the sharp beaks of decapuses and the poisonous spines of sand spites, and once she saw a deep pirate swimming rapidly away from her. The waving weed fronds rose high above, shifting slowly back and forth to the sea's beat, which might perhaps have been the pulse of the whole world. But, for her, such musings were rare. She continued to exist because the memory of the dead god Aeon was within her, and rarely did she consider what purpose she might be travelling towards.

She could not count the days. But at some point in her journey she felt the urge to stop for the first time, crawl down among the broken ruins of old ships that had been swept against an undersea cliff by ancient tides, and hide. The sea itself seemed to pause in its constant movements – there were always currents, cool and cold contacts, but now everything was still. She sat silently for a long time. Crawling things investigated her and moved on.

And then something came close.

She never saw what it was, but she felt it, probing at her thoughts with a mind utterly alien and cold. Its presence pervaded the whole area, and she saw several fluorescent fish swimming so hard away from it that they simply died, slowing and sinking to the seabed, their lights fading to nothing. The shape passed close by, sending a heavy, cool wave across and through the piled wrecks. They moved as though unsettled by the massive thing's presence. It took a long time to drift past, and the sense of size was staggering. Even after it had gone she remained where she was for some time, unsure of exactly who she was or what she was doing anymore.

Then she was moving again, and the memory of her ruined god moved with her.

Much later, when so much time had passed that she could no longer recall the origins of her journey – not then, at least – the sea floor began to rise.

She emerged eventually into sunlight, onto the strange shore of a continent she had never visited before – Alderia. The beach was cracked with spreads of melted, glassy sand, glimmering black in the daylight. Bright blue birds plucked insects from the wing. A slow mammal walked along the beach on four wide feet, not seeming to notice her. Way behind, the horizon glowed with a sickly heat. She was very, very tired, and the world was so far away. She had no wish to see any more.

She found a cave in the cliffs at one end of the beach, its entrance barely exposed even at low tide. It went deep, and so did she.

In that same cave now, she can hear the sea. It is distant, but comforting, a constant that would sound the same one age to the next. And now there is the faintest light as well, bleeding in somewhere and reflecting and refracting through the cave to where she lies. She is all but buried after being there for so long. Even the cave feels new, reshaped around her over time as seasons and years have come and gone, rocks have fallen, and the sea has done its timeless, erosive work.

It will take some time for her to find herself again. Her mouth is moist once more, but her eyes are still gritty and sore. She can feel the weight of slumped organs in her body, though her muscles seem to be reacting to her commands, doing their utmost to obey.

She thinks her god's name, but Aeon is silent. She probes for it, but there is no response. Perhaps over the time she has been hidden down here, it has faded away to nothing. It was a mere shard of what Aeon had once been, after all.

Some time later, Milian Mu sits up at last.

Chapter 3

adaptations

Venden Ugane dropped the cart's reins and fell upon a red-spined snake, one hand clamping hard behind the powerful jaws, the other pressing down halfway along its length, trying to prevent the creature's thrashing and avoid it curling around his arm. A year ago he'd witnessed a specimen smaller than this wrap itself around a hillhog and squeeze until the swine's guts exploded from its arse.

'Calm it, for the bastard gods' sakes!' he hissed. The snake seemed to weaken, and then its movements drew to an abrupt halt. He'd seen serpents feigning death before, a defence mechanism or a hunting ploy. He would not lessen his grip.

'Fifteen spines. Shorter than they should be. Won't catch anything with them.' He lifted the head and pressed, its dislocated jaw dropping open under the pressure. Sickly yellow venom dripped from its long fangs, and he was careful not to breathe in any of its fumes. 'Teeth should be longer to break through a hillhog's hide. Hogs growing heavier and tougher. Don't adapt, don't survive.' He stood slowly, then heaved the snake down the hillside. It twisted and rattled through the air, then fell in a clump of bushes and slithered away. He watched it go, wondering how it could still be alive and whether its offspring would persist for long. It was far from a perfect specimen, but then he was already certain a perfect specimen would no longer exist. On Skythe, perfection was further away than anywhere else. The snake hunted imperfect prey, living among flora that barely understood seasons. That confusion led to beautiful landscapes of many colours – lush greens and blooming wonders, as well as the autumnal hues of orange, red and brown. But such beauty was unnatural, and wrong.

His mind never still, Venden enjoyed retroscrying; trying to discern how these animals and plants might have been in the past, and how perhaps they should have been in the present. And he could sometimes retroscry back to the point when everything had changed – when Alderia's assault had blighted the land, and polluted it for centuries to come.

Back where he'd come from the idea that Alderia had implemented magic was a forbidden concept, but here there was no one to forbid. Not this far north, at least. On the southern shores there were the slayers, and some people still foolish enough to fear uttering the truth. But here he was deep in the heart of Skythe, and deep in the wild past.

The war had changed things more than most people could ever believe. Discovering the truth was a challenge that had become a personal quest since he had come here to live, and every oddity he found only served to pique his interest more. Back on Alderia, his interest had necessitated the gathering of forbidden information – parchments, diagrams, whispered rumours passed on in dingy basement rooms. He had never questioned his strange interest in a war six hundred years old, not even when he was a child. But coming to Skythe meant that he could wander the corrupted site of the war and discover evidence for himself, and his fascination seemed like the most natural thing in the world. It was what he had been born to do, and he felt more at home than ever before.

Especially since discovering the remnant, when in a flash his life had taken on new meaning. Since then, his retroscrying of local flora and fauna had become little more than a way to pass time during his journeys. What he sought now was something far less known.

Venden picked up the cart's reins and started hauling it forward again. He had come this way once before on one of his scouting trips for further remnants, but any tracks he had left behind had been wiped away by the weather. The gentle slope of the hillside was relatively free of trees and rocks, and a good route along the valley towards his destination. Soon he would drop down to the valley floor and follow the river. The cart was small, light, but it was the object on it that might cause him some problems. It had taken eight days to come forty miles, and now he was almost home.

Memories of his previous life – the sad, wasting man who was his father; the dead mother – came clearer in dreams now than in waking hours, an indication that he was leaving his past way behind. It was a long time since he had whispered apologies to his father before dropping into a peaceful sleep.

Sometimes he thought to whisper to that void hiding inside of him instead, but he had long given up trying to understand.

The cart bumped, and the thing it contained thudded against the timber sides. Venden glanced back at it. Every time he looked, his stomach dropped and he felt sick. It was a sickness at his loss of control, at the feeling of *being* controlled. He should never have known where to travel to find it.

It had been the same with every other remnant.

The memory of his long journey north from Skythe's southern shore, and what he had found close to the source of the river, was as fresh now as the time he had first relived it. Each recollection seemed to make it more real, as if his mind was solidifying his experience to hold back the subtle madness he felt. *Everyone blessed with genius is also tainted with madness*, his father had told him on the day Venden was accepted into the Guild of Inventors. But that was a continent, and a lifetime, away.

'I'm not mad,' he said to the wilderness. Each reiteration chipped away at his confidence in the idea, and the watcher inside had never deigned to offer an opinion.

All through his journey north from Alderia to Skythe, he had suspected that he was being drawn to something. After many days stowed away on the supply ship – fearing capture, stealing food – the open freedom of this strange land had refreshed him. It washed out the fears that had built in him, and the regrets about what he had done. And finding himself somewhere he had dreamed of for years, it had not been difficult to follow the lure.

He guided the cart down the gentle slope, turning so that he was behind it and the weight of its contents pulled it down. Staring at the shape exposed to the harsh sunlight, Venden felt that shiver again, the mysterious sense that this hidden thing was always meant to be found by him. The first time he touched it, the smooth shape seemed to fit his hand perfectly, as if he had always known it. It had lain in the ruin of an old Skythian temple for centuries, buried beneath a fallen wall, swathed with sickly crawling plants, patiently waiting. It had taken only a morning to pull back the rubble and cut away the plants that sought to smother the object, and it had felt like granting freedom.

The length of his arm but slightly thicker, the spine-like

object had fourteen protuberances down both sides, each of them as long as his thumb. They were round and smooth, and pocked with between three and thirteen holes. These holes had been home to crawling things, but since loading the object onto the cart they all seemed to have crawled away. The central trunk was almost circular, with one side slightly heavier than the other. If cut it would have the cross-section of a seagull's egg, but Venden would never try to cut it. He wasn't certain it *could* be cut – even after so long, its surface was completely unscarred by anything time, or the falling temple wall, had thrown at it.

With each bump it seemed to slip across the cart's wooden surface, moving as if alive.

But it was *not* alive. When he'd picked it up it had been cold and still, hard.

The cart jumped over a rock and the ropes jarred through his hand, burning his skin and causing him to cry out. He tugged hard, pulled the axle to the left, and jammed the wheels against a rut in the hillside. Panting, Venden released the cart and sat down. The sun blazed. His water skins were empty. Home was near, but the familiar desire to draw out his journey had been nagging at him for the past two days.

He liked being at his camp, but when he was out looking for a relic he never wanted to get there. Deep down, past even that shadow at his core, he was terrified of what he was doing.

Falling onto his back in the long grass, turning his head to the side, he saw a small spiky plant speckled with hundreds of tiny purple flowers. 'Bruised heather,' he said, used to talking to himself. For the past years, there had only been the animals and plants of this place to speak to. The Skythians he encountered seemed lost to civilisation, regressed to more feeble times. 'Haven't seen it this far inland before. Likes the sea breeze.' He leaned on one elbow and examined the plant closer. 'Flowers are catching insects. Drowning them. It's turned carnivorous. Long stems, flowers too heavy when they're full . . .' He lifted several drooping stems with one finger and found that more than half of them had snapped. At the breaks, the bright green stems were turning a rusty brown, as if their drowned victims' blood seeped out. 'Not fit for purpose.' Sitting up, Venden looked at the sky. Up there where the sun burned fierce and the clouds flowed south to north, there was nothing that looked wrong. The sky was pure and untarnished, while Skythe was tainted by the past.

'It should all be dead by now,' he said, because from his studies back on Alderia he knew that such natural systems could not persist if things were going wrong. It was early spring, but down the hillside he could see a swathe of trees whose leaves were smudged orange, yellow and red, a gorgeous array of colours that betrayed the errors imprinted in whatever still drove the trees to grow. Perhaps they drew this corruption up from the soil through their roots, infected water, mutated nutrients. Or maybe even Skythe's air was polluted and wrong.

Down to the valley floor, following the river, he soon approached the place he had come to know as the ruined vale. From a distance it presented a pleasing vista – the river curving in a gentle arc around an area of uneven ground, trees standing sentinel, and the remains of two stone bridges planted either side of the river. One of them was almost unrecognisable, but the other had only lost its central span, the carved stone formations on either side evidence of the graceful structure it had once been. The ground here was sometimes marshy, but not today. The river had not flooded for several moons.

As he drew closer a flock of sparrs took flight, startling

him to a standstill. The commonest birds in this part of Skythe, they were also the prettiest, with luminescent blue wings, long trailing tails, and a green flash on their chests by which it was possible to identify the males from the females. But in flocks their combined song sounded like a stalking creature's roar, and Venden could never get used to the brief moment of shock.

The sparrs flittered up and to the east, higher into the hills, swirling and swooping but never breaking formation. There were hunting things in the air in these high valleys that would pick off any bird straying from the group.

The ruined vale used to be a large village. Destroyed during or soon after the Skythian War, it no longer betrayed any evidence of its violent demise. Nature had reclaimed the village, subsuming it, smothering the buildings with crawling plants and trees, pulling them back into the ground. There were glimpses of upright stone structures here and there, but time had ensured that there was no longer much order left to this place. Walls had fallen and been taken back to the wild.

Once, walking through the ruined vale almost two years before, on the day he had named it, Venden had sensed something beneath one of the small hillocks of tumbled stone. There was no sound and no hint of physical movement, but staring at the plant-covered mound he had been taken with the disconcerting sensation that everything within was in turmoil. A terrible aura of violence projected from the motionless pile, and Venden's heart rate had doubled in the blink of an eye.

The void inside him had screamed.

He'd turned and run blindly, collapsing miles away in a sweating, frightened mess. And later that night, as he stared at the stars unable to sleep, he'd acknowledged what he might have witnessed – a shred of old magic.

It was said by some that dregs of magic still persisted in the darkest, deepest parts of the world, left over from the war. A forbidden thing now, even more so six centuries before, there were still those who sought it. Venden was not one of them. In his illicit studies he had found plenty of evidence to suggest that magic was a dark, insidious power. Some suggested it had possessed a strange sentience. One Skythian parchment, ancient and ambiguous, had even given magic a name.

Crex Wry, Venden had muttered, and dawn's cool light had brought a desire to hunt the magical dreg. Fear had changed to excitement. But upon his return to the ruined vale, he could already tell that whatever had been there had flitted or melted away.

Now, he stood by the river with his cart and the thing it contained, and stared at that fallen building. It remained motionless and dead. The plants growing upon it were a mixture of wild, mutated creeper that sprouted vicious-looking spiked seed pods, and the pale echoes of roses. These flowers were like images faded in the sun, bare memories of the beauty they should project. Their stems were weak and thin. Thorns were blunted by the sickness in the land.

Yet still they grew. For Venden this was the greatest shame, and the worst crime of the Skythian War. Alderia's use of forbidden magic had not killed Skythe, but had destined it to a future of weakness, mutation, and steady, slow decline. It had been six hundred years, and it might be six hundred more until this land was truly dead.

He pulled his cart through the ruined vale and the object rocked on the cart's bed, its protruding parts tapping like fingertips on a wooden table. Past the vale he entered the narrowing valley, beyond which he passed through the fallen shoulder between mountains. That was the hardest part of the journey, when much of the time he was lifting and manhandling the cart rather than pulling it. The solid wooden wheels, though braced, bore some considerable damage on the fallen scree of boulders and sharp rocks, and Venden worked all through the day to make his way east.

As darkness fell, he found a relatively flat area in which to camp. In the flickering campfire light he saw pairs of eyes watching him.

He sighed, hand stealing to the knife in his belt. Venden – a genius, a silent boy, a searcher – was a stranger in a strange land, and there was never any telling how these meetings might end.

Some of them crawled, though their limbs looked little different from their brethren's. Some loped, stooping low. A couple still walked tall. Those who were not naked wore old, torn clothing. They were dirty, scarred, their muscles knotty and worn. The women's breasts hung empty and sad like drained water sacs, and the men's genitals were withered and thin. Venden had once encountered a group of these mutant Skythians rutting beside a lake, and aside from the violence of the group act, it was the apparent lack of success that had shocked him most.

In the forbidden books he had viewed before leaving Alderia at the age of thirteen, images of Skythians showed them as tall, proud and cultured. Their clothing had been beautifully woven, their hair worn in long, intricate braids. They'd been a head taller than most Alderians, and their art- and science-based culture was much more advanced, and less troubled.

We did this to them, Venden thought, though the damage had been done six centuries before his birth. There were others he had encountered who had seemed to haul themselves forward somewhat, establishing camps and even attempting to farm the land. But they were the minority. Skythians today were a wild breed, and Venden found their fall so depressing.

Resting one hand on his knife handle, he raised the other, palm out. The Skythians paused, one woman scurrying forward to within a few steps. She raised her head and sniffed at the air.

'I'm Venden Ugane, no threat to you,' Venden said. 'You know me. You've seen me before.' He tapped his cart, trying to jog the Skythe woman's memory.

She sniffed some more, edging a step closer. 'Venden,' she rasped. She looked at the thing in the bed of the cart, her eyes going wide. They were bloodshot and weeping. She scampered back and cried something else, her voice a high whistle that seemed to contain little sense, and the few Skythians with her drew back as well, a sigh passing amongst them. It was not quite fear, and Venden had seen it before.

'It's nothing to be afraid of,' he said, still holding out one hand. He watched the way they moved, hunkered down on splayed limbs like dogs waiting to leap. Fear seemed to lower them. Evolution was a debatable theory, and for the most devout of the Ald – Alderia's ruling sect and unelected government – it was a blasphemy, because it denied the creation of things by the seven Alderian gods of the Fade. But most intelligent people, whatever their depth of belief in the Fade, accepted evolution as part of what made things the way they were. In these Skythians, Venden could see distinct evidence of devolution. And that made him sad, because it was man-made.

He sat down close to the fire to eat. They would not join him, but he knew that they would hang back in the darkness to watch. He would leave them some food when he left in the morning.

*   *   *

Dawn brought a light sheen of rain that painted rainbows on the eastern skies. Venden remembered a story the Fade priests told children about Shore, the Fade goddess of the air, who cavorted with the sun and moon and sighed rainbows of delight when Venthia, the god of water, cast his seed through her. It had been an innocent tale of gods and dancing for the children, but its connotations had become more apparent the older Venden became. Rainbows were the ecstatic emissions of the gods. As he stood beside the dying fire, he looked at the colours and smiled. They were beautiful, but they were factors of light and water, little more. Venden did not understand the science of rainbows, but that did not mean he had to ascribe them godliness.

There was no sign of the Skythians, but he knew they were still watching. They watched him on every journey. He broke camp and went to pick up the cart's reins, and then noticed a strange thing. The light rain did not seem to touch the pale object. It lay upon dampened boards, but its surface seemed dry. He placed his palm on the smooth body, ran a finger along one of the short, thin limbs, and it was untouched.

He frowned. Perhaps the water soaked in so quickly that the thing could not feel wet. But as with the rainbows, his lack of understanding did not drive him to the gods. Its mystery was not divine.

When he moved on, the Skythians emerged from their hiding places and took the food he had left for them. They followed him for a while, as he knew they would. They mumbled and muttered amongst themselves, and in their language he could hear nothing of the wondrous Skythe tongue he had studied in those books and parchments. So much had been lost.

The rain persisted, but the soaking did not dampen his spirits. The Skythians soon disappeared, and he was alone once more, pulling the cart with the reins over each shoulder. By midday he was close to where he had made his camp, in the fertile land at the junction of two mountain ridges where the river found its source. The flow here was more a series of trickling streams, the land between them boggy, and Venden followed a route he had taken many times before. It involved a steep climb, but then a level, mostly dry path across the mountainside to the sheltered area he called home. Here was the rocky overhang beneath which he lived. Here, too, was the remnant.

He glanced across the clearing to his camp, and for a moment the change did not register. He frowned, trying to perceive the difference, and because it was something taken away instead of added, he had to search further.

It's dropped, he thought. He released the reins in reaction to this, leaning back against the cart, because even from here he could see what the remnant had become.

The first time he'd seen it, he'd thought it was a fallen tree. Eight times as long as he was tall, it arced out of the ground from the foot of another dead tree's stump and pointed north, lifting and dropping again so that he could just pass underneath it without stooping. Graceful and horrible, its surface was speckled and pocked, and close to one end it changed from pale brown to black. He'd shivered and leaned back against a living tree's trunk, eager to touch something not so dead.

He had decided to stay there for a while, camped beneath the overhang, before even looking at the thing again. *Such a delicate remnant*, he'd thought, naming the object without realising it right then.

Now it had relaxed. The action of the remnant's highest point lowering towards the ground had pushed out both extremes, tilting the dead tree at one end, and gouging an uneven furrow at the other. The five objects he had already brought here from across Skythe, and placed close to the remnant in positions that had somehow felt right, remained in place.

'Someone has been here,' Venden muttered, but he immediately knew there was more to it than that. Though there were those on Skythe who would think nothing of invading his space and stealing anything of use – the south coast was home to several settlements where those banished here had chosen to make their homes, and they were wild and lawless places – they rarely ventured this far north. Those who travelled usually did so for reasons more complicated than simple theft or vandalism.

There were no footprints in the long grass, no signs that anyone had been here. He had been away for eleven days searching for the latest object, true, and much could have happened which the weather might have covered in the meantime. But the clearing had the sense of having remained uninterrupted. Untouched. There was a wildness here that he had sensed in many places across Skythe, as if the land had shrugged off all memory of human interaction and returned to its primal state. Even though he had lived here for almost three years, the cave and surrounding area managed to retain that feeling.

Venden had often thought it strange. Now it was stranger still.

He stepped from the trees' shade and crossed the grassy clearing, unafraid, cautious. He listened for any sounds out of place, sniffed the air, remained alert, but he was as alone as ever. When he reached the remnant and held out his hand to touch it, something moved.

Venden fell and struck the ground hard, one hand held out to break his fall, the shadow deep inside him rolling with apparent delight. The wet grass stroked across his face. Everything had moved but for the remnant. It was as if the land had shrugged, the sky shimmered, and the falling rain wavered at the audacity of Venden's touch. The only solidity was the remnant and those objects he had brought to it – the objects he had been guided to by the shadow he carried inside – and he was struck with a certainty that if he had been touching it, he would not have fallen.

The trees were still, and there were no sounds of panicked wildlife or falling rocks. The world had moved for him alone.

Water soaked through his clothing. He lay motionless, looking up at the falling raindrops. Those that struck him seemed suddenly warm.

From the cart came the sound of movement, and he rolled onto his side and lifted up on one elbow to look across the clearing. The object lay motionless where he had left it, yet he was certain he'd heard the sound of its many short limbs drumming against the wood. He gained his feet and walked back to the cart, nervous that the same sensation would strike him again, but he was steady and sure.

The object was almost weightless, motionless, in his hands, cool, and nothing like anything alive. It was only as he started across the clearing with the thing in his hands that the remnant began to move.

Chapter 4

remnant

Days after Milian Mu's awakening in the cave, she catches her first food. Tiredness no longer preys upon her. Yet she is still weak and almost withered away, and it will be a while until she can move again.

There is no day and night, only the ebb and flow of the tide to time her slow heartbeats – five beats ebb, five beats flow. She has been sleeping and ageing with the land. The shard of Aeon has been resting with her, and perhaps dreaming as well, because she can feel it still inside like a forgotten memory.

She has been listening to skittering back and forth on the cave floor. Hearing the animal locates it in the dark, and the warmth of its meagre supply of blood has raised the temperature on Milian's right side. She reaches out slowly and grabs the creature. There are waving, scabrous legs, a spiked carapace. She squeezes, and the sounds of breaking things echo. She puts it to her mouth as it still struggles, keen to feel its life against her lips. The dying animal moves against her mouth. There is no taste, only sensation, and she swallows because she knows she must to grow strong. Her future awaits. The shard swells within her, a cold thing reminding her of where she came from, in preparation for where she must go.

She chews some more. The memory of hunger is a bloom of heat from a spreading fire, rumbling in her stomach, vibrations spreading along limbs she has not been able to feel since waking. The more she chews and swallows – soft innards, spiky shell and legs – the more awake she feels.

After finishing eating she sits for a while in the complete darkness, listening to the water washing against the shore outside the cave. She can almost feel the sun on her skin, the wind blowing abrading sand against her face, and she can taste much more than the crushed dead thing.

She remembers arriving, and wonders how much things outside have changed.

Another animal oozes between the rocks; she can smell it, and hear its moist skin flexing and releasing secretions that allow it to slip along. It is somewhere to her right, easing closer. She prises the thing from a narrow crack and brings it to her mouth, cool and slick. Her arm scrapes as she moves, heavy and weighed down.

How long have I been here?

The shard does not steer her or coerce, but it is aware. She can feel it watching, and has the idea that perhaps it has *always* watched, and kept her alive, and waited for . . .

Something.

Because it is merely a shard, not the whole. The remnant of a god.

Bon was exhausted. After seven days at sea with poor food, sickness, dirty water and a constant belief that his next breath might be his last, he'd had to swim half a mile to shore through vicious waves, with sea things doing their best to take bites from him. His arms and legs no longer wished to function. His stomach was rumbling from the bread and meat, and he wondered whether Juda had succeeded in poisoning him, intentionally or not.

But the memory of the dreadful murder and mutilation he had seen on the beach drove him on. And after so long fearing the light and courting the dark, the realisation that he desperately wanted to live came as something of a revelation.

Juda led them from the small cave and into a narrow crawlspace that seemed to go on for ever. The oil lamp threw vague illumination, but it birthed shifting shadows that deepened crevasses and exposed the sharp ridges of broken rock, and after a few minutes' crawling Bon had slashed his left thumb and right knee. Behind him Leki seemed to move soundlessly, a counterpoint to his gasps and struggles. She had grace. She enchanted and frightened him.

'How far?' he asked, but Juda did not answer, or did not hear.

'Just crawl,' Leki said from behind. 'I think we can trust him.'

'You think?' Bon's voice was muffled in the enclosed space. He wasn't sure where he was, or why, and this journey had become something he had never expected.

Juda had every opportunity to kill them, but so far had done his best to save them. *So he says*, Bon thought. But that image came again – slayer, the man, his guts and severed head.

The route from the cave was barely even a tunnel. A crack in the ground, narrowing and widening, sloping and falling, and at one point it became almost vertical. Juda climbed without pause or comment, and Bon followed, bracing his back against one side and his feet against the other. They climbed for some time, and the thought of what injuries he would sustain should he fall kept his back straight, his legs tense. Leki climbed below him, silent as ever. Whenever he glanced down he saw only her pale face looking up, and he was grateful for her encouraging smile.

Bon lost track of how long they were climbing and crawling. They paused to rest frequently, and it took five stops before he realised that Juda was lost. Their rescuer would sit back against the cave wall with his eyes closed and his hands reaching, grabbing shadows from the air and piling them either side of him. Bon glanced back at Leki, and she merely raised an eyebrow.

The air changed just as Bon noticed the light. The oil lamp had been burning low, but there was a background illumination that seemed to filter down from above. Dusky light was visible through narrow cracks above them, filtering down through spiky plant growth.

'This is it,' Juda whispered, and his obvious relief was also loaded with stress. 'We're out, we're away. But I have to see. See if the open brings danger.'

'How could the slayers know where we're coming out?' Leki asked, but Juda seemed to wave away her question, slapping it from the air with his ever-moving hands.

'I'll crawl out and see,' Juda said. 'They're not looking for me.'

'Wait. Don't move. Don't cough or fart. Don't . . . *breathe*.' He nipped out the oil lamp between thumb and forefinger and crawled into the open.

Bon watched him go, and then Leki was beside him, warm and close. Though he had only known her for days, there was a familiarity that he found comforting.

'He has Outer blood,' Leki whispered.

'You're sure?' Brought to the continent of Alderia from the countless scattered islands way across the oceans – it was rumoured that some even came from the fabled southern place known at the Heartlands, ten thousand miles distant – Outers were regarded as inferior races, created by the Fade gods for Alderia's use. As such they were frequently imported into the south of Alderia as cheap labour, and the north as slaves.

'I don't think he's pure Outer. But there's something to him, yes. Have you seen the colour of his eyes?'

'Piercing green.'

'Regerran.'

'I knew a Regerran once,' Bon said. She had been a thin, striking woman who had worked in a tannery close to where he and his wife used to live. He had tried speaking to her several times in the street but, every time, she had turned away, almost panicked by the unaccustomed contact. It had shamed him then, and it shamed him still, because he had not tried harder. She had been killed in an accident soon before his son had vanished. No one had mourned her.

'A feeble race,' Leki said, surprising him. 'They're troubled, and never rest. They suffer nightmares that make them violent, dangerous to themselves and others. That's probably why he's smoking those cigars – there'll be a drug in there, settling and calming. Where I come from in Skeptin Lakes, they're employed to harvest nark eggs from the Chasm Cliffs. They sometimes spend days up on the cliffs, and they tie themselves on when it's time to sleep.'

'He said he'd been awake for some time,' Bon said. He could still smell the scent of the cigar smoke. 'Do you really see him as feeble?' The comment had troubled him. Leki's past was still a mystery, and he could not simply assume that she was here because she had spoken out against the Ald. For all he knew she was like the priest on the ship – a devout whose banishment was for something else entirely.

'I'm speaking through what I've witnessed of other Regerran,' she said. 'That's all.'

Bon fell silent, thinking about what she had said, and what Juda's heritage might mean. There were still many questions to ask him, but he had no desire to include Juda's race in any discussion. It was irrelevant. Alderia was behind them now, and with it the prejudices and indoctrinations of the Ald's way of life. If being banished had done anything for him, surely it would have granted him such freedoms?

They remained close, but not quite touching, until Juda returned. He scrambled down from the narrow entrance, blocking the fading light and panting as if he had been running. He paused close to them, little more than a shadow, and handed them both dry, rumpled clothing.

'We're . . . okay,' he said. 'No sign of slayers nearby. Close to Vandemon, but we'll have to skirt around and head north. We can't enter the town.'

'Into the wilds, then?' Leki asked.

'Yes. The slayers might expect that, but it's not likely they'll follow right away.'

'Why not?' Bon asked.

'Two others they wanted from your ship evaded them.' His meaning was implicit. While the slayers hunted down the others who had escaped, the three of them could flee.

'You've done this before,' Leki said. 'So do you always run with the people you rescue?'

Juda was silent, awkward. His shadows shifted as his hands waved, grasping at the air.

'Juda?' Bon asked.

'We need to go,' Juda said. He turned and started climbing, and Bon reached out, grabbing his foot.

'What happened?'

'Nothing good. Which is why every breath counts.' Juda

sighed, and when he spoke again his voice was shaking. 'I knew the time would come. The slayers have marked me also. I made contact with a friend in Vandemon, and she told me the slayers have my name and scent. I'm now as much on their list as you.' He shrugged. 'I'm fucked.'

Juda went and they followed. Outside, Bon's first sight of Vandemon was the flames.

Juda was tired, and he could feel his darker, troubled side starting to fill him out, stretching itself through torso and limbs and taking his shape. Aggravating his part-Regerran blood, this darker echo was dangerous. Though dusk had fallen, he could not let himself succumb to nightmares. They had to escape.

He had slipped into Vandemon only briefly, but in that time he had learned everything he needed to know. Built amongst the ruins of an old Skythian sea port, rough wooden buildings stood between the tumbled walls and rubble piles of homes where no one had lived for six centuries. Even ruined, it was obvious from some of the carved stones and barely visible floor layouts that these old structures had been much grander than those now forming the coastal community of banishees. In the hundred years that Alderia had been shipping its worst criminals to Skythe – from murderers to political exiles – there had been barely any attempts to improve these dwellings. They were built, they fell or became dilapidated, and they were repaired or rebuilt. Patched up and thrown together, they reflected much about the people who lived within them.

The new arrivals who had made it to shore and not been marked for execution by the slayers were already being integrated into Vandemon. There were those who sought to welcome new prisoners, and who did their best to reach them before some of the town's less benevolent characters – the pimps who went for the women, and slave drivers who lured with promises of buried treasures in the wilds to the north. If the prisoners could be warned then they might avoid both.

Juda had gone to visit his friend Bindy at Bindy's Tavern, and from the moment he'd entered he had known that something was wrong. Usually pleased to see him, she had been uneasy and twitchy, glancing more at the door than at him as if waiting for someone else to arrive. And moments into their conversation he had asked the question, and her silence provided his answer. *Slayers?*

Juda was now known and marked, and his time in Vandemon was over.

He had always known that this moment would come, and for some time he had been awaiting it. After each prison ship arrival and the resulting executions, the slayers would retreat to their holes along the coast where the cliffs were tumbled and worn from erosion and, perhaps, some ancient cataclysm. They made their dens there, and no one ventured close. But Juda had known that he was destined to be hunted by these inhuman killers one day. Seeking the sparse dregs of magic still in the land – and attempting to rescue those who might be able to guide him to them, knowingly or not – was inevitably going to make him a marked man in the end. Gathering information, such as the names of banishees and the reasons why certain ones were marked for death, was always dangerous. Bon Ugane's name and crime had come to Juda at a cost.

Sometimes Juda recognised the desperation in his actions, and the unlikeliness of success. But he had nothing else left to live for. And there was always a chance.

He was not sad to leave Vandemon, because Bon Ugane and Leki might be the people he had been seeking for so long. Bon's crime had been studying Skythe and the war's ambiguous history, after all. But he could not yet let them know. He did not wish to frighten them away. His needs and aims, he knew, could be perceived as arcane to some, and mad to most.

'What are all the fires?' Bon asked behind him.

'Warding off the spirits of dead Skythians,' Juda said. 'They set fires in the ruins of old Skythe buildings the four nights of full moon each month.' He shivered. The flames always provoked a chill in him.

Bon laughed. 'Spirits!'

Juda paused, squatted beside a thick tree. The light from the settlement played shadows with the tree's branches, dancing them across the ground either side of the trunk.

'What do you know about spirits?' he asked, perhaps too harshly. As ever in the presence of new arrivals, he found that he was developing some sort of pride about Skythe and his place here. It was inexplicable and surprising, but he treasured the feeling.

'Only that the dead don't trouble the living,' Bon said.

'Maybe not where you come from,' Juda said. 'Here, they dance, and you'd better hope they don't want to dance with you.' He headed off, leading away from the coastal village in a curving route that would take them inland along the shoulder of a mountain. They followed their own dancing shadows.

'You believe in these spirits?' Leki asked behind him.

'Do you believe in the sea?' Juda asked. 'The air? The land?'

'That they exist, yes. But I have no need to decorate them with make-believe.'

'And that's how I believe in the spirits,' Juda said. 'They are there, without doubt. No need to deform reality into a myth.'

'Why try to scare them away?' Bon asked from behind Leki. They were moving slowly, cautiously, and Bon's were the heaviest footsteps.

'Nobody wants angry spirits living amongst them,' Juda said.

'Why are they angry?' Bon asked.

'Because they're dead, and we're living on their land. Now, enough with the fucking questions. Stay quiet.'

He led them across the steep mountainside, following a gentler path that would not be too treacherous in the dark. Each time he blinked it was darker still, and he could feel that other self inside stretched almost to fill his extremes. He did not have long, but he had to concentrate, and move them away as far as he could before camping down. The slayers still had other targets to track and kill, but it was possible they would find them quickly.

And the slayers did not tire. Did not stop. Juda had to lead the others to a place where they might lose their pursuers, and that was still a day's hike.

'Where are you taking us?' Bon asked after they had been walking for some time.

'Somewhere safe.'

'From the slayers, or you?' Leki asked.

Juda glanced back. Even in the moonlight he could see her expression.

'Whatever you think you know about me, I'm fine for a little longer,' he said, grinning. 'Important to go further. Up there, over the ridge, there's a place on the other side where we'll be safe for the night.'

'And from there?' Bon asked.

'That's for tomorrow,' Juda said. 'We live day by day on Skythe.'

They crested the ridge in silence and, descending into

the shadowed valley beyond, Juda felt the nightmares closing.

'Tie me . . .' he said, slipping to his knees on the shale. He pointed downhill at the small wooden shelter built within a copse of trees. 'In there . . . tie me . . . keep watch.'

'And if a slayer comes?' Bon asked.

'Won't,' Juda said, and his voice felt like someone else's.

He grasped a handful of sharp stones in his fist and squeezed, trying to hold back the night.

Where in the name of all the fake gods have I been sent? Bon wondered, and their saviour raged and strained against his ropes.

'I thought you said Regerrans sleepwalked?' Bon said.

'Well,' Leki said, but she had no answer. She shrugged. 'Nightmares, too.' She seemed as confused as him. They sat close together as they had in the prison ship's hold, but this time the storm was inside with them.

They had carried Juda the final distance to the rough shelter he had indicated, and even then he had been twitching and hissing like a captured serpent. After tying him as instructed they had sat back, waiting to see what would happen. They did not have to wait very long. The hissing continued, spittle and blood frothing at his mouth, and then he started rolling and writhing against the bindings. His movements appeared agonised rather than strong, flesh bulging where he forced against the ropes, and his constant shifting and hissing reminded Bon of the terrible sound and movement of the sea surging against the ship.

'This is no simple Regerran sleep,' Leki said a little later. 'What do you think's wrong with him?'

'Don't ask me,' Bon said. 'Seems half-mad when he's awake; why should he be any different asleep?'

'He could give us away.'

Bon had been keeping intermittent watch, but the valley was in darkness, and anyone or anything wishing to creep in would do so without him seeing. They had already discussed leaving Juda here and going on alone, but neither relished the idea. He had saved them, he seemed to know where they were going, and for now they both wanted to stay with him. *Until we know more*, Leki had said. And Bon already believed there was so much more for Juda to tell them.

'Did he really put himself in danger to save us?' Bon asked.

'I think he was in danger before,' Leki said. 'And he seems . . .'

'Eager,' Bon finished for her. 'He's done this before.'

'But why?' Leki asked. 'What does he want?'

'Maybe we'll find out tomorrow.' Bon sat close to Leki, pressing against her and feeling her warmth through the jacket Juda had brought for him. She had talked of not decorating the sea and air with make-believe, and those words to Juda betrayed more than she had to Bon. 'You're no slave to anything the Ald tell us,' he said.

'Did you even once believe I was?'

Bon chuckled, and it felt good. That surprised him. Could laughter really find a place against such darkness, when a madman writhed before them? But perhaps that was the best reason for laughter.

'What were your plans when you got here?' he asked.

'Plans?' She shrugged, glancing away. 'I made none. They tore me from my family, my home, my life. I taught in Skeptin Lakes, history and philosophy. Taught everything *they* told me to teach, mostly, but there were always moments when some of what I believe found its way in. By accident, usually. I wasn't stupid. Knew what I'd do to myself if I made it too obvious.' She drifted away, perhaps disconcerted by how much she had said in so little time. Her bitterness did not surprise Bon, but her uncertainty unsettled him. He liked the strong Leki.

'So, plans?' she continued. 'Fuck plans. I wouldn't honour them by making plans. Fuck them.' She trailed off again, and Bon pressed sideways against her, a subtle but obvious movement. Not so blatant as a touch or a hug, but a gesture of comfort.

'Even if you had, I bet I wouldn't have been in them,' he said.

'Right.' She sighed, drumming her fingers on her leg, the air heavy with something unsaid. But they sat in silence.

Before them, Juda rolled on a bed of dried twigs and leaves, a foam of spittle and blood sheened across his chin and lips.

Bon looked out at the shadowy valley one more time, saw no movement, and leaned his head back against the rough wall of the shelter. Tomorrow, he would begin his first full day on Skythe as someone hunted, and scared. But at least he was with a friend.

Someone shook Bon awake from a dream of being chased by a swollen killer, a heavy-cloaked thing bearing a spiked staff and his dead son's face.

He rose from his dream like a god looking down, and in that brief omnipotence he saw himself sprinting across a desolate landscape spotted with bright purple plants, each of them a blooming bruise. The son-thing lurched after him, barely walking and yet closing on him with every step he took. Behind the son-thing came a shadow that belonged to something larger and more dreadful. Its shadow tendrils seemed to emanate from them both. And while he ran and his son-thing lurched, the shadow seemed to dance with unalloyed joy.

'Bon Ugane,' a voice said, and Bon blinked himself awake, leaving the dream behind. For an instant he wondered whether that monster was still closing on his fleeing self, then Juda leaned back from him and smiled down. 'You must have really needed that sleep.'

'How long . . .?' Bon asked.

'It's barely dawn.' Juda's smiled seemed strained, pained. There was blood smeared across his jaw.

'Leki!' Bon said, sitting upright and kicking at Juda. *What has he done where is she why did I fall asleep?*

'The water woman's fine!' Juda said, sprawling back.

'Then where is she?' Bon stood, remaining stooped in the shelter. Dawn sunlight slanted in between the roughly tied uprights, and his clothing was damp with dew.

'I was taking a piss,' Leki said from outside. 'And keep your voice down or you'll scare them away.'

'Scare who away?'

'Come and see.'

Bon's shock settled and he smiled hesitantly at Juda. The man nodded back, wiping at his chin with one hand. He must have seen Bon looking at the dried blood.

Outside, Leki was standing beneath the shadow of the trees, looking out across the narrow, deep valley at a herd of creatures on the opposite slopes. Pale brown, the size of a child, they flitted back and forth across the grassed slopes like a flock of birds. Their hoofsteps sounded as a vague mumbling, and their call was a piping cry that mourned across the valley.

'Anything?' Juda asked from the shelter behind them.

'No,' Leki said. Bon realised that she had been to the ridge to check if anyone or anything was following, but now she seemed more taken with the creatures seemingly performing for them.

'Hat-hat,' Juda said. 'Taste good with rose herb.'

'I'm happy just to watch,' Leki said.

The hat-hat streamed left and right across the slope for some time, and then a pair of hawks swooped down from out of the sun and took one. They tore it apart on the ground, and as they ate the rest of the flock grouped tightly together and fled over the hilltop.

'He says there'll be two of them following us,' Leki said. 'They'll pick up our scent and be on our trail. Today's the day we have to escape them, or they'll hunt us until we drop, or they do. And it won't be them.'

'Then why aren't we moving now?' Bon asked, knowing there was an answer. Today had a strange feel already, as if he had woken into a world with different rules.

'Because Juda is going to try and use some magic.'

Bon caught his breath, staring at Leki, waiting for her to elaborate. Magic? The word was used as a turn of phrase, but Leki had given it weight.

'So what happened when I was asleep?' he asked.

'Our lives changed,' Leki said. She looked at him at last. 'And I found out why our saviour and friend is just a little mad.'

Juda emerged from the shelter and lit a roughly rolled cigar. He breathed in deeply and glanced their way, nervously.

'Magic?' Bon asked.

To begin with, Juda did not respond. He took a long pull on the cigar, shivering slightly and closing his eyes. Smoke drifted from his nose and curled like a living thing, caressing his cheek and forehead before dispersing in his hair.

'Why else do you think I'd come to Skythe?'

'You came here voluntarily?' Bon asked.

'Could say that.' He stood beside them, taking deep, long

pulls on the cigar. Seemingly without noticing, he clasped at the air before him with one hand, searching for something that was not there. *Mad, indeed*, Bon thought, but he was never one to judge madness on simple deviation from the norm. He knew the norm to be an ambiguous thing, a construction of doctored beliefs and prescribed outlooks. It could be that Juda simply saw in a different way. 'I came here looking.'

'For magic,' Leki said.

'Where else would I look?'

'You're not Regerran?' Bon asked.

'I'm told my mother was,' Juda said. 'But the nightmares are mostly my own. Magic does strange things, when you're close to it for a long time.'

'And those cigars?' Leki asked.

'Scamp smoke helps. A problem hidden, not cured. Scamp keeps the nightmares deep, for a while.' He stared across the valley. Even with the cigar clamped between his teeth he seemed to be sniffing the air. 'You need to break camp. Prepare yourselves for a fast, long journey. We must escape the slayers today, and to do that we first have to gain a good lead.'

'So shouldn't we be running *now*?' Bon asked, panic blooming.

'We're about to. But I'm leaving something behind.' Juda glanced back at them and nodded up at the steep hillside beyond the shelter. 'Climb. Snuggle together and watch. But don't come close. I'll join you soon, and then we run.'

Bon and Leki packed up the few things they had with them and left Juda behind, sitting on a fallen log close to the shelter and absently kicking loose soil over the remains of their campfire. They climbed silently, the brief respite already behind them. Bon felt an urgency borne of fear, and confusion about why they hadn't run through the night, why Juda couldn't have smoked and gone further despite the nightmares. But then he thought of the reason Juda said the people of Vandemon kept fires flaming in the dark, and he wondered whether night was a safe place for visitors to Skythe.

The slope soon became steeper, and for the last stretch they were climbing on hands and knees, crawling up from handhold to handhold. Bon tried not to look down, but the knowledge of Juda called him. That, and what their rescuer might be doing. *I'm leaving something behind*, he had said. As they reached the ridge and sat down, panting and sweating, Bon looked down into the valley to see.

Juda was moving slowly around the shelter and the site of their campfire. He paused many times, seemingly listening or waiting for something before moving on. Smoke from his scamp cigar drifted about his head, forming a larger cloud that settled over the area and stole colour and sharpness.

'Why is he taking so long?' Bon asked, but Leki merely shrugged. She was frowning, concentrating, and Bon wondered what she was waiting to see. He had no idea what magic was supposed to look like.

Juda finished patrolling the site and knelt down. He reached into his pack and seemed to sprinkle something on the ground, moving his hand left to right in a casual wave. Then he stood, surveyed the area one more time, and started climbing.

'That was it?' Bon asked. Leki shrugged again. Her silence deepened her mystery. He wanted to clasp her hand, ask what she knew, but he was certain that she would only tell him if she wanted to. She'd had ample opportunity, and remained silent.

'So now we run,' Bon said. 'Maybe I should just go the

other way. Let the two of you flee, I'll go back and meet the slayers on our trail.' He didn't mean that – not after the horrors he'd seen on the beach – but he was trying to provoke Leki into saying something. Anything.

'Self-pity is ugly,' she said. They watched Juda climbing towards them, and no more was said until he arrived.

He scrambled up the slope and sat beside Bon, lighting another cigar. He was breathing heavily, but seemed otherwise untroubled by the climb. Bon wondered how long he would be able to keep up with Juda and Leki. Already his legs burned, his muscles ached.

'That might help,' Juda said.

'What did you do?' Bon asked.

'Left something behind for them. A dreg.'

'What will it do?' Leki asked.

Juda seemed upset and distracted. 'We need to move. I'll know exactly when the slayers reach here, and whether they're still following our trail. And the more distance we put between them and us, the better.'

'How will you know?' Bon asked.

Juda puffed on the cigar and the scamp smoke hung heavy and spicy in the air. He stared at Bon through the smoke, and seemed very far away. 'You don't know much, do you, Bon Ugane? How will I know? I just will.'

Juda set the pace, taking them along the ridge and down into the next, much wider valley. He marched with purpose and determination, and it soon crossed Bon's mind that Juda seemed to be rushing towards something, not away from something else.

Venden Ugane came awake with something dead beneath him. He could feel it nestled under his stomach, an object whose presence was different from the bundled blankets and

82

the sparse mattress he'd made from moss and hat-hat hide. It was cold and hard. It did not belong.

For a while he did not move, staring across the clearing at the remnant and those objects he had spent so long gathering to it. It had now arced up into a perfect half-circle, and the dead tree stump at one end had tipped over to an extreme angle, a skin of dried bark fallen to the ground. It had shifted more while he had been sleeping.

He rolled onto his side and looked down to find what had died.

He had no name for the orange spiders. As large as his fist and the colour of bloodfruit, this one must have crawled down from the low cliff and dropped from the overhang into his bed just as he rolled in his sleep. They lived up on the cliff face, spinning funnel webs in holes in the rock, venturing out at sundown to harvest any prey caught in the web traps they set elsewhere across the cliff. He had observed them keeping to their own traps and not thieving from others, and he had wondered why. It hardly bode well for survival. Catching and examining a spider had crossed his mind, but there had always been something else to do, and he'd never had the chance. Now, the chance had come to him.

It had burst beneath him. Its insides were slick and sticky, stringing from his jacket as he sat up. The creature had seven legs and, search though he did, Venden could find no evidence of an eighth. Lost in a fight, perhaps. But it was just as likely that it had mutated this way. He prodded the sad body, and its ruptured shell was cool and surprisingly soft.

'Seven legs,' Venden said. Whenever his voice sounded across the clearing, it felt like an intrusion into the wild. 'Nature welcomes even numbers. Hard walking. Goes in circles. And the eyes.' He turned the dead creature a little, leaning close and trying to ignore the acrid smell. 'Simple

83

surface eyes. All but blind.' There was a thick line of thread still hanging from the spider's abdomen, trailing across Venden's mattress and disappearing into the grass. He scanned left and right until he saw where the sun glinted from a hanging thread high above his head, drooping down from the overhang and waving in the slight breeze. Perhaps it had been lowering itself down when it fell. Venden touched his face and throat, because he had never known how these things hunted, or killed. He found no punctures.

Beneath the overhang was a rock with a hollow in its surface, and Venden took his morning scoop of water from here and drank deep. It never tasted fresh. Water dripped from the overhang above, and he wondered how long it had taken to filter down the surface of the cliff. Perhaps some of it was run-off from the previous night's dew. Or maybe it originated deeper, filtering down through the cliff and exiting eventually to drip into the hollow, and pass into him. This filtering water might have been many years on its journey through porous rock, and he wondered what this clearing had looked like when the rain fell.

Barely taking his eyes from the shifted remnant, Venden went through his usual waking ritual of toilet, a meal of dried fruit and a silent moment of reflection upon this land. He had been here for years, and he was more certain than ever that the war and its results had banished humanity from these shores. He was only a visitor here. That the unknown presence, the hollow inside, seemed to feel at home disturbed him, but he did not dwell on it.

He judged that it was approaching late afternoon. The sun dipped towards the low wooded slopes in the west, setting fire to the treetops and smudging the landscape with vibrant fire colours. He still had time.

The remnant loomed higher above him than it ever had.

He circled it twice, examining the ground where it appeared rooted with the tree. Though it had moved, its end still disappeared into the ground, soil around it disturbed and upset, wet. Its other end also pierced the land, and there was no sign of any upset from the movement – no disturbing of the long grass, scoring of the turf or topsoil. In order to rise as far as it had, it must have grown.

He moved back to the tipped tree trunk again and knelt to examine it. There were thousands of ants crawling around the exposed roots, gathering countless spotted white eggs and transferring them down beneath the soil again.

'Only just exposed,' he whispered. A breath of air passed across the clearing, rustling plants growing on the cliff face and waving the grass in complex patterns.

The object he had brought back that morning was still where he had dropped it close to the cart. He remembered the remnant's strange movement, and dropping the spined object as he dashed for his place beneath the overhang. After that there was nothing, and sleep must have come quickly. This journey had been a long one, and tiring, and he still felt weary.

He touched the object, and the sense of raw power struck him hard. There was no movement this time, but a staggering potential that made everything clear and defined, smoothing blurred edges of doubt. And he knew what he had to do.

The object was light and comfortable in his arms. He pressed it to the remnant many times – its end, its underside, the edge with the longer projecting spines. When he shifted it in his grasp and presented the shorter spines to the remnant's underside, standing there with the shape arching above him and slicing the darkening sky in two, there was an immediate attraction that tugged the thing from his hands.

The world turned over. Venden fell, fingers digging into

the soil, terrified that he was about to fall off. His heart thudded against his chest, and he squeezed his eyes closed, thinking, *This is what I was always meant to do.* After a pause he rolled onto his back and looked up, and the remnant was more complete.

The object had melded to the arched underside, spines now bent and connected to the remnant as though they had never been apart. Venden stood and stretched up to see, but there was no sign of any connection, no join. The two had become one, and when he reached up and touched the object it felt no different from the remnant.

It was as if they had never been separate, yet, until Venden, they had been forty miles apart.

'And there are more,' he said, looking at the five other objects around the clearing. Each had a story of his finding them – guided by the presence that resided within him, shown and told where to go. Scattered across Skythe, they had been brought together again by his hands.

One of them resembled a network of petrified veins, almost the size of his torso. It looked delicate, yet when he had recovered it from a deep pool beneath a waterfall he had felt the strength inherent in its structure. It was something that belonged inside. He had not applied pressure, but knew that, if he had done so, the object would have resisted, perhaps even pushed back. It had lain in the grass beside the remnant for three moons, and now he picked it up to see where it might belong.

This time he was still clasping the thing when it hauled itself against the foot of the remnant close to the upended tree, and though the mountains seemed to shrug, he retained his balance. Part of the remnant for a moment, he felt none of the upset. It was as if it was keeping him safe.

When Venden picked up the boxy, bony shape he had

discovered in the ruin of a Skythian lakeside town, he thought that his actions resembled something like building. But as this shape also moulded itself around the remnant's underside, he let go and fell back, acknowledging what he had somehow known all along: that he was not building something new.

This was reconstruction.

Chapter 5

seed

Milian Mu senses the sun and moon shifting around her, as if she is central to their existence, and the passage of time is an ambiguous thing. Her breathing fills the cave in rhythm with the tide, and then faster, and faster still as the smell of the sea comes in and the sense of movement fills her torso. Her blood flows, her nerves jangle.

She shifts to a kneeling position, one hand splayed against the cave floor, shelled things falling from her body as she flexes and twists them away. Some of them she picks up and puts to her mouth, sucking out the slick insides and swallowing without chewing. The taste is neutral, but she can feel their goodness spreading through her insides.

Some time later, Milian Mu manages to walk around the cave. Motionless for a long time, her body has lost touch with the world, and being a moving part of it once again is like being reintroduced to a former lover.

She tries to speak. Her voice is a croak, and the shard she carries of her old god Aeon gives comfort. It does not speak, but exudes an understanding that all will be well.

Later, when the tide is low, she enters the water at one edge of the cave and starts making her way outside.

The sea welcomes her in with cold arms. She breathes in the water and panics for a moment, but the shard rises and calms her, urging her on. Those memories of a long, long journey across the bottom of the sea come again – passing through murky depths, and hiding from dark things down there – but they feel more distant now, moved further back in time by her return to life. So she pulls herself past the low stone ceiling, lowering her head beneath the surface when the powerful waters scourge the last remaining molluscs from her skin.

Eventually she feels something different above her, and she surfaces slowly to the silvery glare of the moon. Outside now, she gasps in the fresh night air. The water buoys her, and the shard sinks back down, not cowed, but secretive. She thinks perhaps it has betrayed itself, just for a moment.

Milian Mu walks through the surf and onto the beach. When she had arrived here long ago, the beach had been scorched to glass by the cataclysm way across the sea on Skythe. Now it is a rough surface of sand and sharp-edged black rocks, scattered with evidence of life – empty shells, dead crabs, seaweed, and night things that root amongst the tidal deposits to take their fill. Some of them scurry from her. Some sink down and play dead. She ignores them and looks down at herself, and feels a momentary surprise at her nakedness. She is, she realises, beautiful.

And cold.

She looks around, and along the beach there is something out of place. The building seems empty, an awkward, blocky shape against the dunes. There are nets hanging from racks beside it, and timber and wire pots piled on the beach in front. A fisherman's shack.

As she walks towards the shack, the sand slicks between her toes. The soft sea breeze brings visions of the open ocean and a chill across her newly exposed skin. She drags her feet through the sand, feeling the swish of knotted hair across her shoulders. Her breath is heavy and phlegmy in her throat. *How can I be walking?* she wonders. *How can I be breathing after so long?* But the shard rises again to allay her doubts and drive her forward.

There are many questions, but for Milian they are all answered by the presence of the shard. She is in Aeon's service now, and whatever the bastard Alderians and their Engines did to her god so long ago, at least she carries a trace of Aeon inside. *A memory*, she thinks, but that is too vague. *No, not just a memory.*

A seed.

The shack seems abandoned. The door hangs off, one side wall is split and rotting, but when she ventures inside she finds someone's belongings, heavy with windblown sand. Perhaps a fisherman went out one morning but never returned, and the only evidence of him ever existing remains here.

There are clothes, sandals, a time-blunted knife, some tobacco and a small shoulder bag. As she dresses, Milian feels a growing warmth heating her insides and exuding outwards. She is alive, again. She has risen.

Though terrible memories of what she once did still haunt the edges of her perception, she no longer feels like a relic of the past, and the future is suddenly an exciting place.

Juda viewed the slayers from the dreg of magic he had left behind, and they were terrifying.

Since finding the wisp of magic he had been training it, kneading it to his mind's desires, employing untested techniques which were largely theoretical in an effort to make the weak haze his own. This was his final dreg, a precious thing, and every step of the way – Leki and Bon Ugane following on behind, their silence loaded and nervous – he was anxiously probing back with his mind, eager to discover whether anything had worked. If it did work, then much of what he had dedicated a large part of his adult life to might have had a purpose. If it did not, then there would be so much more left to do. He would not give up on magic. He *could* not. If he did, he might as well wander into the wilds and die.

He and the others were four miles away from where they had camped when he sensed the slayers. He rested against a tree that had half fallen to grow out across the water, and as Leki's shadow reached out a concerned hand, he clasped at the air and dragged it aside, and saw back the way they had come.

The images were erratic, but clear. There were two slayers descending the steep slope towards the camp. They leaped and loped, no caution in their movements, no effort at conceal-ment or surprise. Their heavy feet slapped down and coughed up clouds of bursting fungi, and dark clothes flowed behind them, dragged along like resistant shadows.

'You're seeing them,' Bon said, but Juda waved away his words, closing his eyes. He plucked a cigar from his pocket and lit it, drawing in the spiced smoke and welcoming its calming influence. It made the visions clearer.

One slayer was female, one male. The female was heavy-boned and her large bare hands were scarred where she clasped her pike, yet she had made a grotesque effort at make-up, smearing blusher across her pale, inhuman face. Juda found the effect more disturbing than the various weapons tucked into her belt and shoulder harnesses, and as she went to all fours and sniffed across the camp he diverted his attention to the male. This was a larger slayer, his muscled arms and legs bare, body clad in thick leathers bathed so many times with blood that they had taken on a port-wine hue. His misshapen head jerked this way and that like a bird's, long plaited hair a snake's tongue tasting the air. He strode to the fire pit and kicked it asunder, and the woman scampered across and sniffed at the still-warm embers.

Then she stood, and she and the male slayer moved close, conversing in a shockingly human manner. They turned as one, pointed at Juda, and darted at him.

Juda gasped and cringed back against the tree, and for a moment the visions blurred with reality, a merging of scenes that brought the slayers close. He squeezed his eyes shut and drifted back to the camp, then held his breath as his senses opened up once more—

—and the slayers were circling like wild animals toying with their prey. There was a hint of fear in their stance, perhaps, but it was mostly fury that drove them, shimmering through their swollen muscled bodies as they stepped left and right around the dreg. He could hear them hissing, smell their scent – meaty, sweaty, a tang of something sweet – and the threat they exuded was palpable, scarring the air. They were even less human than he had believed, and he realised that they would never, ever, stop in their pursuit.

He went to his knees beside the fallen tree and brought himself back, blinking the magical dreg away and feeling the hollowness of its loss. It wrenched at his insides like the death of a loved one.

'They've reached the camp, and it's only made them madder,' he said, leaning forward to let the cool mud calm his hot forehead. 'They're coming.'

'We have four or five miles on them,' Leki said. 'We have a head start.'

'Yes,' Juda said, and he struggled not to cry as the sense of loss throbbed slowly away. 'But they're never going to stop.' He sat up and wiped the mud from his forehead, and they were both looking at him as if he was mad. If that was the truth, it was a madness that suited this land, and he was at home here. Bon and Leki were the ones out of place.

'Why did you save me?' Bon asked. 'You've doomed yourself.'

Juda laughed out loud. 'There are always reasons,' he said, puffing on the cigar again. 'We have to move. There's somewhere we can go where we might be able to lose them. But they're on our heels now. They're filled with rage. And if they catch us, there's no fighting them.'

Juda led their way along the course of the stream and looked for a good place to cross. The slayers would see their footprints and smell their route, but any way to confuse them would give Juda and his charges a few more moments. And if they reached the gas marshes, they might just have a chance.

'You were using magic,' Bon said from behind. Juda could hear the fear there as well as fascination. He did not respond. Bon persisted. 'Juda, you were using magic?'

'You doubt me?' Juda asked without pausing or looking back. Bon's change from statement to question had irked Juda's pride.

'Where does it come from?' Bon asked.

'You believe in magic?' Juda asked.

'Strange question,' Bon said. 'Everyone believes it exists, in places. But most don't even consider using it, even if they could find it. Too dangerous. Trying to use magic is like . . . catching hold of lightning.'

'Perhaps that's true,' Juda said. 'Not many people respect it. Fewer still can touch it.'

'And you're one of the few,' Leki said.

'One of the fewer,' Juda said. 'Before I arrived on Skythe . . .' He trailed off, the secrecy even now making it hard for him to continue. Even now, in this wild place where many things were possible and with people for whom his revelation might even be welcome.

'You were a Broker,' Bon said.

'I was,' Juda replied. 'The Brokers found me thirteen years ago.' He pulled out a new cigar and lit it, the scamp smoke his shield against thoughts that would do him harm. Occasionally he wondered whether it was a psychological effect, this shielding. But he was too afraid to not smoke and find out. 'I was in the south of Alderia, looking for magic. Had been for two years, since I found my first dreg on the northern face of one of the Chasm Cliffs. I'd been there since I turned twenty, climbing and abseiling, climbing again, scouring the cliff faces for signs of what I knew must be there.'

'How did you know?' Bon asked.

'Because it was calling me, of course.' Juda paused at the foot of a steep slope and looked past Leki and Bon, back the way they had come. He had to think straight. Had to consider every option, every route, every possibility. And here he knew that they must climb. He started up the slope and the other two followed, already placing themselves in his hands without question.

'I'd heard the call years before,' he continued. 'I left home in New Kotrugam and hiked south, looking for something I didn't understand, and which at the time I couldn't even name. I left behind my parents and friends, and could not make any of them understand. My father always wanted me to be a medic, and my mother doted on me after my sister died at a young age. I'm sure I broke their hearts. I told them I'd return home, but never did, and didn't really expect to. They probably think I'm dead.' Juda forged on, breathing heavily and smoking, enjoying the pressure in his chest and the haze of smoke around his head. 'I wandered for years, and in that time I met a few others who seemed to be searching for the same thing.'

'And you hooked up with them,' Bon said.

'No,' Juda said. 'My search was always a very personal thing. A . . . love. So we'd talk for a while, perhaps spend a few days camped together comparing notes and fulfilling other urges. But then we'd go our separate ways. My route took me south. I found nothing for years. And then I reached the Chasm Cliffs, and from the moment I saw them I started hearing echoes.'

'Echoes of magic?' Leki asked.

'Nothing so easy.' Juda paused halfway up the slope and took a small spyglass from his pack, extending it and scanning the landscape to the south and west of them. A herd of hat-hat smudged a distant hillside, passing back and forth like a mote in Juda's eye. Sparrs and other birds flitted through the air. He instinctively found the route they had taken and scanned its length, knowing that the slayers would be following their scent. He saw nothing, but that did little to comfort him.

'Then what?' Bon asked. The fascination in his voice was evident. And, perhaps, jealousy.

'Rumours,' Juda said. He inhaled some more scamp smoke, feeling the sharp edges of his knowledge being dulled once again by its effect. But past that dullness lay his memories. 'Suspicions of magic, beautiful. The whispered words of hundreds who had come before me, or thousands. All tempting. All . . .' He remembered being drawn to the Chasm Cliffs and standing at the edge of the first ravine, the whole landscape before him a sea of wounds and scar tissue on the land. 'Perhaps some of those before me got so close that their thoughts ... .' He did not complete the sentence, because already his memory was ahead of itself. He was down in that deep chasm, nursing a broken ankle and crawling along a rocky floor that was never touched by sunlight, heading for the dark place that felt like nowhere in the world. 'We should move on,' he said.

'But I want to hear—' Bon said.

'We move on. I'll talk as we climb.' Juda tucked the cigar in the corner of his mouth and started climbing again, grabbing tufts of heathers to pull himself up the steepening slope. He did not look back to check if Bon and Leki were following. In a way he was talking to himself, because it had been some time since he had remembered this much. But he was also probing, planting seeds, and hoping that their own purposes here might collide with his own. 'I don't know how long I was down there. Day and night seemed the same. I was watched, all the time, but I only felt in danger when the watchers revealed themselves. A lyon came close with fire dripping from its nostrils, but my screams and shouts scared it away. Three dusk blights stalked me through the deeper shadows, but I stood my ground and pulled my knife. I cut one. It dulled my knife blade and numbed my arm for the next half a day, but my fearlessness saw them away. And I *was* fearless. I knew I was down there for something else. Not to be scorched and eaten by a lyon, or carried deep by dusk blights. There was something that had drawn me down to the deepest places in those Chasm Cliffs. And whether the gods existed or not, I believed myself touched by something beyond my experience.

'I crawled, drinking from streams and eating sour berries that grew somehow down in those shadows. And then I grew closer, and I could sense it with every part of my body, every sense I knew and some I didn't. It smelled of age and distance.

Its tang was on the air, tasting of something unknowable. It vibrated through the ground and whispered to the shadows, and when I set eyes on it . . .' Juda trailed off again, taking a deep pull on his cigar as panic closed in and teased him with things he had no wish to know. His heart thrummed. Between each blink lay madness, and the scamp closed his eyes to that.

'We're almost at the top of the rise,' Bon said, panting behind and below Juda. 'We should rest . . . once we're up there.'

'It was ordinary,' Juda said. 'A smudge of solid light in the dark. Ice on coal. It looked like nothing but was . . .' He turned around then, pausing just below the ridge and looking down on Bon and Leki climbing behind him. They were both sheened with sweat and panting, and when they halted and looked up at him he saw the caution in their eyes. They were afraid of him. 'Imagine actually seeing a god of the Fade,' Juda continued. 'Being able to touch Astradus, feel Flaze's heat as he passes by. It would make them ordinary, too.'

'But you took it up,' Bon said.

'Of course,' Juda said. 'I put magic in my pack.' He mimed the words, sliding his hand into his empty backpack where a dreg of magic had once rested. He felt naked and lost now that he had left that last dreg behind. But he knew there was something greater ahead. That was what drove him. He was being pulled forward by promise, not pushed ahead by threat.

'So why come to Skythe if there was still magic in Alderia?' Leki asked.

'That dreg I found seemed to be the last,' Juda said. 'And magic is . . . insidious. It had me. There was nothing more to life from that moment on. Except maybe fucking.' He tried to smile, but they all recognised the humour as forced.

'And us?' Bon asked.

You will lead me to more, Juda thought. He had scoured much of the south of Skythe and had even ventured inside the ruins of old, incredible Engines in his search, but he had come to believe that there were others who might lead him to a true source of magic, not just a leftover. His search had shifted from magic to people, and his sense of magic had made Bon Ugane's name sing with promise – an enemy of the Ald who refuted the Fade, and who knew so much about the old war, and perhaps the magic used to fight it.

But first they had to lose the slayers.

'We can't rest,' Juda said, looking over their shoulders. 'Hope you're feeling strong. Now, we run.'

They hit the ridge and Juda led them quickly down the other side into the next valley, not wishing to present a silhouette to the pursuing slayers. They would still be way out of range of their pikes, but if the beasts actually saw them in the distance it would fuel their determination, perhaps drive them even faster. And Juda already had doubts about being able to escape. *If only I knew magic better*, he thought. *If only I could have trained it to act for me, rather than passively observing*. But being able to train magic at his relatively young age meant using Wrench Arc techniques, and though he had started examining their philosophies, that took a whole lifetime of learning. Juda, though obsessed with magic, still retained shreds of those morals instilled by his upbringing and long-lost family. The Wrench Arcs would torture magical dregs instead of training them, twist them to their needs instead of teasing them to follow their desires. Theirs took a special kind of knowledge and cruelty, and anyone in their way would suffer. Murderers and mad people, the Wrench Arcs had left humanity behind. Juda comforted himself in thinking that he had some way yet to go.

The next valley was much wider and shallower, a gently

sloping side leading down to a wide plain of grassland speckled with pockets of trees and undergrowth, and a river snaking along the valley floor. Juda knew that there was a ruined village just across the river, but it would only be visible when they were almost upon it. Perhaps it would be a place for them to rest past midday. But the more they rested, the closer the slayers would come.

'We're heading for a place past those distant hills,' he said. 'Gas marshes. Very dangerous, but there are ways to cross them. And that's where we must shake off the slayers.'

'They'll lose our scent,' Bon said.

'Hopefully.'

'But not if you're still smoking those stinking things,' Leki said as Juda lit another cigar.

He drew in the smoke, and it settled his inner darkness. 'I stop smoking these, and you're on your own. Without this . . .' He exhaled, and the smoke danced around his head. '. . . my nightmares find form. Besides, better this than the stink of you two.'

Juda's legs ached, and he knew the others were rapidly tiring. But they had no alternative. As he took the lead again, he started telling them about the other dregs of magic he had found.

Chapter 6
reborn

When Venden woke up it was snowing, and there were three auburn tadcats sitting in the snow a few steps from his camp beneath the overhang.

He had seen snow in Skythe before, but only in winter, and only when it was extremely cold and the wind blew from the north. But as far as he could remember it was still late summer, and the breeze blowing as he'd drifted to sleep had been from the west. *Maybe even the seasons are confused*, he thought, and it was not such a shocking idea. The flora and fauna of Skythe had been damaged by the war so long ago. Why not the weather also?

The tadcats were skittish, and as Venden sat up with a blanket around his shoulders, they backed away. Still watching him, they settled in the long grass at the edge of the clearing and licked their delicate paws. The long, snow-free grass.

He closed his eyes, breathed deeply and opened them again. Snow still fell. Around the remnant it appeared as deep as his ankles, settling across the smooth lines and jagged parts he had come to know so well. But beyond, past where he had parked the cart, the plants were free of snow, many of them bathed in early morning sunlight.

Venden stood, ignoring the pressure on his bladder. He glanced once more at the tadcats as they scampered away, then stepped forward into the snow shower, convinced that it would fade away as sleep and dreams retreated.

His foot sank into snow. He gasped at the cold and looked up into the swirling flakes. They were fat, floating down slowly enough for him to target one and catch it on his tongue. It melted and freshwater flowed down his throat. Other flakes touched his warm skin, landed in his eyelashes and settled in the soft scruffy beard that had grown over the past year. The snowstorm was troubling but beautiful, and for a moment sleep still haunted Venden enough to relish its beauty.

When he took several more steps towards the remnant, the snow stopped. Sunlight burned through and warmed his face where the ice had recently touched.

'That wasn't normal,' he said. He looked at the remnant again and it was still covered in snow, thick layers that blurred its lines. But elsewhere it was quickly melting, seeping into the ground as though subject to a great, unfelt heat. Grass compressed by the weight popped up again, shaking the memory of snow as if it had never happened. Soon, Venden felt little more than a morning chill, and even that dispersed as he walked around the remnant. For the first few steps his feet squished in muddy ground, but then the soil grew harder, the grass swishing around his feet and whispering dry secrets.

The remnant remained covered in snow. It was frozen, not dripping beneath the sun, and several times Venden went to step closer, to see whether the world around him would stay

101

the same once he touched the great shape. When he'd been attaching objects to it the day before he had been part of it at times, settled by its touch while he felt the world around him shifting, shivering. But stepping forward now, he was afraid that contact with this strange thing would remove him from his world. And much as he had devoted himself to it for some time, he was still afraid.

'So what now?' he asked, and as if in answer the snow on the remnant melted. This was no gentle thaw. One moment it was still there, frozen solid, icicles pointing and snow moulded to the remnant's peculiar extremities; the next moment, everything melted away and washed to the ground, spreading in a puddle through the long grass until the dry soil sucked it down. Venden closed his eyes and breathed in, feeling steam stroke down his throat and into his lungs. He heard movement, felt three harsh thuds against the ground, and when he opened his eyes he caught a glimpse of the shape flexing to motionlessness. It was an insinuation of movement rather than something overt, the air and landscape around him complicit.

The rain came then, great droplets that flattened the grass and splashed from the remnant and the dead tree. Venden cried out in surprise. His voice was loud and lonely, and he reined in the shout because he thought the remnant might frown upon it.

I know what you are, he thought, and it was the first time he had ever formed that idea. Before now he had been too afraid in case he caused offence, or the betrayal of such knowledge might mark him for murder. But the remnant already knew that he knew. His exposure of that knowledge was nothing. He was only a human, not . . .

'Not a god,' Venden said, and rain ran down across his face into his mouth. It was cold against his sensitive teeth, questing fluid fingers inside his shirts. He thought he was being examined. But the remnant already knew him, and had been using him for a long time. It would know him better than he knew himself.

Rain ended, hail began. The remnant flexed, and this time it did nothing to hide its movement from Venden. It movement was fluid and beautiful, harsh and terrible, like nothing alive he had ever seen before. It was more solid and real than everything else, and as the hail drove Venden to his knees he began to cry.

The hail ended and melted away, and sunlight warmed the tears from his cheeks. Wind rose up and faded again, caressing the remnant and the prone Venden, yet not touching the trees at the clearing's extremes, nor the plants hanging down the cliff face. Mist rose and fell, lightning cracked overhead and lit up the shape in a brief, incredibly bright flash. Venden's skin stretched across his face and his eyeballs dried and his hair started to singe, but then a coolness closed around him like a protective hand.

It's coming to life, he thought. *It's resurrecting!* An idea flashed into his mind, more fully formed and detailed than any that had come before, and he realised that was not quite right. It was not yet living again, not in any way that he could understand. Without its final part it was a shape, not a life. Without its heart, this reconstructed god was an old memory flexing its muscles. New thoughts and memories were yet to come.

'Fifty miles away,' Venden said as he recognised the place displayed to his mind's eye. 'To the north.' The void inside him flexed in excitement.

He had never ventured that far north. Skythe was strange and dangerous, and in that direction lay the strangest and most dangerous place of all. Haunted, legendary, a location where myths were still birthed, Skythe's dead capital city, Kellis Faults, awaited.

The heart of the murdered god Aeon rested in that place, and Venden would help it beat again.

Once dressed, Milian sat on the beach and ate again. She'd found a seabird with a broken wing, and after a quick twist of the neck she plucked it and bit in. The warm blood inspired horrible memories, but she stared out to sea and continued chewing. She craved the sustenance. Those memories were of another time, and a Milian driven by something else. The daemon had made her do those things, that mad soulless thing, and then the shard of Aeon had driven it out.

I owe Aeon so much, she thought. But as she ate and looked around, she was far from certain about that. She had no concept of how the world was now – whether Skythe was still there, what had happened to those Engines, whether the daemons had raged on and on – and no idea of her place in it. She supposed that her first act would be to start exploring.

For the first time she noticed how cool the breeze from the north was. It picked up sea scents and spray and salt, and abraded her skin as it rolled up the long beach. It did not make her uncomfortable. After so long sensing nothing, it was beautiful. She stood and stretched her limbs, turning slowly around and inviting the breeze's caresses. The sand was cool and smooth between her toes, and she remembered the glassy sheen across the beach the last time she had been here, the sand melted by whatever cataclysm had occurred to the north.

'Will I find anyone?' She looked at the high, wide dunes behind her and wondered what might be beyond. Then she looked down at herself for the hundredth time since leaving the cave. The memories from before her long sleep were vague and informed mainly by dreams, but she could not recall ever acknowledging these curves, her shape, and the athleticism that should not be here now, but was. Perhaps because she never had. Or perhaps, she thought, because she had awoken anew. Refreshed by dormancy. Reborn. She ran her hands down over her breasts, across her flat stomach, and down her muscled thighs to her feet, half buried in the sand. She could feel the potential in her body, coiled and glad to be awake. Standing bent over on that beach, every ache or pain from her joints had vanished, and her mind was clearing by the moment.

And the shard was there within her, that meagre surviving part of her destroyed god, calming fears and smoothing errant doubts about why she was here, and how.

She had been on Alderia for centuries, and now Milian Mu felt the urge to explore.

She left the beach behind and climbed the first of the sand dunes. Panting, sweating, relishing the exertion, she gained the summit and turned back to look out to sea. Even from this slight elevation she could see much further. A small sailing ship ploughed the water a couple of miles out, flying a flag she could not see and would not recognise if she did. It approached land at an angle, and Milian looked left along the coast to see if she could make out its destination. But dunes, trees and a headland to the west meant that her view along the coast was restricted. She watched the boat, hypnotised by its movement until something inside jarred her onward.

'I'm going!' she said, surprising herself. She spoke a language as old as her dead god, and wondered whether anyone here would recognise the words.

As the sound of the sea slowly faded behind her, she felt a tug of loneliness. *I've been hearing that for hundreds of years.* She was woken, but could she really move on? Her condition was remarkable, but if she attributed it to that thing inside her then she was not wholly herself. *I am me!* Milian thought. But it carried little weight. She felt the shard in the background, and if she defied or denied it, perhaps then it would come to the fore.

So she walked south, because that was the way she felt compelled to go.

The dunes stretched further inland than she had anticipated, and they grew larger than she could have imagined. Those close to the sea were mere sand humps, speckled here and there with grasses and spiked on occasion with driftwood worn smooth by the sea. Soon the slopes became higher, held in place by numerous tall trees hanging heavy with a deep orange fruit. She plucked one and ate it, and it purged the taste of raw meat from her mouth.

Some valleys between dunes were strafed by sunlight, others shadowed by the huge sand hills. She found freshwater streams and drank, gulping down so much that her stomach sloshed when she moved. She soon needed to urinate, and moments after that she was drinking again. She felt herself growing stronger and more whole, and the next time she passed a small copse of fruit trees she ate from them once again.

With every step she took, she moved on from the memories that had haunted her strange hibernation. She welcomed the distance, because with it went the sickness about what she had done. This Milian Mu was becoming a whole new person. And though as yet she did not know how that was possible, or why, simply being was enough.

She walked on through the day. The landscape changed,

sand dunes giving way to a gently rolling plain. It was dotted with rocky mounds that looked artificial, reminding her of burial mounds back on Skythe, and here and there were swathes of woodland singing with bird life. Much further south she could see high hills, hazed with sunlight and glinting with what might have been water or veins of exposed, pale rock. Some hilltops were craggy where rock falls had sharpened them, others seemed smoothed by erosion.

Later, she heard voices from the other side of a low ridge. She paused and remained motionless for a long time. The falling sun caught her shadow and cast it eastward, and she lengthened into dusk without once moving. She was a tree, a rock, a mountain, etched as part of the landscape until the sun went down and her shadow combined with the general darkness.

There were several children, shouting and arguing as they played some game remote from the adults conversing in more level tones. No one attempted to disguise their presence. The glow of a campfire lit the air above the small ridge, and as dusk bled across the hills in the west, the smell of cooking permeated the air. Stomach heavy with soft fruit and fresh-water, still Milian salivated. She could not identify what they were cooking, but it was rich and tangy. That, more than anything, drove her to move closer.

There were two covered wagons and several shires, similar to creatures she had known on Skythe but taller, stronger, with shaggy hair on their legs and much broader shoulders. The wagons were parked parallel, and between them a large cooking fire had been set. Six adults fussed around the fire, and beyond them Milian could see the silhouettes of frolicking children.

The smell of cooking meat was almost overpowering.

A shadow fell across her, cast by faint starlight. Milian froze. A woman spoke. Milian did not understand the language, and did not reply. She thought that to betray herself would be a bad idea.

She turned around. The woman stood six steps away, wary but not threatening. She was short and stocky, with a wild head of hair and intricately woven clothing. A tall man stood just behind her, a long object of some sort nursed in both hands. His clothing was equally fine. He said nothing, but his eyes spoke volumes. Reflecting his camp's firelight, they flickered as they took in this mysterious woman, her stained clothing and the tatty fisherman's bag by her side. He looked her up and down. Milian could almost taste his lust.

The woman spoke again, slower, her words just as incomprehensible.

Milian touched her ears and mouth and shrugged. The woman nodded, seeming to sink slightly as tension left her. The man looked away.

So now I am deaf and dumb, Milian thought. But she knew that subterfuge could last only so long, and that her otherness would be revealed in a thousand ways.

She put herself at the campers' mercy until the shard urged her what to do next.

'That first dreg in the roots of the Chasm Cliffs changed my life. I carried it back towards New Kotrugam, intending to examine and study it. But it started a hunger for more. Thirty miles from the New Kotrugam wall, I spent three days in an inn with a heavy head cold. I drank water and ate rice, and only ventured down to the inn's public rooms late on the third evening for beer and more food. Starting to feel a bit better. Hungry. And that's where I met the Brokers.'

Juda was marching quickly, telling them his story as if to

lure them on. Bon Ugane and Leki followed, apart from Juda and together in their silent acknowledgement of each other. They walked without looking or touching, but a connection had been made which Bon felt would not be broken. Leki might act distant and aloof at times, but he knew that she felt the same. She hadn't needed to tell him.

'I'd heard of them before, and thought them fools,' Juda said. 'Maybe that made me a fool's fool. Because they have records, and knowledge, and what they do can't be denied.'

He's talking about people who openly seek forbidden magic, Bon thought. He had heard and read so much, and his doubts led to him continuing his son Venden's research into the war. That was sedition, and such dissidence had resulted in him being deported to Skythe. Now, Juda was talking about the forbidden magic that Bon and many others believed had been borne by the Ald to assault Skythe's manifested god. There had been no plague, and the war had left dregs of magic scattered across both lands. Bon believed that as fact, but proof had always been much harder to find.

Though terrified, Bon could not help being fascinated by Juda's tale.

'I spoke to the Broker,' Juda said, 'but I've always been . . . on my own. People didn't like my Regerran blood, though it barely meant anything to me. The green eyes are unusual. So I stayed another day, and late that afternoon I showed them what I'd found. I was expecting a certain reaction. A certain . . . shock.' Juda leaped a small stream easily six steps wide and carried on, not once looking back. After Leki crossed she *did* look back, one eyebrow raised, smiling gently.

'Come on, then,' she said softly, and Bon kept his eyes on her as he jumped. He landed awkwardly and tipped back, and Leki grasped his hand and pulled him upright. He staggered forward, exaggerating his momentum so that they ended up face to face with their arms around each other.

'My saviour,' he whispered.

'The Brokers knew exactly what they were looking at,' Juda said. He'd stopped away from the stream but hardly seemed to see them. He was looking elsewhere, at another time. 'Finding it is all very well,' one of them said. 'But do you know how to use it?'

'How much further?' Bon asked. He and Leki disentangled themselves, and he felt a warm flush as her hand swept across his back.

'Far enough to tell you the rest.' Juda looked up the slope they had descended, scanning it quickly with his telescope. 'And we have to reach the gas marshes before nightfall. I don't have many scamp smokes left, and . . .'

'We know,' Leki said. 'Don't worry. We'll tie you tight.'

Juda's green eyes flickered strangely, and Bon realised then that he would never know this man. It wasn't his part-Regerran ancestry that made him a mystery. It was his quest. The Brokers were considered one of the most dangerous criminal organisations on Alderia by the Ald, and there were frequent cases of the Ald's personal army, the Spike, assaulting a suspected refuge. Bon had once passed the site of such an assault in the slums of New Kotrugam's eastern quarter. Five properties had been gutted by fire, a dozen bodies were laid under blankets in the street outside – several adults, the rest children. The bitter memory had always remained with him.

'I found the second and third dregs inside an Engine,' Juda said, and as the shock hit Bon so he heard Leki gasp.

'You've actually seen an *Engine*?' Bon gasped.

Juda continued, ignoring the question and telling the story his own way, at his own pace.

'I came to Skythe . . . on my own. The Brokers are an organisation. And no organisation can be as personal as you need to be about magic. As subjective. Because magic is a personal thing, like love or hate. I love differently from you.' He pointed at Leki. 'And you.' He nodded at Bon. 'And if either of you took to magic, your experience of it would be very different from mine.'

'You won't find me touching it,' Leki said softly, but Juda seemed not to hear.

'We're close to the river,' he said. 'There's a rope bridge a mile upstream.'

'Can't we walk or swim it?' Bon asked.

'You wouldn't want to.' Juda moved on, falling quiet and contemplative.

Bon looked up at the cloudy sky, seeing the smudge of sunlight behind a spread of clouds and comforted by its presence. He had never worshipped the Fade sun god, Flaze, but it was a presence that no one could do without. It bathed his face with warmth, and as he blinked slowly he could almost be somewhere else. He had a sudden, unbidden memory of his wife falling, and his hand reaching out terribly slowly to stop her. How he had loved her. How he had almost feared her, on days when a distance hung between them. She had come into his life, and left it, entirely of her own accord.

They reached the river without Juda saying any more, and Bon feared his revelations had ended. *I want to hear about the Engine*, he thought. *I want to know where it was, what it was like*. There had been much talk of the Engines amongst the circles he orbited – the devices used by the Ald, so it was said, to gather and channel magic during their attack on Skythe. They were almost mythical creations, product of stories told in the shadowy corners of bars and private meetings where fear kept watch at the doorway. Some said that

111

there were ancient Engines, thousands of years old, buried deep in western caves on Alderia, and even older constructs had been taken apart, their elements broken down and melted and scattered to the winds. The further back in history Bon looked, the more mythical the Engines were. But here on Skythe they suddenly seemed so much more possible.

It was obvious from first sight why they needed the rope bridge to cross the river. It was not too wide, and it flowed at a sedate rate, but something in there exuded menace. Silvery, sharp things with membranous wings, leaping above the waters and taking any unfortunate bird that happened to fly too low. The length of a person's arm, Bon could see the stark glint of their teeth even from the river bank.

'They're only the ones that let themselves be seen,' Juda said. 'Sometimes, others come out. There are water pigs, similar to those on Alderia but twice the size, with ragged teeth that seep poisonous blood.' He shook his head as he walked. 'All gone wrong.'

'What's all gone wrong?' Leki asked.

'This place. Don't you feel it? See it? The war did more than destroy millennia of Skythian civilisation and history. It set a rot in the land.'

They walked until they saw the rope bridge – a rickety affair, half of its planks rotten and dropped away. To cover his fear Bon asked, at last, about the Engine.

'They're here, if you know where to find them,' Juda said. 'There's the remains of one on the coast, maybe twenty miles from where you landed. And there are others. More whole.' He tested a plank on the bridge and started across, walking quickly from plank to plank and gripping the rope rails. They were frayed, and strung with dried, crackly growths that crumbled beneath his touch.

'More whole?' Leki asked, probing.

Juda glanced back at her but said nothing.

Bon looked down at the river only a few steps below. Shadows moved across its smooth surface. They might have been clouds or reflections, or larger things beneath the surface.

'So what was it like?' he asked at last, because Juda seemed to be toying with them. But the man simply walked on ahead, checking each board as he stepped across and barely pausing to drop his weight.

'I think we'll see one,' Leki said. Bon glanced at her, eyebrows raised.

'What makes you think that?'

Leki shrugged. 'I'm good at reading people.' She was staring down at the river, and there was a look in her eyes that Bon did not like. It resembled hunger.

'And amphys can read the water,' he said.

Leki started across then, and Bon followed her footsteps over the swaying bridge. It reminded him of the feeling in the hold of that awful ship, and his stomach lurched.

'You won't be sick,' Leki said, her voice almost a laugh.

Bon paused, watching her increasing the distance between them. She moved with such grace, and even beneath her long coat he could see the delicate sway of her narrow swimmer's hips. It had been a long time since he had been with a woman, and—

Leki glanced back over her shoulder, mock-stern. Then she looked down and moved again, and Bon knew that she was looking between the boards, at the water. Using her strange amphy's gift, she had sensed Juda's intentions and let Bon know that she could perceive his as well.

He smiled. And as he crossed he allowed his imagination to swell, seeing Leki lying naked in a warm bath of scented water, webbed hands closed around him and his fingertips playing across her breasts. He chuckled, the image helping him smother his fear of falling. But even if he did drop through into the river, he was sure that Leki would be there to save him.

She had saved him before, after all.

When he reached the other side, Juda was already heading towards what looked like a dozen mounds of moss-covered rocks. Leki was waiting for him, an enigmatic smile picking up the corner of her sensuous mouth.

'So what else did you see?' Bon asked.

'Those mounds are the ruins of a Skythian village,' Leki said. 'He's taking us there to . . . it feels like to meet someone. But the urgency's growing in him, too. The slayers might be closing. And I think the Engine . . .' She closed her eyes, frowning. 'He won't talk about them, because he's going to show us. There's rumour of an Engine beyond the marshes.' She opened her eyes again. The frown remained. 'And you. Your name, in his mind. He thinks you might lead him to magic.'

Bon snorted, confused. But then he asked the real question. 'And what else did you see from me?'

'Something wet.' Leki went after Juda, and Bon thought, *I'm going to see an Engine!*

Following Leki, troubled by what she could see and yet aroused as well, he could not help dwelling on how much things had changed in a matter of days.

Without Juda, the slayers would have butchered him if he'd even reached that beach. Without Leki, Bon might well have let them.

Bon looked back the way they had come. The river whispered behind them, splashing now and then as sharp fish leaped at the sky. Beyond, the hillside they had descended looked innocuous enough. But when he looked up to the ridge and tried to spot where they had crossed, he could not escape the idea that there was constant movement up there. He squinted and shielded his eyes, even though the cloud cover reduced the sun to a smudge. The movement was too far away to focus on, and too uncertain to trust. It was as if the hillside was breathing, or shrugging, or trying to shift closer or further away. He might be seeing slayers reaching the summit and hurrying after them, or he might not.

And then the fear of those slayers struck him again, the terror rich and heavy. He'd seen that terrible murder on the beach, but now he projected it onto himself, and the sheer *unfairness* of it was staggering, the taking of his life when that right should only be his. Until recently to Bon, death would have meant the end of the pain of loss, but now it was the end of hope. Because sheltering behind the grief from his dead wife and missing, probably murdered, son, there had always been a glint of hope that he might continue into the future.

Coming here, meeting Leki, had exposed it.

He turned and sprinted after Leki, and as he caught up with her Juda was waving to them from beside a mound of tumbled stones.

'Here!' Juda said. 'We can rest here, for a while. There's things for you to see. And someone I have to meet.'

'But we have to run!' Bon said.

'Yes,' Juda agreed. 'But I must see someone.'

'Who is it?' Leki asked.

Juda looked away, scratching at his cheek. 'Just . . . a man.' He chuckled. 'We can't get where we're going without his directions, but . . . he'll see no one but me. I'll be back soon.' He left them there, ducking away between the mounds and quickly disappearing into the landscape.

'What's wrong with him?' Leki asked, then when she turned to Bon her eyes opened wide. 'What's wrong with *you*?'

'I'm afraid,' Bon said. His honesty made him naked. Leki only paused for a moment, then came to him and squeezed his shoulder.

'We're in Juda's hands,' she said. 'Let's take a look around.'

'Maybe he's running on his own,' Bon said. They knew Juda hardly at all, and could trust him even less. 'They might be closer than we think, and he could have . . .'

'He wouldn't have brought us this far if he was going to give us up,' Leki said. 'Besides, I'm starting to think we mean more to Juda than he's letting on. I don't think he rescued us out of sheer benevolence.'

'Aren't you afraid?' Bon asked. Weakness had always haunted him, whether or not others saw him in it.

'Down to the tips of my toes,' Leki said. She blinked, and her amphy's clear film swept across her eyes.

They moved past the mound of stones, and as they did so Bon made out a vague order to them. They were fallen, but the mound's base maintained a regular shape, and some of those stones not smothered by moss or purple shrubs exhibited square corners, and even some faded sigils. History swamped this place.

'A door,' Leki said, pointing. Past a huge fallen tree, beyond a copse where a flock of birds seemed to be weaving back and forth between branches in an endless spiral, stood another old building, its roof and one wall collapsed. The doorway was swathed in creeping plants, but some of them were withered and dry, while others were green and lush.

'We should wait for Juda,' he said. 'Ready to run.'

'He said there was stuff we'd like to see,' Leki said. 'And we'll hear him come back. We can't go any further without him, and he won't be long. Come on. Let's see if anyone's in.'

*   *   *

116

Juda did not have to travel far in order to try and feed his addiction.

He had left his last dreg of magic behind and, ever since, a chill had set in him, a hollowness of loss which he knew he must fill soon, or die. Magic was his heartbeat, his breath. It had become his life.

Away from Bon and Leki, he leaned against a fallen Skythe building and took in several shuddering breaths. Talking to them about magic had gone some way to holding back the grief, but the deep emptiness was growing. Unless he filled it soon, he did not think he could maintain his fragile hold.

I've been just holding on for years, he thought. The promise of a big find had always driven him on, and now there was something about Bon and Leki that hinted at greater things to come. They smelled different, and Bon especially had depths that might hold secrets even he did not know. His name on the list of deportees marked for execution, and his crimes, had cried out at Juda.

And here, he hoped to find out more.

He moved away from the other two, assembling his pistol as he went and loading the pressurised steam valve. He would need the weapon if and when the slayers caught up with them, but it would likely do little good. Here was where it might benefit him more. If there were fresh rumours and whispers amongst the Skythians, he needed to hear them.

He had become adept at recognising the gathering places of those wild, sometimes mutated Skythians left alive. They maintained a whispered communication with each other, stories spanning miles, rumours drifting with the winds, as if somewhere deep down they were trying to regain their former glory. He suspected this information exchange was instinctive rather than intentional, and sometimes it had been of use to him. But though the Skythians knew what was happening across their damaged isle, in Juda's regard they were weak things, ill-suited to existence in the place they had once thrived. Time moved on, and he had no pity for them. Like any addict, his empathy had been suppressed by his cravings.

Juda stalked. He went beyond the ruined village, glancing back frequently to make sure Bon and Leki could not see him, and found a trail. He paused and sniffed the air. Closed his eyes. Regerran blood pulsed through his nose, his sense of smell greater than most, and he moved off to the left, skirting around a hillock and then slipping down into a shallow ravine. A stream flowed along its bottom, heading left towards the river. In the stream squatted a lone Skythian male. The water washed around his ankles. He stared along the ravine towards the river, his purpose hidden.

Juda looked around quickly, scanning the ravine's sides in case there were others hidden away in small caves or lying in the fading light. But he was alone. He lifted the pistol and fired. The shot struck the Skythian's left shoulder low down, and he fell forward, splashing face first into the stream.

Juda grunted in satisfaction and reloaded the pistol as he approached the twitching figure. New metal shot, new steam valve, and when he was three steps from the whining man he pocketed the pistol, drew a knife and knelt beside him.

Though his left arm was useless, the man had just managed to turn his face out of the water to catch a breath. Blood flowed with the stream. His hair was long and clotted with mud, his skin pocked with disease, left eye cloudy with cataract. He was trying to speak in their strange language, but the water garbled his words. Juda slid the knife between his ribs and leaned all his weight on it, and it was like putting a beast out of its misery. The man squealed, and then slumped down. His final breaths escaped in a series of bloody bubbles, which Juda watched disappear downstream.

Heart hammering, he looked back out of the shallow ravine towards the ruins, but no one was watching, no one knew. *I can't leave them alone for too long*, he thought. But this part was always over quickly.

Knowing that what he did here was redolent of Wrench Arc behaviour – and still trying to deny to himself that he was one of them – Juda took the fleet clinger from the seam of his boot. Long, thin, incredibly hard and sharp, he had bought it from a Broker in New Kotrugam just days before leaving on his journey north. Used mainly by Spike interrogators and investigators, they resembled weapons, but were in reality sensitive devices designed to snag the final, fleeting thoughts of someone dying. Often those thoughts were random and useless. The trick to using the fleet clingers successfully was to feed the right impetus to the dying person.

He plunged the object into the man's ear and pushed it into his brain. Then he connected the trailing nark-gut lead to the top end, held his breath and pushed the needle on the lead's other end into his own neck. He gasped as the cool metal slid home, the pain immediately simmering to white-hot. But he did not have time to hurt.

Juda leaned over the stinking, dying man and whispered into his ear, muttering the Old Skythian word for *magic* over and over, and soon . . .

He had done this five times before, without success. But this time he found something. This Skythian knew nothing of the magic Juda craved to quieten his soul, but he did know of other things, more incredible and valuable than any Juda had ever hoped to find.

In his confused, dying thoughts, the man held rumours of

Aeon's resurrection, and whispers of the strange young Alderian who was bringing it about.

Venden Ugane . . .

As Juda fell back and tugged the needle from his neck in a spray of blood, he uttered a mad, high laugh at what might come next.

Chapter 7

heartbeats

On previous journeys to search for and retrieve objects associated with the remnant, Venden had taken a whole day to prepare. The location would be a blur in his mind. The distance obscure, like tomorrow seen through a heat-haze. Since the first journey when he had discovered the cart upended at the foot of a small waterfall, he had taken it with him as much as possible, only leaving it behind when the terrain grew too uneven, the journey too long. But this time something pressed him to go alone and unhindered. He had the old clothes he was wearing, some food and water, two knives, some meagre camping equipment, a flint, and cooking implements he had fashioned from shreds of something melted. He had often wondered what they had been before. Perhaps he ate food with deformed cogs from the heart of an ancient Engine.

He readied himself to leave before midday, and then stood close to the remnant, waiting for something else. *It will show me where exactly to find the heart, how to retrieve it, how to transport it back here*, he thought. But the remnant was silent and still, and he sensed a deep weariness cradling it against the cold, wet ground.

'I'll find the heart of you,' he said. There was no response. 'I'll bring you back.' Silence filled the clearing, seeming to steal the sound of movement from the orange spiders and the rustle of leaves on some of the withered trees to the north. Venden wondered where those sounds had gone, and whether anyone else would hear them.

He reached out to touch the remnant, but was repelled. He frowned, but the closer he moved, the further away the shape seemed. It did not shift or flex, but its altered shape was beyond him.

'I only want to touch you,' he said, but his plea was swallowed by the silence.

So Venden left the clearing, looking behind at the things he had brought back, which, together, went to make up Aeon. The reconstructed god looked more innocuous the further he walked, and by the time it passed out of sight, hidden behind a screen of low trees, he could believe that it was a dead thing that had been there for six centuries. Its bone was dulled and unreflective, giving back nothing of its surroundings. A fine camouflage, he thought, but it also left him feeling bereft. He might as well have seen himself fading into nothing.

'I am *not* nothing,' Venden said as he walked. 'And Aeon chose me.' The hollow place inside him seemed to churn with potential, and then settled once more.

He planned his route north to Kellis Faults as a way of occupying his mind, but he had little knowledge to draw from. Already he was in the wilds, further north than most banished to Skythe ever came. He saw amazement in the eyes of the few Skythians who encountered him. There was some fear, but they were also fascinated by him, a reaction refreshing on every new meeting. He had seen some of the same regressed Skythians several times. They knew him and his name, and sometimes he believed they spied upon him. Often they seemed somewhat in awe of him, and if he had been more superstitious he might have thought himself a ghost.

Perhaps I am, he thought, pushing through a whispering forest. He had been this way many times before, but there was no evidence of his presence here, nor that of his wagon. No flattened ferns trampled by his feet or crushed by the cart's wheels. No route worn into the landscape by use, even though that use was not frequent. 'I am not a ghost!' Venden shouted, and a small flock of sparrs took flight, and something larger scurried in the canopy thirty steps to his left. He smiled, pleased that they agreed and content with his own reality.

The shadow inside seemed to lean forward and take note. Venden felt the blank space in his soul that did not belong to him swelling and shifting, and the attention from there was harsher than ever before. He glanced around, but the eyes focused on him were not from without. The sense of being watched was something he had carried with him ever since he could remember – it was one of his earliest memories – but at moments like this it made his skin crawl, and gave him reason to run. He halted instead, breathing deeply and squeezing his eyes closed. *It's just another part of me*, he thought, as always. *Just a part of me I don't yet know . . . my older self, waiting to meet me . . .*

Venden walked on, not a ghost but never quite himself.

They headed south, away from the sea and deep into a continent where Milian had never set foot during her first life. Bouncing along in the back of one of the wagons, she lay with her eyes closed, trying to cast aside terrible memories.

All that time lying asleep in the cave, she had dreamed. And now, awake at last, those dreams had left their taint.

She opened her eyes, and the woman and child were staring down at her. Milian was taller than average, her features wider, and her skin was paler than most on Alderia. But these people seemed untroubled by her appearance, and perhaps they were unaware that she was Skythian. *I wonder if there are even any Skythians left*, she thought, shocked at the idea.

The woman spoke, forming her strange words slowly and deliberately, but still Milian could not understand. She shrugged and shook her head, touching her ears again. The boy giggled and copied her. Milian smiled, touched her nose, and the boy did the same. He shrieked in delight. She sighed, he sighed. She laughed, he laughed, and she found that simple act of laughter illuminated the darkness.

The shard of Aeon is still within me, but I am whole again. The daemon is long gone. Perhaps the things I did – the things it did – went with it. The shard nestled, piercing her heart and soul and the landscape of her memories, but dormant for a time. Silent.

The woman started forming some sort of sign language, but Milian shrugged again. She felt her heavy breasts moving beneath the scruffy clothing, and the woman's disquiet took on new tones. She eyed Milian up and down, and the species of fear in her eyes was obvious. But the last thing on Milian's mind was fucking.

They're not the ones, she thought of the two men steering the wagons. The thought echoed again with the shard's influence. Never *quite* dormant, it seemed.

Later, Milian was woken from an unsettled sleep by cries of delight and children's laughter. She blinked herself awake and groaned as she worked stiffness from her joints, warmed

her muscles by tensing and moving. Whatever strange influence had allowed her to hibernate for so long and emerge
alive had not yet driven all signs of age from her body. *Only
on the outside, perhaps.* If they cut her open, she might be
grey and dead.

She crawled across the bedding and clothes strewn around
the covered wagon's interior and pushed open the small wood-
framed door. She realised that they had stopped moving, and
when she stepped out onto the wide wooden deck at the back
of the large vehicle, she understood why.

The two families stood off to one side, the adult couples
holding hands, children dancing and leaping under the
multi-coloured sky. There was a river not far away, its gentle
movement audible in the background, and it glowed with
sunlight as if possessed of a sun itself. The gently undulating
landscape was interrupted in a score of places by tall, thin
spires, their wider bases supported by heavy buttresses, doorways and window openings shadowing their entire heights.
But it was the pinnacles and what danced above them that
grasped Milian's attention, and held it for a long time.

Rainbows played through the air. Flexing, melding, fading
and reforming, sheets of light frolicked from one spire's top
to another, arcing high above with a sound like a giant walking
through fallen leaves. The hairs on Milian's arms and neck
stood on end, bristling. She caught her breath and held it,
and for a panicked moment a rush of thoughts sickened her:
*If I breathe that in, if it touches me, if it leaks down from
there and drowns me.* But the fear was momentary, because
the adults and children looked back at her as one, and grinned.
The tall man who had first found her shouted something and
laughed, and waved a hand at the sky as if fearing she had
not seen. But how could she not? Milian stood alone on that
wooden deck for a while longer, watching the display and

feeling a sadness inside her, stirred and reborn by the certainty that she had no memories this wonderful of Skythe.

It had been a beautiful place, but much of the beauty evaded her now. Most of those vague, ancient-feeling memories from before the daemon and the shard revolved around something growing dark, or things going wrong.

The sight inspired tears, and the distortion only made the flailing, sweeping light-show more wonderful. *I am truly alive again*, she thought, revelling in the wonder. The light and colours dipped down as if to bounce from the spires' highest points, then streaked up into the sky once more. It was light-ning with colour, and lacking the violence.

Milian examined the closest spire some more, focusing on the openings she could see pocking its surface from the ground all the way up to its highest point. They betrayed no light, and when the colours were right they illuminated part-way inside. There was no sign of anyone standing at the doorways watching the display. Maybe the strange buildings were abandoned or never meant for habitation. Or perhaps the people inside were used to the display, and would not give it a second glance. It shocked Milian that such beauty might be ignored.

She closed her eyes and the colours still danced.

The families returned to the wagons, flushed with excite-ment and chattering amongst themselves. The tall man grinned at Milian, and it was the nervous sideways glance at his wife that betrayed his thoughts. She would have to be careful. She had no wish to cause a problem. They were taking her south, and the shard seemed happy with that direction.

The slayers were pursuing them, intent on slashing Bon's throat and spilling his guts to the ground, and the man who had made it his mission to save them might be mad. And yet

Bon found that he was enjoying these moments alone with Lechmy Borle.

'Leki,' Bon said, voice low. 'Over here. I've never seen anything like this.'

They had worked their way through the half-collapsed doorway, and discovered that there was a set of steps leading down. The cellar was a complex of eight rooms, three of which had been buried by tumbled ceilings. But the others were surprisingly free of damage. Time had imprinted itself in these places – mineral stalactites drooped from the ceilings, pale and delicate, and there were traces of animals' nests and dens in every room – but considering they were more than six centuries old, most of the rooms were surprisingly well preserved.

Leki had found the torches, and lit them with her flint. *I wonder if the last person to carry this was Skythian*, Bon had wondered as she handed him a blazing torch, and the idea was both thrilling and chilling. He could not help wondering what had become of them. Killed by the Kolts, perhaps – those Skythians driven to murderous frenzy by Aeon's destruction. Such a fate was beyond imagining.

'What have you found?' Leki asked. She crossed the room, kicking through grit and rubble and uncovering the remains of the intricate tiled floor. There were mosaic designs there, but Bon hadn't been able to make them out in any detail.

'I think this must have been their Aeon shrine,' Bon said. He nodded at the wall, and Leki added her light to his. There were gorgeous images in ceramics, their colours as brash and bright as the day they were created, and all of them displayed wondrous scenes of Skythian landscapes, wildlife and plants. The animals were powerful, the plants lush and blooming, and much of what he saw was a mystery to him. There were similar species on Alderia, but others were unknown. They had vanished from the world, but still existed here, a frozen history. Bon's breath caught and he swallowed, a lump in his throat. 'This is everything they lost. Everything we took from them.'

'Not "us",' Leki said. 'You and I didn't take anything.'

'The Ald. Leaders of Alderia. Same thing.'

'Six hundred years ago,' Leki said. 'You still truly blame a race for actions that old?'

'Don't you?' Bon asked, aghast.

'I blame the Ald now for continuing to blame the Skythians for what happened here, yes. But when they used magic back then, they were doing what they thought best. They didn't know whether Aeon would be benevolent or not.'

'So they killed it,' Bon said. 'And faced with the same thing now? Don't you think the Ald would do exactly what they did then, to protect their Fade?'

'Protect a lie from a lie,' Leki said. 'Yes, I suppose they would. That's what depresses me most, you know. Always has. The fact that everything that happened to this place happened because of one false belief facing off against another.'

'You don't believe Aeon really appeared.'

'Do you?'

'I don't know,' Bon replied, because he didn't yet want to say yes. But he'd spent years reading forbidden books about the war and its causes, and speaking to academics who had spent their whole lives living a secret. And yes, he *did* believe that Aeon had appeared, because why else would the Ald back then have launched something so devastating against Skythe, and something with such unpredictable results? They would not have used magic to wipe out a rumour, a faith that had always existed. They would have used it to destroy the *root* of that faith – Aeon. The appearance of the Skythian god had proved them, and their Fade religion, wrong. And they could not stand for that.

'Certainly is beautiful,' Leki said softly.

'I wonder who lived here,' Bon said. 'Big house.'

'I'd like the time to explore,' Leki said. 'But we have to move on. Don't know what Juda's up to here, but I'm trusting him less and less. There's just something about him . . .'

'Perhaps the fact that he's mad,' Bon said.

Leki smiled. 'Maybe. But right now, I don't think we can afford to doubt him. We've got to assume those things are still chasing us.'

'And the gas marshes sound like fun,' Bon said, and something growled.

A deep, wet growl.

'Oh,' Leki whispered. 'Maybe we should have checked all the rooms.'

'Juda,' Bon whispered, fearing treachery.

'I don't think so,' Leki said. Something moved in the next room, passing before a fallen length of wall, its bare skin pale yellow with reflected flame. 'I think bad luck.'

Bon drew his knife. The blade felt ineffectual in his hand, no weight to it, no heft. He could use it for peeling fruit, but little else.

'If we move slowly . . .' he began, but the growl came again, and, it seemed, from a different direction.

'Oh, fucking great,' Leki said.

Bon held the flaming torch out towards the room's doorway and the wide hall beyond. The heavy tree roots that had grown through from above were hung shadows waiting to whip. The shaded lines of protruding blocks flickered back and forth as the flame moved in a slight breeze. *Old dead Skythe breathing*, he thought, and the idea of the land having a breath chilled him to the core.

'Come on,' Leki said. 'Don't show fear.'

'What? That could be *anything* out there!'

'Don't think so,' she said. She grabbed his hand and, though her palm was slick with sweat, tugged him gently forward, holding the torch before her.

A shape moved sideways into the archway. Bon thought it was an ape of some kind, like the rawpanzies of the Blane Jungles far to the south of New Kotrugam. Sometimes people kept them as pets, and occasionally they were trained as clowns or servants. But this ape was different. Its body was hairless apart from a thatch between its legs and the long, straggly hair reaching its shoulders from its half-bald head. Its features were human, disturbingly so. And Bon could not help thinking that its keening, clicking voice held something that might have been language.

It was staring at Leki, and the growl came again.

'Where are you?' The call came in from the distance, above the cellars in the open ground. Juda.

'Don't shout,' Bon said. 'Don't startle it. I know what this is.'

'I thought I did too, but . . .' Leki said.

'Skythian,' Bon said. 'This is what they've become.'

'No,' Leki said, an exhalation of shock and sadness rather than denial.

'Keep your hands fisted,' Bon said. The Skythian was staring at Leki. 'Try not to blink. I don't think it knows quite what you are.'

Bon edged slowly towards the Skythian, fascinated and shocked. Such human traits in something that looked almost animal. It swayed slightly where it stood, glancing back and forth between him and Leki, and he knew not to underestimate it. People he'd spoken to had different ideas of what had become of the denuded Skythian race, and in reality there was no way to say what might happen here. Some stories told of primitive herbivores who haunted their ruined centres of population like the shadows of their dead, brilliant ancestors. Others told of savages, and cannibals. To get out of this alive, Bon had to assume the worst.

Juda called again, more urgently. The Skythian glanced back and up towards the stairs leading to the surface. And in that glance Bon saw the first hint of intelligence.

Of scheming.

'Leki, get ready to run for the steps,' he muttered, as more shapes appeared out of the dark room behind the first. Four, then six. Most of these were naked as well, but a couple wore rough garments around their loins, and they all carried basic weapons – rocks, spears, blades.

The first Skythian said something in its rattling, deep voice, and though Bon had studied Old Skythian in its written forms, he could not identify any of this language. Their tongue had changed as much as their appearance. He could smell the stink of them, animal and unwashed. They stalked rather than stood, eyes glittering with basic hunger, primeval fear. Civilisation was no longer here, and Bon felt a surge of sadness for these people and their ancestors. *Who might you have been?* he thought, looking at the first shape. *If things had been different, what might you have done?* The man growled at Bon, baring his teeth, crouching down as if unsettled by the scrutiny.

'Bon! Leki! We have to move, now!' Juda sounded more urgent than ever, an edge of panic to his voice that ignited panic in Bon.

'Bon . . .?'

'When I say run—' Bon began, and then the first Skythian sprang at Leki. She let out a cry and Bon stepped sideways, knocking the leaping shape to one side. The impact was hard,

131

the weight of the skinny thing surprising, and as it sprawled to the ground in a riot of waving limbs its companions started screeching and yelling, high-pitched ululations that hurt Bon's ears.

Shaken, he went to pick up the torch he'd dropped, but the fallen Skythian was quicker. It dragged the torch across the gritty floor and lifted it, waving it back and forth to excite the shadows. The others screeched even more, edging forward, back again, constantly on the verge of leaping into the fray.

Bon knew that if they all came at once, he and Leki would fall beneath them. They might well be a sad echo of what they once were, but they also intended to do him and Leki harm.

Leki stepped forward and waved her knife, slashing at the air in the hope that it would warn them back.

'Bon? Bon Ugane?' Juda's voice was closer, but none of the Skythians seemed to notice. *Why use my second name?* Bon thought.

Another shape came forward – a woman, thin and wasted – and hacked at the air with her clawed hands, mimicking Leki's movement.

'To the steps!' Bon said. 'You go first, backwards, keep the knife ready.'

'Here!' She threw him her torch and started backing along the hallway to the steps. Bon caught the flaming stick and heaved it back and forth, the flame roaring quietly as it burned the darkness. The Skythians backed away, but there was no fear in their eyes. Bon wasn't certain what he saw there. Not intelligence. But . . . a curiosity, and perhaps a desperation to know who and what he and Leki were.

The woman waved her hands again, then reached into her wild hair and withdrew two writhing shapes. She flung them at Bon, and he was so surprised that he backed away and lost his footing, slumping against the hallway's rough wall and feeling age-old plasterwork crumbling beneath his back.

'Snakes!' Juda shouted, and from the corner of his eye Bon saw their guide halfway down the steps.

Bon thrust the torch out and one of the slinky shadows hissed to an end in the flame. Another struck his leg and he kicked it away, waiting for the bite, expecting the cool flush of pain as venom melted his veins and assaulted his organs. But no pain came, and as he found his feet the woman was already reaching into her hair for more.

Something coughed and hissed, and the woman's left forearm shattered in a cloud of blood and fractured bone. She slumped to the floor without a sound. A slick of blood spread quickly across the intricate mosaic floor, painting its new, terrible story across that old one.

Juda was already reloading a new cylinder into his pistol, but Bon knew that their chance was now. The screeching had silenced into shock, and Leki was staring at him, wide-eyed, freckles of blood on her face black in the torchlight.

Bon grabbed her hand and ran, kicking aside the torch wielded by a Skythian man. Juda waved them on and, as they reached the uneven steps and climbed towards daylight, Bon did not feel any sense of escape. He had seen Juda's expression.

'They're here?' he asked.

'Not quite,' Juda said. He stared at Bon strangely, as if seeing him for the first time. He had a smudge on his forehead that might have been blood. 'I saw them on the ridge, and they'll be coming quickly now that they can smell us. They might even see us. So we have to run, not look behind, and you have to trust me completely.'

'We have up to now,' Leki said coldly, but Juda seemed hardly aware of her presence. His eyes glimmered as he stared at Bon, burning with a fire Bon did not know.

'*Completely!*' Juda emphasised. 'Whatever I tell you to do, *when*ever, you have to do it if we're going to live. It's ten miles to the gas marshes, maybe more, and they're faster than us.'

'I don't know,' Bon said, and weariness was smothering him. Tired muscles and aching legs, and the weariness of the soul that had been his curse for years. Leki held his hand, squeezed. *She doesn't seem even remotely scared*, he thought, but he was too distracted to dwell on that right now. Beneath them, he heard the scurrying sounds of Skythians shaking off their shock and coming in pursuit. Above, the slayers had his scent in their nostrils, and would not stop until they could smell his spilled blood. Hopelessness hung heavy, misting the air like the Skythian woman's blood when Juda had killed her.

But then Juda said something that lifted that weight for ever.

'Venden Ugane,' he said.

'Venden?' Bon gasped.

'Living to the north. And we can find him, if we shake the slayers.'

'*Venden is alive?*' Unreality struck Bon, swirling him in its dizzying embrace. *My son. My son!*

'No time now.' Juda remained motionless for just a moment, wide eyes still on Bon as if he saw something more than human, and greater than everything he sought. Then he turned and ran, and Bon and Leki had no choice but to follow.

'Come on,' Leki said.

'But Venden?' *I haven't told Juda his name.*

Leki offered him a tentative, confused smile. Her eyes were alight. *She wasn't really scared back there at all*, Bon thought, and she still seemed rich with potential she had not exposed. A stranger, she had layers he had barely touched.

134

Blazing sunlight did nothing to lessen the sense of doom closing in, and could not match the fire of hope that had been ignited in Bon Ugane once more.

Bon's first act as they rushed across the uneven ground of the ruined settlement was to look back. Through the sparse trees, past the tumbled buildings that hid subterranean secrets, he could see the gentle slope of the valley's side. He scanned left to right and back again but could see no sign of movement. That did not mean they weren't there. It only meant that the slayers were either moving covertly, or were already too low down to the valley floor for him to see them.

If that were the case, they were closer even than Juda had hinted.

Bon thought of Venden, why he could be here, how . . . and it made no sense! If he'd been arrested and deported, Bon would have surely heard news of that. If the Guild of Inventors had turned him in for his seditious thoughts and opinions, there would have been at least a whisper of events, and more likely a shout. The Guild's public face projected a crisp clean image, though any organisation that old surely possessed dark secrets. They would have taken advantage of the revelation that one of their most promising students had betrayed his religion and country, and that he had been discovered and expelled because of those crimes. They would have made an example of him.

It was always something smaller, Bon had believed. A kidnapping by his Guild tutor, a murder, his body thrown into the river.

And now Juda, a stranger, said that he was here.

Bon had so many questions, but hardly any breath with which to ask them. They would have to wait. It had been three years, and now it would have to be a little while longer.

But the mere thought of his son being here – the possibility, however remote and unlikely – had galvanised Bon, and he felt a newfound urgency surging through his muscles. Juda led, Leki followed, and Bon followed her, enjoying the impact of his feet against the soil because that grounded him, relishing the burning in his lungs as he drew shallow, fast breaths because that told him he was still alive and striving to remain so.

Beyond the ruins the landscape changed, becoming less uneven and easier to navigate. *Easier for them, too*, Bon thought, and he risked another glance back.

Three Skythians stood atop one of the ruins, slouched now and unmoving as they watched the escapees fleeing across the fields. Bon had seen gargoyles similar to these on the taller Fade churches of New Kotrugam, statues of Kolts cast into the walls of godliness to evoke the power of faith over faithlessness. One of them stood straighter as if he or she had heard a noise, turned its head, and—

Bon tripped and sprawled, grunting as he stumbled against a fallen tree trunk and struck it with his left shoulder. He rolled and came to rest on his back. Leki pulled him up again.

'Juda's not slowing.'

They stood, Bon shaken, and Juda was sprinting away from them.

'Don't look back!' Juda said. He'd shifted his direction slightly, and now ran even faster. 'Every . . . moment counts. Got to get . . . somewhere.'

They sprinted side by side after Juda. He led them across the undulating fields, places where perhaps the residents of the ruined village they had just left had once grown crops and tended their cattle, but which now were wild. Small creatures scurried through the grass away from them, heard but unseen. Startled birds took flight. Bon's heart thundered with exertion and fear, surprise and excitement. Memories of his son came unbidden and with a flaming intensity. But the timescale of these memories was confused. *Because I always want him with me*, Bon often thought. *Because I never want to let him go.*

'Ahead,' Juda gasped. Even he was panting now. 'Those trees . . . we need to get in there before . . . they see us.'

'Red fruits?' Leki asked, and Bon saw the trees she meant – short, squat, branches heavy with what from this distance looked like an abundance of red apples.

'Not fruit,' Juda said. 'Run.'

The trees grew in a wide clump at the edge of the river's flood plain, and beyond the copse Bon could see the hillside rising out of the valley, speckled with rocky outcroppings and swathes of purple and brown heathers. As they closed on the trees he risked another glance back, and they had run so far that it took him a few moments to place the ruined village.

'Hurry!' Juda said. He was beneath the first few trees now, leaning against a trunk and looking around in a panic, and Leki joined him, pressing her forehead against a tree and breathing hard.

Bon walked backwards towards them, scanning the valley floor until he made out the humps of the tumbled village. The three Skythians were still there, stick figures atop one of the humps. If he hadn't known what they were he'd have thought them bushes or trees.

They fell out of sight, as if startled.

And then he saw the slayers.

He dropped to the ground and crawled backwards beneath the tree canopy, only standing when he was well within their shade.

'They're so fast,' he said softly. And they were. They

137

seemed to be outrunning their shadows, loping across the grassland like the red lyons Bon had seen in captivity in New Kotrugam. From this distance it was difficult to make out any detail, but they moved with an inhuman gait. They pounded the ground with heavy feet, as if it too was a target.

'Find sticks,' Juda said. 'The longer and thicker, the better.'

'We're going to fight them with sticks?' Bon said.

'No. Here.' Juda lobbed a stick at him, and Bon snatched it from the air, wielding it and feeling like all the gods' fools in one.

'Those aren't fruits,' Leki said. She'd been looking up, not across the plain at their pursuers, and now Bon followed her gaze.

'Stark blight eggs,' Juda said. He found another stick and handed it to Leki, who took it without looking. 'I was once close to the Engine I told you about, and I credit the worst pain of my life with driving me to where it lay hidden. One of these . . .' – he nodded at one of the shiny red eggs, hanging very much like fruit, but spiked for protection and slightly opaque. There was something moving inside – '. . . burst against my cheek. The thing inside slithered down my neck and got caught in my collar, and by the time I plucked it out and threw it over the cliff it had stung me enough times to drive me mad. When I regained consciousness I was on the beach, close to—'

'Fuck the Engine for now,' Leki said. 'What do we do here?' She was looking past Bon urgently, and he glanced over his shoulder. He could differentiate between the male and female slayers now. Evil and ugly in different ways.

'They're weak and disorientated when they emerge,' Juda said. 'But that doesn't last for long.' He knocked one of the bulging red eggs with his stick, and when it split open he ran.

Bon had an instant to see what came out, and to try and

make out what it was. He'd never heard of stark blights, and the glimpse he caught gave him few clues as to what species they might be. There was a flutter of what could have been wings, the snap of a beak or claws, the sinuous remnant of a neck or body. Pale red, streaked purple, fluid accompanied it to the ground as it slipped from its egg, like a haze of gas easing it down. Moments after it hit the grass it gave a cry or a growl, like serrated metal grinding across stone, and then Bon was following Leki and Juda into the trees.

They ran line abreast, careful not to stray into each other's paths. The eggs were everywhere, and the problem wasn't so much aiming as avoiding them with other parts of their bodies. They hung heavy and low from some of the lower branches, and Bon had no wish to touch them with his hands or bare forearms, or his face. He watched the ground for obstructions, swung the stick, felt it striking branches and leaves and eggs, saw the things falling from the corner of his eye, and ran on, listening to their deep scratching calls as they stirred behind him.

They reached a clearer area where a rough circle of stones surrounded a flat rock. Whatever it had been was long lost to antiquity, but Juda paused and turned, eyes wide as he looked past Bon and down through the woods. Bon and Leki followed his gaze.

The woods sloping downhill to the plain seemed tainted red. The air hung heavy with it, a drifting mist that was staining trees and lower plants a light pink. Floating through these faint clouds, the stark blights.

'Won't they just run around?' Leki asked.

'This close to us, I'm hoping their caution is lessened,' Juda said. 'Hoping they're blinded by . . .'

Juda was staring at Bon again, but now his eyes were wider. 'Keep still! And don't—'

Bon felt movement in his hair. He slapped at it with his hand, and the stark blight wrapped filaments around his fingers, stinging the back of his hand, his palm, his wrist, and he could feel its toxins pumping along the veins in his arm, a slick of heat that set fire to his hand and moved quickly up towards his elbow.

He glared at Juda, trying not to scream.

Leki came at him, then Juda. Though Bon knew they were talking he could not hear, because his heart was thudding so hard it was all he heard. His treacherous heart, pumping the fury about his body and setting fires.

Bon dropped his stick and fell, thinking, *Not again!* And as he felt the power of the scream leaving his throat the pain exploded, and his heart beat him into darkness.

Chapter 8
breaking

Darkness was closing, and Juda felt the familiar madness readying to take him. He had often cursed his heritage and the tainted sleep it gave him, but he would never curse the magic that aggravated the condition. Especially now, when the man he carried might lead him to discover the greatest source of magic there might be anywhere in the world – a dead god, risen.

Juda had smoked his final scamp cigar, and if they had time he could have searched for more scamp growing between the moist roots of trees. He was sure he had seen some moths fluttering from leaf to leaf as they'd worked their way uphill. But there *was* no time.

If they did not reach the gas marshes by nightfall, and find somewhere to hide away, it would be the end. He could not accept the end when he was so close to a new beginning.

Juda had never been a strong man, but his strength and stamina now came from a bitter determination. Bon lay slung over his right shoulder, head nodding against his back as Juda planted foot after foot and lifted himself up the hillside.

Leki was behind him, helping him as much as she could by pushing against his lower back. She was not so much lifting him as propelling him forward, and her effort aided more than he could have hoped. It was the physical contribution that helped, but also the simple fact that they had the same aim. Juda had always been a loner, but he was finding this company pleasing.

Wrench Arcs craved no company save that of magic. Perhaps, after all, he had some way yet to go.

They had heard the slayers entering the woodland. Their grunts as they ran, animal sounds like swine being herded to the slaughter. The impact of their wide feet on the leafy ground. Clanking of poorly tied weapons, chafing of leather armour, rasping of breath through mouths crowded with too many teeth. Juda had never learned exactly where the slayers originated, but he suspected some sort of interbreeding programmes by the Spike. Steppe warrior and lyon, perhaps. And there were other rumours.

They had heard the squeals, and then the screams, and then the impact of falling bodies as the stark blights had fulfilled their natural function of protecting themselves and their kind from attack.

'Not far to the top,' Leki said from behind him, and Juda knew she was trying to reign in her exhaustion. She could not let herself sound tired when he was carrying Bon's weight as well as his own. He looked up from the ground directly before his feet and saw that she was right. The trees were much sparser here, though still speckled with stark blight eggs. The ridgeline was close, and beyond that would be the wide plateau that led eventually to a deep ravine. They would descend, follow the flow of the raging river, and then enter the gas marshes spread across its flood plain. They were constantly shifting places, a slow-moving sea of mud and gas, rocky outcroppings and swallow-holes, and he had never dared venture across them before. He'd heard tales from one who had, and she had claimed to be the only survivor of a group of eight. *Poison gas and steam to melt the flesh from your face*, she'd told him over a bottle of bad wine in one of Vandemon's saloons, looking into a hazy distance of painful memory. *Bottomless marshes, swallow-holes, wasps the size of your head, and wet-wolves that breathe mud and surface anywhere, without warning. They eat bones. They spit out the flesh and blood.*

He'd doubted her stories, suspecting them to be embellished excuses for a badly planned journey. He'd been *free* to doubt, because he'd had no reason to ever travel within miles of the gas marshes.

Now they were the only place where they might shake the slayers from their trail. Through the marshes, the slayers would lose their scent to the acidic air. Juda and the others would flee north.

North, towards Venden Ugane and what the Skythians believed he had found. Though Juda had considered seeking out Venden on his own, to get the boy's trust it would be best to stick with his father. And with the slayers still on their trail, he hoped there was safety in numbers.

'How long will they be down?' Leki asked.

'Depends how many times they were stung.'

'Bon was only stung once. Maybe they're dead! Maybe those things have killed them!'

'No,' Juda said, too exhausted to explain how he knew. *The slayers might have died many times before.* He'd heard those rumours, whispered in dark saloons, and could not afford to doubt them now.

'You sure we'll lose them in the gas marshes?'

'Yes,' Juda gasped. He had to stop, and it seemed that

momentum was driving him, because the sudden weight dragged him to his knees. 'Help me . . . up.'

Leki lifted, and Juda considered shifting Bon to his other shoulder. But nothing would be comfortable. So instead he thought about how things had changed, and what might come, and he tried to forget the dangers behind them and the promise of madness the approaching night would bring to him. His nightmares would be bad, so he concentrated on his dreams.

Every Broker is a selfish beast, Rhelli Saal had told him. Rhelli was one of the first Brokers he'd met in New Kotrugam, and she had become a friend and sometime lover for the short time they'd spent together. *How can they not be, when magic is such a personal thing? We join forces and give ourselves a name, but we all want the same thing, and that's for magic to be ours and ours alone.*

You want that too? he'd asked, looking at her across the sea of bubbles in the giant bath they were sharing.

Of course, she said.

But we're not like the Wrench Arcs. Not like them.

There's a difference between selfishness and cruelty. I can be selfish but maintain my morals. Selfish, and like myself.

They must start like that. He'd been thinking of the Wrench Arcs a lot since being welcomed, cautiously and tentatively, into the Brokers' embrace. Independent, vicious, cruel, and quite certainly mad, the Wrench Arcs wandered the continent with a shadow of myth and a haze of rumour camouflaging them against being caught. They slipped from darkness to darkness, and only made themselves known when a whisper of magic passed from lip to ear. Then they would come and take it, and whoever might be in their way would suffer.

144

Every Broker is a selfish beast. As soon as he had arrived on Skythe and caught his first hint of the magical dregs there, he had known that to be true. His Regerran blood and night-time madness, the murders of pathetic Skythians . . . he knew that many would see him as a Wrench Arc. But his shame at what he did meant he was not quite there. Wrench Arcs were shameless.

'Juda, the day's wearing on,' Leki said.

'We'll get there.'

'But, your—' Leki stopped. She did not wish to call it madness.

'We'll get there.' He could offer her no comfort. If they did not reach the marshes, he would have to flee from them before the night took him down. Alone, they would all be easy targets for the slayers.

Bon groaned. Juda paused, trying to shove his relief aside. Even if he did stir, the man would not be able to walk on his own for some time.

'Bon,' Leki said softly, and as Juda continued pushing himself uphill, she whispered to the man slung over his shoulder. He responded with groans at first, and then muttered words. By the time Juda hit the ridge and collapsed, Bon was able to break his fall when he slipped from his saviour's shoulder. Juda hit the cool, damp heather and rolled his face against it, relishing the freshness against his sweaty skin. He caught Bon watching him, and saw gratitude through the pain.

'I can walk,' Bon said.

'I doubt it,' Juda replied. Bon's hand was swollen and red, exuding heat he could almost feel from where he lay.

Leki knelt beside Bon and cradled his head in her lap. She looked from one man to the other.

Juda stood. His knees shook, muscles in his legs quivering. He needed food, energy, but they had no time to stop and eat. He looked downhill and saw no movement, but that did not mean the slayers were still down. They could have been moving painfully through the shadows lower down the hillside, slashing their skin to vent infected blood, growling away their pain.

'His hand,' Leki said, moving her own around Bon's, but not quite touching.

'I could cut it to release the pressure, but infection would soon follow,' Juda said. 'Best to let it settle on its own.' He drank the last drop of water from his canteen. It was warm, and did little to sate his thirst.

'He was bitten on the ship, too. Unlucky.'

'Maybe,' Juda panted.

'You can't carry him any further. I can.'

'You?' Juda said, immediately feeling a pang of regret.

'Yes, me. A woman. I'm probably stronger than you.'

'I'm sorry,' Juda said. 'I didn't mean . . .' But he had, and he could not explain it away.

'I can walk,' Bon said again, but he could barely speak.

'How far from here?' Leki said.

Juda pointed across the plateau. 'Four, five miles that way. Then down into a—'

'Let's take one thing at a time,' Leki said. 'Help me get him up.'

Bon waved her hand away angrily, propping himself on his good hand and pushing, falling onto his side and crying out when he struck his stung hand against the ground. So Juda helped, sensing the strength in her as she hoisted Bon across her left shoulder, and he remembered that an amphy could swim as fast as any fish for a short stretch of time, flooding muscles with a burst of power to give exaggerated strength. How long that might last on land he didn't know, but he had to trust her.

No choice.

'We should get away from the slope,' he said. 'They'll see us moving against the sky.'

Bon protested one more time, but then Leki said something to him that Juda did not hear, and he seemed to fall calm and loose across her shoulder. She smiled an enigmatic smile as she started walking, looking at the ground before her and moving with grace and no apparent discomfort.

That won't last, Juda thought. He squatted and looked downhill, back the way they had come. There was no sign of movement, and no sense that those bastard things might be watching him from the shadows. Yet doom still hung over him like the breath of a god. However fast they ran, however close they came to the gas marshes, he suspected that sensation might never lift again.

'Aeon, and magic, awaits,' he whispered, glancing back guiltily. But Leki was already forty steps away, walking steadily and smoothly. Even if she had heard him – even if Bon had heard him – neither would know what he meant.

The time would come to tell. But first they had to survive.

Walking away from the remnant towards what might be the heart of a dead god, Venden found himself dwelling on the past more than he had for a long time. He heard his mother saying his name, as she used to when she watched him playing or reading, or making some complex device whose purpose was pointless but which was remarkable nonetheless. She had spoken with deep pride and love, and he thought perhaps a trace of sadness as well. Maybe it was memory giving her voice that lilt, but he thought not. Maybe it was the fact that her little boy would grow up, and become a person of his own, and eventually leave to make his own life . . . but he thought not.

He thought perhaps his mother had known when she was going to die.

You have further to go than most, she had told him, words once lost to memory but surfacing again now. They had confused him as a child, but remembering them as he walked through Skythe's wilderness, Venden heard something so prescient in his long-dead mother's sad tone.

His destination, Kellis Faults, was way to the north, and he had no wish to travel all that way on foot. Walking there might be easy enough, but returning with the heart of Aeon . . .

'Too heavy,' he said. 'Too precious.'

So he was seeking help. And he went bearing gifts.

Venden watched them from behind a rocky outcrop, wondering how they could even survive like this. He had spent some time thinking about the Skythians – how they were now, and how they must have been before and immediately after the war. And unless the punishment visited upon their old society had in some way hobbled their ability to learn, grow and evolve, then six hundred years ago they must have emerged from that cataclysm little more than blind animals. They had persisted, but not prospered; they existed, but without triumph or joy. Watching them attempting to farm, he could see why.

The field was already criss-crossed with furrows from previous years, scarring the land with barren impressions. He knew from experience that yield from these farming attempts was small – perhaps the soil's nutrients had been scorched away by the war's fallout – and barely worth the effort the Skythians put in. And these were the more advanced of their race. The disparate and somewhat uneven levels of civilisation remaining on Skythe were a mystery to Venden, and he could only put it down to bloodlines. Perhaps the war had damaged and polluted one family branch more than another, and descendants carried those greater or lesser degrees of taint. Even the lesser degrees were sometimes heartbreaking to watch. In other areas of Skythe farming was unknown, and food grew in the next valley or ran from hunters' spears. These Skythians were ploughing against the grain.

They had a wild shire shackled to a heavy scrap of melted metal, similar to the tools Venden had picked up but much larger. Another shire was tethered across the field beneath the shelter of a huge old koa tree, the tree's branches drooping and heavy with parasitic growth. Venden had seen this extended family before, and several times soon after he'd arrived he had tried forming some sort of bond with them. Communication through basic sign language was relatively simple, but a desire to communicate had been absent. They had watched his efforts and sometimes reciprocated in a basic manner, but he'd seen no enthusiasm, no drive to know him better or even to accept the gifts he offered. Wildness hid behind their cautious stares.

They seemed to remember his name, however, and they muttered *Venden Ugane* each time he visited. It was strange hearing those words in the middle of incomprehensible chatter.

He carried those same gifts with him now, and as he watched them he planned how to pass them over. *They have to know what I mean*, he thought. *I have to make them know.*

The shires were wild and difficult to control. The family had tied basic harnesses around the neck and shoulder of the one they were using, and tried urging the beast to do their bidding, dragging the spiked metal shape through the ground. The men stood on the metal to add weight, and if they were lucky – if the shire did not turn the wrong way, the men did not fall, the metal did not strike a buried rock, and the rough ropes did not break – they would plough a furrow deep enough, perhaps, to plant seed bulbs. It was a painful process to watch, because the progress was so slow and success so rare. But Venden sat for a while and took a drink, finding some measure of respect for these Skythians' persistence and determination.

After a while he emerged from behind the rocks and walked down the gentle slope, careful to edge around the field as he approached them. One of the children saw him first, standing from the uneven furrow he had been planting and filling in with clumpy, rocky clods.

'Venden Ugane,' the boy said, walking backwards across the furrows and grabbing his two small sisters by the hand. The children wore only flat wooden shoes, and one girl had a withered arm.

Venden paused, raising both hands palm-out. The same thing happened every time he chose to approach any Skythian group, and for that reason he did so less and less.

'Patience,' he muttered to himself. 'Plenty of time.'

The men dropped from the make-do plough. They scurried close to the women and children, hunkering down as if to present a smaller target. Venden always felt a sadness at this; a proud person would stand straight. The men's hands grasped beneath their tatty clothing for blades, and Venden sank to a squat, twenty steps from them and far enough away to turn and run. He would beat them in a chase, but that was not what he wanted.

He wanted to give them things.

Carefully, slowly, Venden took his flint box from his pocket. He emptied a handful of dried sawdust onto a slab of unearthed rock, flicked the flint, and after only three attempts a spark caught in the sawdust and a flame rose.

The Skythian children laughed, the men gasped. Venden

glanced up at them and smiled. One of the women was slowly shaking her head, though whether in doubt or fear he could not tell. He bent over the smouldering sawdust and blew slowly. The flame was short-lived, and he inhaled the sweet-smelling smoke as he held out the flint box.

One of the men edged forward. He limped on a deformed foot, and wore a rough leather patch over one eye. Venden left the box and backed away, and the man snatched it up, spilling its contents as he darted back to his family. The woman who had been shaking her head scolded him, and he slapped her across the face with the back of his hand.

Venden blinked, tensed. The woman spat at the man's feet and stared at him with eyes full of fire, but she did not retaliate. Venden hoped that would be for later. He watched the man move slowly back towards him, picking up the spilled pieces from the flint box. When he was close, Venden spoke.

In his time here he had gathered what he hoped was a basic understanding of their native tongue. Sign language seemed limited, but several times over the last year he had attempted stilted, confused exchanges, with mixed success. More than anything, he had sensed the Skythians' surprise that he would even try talking with them. Sometimes they seemed to fear him, and on occasion he thought they were in awe. He had no idea why.

'Shire,' he said, holding up the other things he had brought.

The Skythians were startled, the children afraid of this alien speaking their language. But the woman who had been slapped reacted quickly. She glanced at the tethered shire, back at Bon, and he saw an intelligence in her expression which had been absent before. *Perhaps they are merely guarded*, he thought. The idea that they might feign

151

such wildness had not crossed his mind, and he found it chilling.

'More than this.' She reached out and tapped the flint and box in the man's hand.

Venden removed the next gift from his pack and stepped forward to hand it to the woman. She took the folded leaf and opened it. Sniffed.

'Bruised heather root.'

'Treated in a way . . .' Venden frowned, and started blending in some words from his own language. 'A way . . . I know how. Paste it on wounds. It heals, prevents infection.'

The woman looked at him, mistrustful, subconsciously touching an ugly scar across the left side of her neck.

'And I have more. Medicines. Tools.'

The woman glanced back over her shoulder at her family.

'I can give you—'

'See you watching,' the woman said. 'You see us weak, wasted.'

Yes, Venden wanted to say, but he frowned. To understand this she must surely be more intelligent than he'd thought. It should have been easy to come here and buy a shire, but she was entering into conversation with him. It was something he had not anticipated, and he wondered again at his assessment of these Skythians. Perhaps they were further removed from the wild tribes elsewhere than he had given them credit for.

'I see you trying,' he said.

'As do you,' she said. 'Trying to touch the remains.'

'Remains?' Venden asked, startled. How much did they know about him? Him, and the remnant, and what he knew it to be?

'Of the past. We see them, but you need to *touch* them.'

152

You have no idea what I'm building, he thought, but something in her eyes betrayed the lie in that. A chill went through him, and he suddenly wanted to be back at the remnant, safe beneath the overhang and staring at whatever it was he had done. The idea of a people portraying themselves as the Skythians did, purposely, troubled him. Perhaps in the race memory of their past they found a need to exist as they did now. Simply, and out of sight.

'Take a shire,' the woman said. 'Build your thing, Venden Ugane.' She spoke no more, but in her eyes he saw so much. *You amuse us*, her expression said. *We watch you.*

Venden walked past her and pulled a blanket from the back of the plough-harnessed creature. It shook its long head at him and snarled, but he moved away from it, and away from the family. The children whispered, the adults watched him go. Never had he felt so observed, and he feared that by speaking their language he had seen away his advantage, and closed a distance. It concerned him that he could not have seen the gentler reality of these people.

As he approached the tethered shire, he felt confidence return. Fool or not, he would surprise them again. He had never seen a Skythian riding a shire. They were beasts of burden, not a means of transport, and there was little wonder why – the Skythians he had observed rarely travelled more than a couple of miles from wherever they chose to make their home.

The shire snuffled as he approached, regarding him warily yet unconcerned. Its nostrils flared, its head swinging left and right as it gathered his scent. It looked stronger than most shires he had seen, perhaps because it was fed more than those in the wild, where shires' predilection for the meat of their young sometimes drove new mothers many miles to evade those they had previously run and hunted with. He didn't know what meat the Skythians fed them – this one had been munching on a pile of dried grass and fruit – but its muscle tone was defined, limbs long and strong.

That was good. He had a way to go, and on the return he would be carrying more.

He approached the beast and rubbed its flank. It looked at him, blinked slowly, and went back to its leisurely meal. Its brown hair was coarse, yet well groomed. Its long tail whipped flies from around its back end. Its lush mane was beaded with the small, bleached bones of birds, some of them carved into unknown shapes by the Skythians.

'You'll not give me any problems,' Venden said nervously. The shire regarded him with one large, watery eye. He had seen riders sprint after wild shires on Alderia, taking them with a harsh-dart to lessen their speed and then mounting, riding them in three circles to break them to their riders' wishes. Still wild, they would be easier to control and steer, and Venden had watched in astonishment as dozens were herded together and raced for the amusement of the gathering crowds. It had been a long sunny day, and his mother had held his little hand in hers. Even then there had been a sadness to her.

He folded the blanket and heaved it onto the beast's back. It neighed and stamped its forefeet, but did not move away. Lulling it with gentle sounds, smoothing its shoulder, Venden resisted the temptation to look back at the Skythians undoubtedly watching him. The children had fallen quiet, and he imagined their confusion as he stood close to their work beast, whispering in its ear and preparing to make it his own.

Grasping the animal's long mane and tensing his legs, he heard something from the Skythian family that might have been a gasp of surprise, or a laugh. And jumping, hauling himself onto the shire's back and clasping his hands into its long mane, the idea crossed his mind that there might be very good reasons why Skythian shires were not ridden.

For a moment the beast froze, and Venden even allowed himself a small, satisfied smile. *And I was worried that—*

He felt the movement building from deep within, muscles coiling and a heavy growl bursting out at the same moment the shire bolted. It bucked as it ran, hard wide back pummelling against his backside and legs, shaking him, his stomach rolling and vision blurring with each impact. In desperation he pressed himself down low to the animal's back. He held on to handfuls of mane, feeling each strand and clotted piece of dirt against his palms and fingertips. *If I fall I'll break something it'll trample me I'll die*, he thought, images of his demise flashing through his mind like his whole life yet to come.

The shire was snorting. Foam speckled its long snout and head, misting the air as it leaped and spat. Each impact of hooves against ground sent a shockwave into Venden. He could not draw breath. He heard the beast screaming, and then realised that it was him, shouting into the mane waving and flailing him across the face, insult to injury.

They rode them in circles, he thought, recalling those wild shires a continent away, and he pulled the mane down on one side and dug that knee into the shire's side. It did not seem to react, so he leaned a little, right arm tensing so hard that he felt his muscles lock and his elbow freeze.

The shire veered to the left, still stamping and bucking and snorting foam at the air. What might have been panic was now anger. Venden could see bared teeth each time it flicked its head back at him, and its tail whipped at his back as if he were merely a larger than average bug.

As it bounced across the randomly ploughed field, the shire moved in a wide circle to the left, meaning that it passed close to the Skythians. They moved back beneath the cover of trees, watching wide-eyed, the children pointing, and the adults . . .

If they had been laughing before, there was some other expression on their faces now. Venden could not read it, but hoped it was respect.

He pulled harder and the shire stomped in a tighter circle. He was sweating and gasping for air, battered and bruised and shaken, but by the time he passed the Skythian family for the second time he was gaining some control. The shire had gone from scared to furious, and now that fury was giving way to something like acceptance. Still it snorted and stomped, but Venden found that subtle changes in the way he held its mane were already providing results. Wild though it was, he had the measure of that wildness. For a while, at least.

Across the field from the family, he hauled back on the mane and the creature stamped to a standstill. Breath plumed from its flared nostrils and its eyes rolled, and through his legs Venden could feel the powerful thump of its heart. But it did not buck, and did not reach back to snap at him with powerful jaws.

Maybe it was biding its time.

'Good boy,' Venden said, leaning forward and patting its shoulder. 'Good boy. We've a way to go, and you might even learn to like it.'

The shire snorted foamy derision. Venden laughed. Then he sat back for a moment, surprised at his own good humour and relishing the sense of power the beast beneath him exuded. *I haven't laughed for a long time*, he thought. He looked across at the Skythian family, who were already continuing in their efforts to plough the rocky field. If he had shaken them, they were not showing it.

'Move on,' he said, kneeing the shire across the field towards them. 'Time to finish buying you. Though I'm not sure you'll ever be truly owned.'

Chapter 9

him

Milian Mu had never regarded herself as a sexual creature. In her previous life she had been an attractive woman, but not beautiful; wholesome, but not voluptuous. Her husband had adored her, but she had been comfortable with the fact that she did not possess qualities that set other women apart.

It took the men from the travelling family to make her view herself in a new way. Because they looked at her with something more than interest, and something more animal than attraction. They lusted after her.

Not them, she thought, because there was some aspect she – or, rather, the shard – sought in a man that was wholly absent here. She was not quite sure what that was, or why, and that troubled her. She could recall her husband's strength and sensitivity, his shyness, and his love as a father. But when she remembered him, there would be something off inside, as if a part of her was trying to look away. *Not him*, she would think, and the memory of his face would fade away into a visage she had never seen before. A stranger, with harder eyes and a downturn to his mouth that bore witness to a harder, harsher life.

Worst of all, she had no idea why she sought anyone. It seemed to be her prime motive now that she was awake, and she disliked the idea of being steered and used. But the shard of Aeon, the part of her god seeded within her, would not answer her silent questions, and in the darker moments of her journey south with those families, she started to believe that she was mad.

She bore no scars to pay testament to her memories of murder, slaughter and fire. If she held her breath, she soon started to struggle; those dreams of crossing the seabed must be simply that – dreams. She tried to deny herself and give space for the truth, but the shard was an inexplicable presence betraying the veracity of those strange memories. It was something she could not make up. Its heat was obvious as she laid her hand across her belly, as was the taste of the ocean at the back of her throat each time she blinked.

The shard has me looking for someone, she thought, and more and more she found the two men looking back.

Three days north of New Kotrugam they stopped beside a lake, fed by a high waterfall and spotted with small floating islands. Large birds had made these islands their nests, and they sat guarding their young, occasionally flitting up and arcing into the water, emerging with a thrashing shape flashing silver in sunlight and landing again to eat. The setting sun lit the waterfall and cast a pink rainbow across the lake. It looked as if the water was bleeding.

Milian remained the deaf mute, unable to hear their discussions or respond if she did, but their language was rapidly expanding and filling her consciousness, understanding of one phrase dawning from another. This understanding was effortless and frightening, and she knew that a time would come when she would have to begin talking.

For now, though, she was enjoying the peace and solitude of silence.

As the families prepared camp she walked along the banks of the lake, admiring its beauty. The sound of birds' evensong as they settled into dusk was countered with the growl of hunting things, and the undergrowth that grew away from the lake's edge was alive with hunter and hunted.

She rounded a rise in the land and looked back, ensuring that the camp was out of sight. Something she had quickly learned was that the families respected each other's privacy. It was an admirable trait in people existing so close together, and she had welcomed the moments this afforded her.

Milian stood motionless beside the lake. A dozen species of birds worried over the water, and far out some fish broke surface and seemed to twist and bathe within the failing sunlight. It was a tranquil scene, beautiful, untouched, and she started undressing.

The water was so cold it took her breath away. She walked into the lake, feeling forward with her toes over slick rocks, and when she sensed the lake bed falling sharply away she leaped in without hesitation or fear. She went under, and for a while the only sound she heard was her own heartbeat and the fluid whisper of bubbles rising about her head. In that sensation she sought memory, but that long walk she had dreamed of seemed to belong to someone else.

Milian swam, conscious of the depths beneath her. There were things watching. Their attention was not perturbing, and she welcomed their interest. Time passed, she swam back and forth close to the lake's edge, and then she trod water and watched the sun sinking into the water. It bled across the lake as though making an offering of itself, and when it finally disappeared she felt the cold for the first time.

Shivering, Milian emerged and walked towards where she had left her clothing.

'You are beautiful,' the man said. It was the tall man who had first found her, and who had paid her most attention in the few days of their journey. He emerged naked from the shadows beneath the trees. His skin was wet, and the idea of him swimming in the same lake as her, watching, set a chill in her too deep for mere cold.

Milian made a pretence of covering herself, but it was hopeless.

'I've never seen anyone like you,' he said, walking slowly towards her. He made no effort to hide himself; his arousal pointed the way. She went to step back but then he was before her, leaning in so close that she could smell his breath.

Perhaps it is him, Milian thought. But the shard remained cool, urging her away.

'You're not him,' she said in the man's own language, and her eyes went wide in surprise. It had been her voice, but it was the shard doing the speaking.

'So you *do* talk,' the man said softly. He smiled and moved back imperceptibly, then took up her hand and pressed it to his lips.

Milian shoved him, hard. The man staggered back, tripped over his own feet and fell, crying out as he hit the ground.

This is when he gets up and comes at me and I have to fight back . . .

'I'm . . . sorry,' the man said. He stood quickly and backed away, head bowed. His excitement waned, and Milian felt a rush of fury towards him, not pity. As he scampered into the shadows, she quickly dressed, worried that he might change his mind and return. *I could tear him apart*, she thought, but

161

though it had been her hands doing the tearing so long ago, it had been that bastard daemon steering her. And Aeon's shard had saved her from that.

She ran along the shore, away from the camp and the people who had helped her, because there was no way she could return. She fled into the night, abandoning herself to the wilds of Alderia and wondering what would come next. *I am my own woman*, she thought, a flush of triumph making her smile. And then the shard rose again, its power obvious and untouchable.

And Milian wondered if she was her own woman after all.

He was not the one, the shard said. Its voice rang out loud, leaving her and filling the darkness around her, the lake, the shadows that waited at every corner.

By the time they reached the ravine Bon's pain was manageable. He could walk on his own and the faints no longer came over him, and Juda had rigged a sling so that he held his left arm across his chest, hand fisted and pressed almost to his right shoulder. The steady, hot throb of the stark blight venom was receding, or he was becoming more used to it. Either way, he no longer felt like a liability.

Juda, however, did not have very long left.

'Two miles,' their guide said. He was snatching at the air before him again, as if ripping the failing light aside and storing it for later. 'Two miles, gas marshes, hide . . .' His madness was falling, and he had no more scamp cigars left.

Bon had heard of these places, scattered widely across Skythe. Some of the old histories he had read of the island – forbidden books, rarer than rare – regarded them as deadly, mysterious places where only those strange creatures adapted to such environments could survive for long. One tome had called them cursed by Aeon, but even that ancient book

162

had the air of a scientific text rather than a religious tract. He hoped that Juda knew what he was doing.

And beyond the gas marshes, once they had, hopefully, evaded the slayers, perhaps they would find Venden.

He so wished to stop and tell Leki more about his clever, bright son, the things he had invented and built himself, his interests and talents, the books he had loved and the thinking he had done on his own, analytical thoughts on the politics of Alderia and the veracity of the Fade, ideas untainted by parental influence and arrived at through his own incredible mind. He wanted to tell her about the good times they had had together, but found there were few. He wished he could reveal to Leki the love he had for his son, and which was reciprocated in an unconscious way. But along with these desires came the understanding that nothing about his relationship with Venden had ever been normal. He could not blame all of that on his son's uniqueness.

Bon heard the river before they reached the ravine. He could smell it, such was its violence and the moisture it threw into the air. Juda paused on the deep ravine's edge, looking down the steep sides at the raging white beast below. He swayed, slashing at the air again, then turned and glared at Bon and Leki.

'Can't we go around?' Leki asked.

'Quicker down there. And some cover from them.' He indicated back over his shoulder, as if the slayers were in sight. Bon could not help glancing back, but the plateau was wide and barren, with no signs of pursuit.

'You've done this before?' Bon asked, but Juda did not respond. He had dark rings beneath his eyes and his face was slack, as if sleep was already pulling him down.

'I don't have long,' Juda said. He glanced left and right, then started down into the ravine, following a rough path that might have been worn there by animals of some kind. Narrow, rocky, it followed the easiest route down towards the raging river.

'You sure you're able to do this on your own?' Leki asked Bon. The concern in her gaze was obvious as she looked at his painful hand.

'No choice,' Bon said. He was right. It was too dangerous for Leki to help him down. From up here the path looked almost too narrow to pass in places, and if one slipped, they both would. The ravine sides were sprouted with plants and ledges, so a tumble would not necessarily be fatal. But he had no desire to put Leki at risk. He had already seen one woman fall, and he had been unable to save her.

They descended into the ravine and followed the river's course, walking through flutters of strange-tasting snow. The river's roar allowed no communication, and its noise filled Bon's head, trying to drown other thoughts. As they descended, the roar grew greater until it became something that intruded into every sense – the taste of river water, strangely stale; a vibration to the air, the shaking ground; the smell of dead things carried on the river and the stagnant dampness of places never touched by the sun. Bon's pain seemed to recede the deeper they went, whether because of the overwhelming effect of the river or a dispersal of the venom, he did not mind.

Some time passed. An early dusk closed over them, but it was not darkness that tracked the passage of time for Bon, but Juda's behaviour. He stumbled several times, and then started falling over. His hands continued to wave at the air, the actions changing from grasping to punching, clasping, slashing.

Bon grabbed Leki's arm and pulled her close. 'We have to tie him and carry him!' he shouted, and he could hear his own voice again. Leki nodded and heaved off Juda's backpack. He carried rope and tape, and as Bon took a moment to glance around, she went about binding his wrists together.

The ravine had widened considerably and the river's violence lessened, flowing past confident and brash. *Where has he led us? What by all the false gods is that?*

It was only a river. Only a river . . .

He helped Leki tie the twitching, sleeping man, and Juda's eyes opened, white, rolled upwards.

'Into the marshes . . .' he shouted. 'But . . . dangers . . .'

'The air!' Leki said.

'Tadcat . . . liver oil. In my pack. A paste . . . leather pouch. Rub it . . .' Juda gasped, clasped at the air, and then very deliberately drew two fingers slowly across his top lip.

'I know a little about the marshes,' Bon said. Leki glanced at him, one eyebrow raised. Bon shrugged. He knew *something* about them.

But his comment seemed to ease Juda into a more peaceful sleep, and they finished tying his wrists and ankles.

Leki rummaged in Juda's pack and brought out several items, looking more and more concerned as she did so. One of them was a long spike, a length of gut trailing from one end. Another consisted of several glass vials melted together, fluid in some of them showing different colours depending on the angle Leki held it at.

'What?' Bon asked.

'Things he shouldn't have.' Leki did not elaborate, but opened a small leather pouch, sniffing and nodding. She plunged two fingers inside and then smeared them beneath her nose, so that her top lip glistened with a faint pink gel. She dipped again, and Bon leaned forward to receive the paste. Lastly, she did Juda.

'Stinks,' Bon said.

'Better than being poisoned by marsh gas.'

'You think this will make us safe?'

Leki shrugged, and looked faintly disapproving. 'You're the one who said you know about the marshes.'

'Well . . . some.' They left it at that. Time was moving on, dusk had settled, and they both felt the pressure of pursuit building behind them. Whatever things Leki had found in Juda's pack, Bon knew they had to trust Juda, for now. He would ask Leki about the objects when they were safe.

The river – ice-cold, the frozen artery of this degraded, dying land – pointed the way to the gas marshes.

Juda was heavier than he looked, and they carried him in short stints. Tall, skinny, clothes flapping about his sticklimbs, Bon thought he must possess bones of steel and organs of rock. His heart, at least, was still a mystery, and Bon did not mind sharing that doubt with Leki.

'We still don't know why he saved us,' he said.

'Does kindness need a reason?'

'Really?' Bon frowned at Leki where she carried Juda's legs. 'After whatever you found in his pack, you really believe it's just kindness?'

'No,' Leki admitted. She looked down at the man slung between them; his bound wrists, tied ankles. He was twitching in his sleep, and muttering things they could not yet hear. His talking would increase in volume soon. They would need to gag him.

'He's led us from the slayers into this place, which is even more likely to kill us,' Bon said.

'He's here himself.'

'A madman might not know fear.'

'Hang on,' Leki said. 'Wait.' She was panting. They eased Juda to the ground. 'Just a breath.'

Bon looked anxiously behind them, into the narrowing ravine where the river and its misty spray seemed enraged, filling the whole space. He wasn't sure just how they'd managed to come through there.

'This river . . .' he said.

'It's just a river,' Leki said. 'I know what you're feeling. I feel the same. But I think it's just . . . picking up on the cold in the land.'

'The cold?'

'The frozen heart of Skythe. Maybe it's only us amphys who sense it.'

'Not something I've heard of,' Bon said, surprised to feel a little put out. He'd thought himself an authority on Skythe, and the cold river had frightened him without his knowing why.

'All the waters of the world are joined,' Leki said. 'They merge and mix and flow, and tell their stories. And the story goes that deep beneath parts of Skythe, the underground has gone from molten to frozen. The heart of the land, frozen by what happened.'

'That sounds like something the Ald would have us believe,' Bon said, only part serious.

'You'd suggest that of me?' she asked, suddenly cold herself.

'No. No.'

'Come on. The ravine's ending, the gas marshes beginning. I can smell them even past this paste. You say you know something of the marshes, so it's time to use what you know.' Leki heaved at Juda's legs, and Bon picked him up under the arms once more.

'We can't carry him far like this,' Bon said. His poisoned hand was still swollen and its muscles and bones ached.

'Hopefully we won't need to.'

167

The river's anger lessened as the ravine sides fell away, flattening into the beginnings of the marshes. The gas was noxious, rotten, stinging the back of Bon's throat. Juda had said that they could lose the slayers here because their scent would be lost amid the gaseous exhalations of the wet ground. But there was much more to the marshes than wetness, and gas. In losing the slayers, Bon began to fear they would expose themselves to dangers even more terrible.

He had not been entirely truthful when he said he knew about the marshes. Dangerous, wild places even back when Skythe had been a thriving island with commerce, art and science, they had interested him little in his readings. They were almost the same now as they had been back then – larger, perhaps, and less well fed by wandering, lost humans. And though undoubtedly the flora and fauna of Skythe had changed since the war, and was still changing now, the marshes themselves stood testament to the differing touch of time. Not timeless, but ancient. The matters of humanity held little significance for such a place.

Bon had heard rumours of the marshes' changing geography, steam and gas geysers, and wildlife peculiarly adapted to the environment. But the detail would be for him to discover along with Leki.

The river spread into the land. In places it seemed to vent into underground routes, clouds of spray catching the last red touch of the sunset. Elsewhere it parted around islands on which grew short, craggy trees, and flowed into wide areas of water that seemed hardly to move. In these watery landscapes, bubbles rose and broke as if the ground below were breathing. The air was already tainted. Bon breathed lightly past the tadcat oils, afraid of what that taint might do, and whether he would even know.

Juda grew heavier. Leki's face mirrored Bon's own

weariness. But they had to move on into the vast marshland. Somewhere, soon, they would need to hide.

Their night in the gas marshes became a blur of vision and a haze of sensation. The sense of being elsewhere was overwhelming – Bon soon felt dislocated from Skythe, and from the whole of the world. Juda was a sleeping creature slung between them, Leki a stranger, and Bon even grew distant from himself. His history became an echo in another mind, and his present lacked definition and importance.

The slayers – the main reason for them venturing into the gas marshes in the first place – were very far away. Bon barely thought about those monstrous killers that whole night.

Later, he would remember their experiences there like recalling a dream from his youth. And thinking back to the few clearer moments he *could* remember – constructing them piece by piece, like writing a letter with words he barely knew – he would begin to doubt himself. Had he lived those moments, or were they simply a dream? Had he truly seen those things, and run from them, and found that place to hide? Or perhaps he and Leki had simply collapsed beneath the weight of their exhaustion, urged down into dream-haunted darkness by the noxious fumes of that place.

Bon was left wondering at reality, and how real anything might be.

And those few clear memories, like dreams given life . . .

As the marshes grew wide and the water sluggish, and it became impossible to define the river any more, the air was heavy with steam and gas. It was difficult to distinguish the two, and they coated Bon's nostrils and the back of his throat with slick sourness. They paused often, lowering Juda to the damp ground and trying to catch their breath, regain strength in their straining muscles. Bon's hand still burned. And once,

169

standing beneath the cover of tall trees whose multitude of roots stood proud of the ground like exposed bones, Bon rubbed at his ears. Something was making them buzz. *Wet air*, he thought, *gas nestling inside my ears.* He pressed in with his fingertips and the buzzing ceased. Seeing Leki doing the same, he realised that the sound came from outside.

They ducked down beside Juda and looked up. Noticing the sound made it louder, and also gave the previous silence more weight. Gas made no sound when it drifted, and water sat quietly with no ravine to power along.

Leki leaned across Juda and clasped Bon's shoulder, other hand pressed to her lips. Then she pointed up through the sparse tree canopy. He looked, and Bon's first thought was that fumes had reached his brain and he was passing out. He blinked several times, but the shifting dark blots were still there.

Above the trees. Flitting back and forth, drifting, searching. Hunting. Buzzing.

'Are they *wasps*?' Leki whispered.

Bon nodded, because he had already recognised their sleek bodies, pale yellow and black markings, and the blur of wings keeping them aloft. The buzzing sounded angry and loud, yet they moved with an easy grace. They owned the air.

'What in Fade do they *eat* to get that big?' Leki whispered. She was still leaning across Juda, maintaining the contact. Her hand on Bon's shoulder squeezed. It was warm.

Juda muttered and then shouted, and Bon's heart sank. *We forgot to gag him!* Leki stared at him wide-eyed, panicked into stillness. The wasps' buzzing changed in pitch, but Bon did not look up, could not, as he bunched up the front of Juda's jacket and shoved it into the sleeping, nightmaring man's foam-flecked mouth.

The wasps came then, drifting down through the branches

like unnatural windfalls. Bon sensed them drawing closer. He heard their drone increasing in volume and changing pitch, and he was the focus of their attention. He could feel them against the back of his head and neck, as surely as if their wings were already caressing there. He looked up from the writhing man to Leki, but she only had eyes for the wasps.

He has a pistol, Bon thought, going to root through Juda's clothing to find the weapon he had seen him bearing more than once. But he was already out of time.

A wasp drifted down before him. It was even larger than he had at first thought – the size of a newborn child, body heavy and bristled, wings tearing the air, buzz almost as loud as the river had been in the ravine, breeze lifting the hair from his forehead. It moved back and forth before him. Up and down. As if attempting to hypnotise him, yet so inhuman. Another fell slowly behind it, turning, looking around as if watching for dangers, though Bon had no idea what could be a danger to these things.

They carried a smell with them. *Rain on a summer day*, Bon thought, and each time he inhaled he caught a memory flash of his wife walking by the river in Sefton Breaks, Venden laughing and running before them.

He looked across at Leki, and she seemed rapt. There was no fear on her face. Ten, twelve, fifteen wasps hung in the air around them. The creatures hung in the air around them and temporarily stole fear of the slayers.

Bon could see stings glistening at the blunt tips of their abdomens. The stings were as long as his finger, and even if their poison did not prove fatal, the stabbing might.

Are they going to kill us? he wanted to ask, but Leki was smiling. He wondered what memories she was living, and what scent she gained from these beasts.

The wasps might have been there for heartbeats or days,

but then they started to drift away. Interest sated, perhaps. Or maybe the fleshy, bloody humans would simply not make much of a meal. Leki watched them go. Bon watched her, trying to define the strange expression on her face. It might have been nostalgia, or loss, or a species of both.

They rested for a while, not speaking. Juda struggled in his sleep. Marsh fumes hazed the air.

One memory faded, melting away into quiet confusion while another rose, slaughtering it with the promise of terror . . .

They crossed the marsh on stepping stones of dryish land, trying to avoid the sucking depths that might pull them down to viscous darkness, feet permanently wet, looking for somewhere safe in case the slayers could still track them this far, still catch their scent through the masking odours of the marsh gas and mysterious darkness. A steam geyser exploded barely a hundred steps to their right. It blasted at the sky and ripped it open, gushing a shower of hot mud, water and steam into the night sky. It spattered down around them, speckles of muck scorching their exposed skin where they hunkered down and held their hands over their heads. Bon felt it splash heavily and wet across his back, scorching skin through his jacket and shirt where he lay protecting Juda from the downfall.

'The ground is spitting at us!' Leki said, 'And it's hot!'

Strange words, but then something made Bon sit up and turn around. The geyser still steamed and roared, but there was something else moving closer to them. Slick and wet, shifting like thick boiling blood, there was nothing sharp about the movement, but still he knew it could bite. His hand stole into Juda's jacket in search of the pistol once more.

Electrical light flickered back and forth through the atmosphere, illuminating the marsh gas and the thing that had erupted from the geyser with greenish light.

172

'Leki!' Bon whispered, but she had already seen.

'Out of the ground,' she said, 'and it has teeth.'

It had a body of mud and filth, thick enough to retain form but fluid enough to be in constant movement. No eyes, unless they were also of mud, but Bon could see several slippery gashes moving across its surface that could only have been mouths. Teeth shimmered there, formed of steam; mini-geysers, perpetuating the promise of danger the main geyser had made. When the teeth dispersed to the air others replaced them. The thing moved closer, slicking across the wet ground.

Bon brought out the steam pistol and registered the irony of using it against this thing.

'That won't touch it,' Leki said, but Bon asked her what other hope they had.

It closed on them, he fired, a splash of mud. Another venting of steam, more mud, even closer than before and hard enough to punch the ground and bounce them from it, a momentary freefall that seemed to continue for ever. His memory took the same plunge.

Whatever followed was ambiguous in his mind as the marsh hazed his sight, and for a long time after Bon was not entirely sure they had survived. *In the belly of the beast*, he thought, scooping mud from his ears and picking it from where it had dried on his stubble. *Still in the belly of the beast, remembering as I am slowly digested . . .*

And the next moment in those marshes that persisted as memory . . .

Deeper into the nightmare landscape, changed so much. Islands were less frequent, but they could follow the higher ground by aiming for where the moon did not reflect. Juda moaned and struggled, but Bon and Leki seemed to marshal more strength, sensing that they would find somewhere to hide soon. Juda had not told them where, or how long they needed to run to evade the slayers. He had not told them what to do. But somewhere there was a haven, and they were close to finding it. Once inside, the slayers would pass them by, their terrible persistence confused by the mixed odours of marsh gas. Perhaps Bon would know they had passed, perhaps not. But once settled, they could wait out the night.

Maybe the ghosts would guide them. They rose like drifts of steam, glimmering with promise. Some drifted with the breeze, enclosed in clouds of gas that Bon and Leki did their best to avoid. Other moved against the wind and came closer. They did not last for long – lost to the air before Bon had a chance to really see – but those that approached close enough seemed to whisper to him. He could not hear their words or sense their intention. Leki would not meet his eye.

Juda became heavier, as if absorbing the air of this place and ingesting it. They had to put him down to rest more and more, their brief burst of strength failing.

'They're gathering,' Bon said, looking around at the wraiths haunting the landscape.

'Watching,' Leki said. 'I can't go on. Not any more, not with him.' She dropped Juda's legs and stretched upright, hands pressed into the small of her back.

'So we leave him?' Bon asked. He did not mean it, and hoped that Leki would not agree.

'No,' she said. 'No . . .'

'Leki?'

She looked at him, and her eyes seemed distant.

'Leki?'

'I think we should ask them for help.'

'Them?' He nodded at the strange figures, some fading and manifesting again, others drifting. They exuded no menace.

'I think they were all someone,' Leki said, and she started

down the gentle slope. They had paused on an island of dryness in a sea of marshy land, and it took Leki only a dozen steps until her boots sank into the ground. Dirty water seeped around her feet, and when she knelt her boots squelched in the muck.

'Take a breath, Bon,' Leki said. 'We're looking for somewhere we might never find on our own.'

Leki leaned forward and pressed both hands down into the mud.

Reading the water, Bon thought, and he knelt down beside Juda to watch. Juda was stirring again, struggling feebly against his bonds and humming behind the temporary gag. He had brought them here, and then abandoned them to weather his own nightmares.

Leki remained motionless for some time, head dipped down and hair hanging around her face. Some of the wraiths faded away, and others drifted off into a darkness the moon did not touch. But some remained, seemingly more solid than before. Bon thought that he could make out features – a mouth here, deep, impenetrable eyes there. It was as if they were remembering themselves, and he suspected it was Leki, the amphy, inspiring those memories.

As Leki read the waters, Bon caught his breath.

'A mile to the north,' Leki said at last.

They went that way, and all the time those wraiths seemed to merge from the darkness and the mists to follow them. Juda moaned, Bon's shoulders ached. Leki remained silent, answering nothing, and it was only as they neared a forest of huge trees that she revealed what else she had heard.

'The slayers are here,' she said. 'Searching the marshes. Their senses harried by the environment. Juda might have been right – if we can hide in here away from them, they might just miss us.'

Leki led them to a massive tree that had rotted from the inside, forming a hollow tree cave in which they might find protection.

'They'll smell us around the tree's base,' Bon said. He was panting now, sweating, exhausted from carrying Juda so far. He so wanted this to be the place where they would hide, but he could not avoid his doubts.

'Maybe,' Leki said. 'But Bon. Do we have anywhere else to go?'

So they entered the hollowed tree, climbing a little so that they were above ground level, inside the trunk that might have been five thousand years old and which perhaps had housed a hundred refugees fleeing a hundred different dangers. Things grew in there, plump, damp fungi that whistled as they pushed past. Insects and other creatures scuttled in the darkness. But Bon found that he was too tired to be afraid, or to care.

They perched halfway up the inside of the hollowed trunk, settling within creases of wood and wedging Juda tight onto a ledge. Leki found a rent where an old branch had fallen away, and she watched outside. Bon was so tired.

'What did you find?' he asked, nodding at Juda. They'd strapped his pack to his stomach, and one hand seemed to rest protectively on the canvas.

'Things he shouldn't have,' Leki said.

'Such as?'

She did not reply for a while. She watched outside, and Bon felt the tension in the silence as she strove for the right words.

'I think he might be a Wrench Arc,' she said. 'Or close enough that distinctions barely matter.'

Wrench Arc, Bon thought. Juda was a danger, perhaps a murderer. Yet he had hinted that he could lead them to Venden.

176

Bon was so tired. He could hear, taste and smell alien things. Venden smiled in his memories, the joy of a young child untouched by the concerns that came with age.

It grew no darker, and yet Bon Ugane slept.

'Bon!'

The first thing he noticed was the smell. Then he felt something pressed over his face, bunched beneath his nose, and Bon snapped awake. He opened his eyes to complete darkness – even the moonlight that had filtered into the ancient tree was absent. He tried to breathe in but was hampered by the thing pressed there. A cloth, bunched and pushed hard against his nostrils. Odours from it played with his senses.

'Bon! Keep quiet.' That was Leki. Bon pawed at his face and felt a hand there, and then another hand grasped his and entwined fingers, squeezing softly, comfortingly.

Bon inhaled slower, and found that he could breathe through the cloth.

'Keep it tight to your nose and mouth,' she whispered into his ear. 'Sit up slowly. Lean into me. Look.'

Bon did everything she had told him. Leki was warm, and when he put his arm around her she did not pull away. She touched the tree beside the crack in the trunk to show him where to look, and then her own arm went around him. She, too, held a cloth to her nose with her other hand. She had gathered the scents of marsh, tree and filthy water; added camouflage to the tadcat liver oil.

'This is when we see,' she said, and she was talking about Juda. This was when they saw whether he was telling them the truth, or not.

The slayers were outside. They crossed the marshy land-scape, moving slowly and without deliberation. Their faces were upturned, and Bon could see the glimmer of moonlight on mucus spread across their mouths and chins. They were too far away to hear, but he knew that the hunters were sniffing for them, and breathing in only the scents of the gas marshes.

The female slayer was closest. She moved with a grace that belied her bulky form, spiked with the points and blades of packed weapons, stocky legs sinking into the marshy ground. She was covered in mud, from her toes to the top of her head. She must have been wading straight across the marshes rather than going for higher ground, and Bon was not sure what this meant. It was either foolishness, or a need to move faster in a straight line. And they could not assume that the slayers were fools.

The male slayer moved further across the landscape. He shifted like the land itself, shrugging and moving.

How can we ever hope to escape them? Bon thought, and a chill hopelessness passed through him.

Juda moaned and struggled, immersed in his nightmares, and for a moment Bon expected the slayers' heads to turn their way. The hunters might not be able to smell them, but they would surely hear.

But there were other noises outside that drowned Juda's unconscious struggles. Unseen creatures howled somewhere in the far distance. A deep, almost sub-audible rumbling – great ice-lakes changing position below them, so Leki claimed. And close by a geyser hissed, the explosive emission followed by the heavy impacts of wet mud and . . .

. . . and perhaps other things.

Those mud-wolves will take them, Bon thought. He watched the darkness for shadows that did not belong, wishing them nearer, urging the shapes to take form and fall upon the slayers. Nothing came. The hunters moved off to the north, heads tilted as they sniffed at the tainted air. They were not being quiet about their movement. There was no subtlety there.

Leki sighed and relaxed into him, leaning her full weight upon him. He smelled her breath in the darkness as she leaned close, and it was precious. He kissed her. It was a kiss of peace, not passion, and they both took comfort from it. Their mutual hug was one of safety, not lust.

Juda seemed to calm, and Bon and Leki remained close together for the rest of that night.

Bon slept no more. Every time he closed his eyes he saw Venden running across the swampland of his memory, phantom shadows chasing him away.

Chapter 10

heart

Venden Ugane rode through the afternoon, drawn by Kellis Faults's call. He could feel it tugging at the heart of him, as the remnant pushed from afar. The sense of being a pawn troubled him little. Intellectually he knew that he was not his own man, but that had changed little since he was a small child. He had always been waiting for this.

The shire rode strong and fast. Venden did not push it too hard, but he also did not hold back. There were miles to cover, and at this rate he could ride for the rest of the day and through the night, and reach his objective by morning. Walking, it would take him days.

On this final quest of discovery and retrieval he wanted to be away from the remnant for as little time as possible. He knew that, upon his return, something was going to change.

Perhaps everything.

Yet he relished the journey, enjoying the feel of the powerful beast beneath him, the breeze in his hair, the movement, the sense of time passing and progress being made. He had not ridden a shire since childhood, and he soon realised it was one of the few things he missed from his time back on Alderia. The beast was tireless, and several times Venden urged it into a sprint, laughing in delight as he bent down across its back, hands tangled in its flowing mane, hanging on for dear life. If he fell he might be badly injured, and deep down he knew that he was taking a foolish risk. But the occasion overcame him. He had been in danger many times since coming to Skythe, but this was a danger whose parameters he knew. He felt in control of this headlong rush.

Following the course of a wide, slow-moving river back towards its source, Venden knew that he would come eventually to Kellis Faults, the remains of Skythe's capital city. And as afternoon turned into evening and the sun smudged across the western horizon, the landscape he was used to began to change. Sparse clumps of trees spotting slopes and valleys became denser, deeper woodland. The land became flatter and yet more mysterious, and as darkness fell Venden found himself negotiating a thickly forested landscape the likes of which he had not seen on Skythe before.

Even in the shadows, he could understand how unsettled this scenery was. Many of the trees were squat and deformed, unsure of which way to grow, as if they could not find the sun. Their limbs were half grown and ended in gnarled knots. Spindly bracken grew across the forest floor, and great swathes of it was browned with poor growth, crackling underfoot. It would die and fade back into the ground, and whatever descendants it might have seeded would possess the same faults.

The woodland slowed the shire, but still he rode through the night. He paused only when his bodily rhythms demanded it, and to eat food he'd brought with him. Several times the beast slowed and edged closer to the river to drink. Venden took the opportunity to rest. Clasping on tightly as he ran the animal was hard work, and as it drank its fill he relaxed on its back and looked out over the river.

It was narrower now, younger. From his studies he knew that its source was far to the north, way past whatever remained of Kellis Faults. He looked at the calm waters in the darkness, moon reflecting from the river in silvery shards, and wondered what it had seen. He knew that some amphys back on Alderia were adept at reading waters, but he had never seen the feat himself. He would have given anything now to be able to do so.

Through the night, when stars sparked the sky and the moon shifted its imperfect sphere, Venden kept his perception open and free. He felt the urgings of the remnant – encouragement from that great, fallen Aeon. He also felt the void deep inside him watching with interest. Somewhere before him lay Aeon's heart, and he was fated to find it.

As dawn's early light threw the woodland in the east into silhouette, he started seeing the first buildings.

Perhaps when they had been built and lived in the whole area had been open plain. The ruins were difficult to make out in the forest's undergrowth, and here and there trees seemed to have burst through the middle of what had once been a structure. Venden felt a chill each time he passed such a place, as if the memories of what had happened there had found homes in the new, living things growing where others had once died.

Terrible deaths, he thought. He had read much forbidden writing about the Kolts' rampage across Skythe. The Ald claimed they were the product of corrupted Skythian science, but Venden knew the truth – that they had been forged by Aeon's destruction. Some rumours had it that the Kolts were corrupted souls who had never been born. Given to living bodies, they turned on family and friend, killing, raging on until they found others to kill. Strong and ferocious, virtually unstoppable, cannibalistic to fuel their rampage. Beyond human, and inhumane. Terrible deaths.

With each ruin he passed, Venden wondered what history those tumbled blocks and shadowed innards might contain. But he had no time for archaeology. His was a more urgent intent, and, though a loud echo of the past, it more concerned the future.

The forests lessened once more, giving way to areas of open grassland. Venden continued following the course of the river, its timeless erosion providing the only real contours in this landscape – a shallow valley here and there, within which the river must twist and writhe like a snake over thousands of years. The plains were windswept and barren, and there were more ruins.

He thought perhaps they were burial mounds. Roughly pyramidal in shape, the mounds spotted the plains seemingly at random. Sometimes he passed close by, but if he saw one in the distance he rarely diverted his course to investigate. None of them had an entrance, and whatever lay inside would remain untouched. They had a sense of eternity about them.

Around midday he came across another collection of ruins, much larger than any he had seen back in the forests. The settlement must have been home to thousands of Skythians. It spanned the river, and the remains of several bridges were evident on both sides of the waterway. And here were also the tallest ruins he had yet seen on Skythe, two structures reaching weathered fingers to the sky that were ten times his height. One was the wreck of a much larger, wider building; the other seemed to be the surviving wall of a tower. Their uses were unknowable.

As the afternoon wore on he passed more remnants of Kellis Faults's satellite towns. They were all testament to that great civilisation's sudden and cataclysmic demise, and they were all deserted. No surviving Skythian lived there now. Perhaps their race memory was still too painful, or maybe they were simply different people, no longer needing whatever the ruins of their ancestors might offer. But though Venden considered the current Skythians to be barely an echo of what they once had been – a simple race, now, scratching at the ground to subsist from one year to the next – he found their absence troubling and unsettling.

Perhaps they knew something he did not.

The hills started rising again, the ruins more elaborate and ringing with a greater history. On one low hilltop stood a solid stone tower, broken high from the ground so that whatever might once have topped it was now lost. Plants grew around its base, creepers clawed across its grey sides, but nothing could hide it from view.

Across another hillside marched a line of immense stone arches. A few had half fallen, but most remained impressively upright, their curves a natural defence against the ravages of time. Venden remained in the valley and examined them from below, assessing that at their highest points they were perhaps twenty times as high as the ruined Skythian homes he had seen elsewhere. There was nothing behind them but hillside – no tunnels, no welcome doorways to somewhere special – and he found that looking through them gave him a chill. Their size was astounding, and he could not help but imagine what they might have been built to allow through. If they were decorative or symbolic, that was impressive enough. If they had been built for a practical reason, then that reason was long lost. Were he to climb and pass through them, he dreaded to think where he might go.

The river narrowed drastically, and he heard the waterfalls long before he saw them. They were wide and low, but meant that he would have to climb the shallow hillside beside them to proceed. It looked steeper than it probably was, and was scattered with rocks and the remains of buildings. There were also long, low walls that he thought had probably been built to terrace the entire hillside, either for farming and irrigation, or perhaps for more obscure reasons.

'It's not high,' he said to the shire. 'It's not steep.' He had not spoken since sun-up, and his own voice startled him. He was in the beyond now, way further north than he had heard of anyone venturing, and these were probably the first words of any language spoken here in centuries.

The shire was tired and hungry, continuously pausing to dip its head down to take grass or berries. But the afternoon was moving on, and Venden was beginning to sense that he was drawing close. He urged the beast on. He forced *himself* on, fighting exhaustion, denying the pain in his limbs and body from the long ride.

The hill was higher than it had looked from below, and scattered with more obstacles. The falls were higher also, and louder, and their roar accompanied Venden as he urged the shire onward, over fallen walls and trampling ground untrodden by man for centuries. By the time he reached the top he was as exhausted as the shire. He fell from the creature, legs refusing to hold him upright. The grass was long and damp from constant spray from the waterfalls. A stone wall stood surprisingly free of plant growth and mosses, especially this close to water, and there were several vague, shadowy shapes blasted onto its surface. Limbs twisted, heads thrown back, Venden found the outlines of tortured humanity in the darkened stones.

When he rose unsteadily to his feet, he looked north. A wide, shallow valley was bordered by a range of six hills, and within their protective influence lay what remained of the massive city of Kellis Faults. Skythe's capital sat untouched by all but the slow, insidious caress of time. Vegetation meant it belonged to the land once more, yet the city's layout was still obvious in many areas, its streets, parks and squares a green-blurred map of what had been. Crumbled stonework rose from the forested carpet. Towers pointed fractured fingers at the sky, some of them solid and seemingly decorative, others bearing windows, balconies and separate turrets, now home to birds and other flying things. Many had tumbled, some had not. Over time perhaps they too would fall, but now they stood as testament to the proud civilisation that had once existed here.

At the city's centre stood the remains of a statue, so vast that he could make it out even here, perhaps a mile or more away. Its arms had fallen and its features were abraded by the seasons' onward march, but its Skythian form was obvious, and defiant.

Venden gasped in shock, and with a sense of invading some private place, an open mausoleum to a dead world.

And walking towards him uphill from that shattered city, four tall figures carried something amazing between them.

'Who are you?' Venden asked as they drew closer. He realised that, in his shock, he had spoken in Alderian, and the people seemed not to have heard. So he asked again, in the regressed language Skythian had become. 'Who are you?'

His heart sprinted, faster than it had done following the shire's anguished hill climb. The presence he had always carried inside him stirred, becoming alert and . . . excited. A wolf sniffing food.

They came closer, heading directly at him as if he had always been their intent. They carried an object on a wooden stretcher, a heavy blanket covering it and hanging over the sides, dragging through the grass, edges darkened with moisture. The object was small but seemed heavy. They took a corner each.

They were not the Skythians he had come to know.

'Some of you survived?' he said, glancing past them at the remains of the once-great city. Perhaps down there, buried in the ruins, dug deep and hidden away, a whole society had moved onward without outside interference and without betraying themselves. The idea was incredible, wonderful. Impossible.

This city was as dead a place as he had ever witnessed. And there was something strange about these Skythians.

They came closer up the slope, and Venden began to make out how they were different. They did not seem to be panting, or even breathing hard, though the slope was steep. They walked without expression, steering around rocks, stepping over cracks in the hillside, finding the easiest route up to him without seeming aware of quite where they were. There was something mechanical about their movement, not natural.

'What are you bringing me?' he asked, and something inside him shifted. His gut fell, sickness rose. He went slowly to his knees, careful not to strike a pose of worshipfulness, his shaking legs barely letting him kneel gently.

The shire stomped its hooves, kicking up clods of mud and shredded grass. Its mane hung across its face, and when Venden glanced its way, its eyes were wide with fear rather than defiance.

The tall figures came, fifty steps away, thirty. The stretcher remained completely level between them, whatever the lie of the land. Venden could not make out their sexes. They had long hair, long limbs, narrow bodies that somehow exuded strength. Their clothes were old and holed. Their eyes were dead.

He tried to stand, back away, but his limbs would not obey. The idea that they were not bringing something to him, but were intending to take him away, struck him a blow to the head, and he leaned to his left in a half-faint. But the thing inside squeezed him awake again, stabbing him in the side and insisting that he watch.

When they were five paces away the figures halted. They *were* Skythian, Venden was sure, but unlike any he had seen, either in the flesh or in old books and parchments of the past. And when they lowered the stretcher and each lifted a corner of the blanket – exposing what it carried without flourish or ceremony – he began to understand.

His heart stopped as he laid eyes on the heart of Aeon.

Venden went away. He retreated into memory, carried there unwillingly, subjected to his past and having to submit because there was little else for him to do. He was not in control. He saw his mother leaning over him and smiling sadly, and it was a memory older than any he had ever experienced before. He lay in his crib, baby hands fisted before him as he examined them, and his mother's smile filled his vision and his heart. Her eyes were distant and wet, the smile one of gentle mourning rather than motherly love. *She* did *love me*, Venden thought, and though that was true there was something more. He saw his mother again later, when he was old enough to run and she was older than her years. His father ran with him, trying to launch a kite from one of the hills outside Sefton Breaks, laughing as the wind whipped the kite from his hands and flung it to the ground. The cross-brace was broken, he remembered, but his father would fix it later that day and make a successful launch. By then his mother would have returned home.

I know where this is going, Venden thought, but he could not fight his memories' impetus. He was being shown rather than reliving, and the part of him that had never been his own rejoiced.

They ate as a family and discussed their trip to New Kotrugam, where Venden might view the Museum of Inventors and perhaps gain some ideas. He was already a clever boy, and his creations using wood, moulded metal and steam pods were impressing his teachers. *You can make something to be pleased about*, his father said. *You can make us proud*.

Their journey, New Kotrugam, the staggering size of the city that went up from the land as well as across it, metal bridges, steam ships fogging up and down the river, towers of wood and metal—

And after the Museum of Inventors when they were climbing Aesa's Tower to see where that famous architect had completed his most celebrated work, his mother grabbed his hand and pulled him close. His father was ahead, ascending the curving staircase and chattering with delight as he related facts and stories about Aesa and his theories. *I've always served you*, his mother said, and even then Venden was not sure who she was talking to. Her son, or her son's inside. His shadow. His future.

She stepped through the narrow doorway onto a metal balcony, and without looking back tipped over the railing. Venden rushed onto the balcony in time to hear the impact from the street below, and then the screams. And though young and painfully uncertain of himself, he reached the railing and looked down, down at the circle of people gathered around—

Venden screamed himself back into the present. The shire shifted slightly, but its main source of fear was not the screaming, crying man kneeling beside it.

The Skythians were retreating. As they backed away from what they had brought, they changed. They lost their threatening

189

aura, though Venden was not sure why – because they had placed down the heart, perhaps, or maybe because they were moving away from him now, not towards. And they began to lessen. As they stepped away they also shrank, in his vision and his regard. Their skin sagged towards the ground, their shoulders drooped. Their long, strong legs bowed beneath their weight, though that weight seemed to be decreasing. From dangerous to wretched, when at last they turned their backs on Venden to walk away they were even less than the Skythians he sometimes dealt with now. And then, only a little more than ghosts.

He hauled himself to his feet to watch them go, leaning on the shire for support. The creature was shivering.

'I don't think they were what was left,' he said. 'I'm not even sure they were what once was.' As Venden saw those four figures drifting down the hillside and merging with spidery shadows, his attention was snapped back to the stretcher. It was suddenly the focus of everything. His mother's final words hit him again, and he could only wonder why.

'They brought it to me,' he said, the hillside whispering a breeze that might have been agreement, or wonder.

The heart of Aeon was the size of Venden's head. Grey and purple, motionless, unremarkable looking and yet the most amazing thing, still it bled. The blood oozed, but did not drip. The stretcher was unstained. The heart vented itself and then reabsorbed, blood emerging and then running deep. Almost as if it had no desire to touch this world.

'I have you,' Venden whispered. The object did not respond. His own heart hammered, and for a time he simply stood and watched, expecting Aeon's heart to start doing the same. But it was aloof and unconcerned.

He sat and breathed deeply, allowing himself to regain

strength and come to terms with what was before him. Aeon allowed this pause. Venden drifted off, and when he awoke it was dusk, and ghost lights haunted the great, dead city.

When Milian Mu first heard the noise she was convinced she could actually feel it vibrating up into her feet, a roar whose promise she could not understand. She had never heard anything like it. She hid. She was exhausted from her long walk, and the sound set her nerves jangling.

Since fleeing the families and the man who had tried to love her, she had walked non-stop in a southerly direction, heading for Alderia's capital city. *He will be there*, she thought several times during her journey, the words bearing that peculiar sense of coming partly from her, and partly from somewhere deeper. And then the growling rumbling sound in the air, and the ground shaking beneath her feet.

There were a thousand places to hide on the hillside. Rocky outcroppings were numerous, as were holes in the ground, as if something had scooped and dumped great masses of soil and rock and left the wounds to fade with time and weather. The depressions were alive with masses of bright red flowers, the colour of blood and scented with a heady perfume that should calm her, had her mood been more even. The landscape appeared man-made, but Milian could make out no purpose. Things of long ago were often like this. She hid in a dip almost clear of the red flowers, a mound of rocks above and between her and the valley floor, and closed her eyes to sleep.

But sleep did not come. Tiredness urged her down but she remained awake. She thought it might be an earthquake, or the rumble of something huge turning over deep beneath the land, or even the impact of dreadful weather a hundred miles distant. The shard kept her sharp, and eventually urged her back out to face the source of the noise.

She had to walk almost down to the valley floor, such was the profusion of rock piles and flowering holes. The noise increased and became more complex, and when she peered from behind one of the last rock piles she saw its cause.

The wagon train stretched from left to right as far as she could see, snaking along the undulating plain between her hillside and the next, miles in the distance. It was so far away and so large that it barely seemed to move. But as her attention was drawn inward from the train's flexing mass, so she began to make out individual details.

There were hundreds of wagons of all shapes and sizes. Some were small enough to be family caravans, pulled by shire-like creatures with longer legs and faces. Others were much larger, running on multiple wheels and driven by steaming motors, gasping clouds behind them that drifted across the plain towards Milian with the breeze. The clear steam exhalations were interrupted now and then by darker, dirtier clouds. Their upper structures were a chaotic collection of storage and passenger compartments, some flying family colours, others dark and perhaps abandoned. It was like nothing she had ever seen before, but she kept her wonder restrained. She was in a foreign land, and the world had moved on while she slept.

The train of vehicles followed a scar carved across the landscape. Nomads, miners, hunters, farmers, whatever these people were, they had a history of moving in this way. They were heading south towards New Kotrugam, and that was the direction Milian needed to take.

She made sure she was well wrapped in the clothing given to her by the travellers, then started out across the plain. She moved at an angle to intercept the tail end of the wagon train, and long before she reached it there were riders, and running children, and pet wolves frolicking in the long grasses.

All of them made her welcome, despite the fact that she could only speak a few words of their language. They called her an Outer – foreigner, she assumed – and that suited her well. It seemed mostly not to lower her in their estimations. Using a mixture of signing and basic language, some offered her food and water, others pointed towards where she might find accommodation and work. Milian Mu nodded her thanks. Inside, the shard was quiet and content.

Every man she met might have been the one, and she examined them all with frank, hungry eyes.

The wagon train took two days to reach New Kotrugam. In that time Milian learned that it was comprised of a variety of people, she applied herself to learning more of their language and she caught a glimpse of the man who might be the one.

A surge of heat flushed through her when she saw him. *Him*, a voice said. Her voice, but not her thoughts. *Him. It might be him. Watch and learn.* But he was gone as quickly as he had come, disappearing into the shadowy maze of corridors and rooms in the heart of the big wagon.

The smaller wagons generally belonged to families or groups of friends, so Milian settled on one of the huge steam-driven structures. There were cabins to let, and though barely large enough to lie down in, the one she was allocated suited her perfectly. Having no money to pay her rent, she was directed to one of the several huge engine rooms, given a shovel and instructed to shovel coal.

This she did for much of the first day. The exercise was exhilarating and freeing, and she glanced at the other stokers, looking for him. *He won't be here*, she thought. He was learned, an academic. Strong. Not physically, perhaps, but she had seen the strength in his eyes, and the books and parchments he carried. The shard observed from the background, neither feeding nor detracting from her thoughts about the man. It seemed content that he had been seen, and would be seen again. Of that, Milian was certain.

She would see the man again.

The train stopped for the night, and a large proportion of passengers disembarked to make camp, start fires, hunt and cook meat and sing songs. Milian wandered the length of the train, drinking from a wine bottle she had been given by the engine room's foreman as part payment for her day's work. Her muscles ached pleasantly, the wine imparted a calming haze. She felt good about herself for the first time since emerging from that cave on the beach.

Out in the open, the full breadth of the wagon train's inhabitants became obvious. There were fishermen here, their families busy fixing nets and rods, the fishermen talking amongst themselves about catches they had made and others that had got away. Milian drifted close to one group and listened for a while, gleaning what she could from a language still mostly alien to her. She recognised the tones, the sharp peaks and soft slopes of the words, and she found herself quickly learning more, and more. The fishermen had been working the lakes to the north, not the sea itself. None of them even mentioned the sea. It was as if the ocean between Alderia and what had become of Skythe did not exist.

She moved on, drinking and observing and in her silence remaining unobserved. Hunters butchered and hung their kills, smoking meat and stretching hides. Mystics washed stones and crystals, beaded necklaces, drew shapes in the soil, and chanted over fires turned purple by the addition of powdered minerals. Several soldiers gathered together away from the crowds, sitting around their own fire and talking in hushed tones about their own secret plans. *If they knew who I was*, Milian thought. *If they knew what dwelled within me.* She hurried on in case such thoughts betrayed her.

She saw families gathered protectively around nurseries of playing children, lonely people staring into firelight, even lonelier people lying back and looking to the stars. There were printers transcribing writing onto ink pads, herb sellers packing their wares, and some families cooked and sold food from huge iron pots. It smelled wonderful, and Milian drifted close to one group until they waved her over, handing her a free flatbread sandwich when they realised she had little language and believed her to be an Outer. *Such treatment for someone so different*, she thought, and a tang of bitterness soured her smile. They asked her to stay and she walked away, because her memories of before were suddenly blood-soaked by these people's ancestors. Their bloodline had come to Skythe with Engines to channel magic, and caused the deaths of everyone Milian had known.

A large group of people sat listening to a Fade priest. Some of them smiled, some of them cried. Milian could have told them about a god, and the shard bristled at such an idea. Her hands clawed, and the wine bottle in her left hand cracked beneath the pressure. Smothered by loud prayer, no one heard the sound of breaking glass.

And then she saw him again, passing not ten steps from her with a bag over one shoulder and a heavy roll of wrapped parchments beneath his arm.

There he is, she thought, and the shard exuded those words at the same time. They matched so perfectly that she and the shard might have been one.

She followed, and practised what she might say.

*   *   *

He was tall, with long hair bound and clipped with metal ties, a heavy leather jacket hanging open to display a rough cotton shirt, and a wild blond beard. He walked with his head up, looking around but with an air of detachment that Milian found compelling. He did not feel like part of this wagon train. Other people seemed either to fit in, or were content to belong at least until the journey was over. Even those on their own were incorporated in some way, identifiable by their clothing, manner, or belongings as part of a whole. But this man walked alone, and she knew that he was very far away.

She followed him from the camp, out onto the plain and away from the influence of the dozens of large campfires. She stayed far enough back so that he did not see her shadow thrown before him, but the further they went the longer their shadows became. When he paused and looked down at the ground beside him, she too halted.

'I've seen you,' he said. The words were not familiar, but their meaning filtered through, given weight and sense as the shard repeated them. The seed of Aeon she carried was allowing her to hear.

'I'm sorry,' Milian said. 'I saw you and . . .' *And what? And you are the one?*

He turned around and stared past her back at the wagon train. She glanced back over her shoulder and caught her breath, because she had missed out on its beauty. Fires burned, lights blazed, people cooked and laughed, played music and danced.

'You don't want to be there?' he asked.

'I want to be here.' She walked closer to him, and something passed between them. She saw that he felt it too as his eyes opened wider, pinprick pupils dilating as he shifted focus from the wagon train to her, and her alone.

Milian had not felt the true warmth of another human being for so long.

'Cold,' she said.

'I was just about to build a fire.' He retained his grip on the rolled and wrapped parchments, but dropped the shoulder bag and squatted beside it, inviting her to join him.

'But you have . . .' She nodded at the parchments, and when he put them down she saw that there were two books folded in there as well, rolls of bookbinding string, and a pocket of pens and ink.

'I study Skythe, but it will wait,' he said. He watched her as he said it, examining her for any reaction.

'An amazing place,' she said. She was not surprised at his interest in her old home. In the darkness between blinks she lived a hundred memories, and her vision blurred.

'They're conducting a Fade mass back there.' He nodded past her at the wagon train.

She shrugged, dismissive. *Testing me*, she thought. He scratched his bristly cheek. She sensed his doubt, but not suspicion.

'Let me help you with the fire,' she said.

'I've seen you,' he replied, repeating himself. 'Yesterday, on the big wagon.' He said no more, but his silence spoke volumes. *He's seen me and noticed me, and he is the one, and surely there's more than chance to that?*

The shard remained silent, heavy with intent.

'My name is Milian Mu,' she said.

'An Outer name, I assume. I knew by your accent, and your . . . way with words. As if they're new to you.'

'New,' she said, nodding and smiling. She helped him set the fire. 'What's your name?'

'I'm sorry,' he said, 'how impolite of me. Bon. I'm Bon Ugane.'

197

'I am happy to meet you, Bon Ugane.'

'And I you.'

He is the one, Milian thought, and the shard agreed. This was a man who was destined to discover truths and eventually act upon them. Any child of his – and hers – would take on the precious shard, and strive to know the secrets of Aeon. Perhaps, in time, this child might act upon those secrets, and find what remained of that murdered god.

The fire made an island of their first meeting, and she and Bon sat together and talked until dawn.

Chapter 11
dregs

Juda surfaced to a smell he could not identify, and sounds he did not know, and the feel of rough hands pressing his arms against his body. *They have me!* he thought, because his nightmares had been of the slayers. They had caught up with him, Leki and Bon just before they reached the gas marshes, crucifying the other two on sparse trees. Then they had slashed Juda's ankles to the bone, so that as he lay in the mud he could watch the two people he'd tried to save die. They had screamed as their weight hauled them down against the nails in their wrists, suffocating slowly.

The rest of his seemingly endless dream had been the slayers turning to him and considering what his own tortures should entail. The nightmare was not in witnessing what they had done to Bon and Leki, nor even seeing their horrendous, dead-but-living expressions. It was in his own imagination as he wondered what might come next. Juda had seen a lot on Skythe, and heard a lot more. He could imagine so much.

He opened his eyes and struggled against the slayers' hold, but then he saw Bon and Leki looking down upon him, not from the sparse trees but from where they knelt at his side.

'Shh,' Bon said, but it was not in warning. It was a comforting sound. 'Shh. It's dawn. I'll free you, but tell me you're awake.'

'Am I?' Juda asked.

Bon and Leki exchanged glances. There was something between them that had not been there when Juda had been pulled down into disturbed sleep. An affection, but also experience. They had been through a lot.

'You are,' Leki said. 'We should know, because we've been with you all night.'

Juda nodded down at the bindings, and Bon went about untying them.

'We're in the marshes,' Juda said. 'Nice smell.' They were inside a huge old tree, the inner walls rough and smeared with patches of moss and decay. It was large enough to accommodate the three of them comfortably, and when his bindings fell away and he raised himself on one elbow, he realised that they were propped on ledges above the ground.

'The slayers went by a while ago,' Leki said.

Juda glanced at her, eyebrows raised. 'Close enough for you to see?'

'But not smell,' Bon said. He was grinning.

'It stinks in here,' Juda said. 'It'll stink out there too. We should leave the marshes as soon as possible. This gas . . .'

'It's done us no harm,' Leki said. 'You gave us oil.'

'I did. Paste from my pack.' Juda glanced around for his pack, and saw it leaning against his feet, strapped shut. *I sent them in there.* He was unsettled, but still too groggy to realise why.

'So the oil worked.' He sat up, wincing at the stiffness in his limbs and his stomach's hollowness. 'First time I've used it.' He craved some scamp cigars, but he was out of the drug. Perhaps they would find some on the way out of the marshes, and then—

'Juda,' Bon said, 'take me to my son.'

'Yes.' Juda rubbed his legs, working feeling back into them. He felt their eyes on him. When he slept he was mad, but they were still looking to him for guidance, and leadership.

Even after everything they had done.

'You carried me in here,' he said. 'All across the marshes. Slayers on your trail. Found this tree. Came inside, climbed, hid. Watched them passing by, and you knew what they wanted to do to you.' He remembered his terrible dream, and perhaps it showed on his face, because he saw a shadow of fear pass across Bon's own features.

'Yes,' Leki said. 'And the marshes were . . .'

'Not easy,' Bon finished. 'But now it's your turn to lead us. Get us out of this place. To where my son is.'

'*Might* be,' Juda said. He dangled his legs over the edge of the wooden ledge, then dropped to the floor of the hollow tree. His feet sank into mud. It released a smell, and the gas marshes made themselves known once again. 'The man I spoke to . . . he wasn't certain. Your son *might* be there. But, yes, I'll do my best.'

And the dead god, Juda thought. But talking about gods living or dead to these people would not aid him. They all had a quest, and their journeys might well end in the same place. The fact that they sought different things mattered little.

He glanced at his pack again. Leki seemed preoccupied, adjusting her clothing as if she had only just dressed. If they had found anything that troubled them, they would have said by now.

I'm no Wrench Arc, Juda thought. He repeated the phrase

to himself on occasion, but the more he considered the way his personal quest was taking him, the more confused he became. He had killed Skythians. Magic danced at the fringes of his mind whatever he was doing, at every moment of the day, and it passed through every one of his nightmares. He grasped onto his sanity, but worried that such desperation marked him as something very much other than sane.

I'm no Wrench Arc . . .

They gathered their belongings and left the relative safety of the tree. The morning marsh was a busy place, with night creatures going down and daylight dwellers already beginning their hunt for the day's food. Birds dived into areas of open water, insects buzzed and bit, amphibians squelched and jumped. High above, a marsh hawk circled on invisible currents, its size impossible to make out for certain. And below their feet something turned and flexed, sending shock-waves that bubbled mud and rippled the water's surface. Juda never stopped walking, because he did not wish to perceive its movement in more detail.

Leki and Bon were wide-eyed, glancing all around as they moved and keeping close. There was a link between them that hadn't been apparent before Juda had fallen into sleep, and that troubled him. They had also acquired an awareness of their surroundings that only came with experience. He had no wish to ask what they had seen, because he'd heard all about the marshes, and knew that it must have been terrible.

They passed across the gas marshes. Juda's vision swam, his lungs ached, his limbs felt heavy. He knew they were being slowly poisoned, but they had no alternative. The marshes' emissions were more active during daylight hours when the sun heated the water and swelled subterranean gas reservoirs, but the idea of staying for another night could not be considered.

The slayers might have turned around by then to retrace their tracks.

Close to the edge of the marsh, Juda found some scamp bushes. Bon and Leki took a drink while he plucked as many of the seed pods as he could, crushing them in one hand and collecting the fine seed grains in the other. He had no tobacco left, so he would have to crush and chew the pods, and take care about how much he took. In this purest form, scamp would temper his nightmares but might raise demons of its own. But even having the seeds drying in his pocket made him feel more relaxed. More in control.

They started to leave the gas marshes as the sun passed its zenith, and kept walking until they were clear of the smell. They headed north-east, and the autumn breeze came from the north, so they were saved from the fumes drifting after them to remind them of where they had been. Yet the gases remained with them in other ways. Leki started vomiting, and her skin paled to a ghostly white as she struggled to keep up with them. Bon Ugane helped her, but his eyes and nose were running freely, almost blinding him to the trail. Juda felt the sickness also, but he swallowed it down and chewed on a few scamp seeds. He had no idea whether they would aid him, but there was a familiarity about their calming effect. When Leki and Bon both refused his offer of a few seeds, Juda did not force the issue.

They stopped to eat around mid-afternoon. The land was rising now, and they were heading into mountainous countryside that Juda had never explored before. He'd rarely had cause to stray away from coastal areas, but now he was consulting his sketched maps more and more.

The rumours of Aeon lay ahead. All the magic he had ever wanted – a source beyond his imagining – might be present at the site of the murdered god. That was his goal, and having found Bon Ugane, and then heard whispers of his son's name from the dying Skythian, he believed he had come by the luck he had been painstakingly seeking for years.

But there was something else out there. It edged him aside, away from the route he believed they should be taking. It was a weight pulling him with dreadful gravity, or a force repelling him from the path. And when he closed his eyes, Juda felt the familiar tingling sensation inside that told him what might be close. He had never decided whether it was a manifestation of his excitement, or a physical reaction to magic. But right then he did not mind.

They moved on, and Juda changed their course. The other two seemed not to notice – Leki had stopped vomiting but looked weak and pale, and Bon's eyes and nose were red and raw. Memories of the gas marshes came with them.

Juda felt it close by. An Engine. One that no one knew about on Skythe; he was sure the other four he had visited were the only ones anyone else was aware of. He'd questioned many people, listened in on enough whispered conversations in shadowy corners of taverns in Vandemon and other places to be certain. He had only ever heard vague whispers of an Engine this far north, and that was because few people came this far. There was no need, and though few would admit it, Skythe exerted a fearful miasma that pushed most people against the coast. Perhaps with a few, Alderia to the south called and they could no longer answer.

With the possibility of an Engine so close, the temptation was too great. *Magic lures me on*, Juda thought. Not for the first time, he sensed a terrible sentience behind its allure, and the more obsessive he became, the more intense its stare.

When they stopped again to take a drink, he took the calm moment to broach the subject.

'I believe there is an Engine close by.'

'Really?' Leki's eyes widened.

'No,' Bon said. 'Not now. My son, Juda. You tell me he's alive and out here somewhere, and now you want to show us an Engine?'

'You were interested before,' Juda said. He began to shiver, fearful that they would insist upon passing it by. He had long known himself an addict of magic. His scamp dependency was nothing in comparison.

'That was before you told me about Venden!'

'Bon—' Leki began, but Bon threw down his water canteen.

'Neither of you have children. You have no fucking idea!'

'The Engine is on the way,' Juda said. 'I can sense it close by. We'll reach it by nightfall.' His heart was hurrying with need, and with a fear that the chance might be taken from him. He knew it would not, and *could* not, because he was in charge here. But with a chance of dregs close by, his reasoning was wavering. The feel of it the taste of it the sensuousness the touch . . .

He would not let them sway him.

'I don't care!' Bon shouted.

'I used all I had left to spy on the slayers. To save *you*. If I find more, it will help us track your son, and find him. And protect us on the way.'

'How?' Bon said. 'You told us yourself you're clumsy with it.'

'Being clumsy with magic is as good as being an expert at anything else,' Juda said. 'And besides . . . *you're* following *me*.'

Bon paused, staring at him.

'Isn't that right?' Juda asked. His heart settled a little, because he felt the solidity of his control.

'You're threatening me?' Bon asked.

Leki looked back and forth between them. *Something about her*, Juda thought. But she was beyond his concern right now. He turned away from both of them and examined the rough map once more, trying to place where they were. Though this map had been Rhelli Saal's, there was nothing to mark even the approximate location of the Engine. Perhaps most of it was guesswork.

'You haven't even told us how you know about Venden,' Bon persisted. 'Who did you speak to back at that old village? How did *they* know? And right now I don't care. But . . . you'd threaten me with not finding my son?'

Juda felt a faint wash over him. He chewed more scamp, then slashed at the air with his hands, tearing aside a curtain of flitting shadows. *I should just kill them both*, he thought. *But . . .*

But there was something about Leki that made him suspect she would be hard to kill. And he was not that sort of man.

He was *not*.

'I'm no Wrench Arc,' Juda whispered at the shadows, not for the first time that day. He was not sure whether it had been loud enough for the other two to hear. He wasn't sure he cared.

Without responding to Bon's outburst, he started walking again. He knew that they were following him, because they had little choice. If there were dregs of magic at this long-lost Engine, they might prepare him for the encounter to come. Even the remnants of a god would be something amazing.

Juda did his best to follow his senses. He gauged direction from the falling sun, and close to dusk the Eastern Star emerged above the shoulder of a mountain.

The familiar twinge of dread nestled in his heart as dusk approached, but he chewed more scamp seeds to mush between his teeth and swallowed them, feeling its gentle effect settling his twitching muscles. It illuminated the promised shadow of nightmare in his mind, and gave him room to search for the Engine.

As daylight waned, they topped a rise, and something looked so wrong.

From a distance it resembled a rocky deposit at the mouth of a deep valley between sharp mountains. Juda paused on the sloping ridge leading to the mountain on the left, looking to the left and right of the object, trying to see past and through the shadows. Trees grew across the slopes, all of them leaning away from the thing, and the sides facing the object were unhealthy, branches drooped and leaves sickening.

However much scamp he ate, his excitement would not be dimmed.

'I'm exhausted,' Leki said.

'We can't stop now,' Bon said. 'Venden could be in the next valley. He might hear us if we shout.'

'He's not in the next valley,' Juda said. In truth he might have been, because the rumour he'd gleaned from the dying Skythian had been hazy at best. *Venden Ugane, a stranger, seeks to bring together Aeon long gone* . . . The closer they drew, the stronger Juda believed he would sense the pull of the dead god Aeon. It could be that Bon and Leki might feel it as well, though perhaps they would attribute it to something else.

But right now he felt nothing but the lure of the Engine.

'There,' he said, pointing down the slope.

'I can't see anything,' Bon said.

'That's because there's nothing there,' Leki said.

Juda started down the slope, his heart beating so hard that it filled his hearing, turning everything else into something distant, insignificant.

'And he's been chewing on that stuff all day,' Leki said. 'After we carried him . . .' Her voice trailed off.

This might be an Engine no one has ever found, Juda was thinking. *Untouched, unplumbed since . . .*

'. . . through the marshes, and he's so drugged up we might as well . . .'

. . . since the war. And what will that mean? What will I find there? Will there be bodies? And magic. Dregs of magic, for sure. His head throbbed, limbs tingled.

'I don't see why you even believe him about Venden. What if he's . . .?'

The voices faded further as Juda began to run.

'I see it now,' Bon said. 'But what *is* it? It shouldn't be there. It's horrible.'

Bon and Leki must have run to keep up with him, because they stood either side of him now, staring at the Engine.

'I told you what it was,' Juda said. 'You're in my world now. You need to listen to me. You need to . . .' He trailed off, every sense possessed.

'An Engine,' Bon said, voice filled with dreadful disbelief.

'Need to what?' Leki asked.

Juda stepped forward so that he could not see them in his peripheral vision. He wanted to be alone.

'How can the Ald deny the existence of something like this?' Bon whispered.

'Need to *what*?' Leki asked again, insistent. Her voice shook.

'You need to watch.'

Juda walked away from them and towards the Engine. He could smell magic, hiding in the depths of this great structure like blood pooled in a corpse's lowest parts. He could taste it on the air, a touch of something other tainting the breeze that dared flow around and through the apparatus. He could almost hear it, absorbing and giving out noises like nothing natural – it voiced sunlight and time, gave music to history and dark drums to deeds long gone. It was his everything, and he would do *anything* to acquire it.

Though he knew magic would never be owned. It had *never* belonged to the Ald, and Juda and all other Brokers understood that. It was a thing unto itself.

That's giving it a mind, Rhelli had told him at one of his first Broker meetings, *and naming it as a god. That's something the Wrench Arcs do, and they even have a name for it – Crex Wry. Crex Wry, the Skythian god of the Pit. Don't go that way, Juda. Don't give it a mind, or your own mind will be doomed.* But Juda had always understood the difference. People worshipped gods because they believed the gods cared about them. But magic had its own concerns, and they were way beyond the petty ministry of humanity.

The Engine loomed before him. Resembling a pile of tumbled boulders, it was larger than those he had seen closer to Skythe's coast, and seemed more complete. Untouched by time and inquisitive hands. His Broker's selfishness had led here, and he had lived that life for so long that he could feel no remorse. Not over the lies he had told, nor the people he had betrayed, killed. This was a construct intended solely for the gathering and placement of magic, and it stood for everything he lived for.

Brokers don't murder, a vague voice whispered, but he ignored it. Broker, Wrench Arc . . . in the presence of the Engine, such definitions ceased to matter.

Here was a source of his true drug. It was beautiful. And yet he could not linger, because the ultimate source might be closer. This thing had helped destroy Aeon, and what he might find here would be nothing compared to the magic that might still smother that dead deity's remains.

'This will be quick,' Juda said, though as he broke into a run and approached the Engine, he knew that was not the case at all. Once he touched it, he would be possessed, and time would be lost to him.

The sun was setting, but for the first time in years he did not fear the night.

The Engine looked as if it had grown from the land, an imposition that could have been grotesque, and yet Juda found it beautiful. Great metal limbs curved up and out from its main body, burying themselves in the rocky ground, and the stone had melted and reset around these piercings. There were five limbs, smeared and dulled with corrosion and swathed with creepers and a crawling, flowering cactus. The main body of the Engine was bulky and inelegant. It seemed to have tilted to the west over the centuries it had been here, and now it presented its uneven upper surface to the setting sun. There was no real order to its design, and that set it aside from the four other Engines Juda had seen. They had been curved and regular, whereas this was blocky, as if parts of it had been attached with no consideration to order.

Fine metal bracings arced way above the main structure, and something might once have spanned between them. There were rumours of flesh and blood in these things, long since rotted away. There was talk of a mind.

He walked around the Engine. Over time it had truly merged with the ground, sinking down, plants growing against it, and in a couple of places rocks had tumbled from the slopes above and impacted against the shell, shattering or coming to rest as they subtly altered the landscape. The Engine might have been here for ever, as much a part of the landscape as mountains and rivers and valleys. But Juda knew otherwise.

'Is there anything?' Bon asked from where he and Leki watched from a distance. But Juda did not reply. He felt a brief rush of anger at them for intruding on his moment, but then he simply shut them out. This was him, and his Engine.

Somewhere there would be a way inside.

He skirted the Engine twice more and sensed no dregs. It was not surprising. After so long, any dregs left outside would have faded away or been subsumed into the ground. But it troubled him, because it could also mean that this Engine *had* been explored and plundered. Even six centuries ago, there might have been people here who knew what to look for. He didn't know who – not the surviving Skythians, for sure, because that far back they would have been hauling themselves back onto two feet. But who did not really matter. The thought of missing out was awful.

'It'll be inside,' he said softly. 'Near the heart of the thing.' He had to find a door.

He felt Bon's and Leki's eyes upon him, but he ignored them. He circled the Engine one more time, and then started to climb. There was no way in at ground level.

The metal was rough to the touch, abraded, dented. Grasses and moss grew in pockets where windblown soil had gathered. He found handholds and footholds and hauled himself up, pressed close to the metal walls and feeling the subtle warmth stored in the Engine during the day. The sun was touching the ridge to the west now, and the huge device was releasing its heat. *That's all*, Juda thought. *Nothing else. It's dead, now.* But he remained alert as he climbed, expecting at any moment to hear the growl and grind of metal from inside, and the whisper of softer things, as it became aware of his presence.

'Juda, the sun,' Bon called.

'I'm fine.' He did not even look their way as he answered,

211

because he was scrambling across an almost-level platform covered in moss and bird droppings, and something ahead had grabbed his attention.

Juda paused and took a pinch of scamp seeds from his pocket. Shadows danced at the extremes of his vision; bad dreams waiting to pounce.

I'll not sleep, he thought, determined. *There's too much to do and see.* He crunched the seeds between his teeth and closed his eyes at the fresh flow of scamp. When he looked again the shape was still there, atop the Engine. An invitation to explore. A warning to stay away. Juda was not sure which, and he did not care. He was going only one way.

The touch of magic was there, exposed to the elements for centuries and yet still so obvious. Elsewhere, the uneven upper surface of the Engine was spiked with the severed remnants of pipes and cables, and pocked with countless holes, most of them filled with dirt and home to a variety of heathers. It was an old Engine left to the elements, something out of its time, belonging to an age centuries old.

But magic did not age.

Juda went slowly to his knees, muscles weakened by desire. Leaving that last dreg at the camp to observe the slayers, he had been bereft, but had comforted himself with the knowledge that he would touch magic again. Facing it now, he almost wished he followed a god to thank. But magic was his god.

Thank you, Aeon, he thought, because if it were not for the Skythian's murdered deity, this dreg would not be here.

He crawled forward, past sharp protuberances and over dips in the Engine's shell that gave slightly beneath his weight. The smear of magic was settled in a circular pattern around what must have been a hatch to the Engine's insides.

'It's untouched,' Juda whispered. The reason for it being there – placed, or settled by accident – concerned him little. He was a Broker, and he knew what to do.

It was warm when he reached for it, like a living thing. He opened his mind and felt it touch him, an alien contact that was nothing to do with intelligence. He felt its weight against his skin as he passed his hand through the pooled mass, and yet there was nothing solid. It was touching heavy gas, his skin having a memory of its own, and he scooped up the magic and twisted it, turning his hand back and forth and watching the absent shadow curling itself into a smaller shape. Another turn and it lay in the palm of his hand, a seed of potential.

Juda breathed heavily, grinning. The night probed at his mind, but now he felt strong enough to fight it. His Regerran curse sang, but he was not full Regerran, and the aggravating factor of his addiction had been sated. Tonight, he would fight the nightmares down.

The joy was more intense than anything he had ever felt before. He remembered his first orgasm with another person, the girl giggling as he spurted over her hand and wrist. He recalled his first taste of silk wine, his first look at something undeniably beautiful, and the moment he had finally believed without question that magic could be his. None compared to this.

The dreg seemed purer than those he had touched before, and more filled with a potential that expanded even as he considered it. But there was no room in his mind right now to wonder why.

He tugged a small bag from his jacket and dropped the shrunken dreg inside, pressing it back deep into his pocket so that it could not slip out. There was no mass to the dreg, but it was a thrilling weight against his skin.

Removing the dreg had revealed an opening in the Engine. It had not been visible before, but Juda did not hesitate. He lowered himself inside, feeling around with his feet until he found something solid to rest against.

'Juda!' He twisted around and saw that Bon and Leki had come closer, but not by much. 'Stay away,' he said. He dropped into the Engine, and kept falling.

'What do we do?' Leki asked. She had come close to Bon again, clasping his hand as they watched. Bon felt sick, and wondered if Leki did as well. It was not a sickness born of fear or urgency, but something deeper. A sickness of the soul. They were close to something wrong, and Juda was revelling in it.

'Who have we allied ourselves with?' he asked softly.

'No one!' Leki said. 'We're allied with no one. We're following him, that's all.'

'He's mad.'

'Maybe.' She nodded at the Engine, the impossible machine. 'But haven't you always wondered?'

'No,' Bon said, 'I've always been completely sure.'

'But to see it,' she said. 'Unquestionable.' He looked side-long at her and saw the open wonder in her eyes. He was glad, because things were changing for her as he watched. Beliefs hardening, solidifying, and hatred of the Ald and what they stood for taking on form. The existence of the Engines of magic had always been denied by the Ald, because to admit to them would be to admit the truth. And yet here was an Engine. Proof that the story of the Skythians causing the terrible plague of Kolts, not the Ald's forbidden use of magic, was a lie. It lay naked in the sun for anyone to see.

'Do you want to go closer?' he asked, and Leki shook her head. He was glad.

'No,' she said. 'I think we should just wait here until he comes out.'

'I can't wait all night,' Bon said. 'If he's crawled inside and fallen asleep, I can't wait all night.'

'He's found his drug; he'll be all right if he *does* sleep.'

'I don't mean that. I might be close to my *son*, Leki! I've thought him dead for years, and Juda has to keep his promise and lead the way.' Bon closed his eyes briefly against the dusk. A rush of images washed over him, all of them featuring Venden.

Even if Juda *was* telling the truth, after so long, there was no telling who Venden would be.

'So we wait a little while, at least,' Leki said.

'A little while,' Bon agreed. 'But then I'll be going in after him.'

They sat together in the long grass and watched the Engine. It was as dead, and as still, as a pile of rocks.

The Engine is alive! Juda thought, and his fall might never end.

There was no light within the Engine, and no way to see. His senses were smothered by the fall, though he could not feel space passing him by, nor time. He waved his limbs and opened and closed his mouth, striving for something solid or recognisable but finding nothing. He should have struck bottom long ago, unless the Engine was plugged into the heart of Skythe, and that metal shell on top was merely the head of a deep, perhaps bottomless hole into the land.

But there was no real sense of falling, and no idea that the bottom might be approaching.

Juda tried to shout, but he could expel no air. He tried to breathe in, but he could not fill his lungs. He could not tell whether or not they were already full. And then his hand

215

brushed across something solid, and he recoiled with a terror he had never felt before. Not because it was alive and a threat to him, but because it was so, so dead.

Let me out let me out! he thought, but he had invited himself inside. His escape would be no one's choice but his own.

Slowly, light started building. His feet touched something solid, and the muscles in his legs flexed as he stood upright. He looked around in a panic, searching for that thing he had touched, the dead thing with rough skeletal promise, but he could not turn his head quickly at all, and he moved as if submerged in water.

Illumination grew, and with it understanding.

Juda was surrounded by magical dregs. Wisps and whispers of it pressed into his mouth and touched his eyes. Its touch was dreadful. Magic had always been strange to him, but here and now, he realised that there was so much more to it. These dregs echoed with awfulness, and he thought once again of Rhelli Saal's warnings to him. *Don't give it a mind, or your own mind will be doomed.*

'Crex Wry,' Juda whispered, testing the name. The dregs paused in their movements, as if holding breath. Juda held his own. Then they swirled again, parting to reveal what else shared the Engine's interior.

There were several bodies, and they wore uniforms of the old Ald priesthood, Fade sigils sewn into vestments that should have rotted away centuries before. Their hair waved to magic's rhythm of ebb and flow. Their empty eye sockets glared at him with the darkness of their deeds; he felt their horrible stares.

Juda wanted to scream, but he had no voice. Instead, he moved his arms, hands cupped, to try and swim away from the monstrous dead. But they surrounded him, and the swimming took him nowhere.

He could not breathe, scream, or move, but he could think. He realised that he was in the heart of the Engine. He understood that remnants of magic persisted here, in far greater strength than anywhere he had ever seen before. And he believed that this was but a shadow of what he would find around Aeon.

Working slowly, carefully, doing his best to keep fear at bay and remembering everything he had been taught by Rhelli Saal and the Brokers, Juda started to twist and turn the dregs of magic into his hands.

Always a mystery to him, the Engines were an enigma that kept him awake for those nights when he was not nightmaring. Now, he took time to try and make sense. He looked around as he collected, trying to pinpoint parts of the Engine that he might know. Between walls that looked less than solid, a white flame seemed to dance, spiked like lightning. *That could be to honour Flaze, Fade god of fire.* The ceiling above him was formed of a network of veins and fine limbs, opened into blooms that had long since petrified into metallic simulacrums of flowers. *And that's for Fresilia, god of growth and life.* From around his feet, water droplets rose to splash on the ceiling, defying the sciences he knew. *Venthia, who lives in every drop of water.*

The Engine was home to aspects of all gods of the Fade, some obvious, others less so. Though he was nowhere near devout, the idea that the Engines might bear some divine origins shook Juda somewhat. And yet, holy or not, he honoured the magic that resulted.

'Holy or not,' he said, thinking of the name of Crex Wry once more. Juda did not care about names or no names, minds or no minds. All he cared about was what the touch of magic could do for him. That was his true addiction, and his true need.

217

He swam through the Engine by collecting the dregs. It was the only way he could move, and sense time moving on. As the dregs lessened, and his bag began to fill, mad laughter echoed within the mysterious confines of that forgotten Engine. It sounded like a thousand men laughing, but it was all Juda's voice.

Chapter 12

aeon

Time moved on, but Bon could not approach the Engine. He paced back and forth at a distance, staring at the structure and fearing it. It was a monstrous creation, made more so by its persistence, because it stood testament to the evil it had perpetrated, while around it Skythe was far less than it had been. He feared the Engine so much.

But Venden might be close by. And the longer Juda remained inside, the more Bon knew he would have to enter the Engine to bring Juda back out.

He could not allow the half-Regerran to lose himself to madness.

'Stop pacing,' Leki said.

'It helps time pass quicker.'

'Does it?'

Bon stopped and looked at Leki. She was sitting on a fallen tree, chewing idly at a shred of dried meat.

'Don't you understand?' he asked, meaning Venden, and his hope, and his frustration now that discovery might be close. Leki glanced away nervously, still chewing. No, she did not understand.

'He'll be out soon,' she said. 'Juda!' She stood and cupped her hands around her mouth.

'Leki!' Bon said.

'Juda!'

He rushed to her and grabbed her arm. 'We don't know what's out there.' He waved at the darkness, growing rapidly deeper as the sun dipped below the horizon. All horizons were close in the mountains, and there could be anything beyond them.

'Make up your mind, Bon,' she said, exasperated.

'Shit.' Bon took several deep breaths, then marched towards the Engine. He expected Leki to call him back, warn him away. But she did not speak up. He wondered what she was thinking as she watched him approach the brooding construct, but realised he would probably never know. Whatever bond might be forming between them, Venden would always be there to prevent them joining fully.

Alive, Bon hoped. But even if he were dead, his son would remain a strong presence in his heart. He always had. New hope, whether proven or dashed, could never change that.

As he left Leki behind and approached the Engine, Bon felt as if he was moving from one world to another. Realities seemed to shift, because the solidity of the Engine was something he had never expected to see. His beliefs were firm, but fed by rumour, old documents, whispers. Fleeting things. Before him was something substantial. Proof.

The ground around the Engine was hard. He thought he heard his footsteps echoing, but it might have been a heartbeat, his own or another.

The Engine moved.

Bon's fear blossomed into terror. He crouched, trying to

be nothing. He had no wish to draw the attention of the Engine, or whatever was moving within. He heard Leki shifting behind him, and hoped that she was hiding rather than coming forward. He would welcome her closeness, but not what it might cost them both.

Should have gone on without Juda, he thought, and the shadow upon the Engine stood, growing larger, silhouetted against the dark mountains as something darker.

'It's Juda,' Leki said, and Bon closed his eyes and sighed in relief. He stood as Juda climbed down the Engine's uneven side, jumping the final distance to the ground and landing with a thud. He straightened and turned back to the bulk, reaching out and laying his hand flat against its side.

'Did you find anything?' Bon asked, but Juda did not reply.

'It's dark,' Leki said. 'Do you need us to camp and tie you?'

'No camping!' Bon said, because they had to move on. Time teased.

Juda ignored them both. He stroked the Engine, his hand moving slowly, almost lovingly across its surface. He seemed larger than he had before he had entered. Bon frowned, squinting. Perhaps it was the darkness that made him grow.

He moved away from the Engine at last and approached Bon. He was moving like a different man; slower, more confident.

'We need to find your son,' he said.

'Yes!'

'The scamp is working?' Leki asked. She had come closer, and now stood beside Bon. He sensed her uncertainty.

'It's working,' Juda said. His voice slurred slightly, but it did not sound like tiredness to Bon. It sounded like he was drunk.

Juda kept his back turned on the Engine as he led them

away, as if he did not wish to look upon it again. Bon and Leki followed, and Bon was glad to leave the thing behind. There had been something awful about it. Not because of what it had been and done, but because of what it was now. Bon could not shake that from his mind.

The Engine watched them leave, and he felt the cool strength of its regard.

'Is it alive?' he asked, but Juda did not reply. He walked silently ahead of them. Bon and Leki walked side by side, and it was only as he looked at her that Bon realised how tired he was. Even in the darkness he could see the weariness in her features.

'Do you think he found what he was looking for?' he asked Leki.

'I think so, yes,' she said.

'How do you know?'

'A feeling.'

Juda led them higher into the mountains, the air grew cooler, and when the moon emerged from behind a bank of clouds it glimmered from the frost already forming on rocks and trees around them. The wildness of this place was palpable, but Bon felt in less danger than he had since arriving on Skythe, swimming towards the shore where murder was already happening. They had shaken the slayers from their trail, and he supposed that contributed to his more relaxed feeling. But it was also the fact that he had come here hopeless, and now bore hope. It lit a fire in his heart, and that was enough to see away some of the darkness, at least.

Close to dawn, Juda stumbled and fell. Leki ran ahead to him and Bon stood back, his hand stealing into his pocket to the small knife there. The man had not slept all night, and perhaps it was only now that his Regerran nightmare-curse would take him. One swipe at Leki, one punch or kick, and Bon would be on him.

But there was nothing uncontrolled about this fall. Juda pulled Leki down beside him, and Bon crouched and knelt with them, waiting for the other man to talk.

Juda breathed heavily, looking around at the landscape. They had been descending for some time, and though frost still glimmered on trees and grasses scrunched underfoot, they were no longer in the heights. Below them were gentle valleys, not sheer drops.

'What is it?' Bon asked.

'We're close.'

'How do you know?'

Juda ignored him. Instead, he felt around in his pocket, then brought his hand out fisted around something. He glared at Leki and Bon, the mistrust in his eyes sharp and piercing. He pursed his lips. There was sweat beaded on his nose, even though it was cold, and his eyes flickered left and right.

'How do you know we're close?' Leki asked again.

'Can't you *feel* it?' he growled, his aggression sudden and shocking. Bon brought the knife from his pocket, and Juda smiled. 'You won't need that.'

'No?'

'What good is a knife against a god?' Juda opened his hand to reveal something small and black, like a seed or a chrysalis. Bon could not look at it properly; it seemed to change, flex, pulse, repulsing his vision even though it remained the same size and shape, and motionless.

'What by the gods is that?' Leki asked, but Bon already knew.

'Wait here,' Juda said. His voice was deep, and brooked no argument. He moved away, past a fallen tree trunk that was thicker than he was tall, and soon disappeared from view.

Leki was nervous. Looking around, fidgeting.

'Can you feel it?' she asked.

'No.'

'Something . . .'

Bon put his arm around her and pulled her tight. Dawn was breaking. He hoped today might bring Venden.

'I wouldn't want to touch what he has,' he said. 'I don't even like being close to it.'

'It has an odour,' Leki said, wrinkling her nose as if she'd just stepped in shit.

Juda returned moments later, the thing no longer in his hand. 'I'll look ahead,' he said, and he sat down with his back against the fallen tree and closed his eyes.

'We should go,' Leki whispered to Bon. 'I fear this. Something isn't right. Something is wrong. We should go.'

'After we've come all this way?' Bon asked, his voice low. He did not take his eyes from Juda.

'You only have his word that your son—'

'I told no one his name,' Bon said. 'Yet he knew.'

'And you trust him?'

'No. But I can't just run away from this. Not after we've come this far.' He glanced at Leki, saw that she was shivering. She didn't seem to him like someone easily scared. 'What is it?'

'Can't you feel it?' she whispered.

'I feel hope.'

'No,' she said, waving one hand. 'No, no.' She gestured at their ice-speckled surroundings, fine webbing between her fingers transparent in the rising sun.

'Just hope,' he said, searching for something else, not finding it.

'I think it's *terrible*.' She pressed close to him, sounding so wretched.

'Leki—'

'It's here!' Juda shouted. He stood, eyes wide and a grin making a mask of his face. 'It's so *close*!' He dashed around the fallen tree, staring across the wooded hillside towards a depression in the land. He looked back at Bon and Leki, but his eyes barely settled on them. 'So close,' he said, quieter and almost to himself.

'Venden?' Bon said, but he knew that was not right. Leki had pushed away from him and moved forward, reaching for Juda.

'What's close, Juda?' she asked.

'Aeon,' Juda said. 'The murdered god.' He laughed, and several large birds took flight from a nearby tree. Another laugh chased them away.

'Aeon,' Leki said. It was not a question. As Juda broke from her and ran, she turned to face Bon, and her expression of hopeless terror made his heart sink.

'Leki?'

'Again,' she said. 'If it's really true, then it's all going to happen again.'

Venden could not bring himself to touch the heart. Every other artefact he had found and brought back to the remnant, he had excavated from the ground, dragged from their hiding places, and manhandled onto the cart. He had felt no fear whilst doing so, and no sense of being disrespectful. But the heart, he could not touch. It was Aeon's centre, lost for generations. And it was still wet.

When the figures who had brought it vanished, dusk allowed mysterious lights in Kellis Faults to rise, drifting like mist with a sense of direction. Venden dragged the blanket from the stretcher, and the heart came with it. He felt observed in everything he did more than ever before. Trying to ignore

225

the sensation, he folded the blanket's corners and tied them together.

The heart was lighter than he had expected. *As heavy as light*, he thought, turning his back on the city where wraiths might dance. He tied the blanket sling to the saddle and mounted the shire, expecting it to be skittish and unresponsive bearing what he had loaded onto it. But the creature seemed unconcerned.

Not once glancing behind, Venden kneed the shire and headed back the way he had come.

He rode hard and did not camp for the night. The shire obeyed his urging, but still trotted slowly enough to watch its way, avoiding trips that might have broken a leg and spilled Venden, and his cargo, to the ground.

Venden glanced back constantly to ensure the blanket was still adequately tied. Sometimes he sensed the thing hanging there against the shire's right flank, bobbing occasionally when its swing matched the shire's movements. Other times it was a blank to him, as impenetrable as if he was trying to see inside the mind of the shire itself. At these moments he feared the heart had spilled to the ground, and he leaned from the saddle to ensure he could still see its bulk within the material.

Dawn came, and Venden stopped to water the shire. He slipped from the saddle. If the heart still bled, it did not stain the material. *If it bleeds, it beats*, he thought, but there was nothing about Aeon that could be obvious, or which must obey rules. He had learned that even before leaving Alderia and coming here.

He rode through the day, back towards the part of Skythe that he had never called his own, but which sang with the presence of the remnant. Sometimes he felt eyes upon him again, and he rode with caution, scanning the surrounding countryside for any signs of trouble. But if someone or something did watch, they left him alone. Perhaps they recognised what he carried. Maybe from a distance, he and the heart exuded the same kind of wraith-like glow he had seen above the ruins of Kellis Faults.

The shadow inside rested comfortably. It did not stir, even when Venden probed. There was contentment there, and excitement, a potential that the near future might realise. Relaxed as the shadow was, Venden had never felt so apart from it.

He did not question what he was doing, or why. He did not try to project forward. This was simply his meaning, and the task that fate had set him. This was what he had come to Skythe to do, whether or not he had known it at the time.

Late that afternoon he entered the valley he knew as his own. He approached the remnant's clearing from the north, and the first thing he recognised was the sheer cliff where the orange spiders made their home. He breathed a sigh of relief. Without knowing until now, he had spent his whole life waiting for whatever might happen next.

A shred of fatigue settled over him as he arrived in the clearing. The remnant was arched across from the dead tree; perhaps it had shifted a few steps to the east, perhaps not. Neither possibility troubled him. He rested the shire and prepared to dismount, and then—

The shadow rose inside, greater than it had ever been before, more terrifying and deep and expansive. And sharper.

From the far end of the clearing, past the remnant, a man emerged and ran towards Venden.

And behind Venden, resting against the shire's sweating flank, Aeon's heart let out one delicate, thunderous beat.

'Venden,' Bon whispered when the figure rode into the clearing. He recognised him instantly, even though he was

227

no longer a boy. Though only sixteen, Venden was a man now, as tall as his father, thinner, stronger. His face was tanned and weathered. He looked tired but excited, and as he came into view of the strange shape—

(Juda calls it a god, says it's the remains of Aeon, but can a god be stone, or wood, or whatever else makes up that shape? Can a dead god really be touched?)

—his face lit up. The creature he rode looked like one of the wild shires from Alderia's northern plains, but almost twice the size and with heavier features. There was something bulky slung across its back.

Venden's gaze flickered across the shape, and the hairs on the back of Bon's neck rose.

What's that in my son's eyes? He recognised a flash of it from when Venden had been younger, and the boy had asked his mother or father about things that were forbidden in schools and polite conversation. Why did Skythe die? Was there really a god, and who killed it? Did anyone ever say sorry? It was intelligence and fascination, and a love of hidden, dangerous things.

The three of them were hiding behind a howthorn bush. Juda had been shivering and sweating since arriving close to the structure, and countless times he had reached into the small bag tied at his waist, bringing his hand out empty again. His fever was madness and fear. He muttered words that Bon did not know, and Bon wondered whether they were now seeing the real Juda at last.

Leki had remained close to Bon, staring out at the thing in the clearing. He'd asked her whether this could really be the remains of a god. He could not believe, but saw in her silence that she did. That frightened him more than anything Juda could do or say, and even when the man brought out a smear of light and spread it across the soil, and started

228

working it with hands that seemed to flex and bend unnaturally, Bon kept his attention on Leki. There was something more to her that he had never seen before. A look of determination beneath the fear.

'Venden,' Bon said. Leki looked at him, and she understood. Juda worked at his dreg of magic, sensing things neither of them knew.

Bon stood and walked around the howthorn bush, and when Venden looked up he began to run.

'Venden!' he shouted. 'Venden, my son, my lost son!' His heavy footfalls shook his voice, but even motionless it would have broken with emotion. He had come so far, and spent so long never expecting to see his son again – indeed, in his darkest moments believing him dead – and now they would be reunited.

The shire reared slightly, its stomping feet shaking the ground. Venden's mouth fell open. He brought the beast under control.

Bon ran past the shape arching out of the ground from the foot of the dead tree. His attention was on his son, but this close his eyes were drawn to the shape, and the strangeness presented there. It was like nothing he had ever seen – a tree, living or dead; a sculpture; a skeleton of something huge, like corpses he'd heard about washed up on Alderia's southern shores. This thing was static and yet exuded life, the potential of movement made solid. Every part of it seemed about to shift from where it was frozen, and Bon thought perhaps it was stuck in a moment between perceptions. Each facet of the shape was moving, yet he was seeing it in a blink. *If I only let it move on*, he thought, but such a feat was beyond him. He was only a man.

He passed the shape and slowed, stopping ten paces away from Venden and the huge creature.

'Venden,' he said. 'I know you. I see you.'

'I felt its beat,' the young man said.

Doubt flickered briefly at Bon's mind. But these *were* his son's eyes, and that *was* his voice. He had his mother's face; strong, defined. He had Bon's eye colouring.

'I'm your father, Venden. I can see that you remember.'

Venden's eyes narrowed slightly, and he looked past Bon at the shape.

'I can't believe I've found you,' Bon said, more to himself than to his son. He thought fleetingly, powerfully, of his dear dead wife, and how she had seemed to change from the moment they knew they were having a baby together. It had caused arguments, because Bon believed she did not want a child. And those arguments were the only times she had seemed to find her passion, because she had raged at him that a child was all she had *ever* wanted, and that he might save her life. There he had found the only hint in Milian that her history was, perhaps, more complex than she had ever revealed, even to him. He had pushed, and she had pushed back. She had died revealing nothing.

Now, here she was again in this young man's face. For the first time in years Bon felt close to his wife once more, instead of remembering her as a memory with fading sharpness and bleached colours.

'What are you . . .?' Venden asked. 'How . . .?'

'After you left, my interests in Skythe caught up with me,' Bon said. 'But what about you? What happened to you? How did you come to be here?'

'Father,' Venden breathed.

'Son.' Bon went to step forward, but Venden kneed the animal and it backed away several steps. It snorted, stomping one heavy hoof. Bon glanced back, and Leki was standing beside the howthorn bush. He had never seen her so naked and exposed. She had something in one hand, and the other hand was delving into a pocket.

Of Juda, there was no sign.

'Aeon needs me,' Venden said. The words slammed home, shaking Bon as surely as if the ground had erupted. The strength with which they were spoken made him realise how different his son now was – a man, where once a boy. And the words themselves exposed a possibility that Bon had not been ready to entertain.

'Venden—'

'I'm not your son any more. I'm not Venden.'

'Yes you are!'

'No, I'm . . . no name. I'm all for Aeon.' Venden's eyes lit up as he spoke. He turned on the beast's back, looking down at the object suspended from the rough saddle.

'What do you have?' Bon asked, and Leki echoed his question, louder, more fearful.

'What do you have?' She came forward, skirting around the clearing to keep as far from the shape in its centre as possible. She pressed against the cliff face, pushing past creeping plants, gasping and shoving aside a fist-sized spider that fell onto her shoulder. 'What do you have? What have you done?'

'Only what I wanted,' Venden said. Bon saw a flicker of doubt in his eyes.

'Venden, will you come down? Can we talk?'

'Who is she?' Venden asked. 'Who have you brought with you?' For the first time, his own voice was edged with fear.

'She's a friend. She—'

'She doesn't *look* like a friend. There's deceit in her.'

'No,' Bon said, shaking his head and thinking, *I've only known her for days*. She was warm pressed against him in that giant tree in the gas marshes, and they had supported each other on the journey Juda had brought them on.

Venden calmed the shire. Bon noticed that he could not look away from the shape for long. *Is that really Aeon?* he wondered, and realised that he did not care. If it was, that was amazing and staggering and terrifying, because they were in the presence of a dead god. If it was not, it altered nothing. The thing at the centre of his world now was his son, his beautiful son, vanished and laid to rest in all but Bon's most optimistic, unrealistic moments.

'There's so much we need to do together,' Bon said. He thought of everything he had done with his own father, and how that had shaped him – the learning, the sports, the exploring and work. There were still such sights to show his child.

'Bon, we need to leave here,' Leki said.

'What?'

'Bon . . . I need to tell . . .' She was looking at the shape, not at him. Had it moved? Bon was not sure. Was its arched spine slightly higher? Had that gouge in the soil where it touched been there before? Motionless, it resembled nothing alive, nor anything that should live, and yet it was the most animated thing he had ever seen.

'It's too late, father,' Venden said, and he rode past Bon towards the shape. The shire snorted and shook its head, agitated, but Venden steered it true. He could ride well. Bon's father had taught him how to ride, but Bon had only ever taken Venden a couple of times. *One more thing I have yet to do*, he thought, and then everything changed. The past ended, the future began.

'There's no more magic!' Juda shouted, his voice a wretched cry.

Previously so static, the scene exploded into movement.

Juda's heart strived to betray him, but he grasped on to life. Holding it tight, dear to him, even though his reason for being seemed so small now, and so pointless.

Because there was no magic here.

The dregs sat in his bag, weak, pitiful echoes of what had been. They might show him sights from afar, perhaps. It could be that, used properly, the magic would heal one wound, or cause another.

But the great magic he had expected to discover the moment he found Aeon . . . there was none.

And there never had been.

'There's no more magic!' Juda said. It did not sound like his voice, though it came from his throat. It was the sound of a man bereft, the whimper of a wretched someone who has discovered one of life's truths is a lie. Life is dead, moving is stillness, love is hatred . . . Aeon is not magic. It might have been used to put the god down, but it had never been wielded by the destroyed deity.

The ground here, and the air, was as empty of magic as anywhere Juda had ever been.

Behind him, along the valley where a stream cut down from the hillsides with deceptively cheerful music, he heard movement. Stamping feet, harsh breathing. The clank of metal against metal.

Juda could not turn to look, and the noises were remote to him. Everything was remote, all reality circling the huge empty space that had formed inside him. It was the void where all his desires had dwelled, along with everything he had ever lived for. The Brokers sought magic like people who climbed mountains or navigated long rivers – they wanted it because it was there.

But Juda sought magic to live. It had become his heartbeat, yet to be found. It was his love and desire, waiting for him in the wild. It was—

The movement came closer, and he slowly looked up.

The female slayer emerged from behind a copse of trees further down the valley. She ran at him, unhitching the bow from over her shoulder, sweating and foaming at the mouth like a shire that has been pushed too far, too fast.

The male slayer was close behind, swinging his pike from his shoulder and aiming it as he ran. There was a burst of steam from its end, a low whistle and a heavy impact against Juda's booted foot, twisting his ankle. The stench of shellspot poison wafted around him and scorched the insides of his nostrils. A finger's width higher and the shot would have broken through skin and flesh and killed him.

Juda did not care. He stood and stumbled into the clearing, and all eyes turned to him. The young man on the shire, Bon behind him, Leki sheltering against the cliff from the thing at the centre of the clearing . . . none of it mattered. Tears blurred his vision, so he only caught a shadow of Leki rushing across towards Bon.

'Behind him!' she screamed. 'They've found us!'

I've found them, Juda thought. He imagined himself in the belly of the Engine once more, swimming in dregs and thinking himself immersed, but really only touching ancient, ineffectual echoes of what magic really was – Crex Wry, another fallen god. Perhaps the dregs were its final, dying exhalations. Perhaps Juda had spent his whole life chasing ghosts.

And in a flash of revelation he knew, suddenly, what he had to do.

He turned to run, and something punched him in the

shoulder. Blood sprayed the air before him, turning his view of the bleached, dead god red. He looked down at the arrow protruding from his armpit and it did not matter. The pain was fuel to him as he ran.

He touched the wound with his dreg-soaked right hand, and the heat began to fade.

Yes, he thought, *now I know the way.*

Another arrow hissed past his ear and tugged at his hair, and behind him he heard a scream.

Everything is moving so slowly, Venden thought, and he nudged the shire closer to the remnant. The creature was antsy, but Venden exuded calmness and control.

The man rushed across the clearing, and his raised hands seemed to blur with the air. Venden's shadow winced back, shrinking deeper within him, but it quickly rallied and came to the fore again. He felt its shock, and knew that it did not mind him knowing. Even great things cry, have fear, and become triumphant.

'Almost there,' he said softly, and something whistled at the air. An arrow struck the running man and he barely seemed to notice.

Venden saw the things rushing towards the clearing. He knew what they were, but they were as much removed from his world as his father. Aspects of long ago.

The running man seemed mad. Tall, thin, he had the look of obsession about him, and addiction, and his right hand was opaque with something revolting. It repulsed the remnant and the shadow within Venden, but the man was beyond noticing. He was raving, laughing and crying as he held this strange hand to the arrow wound, and then rushed from the clearing without a backward glance.

The woman to Venden's left shouted something, then dashed towards where Venden's father still stood.

Another arrow slashed at the air. Beneath Venden, the shire screamed and reared, the shaft buried deep in its broad, muscled neck. Venden felt a stab of pity for the creature that had carried him so far, but the shadow smothered such emotion and urged him onward.

Through the shouting and screams and growing chaos, Venden felt a calmness that even drew a smile to his lips as the shire stumbled forward into a fall. He grabbed the tied blanket in one hand, holding tight, and felt movement from inside. Impossible, wonderful movement.

There was a brief pull from behind him as he heard his father's voice. He did not understand the words – it was a shout, a warning, or perhaps an exhalation of loss – but as Venden experienced a sinking feeling inside, the shadow bore him up and held him in its caring embrace. Without using words, it told him that everything would be all right.

The shire fell and Venden tumbled from its back, but it no longer mattered.

He reached out his hand.

'Behind him!' Leki shouted as she ran from beneath the shelter of the cliffs. 'They've found us!'

Bon had already seen the slayers further down the valley, the shot from the pike, and the arrow that burst from Juda's armpit in a spray of blood. He had seen Juda running on, face mad, hand pressed to the wound. And he had already thought, *It's all over now*, as his son Venden urged the animal away from him and towards what might be a god.

The female slayer fired another arrow, and although Bon could barely believe she could aim over such a distance, this one flicked past Juda's face and struck Venden's mount.

The animal screeched, stumbled, and tipped forward as its front legs folded.

'Bon, we've got to go *now*!' Leki said as she reached him. She grabbed at his arms, nails scratching through the material of his shirt.

'I can't leave—' he began, but Venden was already falling, the wrapped object swinging in one hand, his other hand reaching for the object he had been riding towards.

Juda fled the clearing, bleeding, laughing or crying.

And the slayers were upon them. The female paused just by the howthorn bush where they had been waiting moments before, and the male caught up with her. They stood apart so as not to offer an easy target for whatever weapons their prey might bear. They sweated, snorted, steam rising from their sun-darkened skins, foam bubbling on their chins, and they were more base than animals, less human than a rock or tree.

'Too late,' Leki said. She shrugged off her coat and stepped forward, entwining her fingers and stretching her arms above her head.

'What?' Bon said in confusion.

Venden crawled from beneath the fallen shire and reached out to touch the object that had stolen his mind.

'Venden!' Bon called, and the female slayer came for him. She raised a hand to brush Leki aside, her arm thick and spiked with heavy bands of rough metal. Her eyes were on Bon Ugane – her target, her quarry since the beach, in her sights now and destined to evade her no more.

Bon tensed himself to fall to one side, knowing it would be useless. He would be dead within moments. He had found his missing son, and he would never have a chance to hold him close.

And then the slayer grunted and fell to one side. Leki was

upon her, punching and kicking so quickly that Bon could barely see the movements. The slayer lashed out, recovering quickly from the shock, but perhaps not fast enough. Leki – a blur, a flitting thing – stabbed again and again with one of the slayer's own knives, plucked from the murderous thing's belt. Her victim groaned as black blood splashed the grass. Leki hit the ground, leaped, slashing and kicking.

The slayer staggered backwards across the clearing with her arms waving around her head as if at an annoying insect. None of her punches or kicks touched Leki.

Bon was unsure what was happening, though he had an idea. It was crazy, and it was shattering, because it suggested things about Leki that he had no wish to confront. But the only people trained in such forms of combat were soldiers in the Ald's own army, the Spike.

Leki paused briefly, squatting in the grass with legs splayed, head down, hand held out and covered with black blood. She was panting, eyes wide from the fight. She glanced once at Bon, and then leaped into the fray once more.

The female slayer was more prepared this time, but her wounds were already wearing her down. She glistened with leaking blood. One arm hung loose and useless. Leki flitted around her on light feet, stabbing and slashing.

The male slayer came for them both.

She can't take two, Bon thought in a panic.

Then he saw Venden, and what he was becoming. And for a moment everything stopped, the whole of the world taking a breath to watch.

Venden was aware of the chaos around him, but he was apart from it all. It was in a world beyond his own. He grasped the heart of Aeon in one hand, and was in turn nursed by the hand of the shadow.

The shadow that rose within him, and was becoming more than he had ever believed.

Venden stepped away from the dying shire and reached for the remnant. He knew he did not have to press the heart to the remnant's surface too hard, and that wherever he touched would suffice. This dead god was almost whole once more, and Venden felt his own short life drawing to a close.

He had achieved much, gathering the disparate parts of this murdered, scattered deity. He had learned a lot about Skythe in the process, but he realised that had been purely for his own edification. He had been *allowed*. It was the fuel to his knowledge, and his knowledge was merely a means to an end. Something to drive him. A reward.

There would be thanks from Aeon, both for him and his mother. They had carried a spark of the murdered god – its mind, its soul, its memory or essence. His mother had passed it to him. And both of their lives had led to this moment.

'I wonder how things will change,' he said, and the weight of Skythe pressed against his skull.

Someone screamed, someone else shouted. Venden touched the remnant's underside.

He felt the change commence, and there was a momentary, blazing agony that belonged to someone so alive. The agony faded, the remnant flexed around him. The heart beat like an earthquake.

His vision grew dark, and then everything was red.

Bon went to his knees, forgetting the slayers, and Leki, and Juda fleeing with an arrow through his torso. He forgot where he was and why he was here, and the trials he had passed through since arriving. He saw only the boy he had raised coming apart, and he did not understand.

Bon Ugane felt his own wet insides ripped as his son's

were opened, his own bones breaking and crumbling. He could not even scream.

Venden touched the god-shape and disintegrated before it. His hand spread on the sun-bleached, bony surface, the red stain soaking in and pulling at his arm. He was tugged closer, lifted from the ground and sucked against the shape's uneven underside. The object in his other hand blistered through the blanket and was lifted up against the shape, penetrating like a sword through flesh and disappearing inside. It left no wound, but a single stain of blood, which was quickly swamped by Venden as he ceased to be a man.

In the space of a few heartbeats, Venden was sucked against the thing's underside and crushed there, his body spreading in a haze of blood and flesh. But the blood did not drip, and neither did his exposed insides fall. They spread around and over the pale shape, darkening where they touched, leaving vibrant colour behind. Blood-red, the hue of life.

Bon started moving backwards on his knees. His son was gone, become something else. He glanced across at the slayers in time to see the female slayer's head tugged back by Leki, her throat opened to the bone by her own knife, and then a blur as Leki hacked and slashed, tugging the head free of the slayer's shoulders and flinging it towards the other attacker, now shaken from his shock and advancing quickly upon Leki.

The headless slayer stood. She remained motionless, other than her left hand fisting and unfisting at her side.

I'm not seeing any of this. Bon gained his feet and backed away towards the sheer cliff. The mass of it behind him presented some false security.

At the centre of the clearing, the spread of Venden's disintegrated body animated the thing that he had claimed was a god. *And what, if not a god?* Bon wondered. The end of his journey suddenly felt like a beginning.

The decapitated slayer fell onto her side, a black slick gouting from her neck and steaming in the long grass. Her partner fired his pike at Leki. She dodged the shot with an incredibly quick sidestep, and the poison pod shattered against a tree. The slayer ran at her, fired an arrow from his quickly drawn bow, rolled, and then he was upon Leki, grasping her in two massive hands and swinging her up and over his head, dropping her behind him, falling back and turning as he fell, mouth gaping to reveal the long, rotten teeth with which he would rip out her throat.

But Leki was no longer beneath him when he hit the ground. She kicked out at his head and leaped aside, slashing out with his fallen comrade's knife. It sparked from a band of metal armour across his chest.

Possessed with the fight, Leki and the slayer did not seem to notice the movement behind them.

But Bon did.

Using the flesh of Venden's remains, Aeon had clothed itself. But its body was thirty times larger than Venden, and his parts must have merely been a catalyst for regrowth. It expanded into being – limbs thickening, torso widening, and Bon could not look upon it. It was *becoming* again. His mind could not cope with the impossibility of this, nor the implications. His body could not bear the weight of its presence without going down again, slumping against the cliff, feeling wet grass around him and the comforting solidity of rock.

'Venden, what have you done?' Bon asked, and for the first time in his life he feared his son.

Milian whispered from his memory, so sad when Venden had come along, so bereft when she should have been so alive. *See what he became*, Bon thought, and he thought perhaps she had always known.

Aeon ripped itself from the ground and became independent.

It lifted each of its limbs in turn, shaking mud and clinging plants free. Then it raised its long tail from beneath the fallen tree. Still forming, its flesh and skin tones changing as shadows passed back and forth across the appearing body, it turned what might have been its head.

It looked at Bon, and he closed his eyes. But he could still feel the unbearable weight of its regard.

He heard Leki scream, then the thump of a body.

And then another thud, a shocking impact, and the crunching sound of someone meeting their end.

Venden was now the shadow. He was the shade in the great mind of a god, whereas before the mind of Aeon had been the shadow within him, and in his mother before him. Borne over centuries, the god had emerged from its chrysalises to find its home again, at last. It revelled in its rejuvenation.

Venden's pain was no more, because his body was no more. But there was a peculiar awareness. He retained a form of consciousness, though he was unsure of his senses, and thought perhaps the old way of seeing, and understanding, was long behind him.

Aeon rose, and Venden rose with it. He wondered how long this would be. Around Venden, circling like stars surrounding the speck of dust he might barely be, Aeon's mind was so vast that he could barely conceive of it. It extended in directions he could not even begin to comprehend – past and future, sure enough, but other ways too. Across boundaries he did not understand, and through histories his limited mind would never know.

As Venden sensed action being taken – and Aeon's great mind interacting with the world for the first time since its death – his human emotions echoed Aeon's disgust and loathing at what it saw: *Dead things should stay dead.*

Carried within Skythe's resurrected god, the irony of that idea was difficult to escape.

Aeon was standing straight and tall like a man, only many times taller. Its fleshed-out body resembled nothing Bon had ever witnessed before. He squinted, trying to make sense of what he saw, but there was little sense to be made. Not yet, at least. His mind recoiled, and he felt a subtle madness descend in what might have been a protective cloud.

Yes, I'll go mad, Bon said, inviting it in. *I'll go mad and thank you kindly.*

Aeon moved. As it lifted one limb, Bon saw the crushed remains of the male slayer squashed beneath it, the monster's slick insides spewing across the clearing as the god walked away.

Don't go! Bon thought. He reached for Aeon, standing, stumbling after it. But then it ran, and in three bounds it was as if it had never been there at all.

Complete silence. Bon had never before experienced such stillness, such solitude. No birds called, no breeze blew, no living thing made a sound. The world was frozen in the moment.

Then Leki groaned, and Bon went to her. She was warm, and that felt good. Whoever she was and whatever lies she had hidden behind, she felt good, because she was alive.

'Did you see?' Bon asked.

'I saw,' she said. He thought it was pain, but when he looked at her he realised the quiver in her voice was dread. 'I saw our doom.'

'Aeon,' Bon said. *Venden*, he thought.

'It's the end of us,' Leki gasped. She grasped his hand and stood, leaning against him for support. She was slick with sweat, speckled with blood from the slayer she had slaugh-tered. 'It's back, and there will be war.'

She's a soldier of the Spike, Bon thought, but the idea still did not seem real. 'You can't believe that,' he said. 'Aeon is . . . the one god, true and real.'

Leki actually shivered. 'Of course it is. And it will be looking for revenge.'

Slowly, as Bon and Leki held each other up, the blood-spattered clearing came back to life.

Milian Mu and Bon Ugane travelled with the wagon train for two days until it reached New Kotrugam. They kept separate rooms, but spent all of their waking hours together, shovelling coal in the largest wagon, taking breaks, perusing the impromptu spice markets set up along the wagon's wide roof. Sometimes they held hands, and Bon felt the thrill of what he had been yearning for his whole life. The first time they kissed, Milian felt the shard shifting, but the greatest move-ment was undeniably in her own heart.

They were falling in love.

New Kotrugam was an amazing place. Milian and Bon stood on the wagon's roof along with many others as the long wagon train approached the city. Built in a huge crater several miles across, the city had a natural defensive wall around two-thirds of its perimeter, a high ridge of land that Bon explained was supposedly the ripple of an impact. It was said, he told her, that a giant rock had fallen from the sky before history and smashed the hollow in the land. To scientists it was a valid proposal, and there were those who spent their lives examining the evidence. To others it was a creation myth, and in the caves and potholes deep beneath the city it was believed that the god who fell from the sky still dwelled.

When Milian asked what Bon believed, he smiled and looked up. 'We have no idea what's there,' he said, and she supposed that was no real answer at all.

They passed satellite communities as they approached the city's great wall, and some of the smaller wagons broke off to make camp. The bulk of the train went forward, and as it approached the wall a set of huge gates opened, swinging on hinges the size of the smaller wagons, so heavy and wide that its movement caused a breeze that stirred dust and sand across the plain. It took some time to open fully, and a flock of birds swirled and fluttered around the door's hidden upper edges, swooping in and out again with long thrashing things hanging from their beaks. The hinges sang like thunder, grumbled through the ground, and reflected sunlight made the darkness behind them seem deeper.

People drifted down from the sheer cliffs above the yawning gates on wings of gossamer material, opaque and yet obviously strong. They steered their kites and landed on the larger wagons. They were short, thin people, with bright red skin and flaming yellow hair. Milian thought they looked like flame given life. Bon told her that they were also Outers – he believed her to be one, and always would – originally brought to Alderia as slaves because of their skills with medicine. That skill had since earned them some respect, and in many cases an element of freedom. The fire-people folded their false wings when they landed and started to trade, and Milian watched in fascination. They moved with such grace and certainty that she was not quite sure just how false those wings were. She would ask Bon when they were through the gates. There was so much for her to ask him.

But faced with the wonders of New Kotrugam, the fire-people would be all but forgotten.

Milian grew cold inside as they passed from sunlight into

shadow, and Bon held her hand and smiled as they were swallowed into the tunnels beneath the cliffs.

'It won't take long,' he said. 'And I'm here to hold you.' He was not quite telling the truth. The tunnel ran for over a mile, thundering to the sounds of the wagon train's wheels and coughing steam engines, lit by lights in caves along its edges where people went about obscure tasks or simply sat and watched, and heavy with the smells of industry. But Bon *did* hold Milian, and they kissed as New Kotrugam opened to them.

She had not known what to expect, but nothing could have prepared her for what she saw as they emerged from the tunnel. The city was huge. Some buildings seemed to touch the sky, and there were floating walkways between them, the air above almost as busy as the thriving streets below. The wagon followed a wide thoroughfare apparently emptied for its arrival, and either side were bustling markets, theatre squares, recreation parks where people played sports and games, bathing pools, fire pits where all manner of foods were being cooked, open-air Fade churches, and countless shops and display rooms swathed in materials, books, paintings and weapons. There was too much detail for Milian to take in, so she closed her eyes frequently. But every time she opened them again, there was something even more amazing to see.

Above the city floated huge shapes, their impossible shadows moving across the streets and squares and slinking over the sides of tall buildings.

'The steamships,' Bon said. 'The Ald ride up there, supervising the city.'

'Don't they ever come down?' Milian asked. She felt a stab of hatred for the Ald, but also amazement.

'Sometimes, I suppose,' Bon replied. 'I don't really know.'

The steamships drifted slowly high above, mostly silent, sometimes hissing and emitting clouds of vapour that quickly dispersed to the air. They were incredible, and Milian watched one until the train turned out of sight behind a tall, wide building. *Watching down on us like gods*, she thought. The shard shifted inside her, and she silently told it to grow still. It froze. She caught her breath. She had never spoken to it like that before.

'Fade church,' Bon said, indicating the high building they were passing. If some of the buildings they had seen were grand, this was ostentatious. Milian could barely imagine how long it had taken to construct such a complex, beautiful, frightening building, with its towers and sharp edges, coloured glass façades, dark openings, and gargoyles that caused her to clasp Bon's hand and squeeze tight.

'What are they?' she asked.

'The gargoyles? Kolts.' She heard the doubt in his voice. 'Monsters, supposedly called up by the Skythians six hundred years ago. Do you not know . . .?'

'Not where I am from,' she said. Six hundred years! She had supposed centuries, but not so many.

Bon nodded uncertainly at this, because he had not yet asked her about her home. 'Nothing to be afraid of,' he said. 'All in the past.'

The shard of Aeon shifted once more, and Milian closed her eyes until it grew still.

They moved on, and wonders assaulted her from all sides. Later, she asked, 'Why is it New Kotrugam? What happened to the old?'

'There are those who believe there was a city here before the crater was made.'

'And you believe?'

Bon shrugged, cautious. 'There's always something before.'

It was a day of discovery and wonder, and when they left the wagon at last and Bon took her through the streets to his home, Milian became a part of New Kotrugam. The place evoked obscure memories of Skythe, but she did her best to drive them down. A vague grief threatened to engulf her. *They called the daemons Kolts, and blamed them on us!*

Having Bon beside her made her calm, and the grief and rage existed only as a distant ache.

A day after arriving, after a meal at a local tavern and several glasses of wine from a vineyard in the hills south of Kotrugam, they made love for the first time. Clumsy, awkward, yet there was a passion Milian could not deny, and which Bon had been searching for his whole life. There had been several women through his twenties, but none of them had possessed him in the same way as Milian. There was something about her. Exotic, perhaps, with her obvious Outer origins. But she seemed larger on the inside than out, as if her capacity for secrets was deep. And her eyes. And her body. And her laughter, always with a hint of melancholy that Bon believed was the sign of a good heart. Anyone could believe that things were good, but his true love could only be someone who believed they could be better.

The next morning they awoke with sunlight slanting across their naked bodies, smiling shyly and with eyes heavy with memories of the previous night. They made love again.

Milian felt the change. As they came together and a tear leaked from her left eye, she sensed the shard leaving her and filtering down into the new life seeded in her womb. She rolled from Bon and fell onto her back, crying out, bereft and shattered at the sudden hollowness. *Countless years*, she thought, and she knew she could not lose something she had carried for so long without it ripping the heart from her.

The shard left no apology. She still sensed it, nestling

into the potential child she and Bon had made. She could feel its weight, if she squeezed her eyes shut and concentrated. But it was no longer a part of her.

The loss was an agony, and as she began to sob uncontrollably Bon hugged her tight. He wanted to care for her even though he had no idea what was wrong, and for that she loved him more.

There should have been a future laid out before them. There should have been pleasure in each other's company, and joy, and lovemaking and being together. And to some extent there would be. But from that moment on, Milian Mu was dying inside. She found it ironic that she had existed for so many centuries, yet was not destined for a long life.

Long enough to protect the child, she thought. That was as long as she would bear to live, trying to hide her origins, her age, her sense of loss and hollowness. Live, in this city ruled by the people who had ruined her world and destroyed her god, condemning her to this fate. *Protect my child until it's old enough to know what is required of it, and what it is here to do.*

'Everything feels so special,' Bon said, drawing a circle around her navel with his finger.

Milian found that her fake smile came easily.

Old enough to raise a dead god.

PART TWO

FALL

Chapter 13

wound

Calm, calm, douse the fire, quench the pain.

Juda ran, each footstep driving agony deeper.

Sink in, seep down. Remove the damage, separate, slice it away.

From where he had fled, the sounds of conflict and shouting and chaos, and then a stunned silence filled with a held breath of impossibilities. The world behind him had been erased – much as he sought now to erase the wound from his mind, his body's systems – and a new history was being formed from the stunned moments between moments. Juda could feel the force of this, though he did not turn to look. He *could* not turn. To turn would be to lessen his onward pace, and that would submit to the pain.

So he forged onward, digging deep to recall the teachings of the Brokers he had met, and Rhelli Saal's gasped words of wisdom into the sex-soaked rooms after they had rutted. It had never been love between the two of them. Brokers were too selfish for that. Even while they licked and fondled and came, it was magic that possessed their thoughts.

You can mould dregs to your ways, because what's left is weak and old and can be manipulated. You need strong hands, a hopeful heart, and desire. Sometimes you need pain.

Juda had pain and desire aplenty, and his hands had been made strong over the years, lifting and sifting those few dregs of magic he had been lucky enough to find.

Dilute the pain, hold it away, swallow it, lose it to the air.

As he ran he pressed his right hand to his left armpit, letting the dreg do the work he urged. He kept his left arm raised and held away from his body. The arrow had entered his back, struck his shoulderblade and been diverted down, emerging beneath his arm and slashing across his left bicep. His sleeve and jacket on that side were soaked with blood. He had yet to inspect the damage closely.

Wash away the pain . . .

The arrow's shaft felt splintered, its sharp metal head sticky with clogged parts of him. That would make it almost impossible to withdraw, even if he could somehow snap off the flight and tug it through from the front. The fractures in the koa wood would act as barbs.

He pressed hard against the wound, shouting out at the agony and screaming the faint away. He could not stop, could not fall. The precious dreg spread around his arm and shoulder as he willed it, warm against his skin, cool against the burning fire in his flesh.

Something more than wood in there, he thought, and, really, he had known that from the moment of impact. His shouting, the running, the attempt to flee what had happened and what might still be happening behind him, all were part of his attempt to deny the truth: that slayers never used one weapon when two would work better. Their arrows would usually kill, such was their proficiency at firing them. But if not, the shellspot poison they were dipped in would finish the job.

Juda was fighting to survive. *If I was a Wrench Arc then madness would save me.* He chuckled at that, and thought perhaps that madness already was doing so.

Everything had changed for him in moments, a dance of transformation played out against the presence of an old dead god. First, the realisation that he had always been utterly wrong about the magic he had expected to find around Aeon's remains, and that the opposite was true – the god had been destroyed by magic, so its remnants would repulse even the smallest dreg, not attract it.

And then the arrow.

Perhaps under such an onslaught his life would have changed, or neared its end. He had lived with a kind of madness for years, and that rode higher now, surfing the waves of change like spinebacks on violent seas. It insulated him, as he was urging the magic to insulate against pain. But it also allowed him a particular focus. Bon and Leki were vague shadows now, and already he could barely remember their names. His purpose was all. And there was something ahead that lured and dragged him across this landscape of madness and pain, just as surely as old dead Aeon had repulsed the magic that Juda so coveted.

There was the Engine. The possibility that perhaps, with the dregs, he might start it again – initiate its systems and parts, and use it to draw bountiful magic once more – gave Juda a blazing point of light to aim for in the growing darkness of his poisoned, dislocated mind. *No one has ever done it before*, he thought, but that was part of what drove him.

The idea was all he had left, so, as he ran, it grew.

Night fell, but pain lit his way. As if it were precious medicine, Juda had plucked another dreg from the small bag and massaged, moulded, pressed it to his will and then his wound.

He could sense the terrible damage done to his back and arm, but it was a remote realisation, tempered by the dark. He panted as he ran, breath rattling in his chest. *Bleeding in there*, he thought. The dreg sank deeper and soothed.

The shellspot poison was in him, and he was an observer of the battle to expunge it. He had seen three people die of shellspot in his time on Skythe, and their deaths were as hard as any he had witnessed. Two had been victims of the slayers, newly landed banishees from Alderia who he'd not had a chance to help before they reached shore. Few of those marked for death dodged the slayers, but when they did the chase was brutal, fast, and merciless. One woman had just left the beach and ducked into a hengrove swamp when an arrow sliced off her earlobe. She'd screeched, run on and then fallen. Even from a distance, Juda had seen her body convulsing as the poison from the arrow's tip surged through her veins and touched each muscle alight. There had been no fight when a slayer reached her and buried a short sword in her stomach. The other had been a man who had tried to land on Skythe prepared. He'd brought out two small crossbows he'd somehow managed to procure on the prison ship and fired them both at the slayer rushing towards him. The slayer had plucked the bolts from her body – one from her chest armour, the other from her exposed throat – and stomped them into the sand. As she tended the wound to her throat, she had kicked the man over and dropped a small object into his mouth. His death had been slow and agonising. The slayer stood over him, watching. It had been more vicious than the stabbings and guttings Juda had become used to seeing.

The third person he'd seen die from shellspot had been at his own hand, and he had stood well back from her final throes.

His muscles burned, but mostly from exertion. He was still

master of his own body, and there were no spasms he did not order, no movements that were not of his own will. He could feel the poison in his veins, like a stream of ice flowing around his body and striking, every few steps, his rapidly beating heart. Its journey to kill him was a pulse in itself, yet with each attack he sensed it growing weaker.

There was a change across Skythe, and it took him a while to place exactly where and what it was. Rushing headlong through the darkness with an arrow piercing his body – an injury that should have mortally wounded him, tainted with a poison that must have finished the job – he noticed nothing different in the world around him. The shadows still echoed with the calls of night-hunting things, the silhouettes of trees guarded the dark. Skythe exuded the same sense of frantic wildness it always had; confused, condemned. But the promise of things to come had changed. Even beyond his tumultuous self, Juda could sense that. The potential of tomorrow was shocking in its scope.

He grew tired, but would not allow himself rest. Movement was all. If he stopped, his heart might follow, claiming its own rest as a result of the wound and poison given by the slayer. The dregs did the work he bestowed on them, but he needed to be strong also.

With dawn behind him, Juda found himself somewhere familiar, and felt the tugging of those splinters of magic for what might have been home. The sun did not yet light the small valley, but he could still see the bulk of the Engine down there, waiting for him now, hiding no longer. He stopped for the first time since being struck by the arrow. Standing motionless, he felt the exhaustion sweeping over him.

'Not yet,' he gasped, starting down the slope towards the Engine. The arrow protruding from his back and armpit had become a weight, pinning him to the world. The left side of his chest felt heavy. Blood ran cool in his veins, but his muscles were still his own, and he sensed the remnants of the poison weakening with each surge of his heart.

He reached the Engine and leaned against its side, the metal shell not as cold as he remembered.

'This must work,' he said. He had spent his whole life coveting magic, and the Engines had been old, dead things. Now, with the sense that another old, dead thing was stirring again, perhaps this Engine of magic might roar once more.

Aeon moved. It strode, floated, sprinted, passing from place to place with a blink of an eye. Venden could detect no sense of effort being expended as it travelled across the huge island where it had been murdered. Perhaps reformed, it had the properties of a spring coiled and ready to unleash. All those years put down were passed now, and Aeon was relishing its new existence. Its senses were nothing familiar, yet Venden's mind was allowed full sight and sound, smell and touch, and other experiences he had no name for. He lived the lives of flowers, and was a breeze flitting high in the atmosphere. He aged slower than rock, and knew the power of existence so brief that a blink of an eye was an eternity.

He thought for a while that he was allowed by Aeon because he had carried a seed, as had his mother before him for so long. Venden's body was gone, and the pain of its departing had been bright but brief. Perhaps persistence of existence was his reward, a kindness from the god.

But then he began to see and experience things that indicated otherwise. Through Aeon's strange senses, Venden was made aware.

At first, the landscapes they passed across were familiar to him. He caught flashes of where they were. A valley here, a lake there; a mountain with one side fallen away in an ancient tremor; a deep woodland, trees incredibly tall, multiple trunks thin and flexible. He had been to these places in his search for Aeon's parts, or seen them from afar.

Kellis Faults appeared, its tall spires and towers still somehow stretching for the skies even though they had been abandoned for so long. Aeon flinched as they passed quickly through the byways of the once-great city, because in places there was a stain on the past, a dreg of magic keeping wretched memory alive. It was not afraid of these places, but would rather not touch them. Magic repulsed it.

And then there were places that Venden did not recognise, and he realised that these travels were places in Aeon's memory . . .

A lake of ice cracks and groans as massive forces play on it from below. Ice geysers erupt so far into the air that they haze the atmosphere. The ice is deep green and blue, and here and there are shadows of things below the surface. Time has blurred their edges.

A man walks across a scorched plain of bones, and in the far distance a huge city hovers above the horizon.

An armada of fighting ships closes on a long, deep beach, beyond which a wall stands defended by thousands of shapes. The air is thick with violence yet to come. The sea is placid, the beach smooth, the sun ambivalent, and it will rise and fall as always, the battle's outcome troubling it not at all.

More images, more events experienced and witnessed in a brief, passive flash, and yet Venden understood most of what he saw. He knew the implications of those images, what had gone before, and sometimes how they would resolve themselves. He could almost smell the rotting hulls of that armada as they decayed over centuries on the long, wide beach.

He was living Aeon's memories, though he was not being shown them. He was simply awash in a sea of recollections, a mote in Aeon's eye. Some were so ancient that their incredible age was palpable in their hazy image. Even a god, it seemed, could see its memories fade.

Venden was also a memory. And as he saw them, so these other memories saw him – a young man hauling a cart across Skythe; that same man sheltering beneath an overhang; a boy watching his mother plummet, ending the fall that had begun for her the moment he was conceived. Venden's own memories were fresh and fiery, and he would have cried had he still possessed eyes.

They sat beneath the overhanging cliff, and Bon knew that this was where his son had made his home. There was a rolled sleeping mat and some clothing stored beneath a tightly woven waterproof mat, a solitary pair of worn boots, and a campfire formed from scorched stones and half-burned kindling. A few cooking implements were piled beside the fire, some of them still stained with the hardened remnants of a meal. There were footprints in the soil.

This is where Venden lived, Bon thought. *He sat here and ate, staring at the thing he was rebuilding. He laid his head here, and slept, and perhaps he dreamed of me.*

'Perhaps he dreamed of me,' Bon said. He sat close enough to the bedding roll to touch it.

'Maybe he still does,' Leki said. She knelt close to Bon, cleaning and binding her wounds with a proficiency that illustrated her lie. She had been taught how to treat battlefield injuries. Expressionless, shutting off the pain, she clamped several cuts closed and treated them with a chewed paste. A deeper wound between her thumb and index finger she cleaned with water before slicing at it with her knife and forcing the paste into the gashes. She was sweating, shaking, but her face was stern and determined.

'You've kept so much from me. *Deceived* me.'

'Would it make any difference if I said I'm sorry?'

'I don't know,' Bon said. 'Would it?'

Leki glanced at him, then returned to her careful ministrations. Watching her, Bon tried to analyse what he might still feel about her. *It's complicated*, he thought, and he almost laughed. What had happened here had been so amazing that he still felt the mists of madness promising to close around him. If that meant calmness and understanding, he would welcome it. But he knew in truth that it would merely mean confronting events later on.

Venden . . . Aeon . . . Leki. Three names that meant different things to him, and about which everything had changed in the blink of an eye. Venden had been found and lost again. Aeon, the old god in stories that some still believed, had risen before him. And Leki had revealed herself as an impostor.

'What do you think happened to Juda?' Bon asked.

'Ran off and died somewhere,' Leki said. She relaxed back on her haunches and sighed, closing her eyes, still shivering. From the shock of her wounds, perhaps. Or fear.

'You don't sound concerned.'

'There's nothing either of us can do for him.' Leki looked at him, and her eyes were the same as before. Her *face* was the same, though more lined, more tense. 'The slayers' weapons are almost always tipped with poison. Shellspot, or sometimes dusk blight venom. And even if venomless, they never clean their blades.'

'You have wounds,' Bon said, nodding at Leki's hand, her upper arm.

'I'm inoculated.'

'Against such poisons?'

Leki did not answer. She stood, groaning at her aching limbs. 'We should go.'

'I suppose the Ald retain plenty of such knowledge for themselves.'

'We have to track Aeon,' she said. 'Find out where it's going.'

'And if I'd been slashed by a slayer's blade?' Bon asked.

'Then I'd have fucking saved you! What, you think because I'm Spike-trained I'm without heart?'

'I don't know, Leki.'

'If you don't know, then you've not felt a thing between us all these days.'

Bon looked away, confused. He started rooting through Venden's belongings, sparse though they were.

'Bon?'

'Can I trust any of that?' he asked. He did not look at her. He wanted to judge her through her voice, not the face he was growing so familiar with.

'I cannot lie with my emotions.'

'They don't train you in that, then?'

'They try,' she said. 'And it does work sometimes. But mostly with devouts.'

Bon turned on her, angry, confused. He hated the idea of his affections being toyed with, and he felt open to her, as open as if a slayer had split him neck to groin. He might be an object upon which she practised her intense Spike training. Or she might be telling the truth.

'You expect me to believe you're not a Fade devout?'

Leki shrugged. 'Pile of nark shit.'

Bon could not hold back his smile.

'We should talk as we walk,' Leki said. She was looking around the clearing like a trapped bird now, alert and anxious.

'I'm not sure I . . .' Bon said. He closed his eyes, but his son was still gone.

'He's dead, Bon,' Leki said. 'As dead as you've believed him to be these past years.'

'But he's done something.' Bon opened his eyes again. The clearing looked so empty, sparse, as if something vital had been removed from it that might never be replaced.

'Yes, he has.'

'Why are you here?' Bon asked. 'What are you looking for? Who sent you? If you believe that was Aeon, how come you still work for the Ald? And I didn't think the Spike recruited floaters.'

Leki ignored his use of the derogatory word for amphys, and it hung between them like a sour smell. It tasted bad in his mouth.

'Sorry,' he said.

'I'll tell you, Bon. But can we agree on something first – we have to follow that thing?'

'Follow Aeon,' Bon said, and it felt ridiculous to suggest anything else. Of course they had to follow the risen god. It was what he had spent his life believing in, researching, mourning. And Venden had given his life for Aeon to walk again. 'Yes, of course.'

'Then come on,' she said. 'Everything else can wait until we're moving. Come *on*!'

Leki moved off, and Bon followed. He walked backwards for a moment, looking at the last place Venden might have called home. He hoped his son had found happiness here, of a sort, but he would never know.

He turned his back on the cliff and followed Leki. They passed the dead tree and the wound in the ground from where Aeon had torn itself to leave, standing to an impossible height, running with impossible limbs and disappearing as though it had never been here at all. They passed the smear that was all that was left of the male slayer, and off to the left Bon

263

saw their other pursuer, head parted from her body by Leki's vicious attack.

They might write songs about today, Bon thought as they left that place. Leki was running, and he struggled to keep up, determined to survive to hear those songs.

Bon expected to find Juda's body at any moment. He'd seen the man struck by the slayer's arrow, fall, then rise again and flee shouting, screaming, as the arrow's poison seeped into his system and started attacking his vital organs. Leki's dismissal of him had felt harsh, but his death was assured, and so there was no reason for her to consider him further.

Perhaps she had seen and known many dead people.

But they did not discover his body. Once, Leki paused and pointed out a splash of blood on a plant's leaf, careful not to touch it herself. But she followed the more obvious trail made by Aeon, rather than tracking the still-wet traces of doomed Juda. Poisoned, even carrion creatures would not touch him. He would rot into the land.

Leki did not keep her promise that they could talk while they were moving. They ran too quickly to talk, and whenever Bon urged her to slow down she either shook her head, or ignored him completely. She was so much more than he had ever suspected, and the idea that he could never trust her again came as a shock.

Initially, Aeon's route was easy to follow. Its limbs had made obvious marks as it ran – impact depressions, prints in soft soil or mud, crushed plants. Occasionally, a footprint was still smeared red with the remains of the slayer. They found a shred of scalp and a bent knife. But the reality of what had happened was still blurred, too close for true analysis and acceptance. The haze of madness he thought he might welcome in was, he realised, of a very personal kind. This was self-preservation.

'What are you going to do if you catch up?' Bon asked, but Leki did not reply.

The footprints grew further apart. Several times they had to backtrack to the previous print and search outward for the next. There seemed to be no design to the directions Aeon had taken, and it appeared to turn on a whim.

The landscape around them was silent, observing, perhaps stunned into immobility by what had passed.

Leki became more frustrated and anxious, muttering to herself and only glancing at Bon if he offered an opinion, or asked a question. The sun was close to setting, and though they had followed a series of prints across the Skythian land-scape, they were no closer to setting eyes on Aeon.

'I've lost it,' she said at last. They had paused beside a small lake, smudges of pastel sunlight reflecting from the water and shimmering where fish broke the surface and jumped for insects.

'The last track wasn't far back,' Bon said.

'And if it goes that way, it's beyond us to follow,' Leki said, indicating the lake. 'And if it doubled back, or made a turn along the lake's shores, it's too dark to see.' She was struggling with something, an internal conflict that Bon felt he was not part of. 'No,' she said, shaking her head.

'No what?'

'I've wasted too much time already.' She looked at Bon, and it felt like she was seeing him for the first time since her fight with the slayer. 'Bon, I need to do something, and I'd like you to help.'

'That depends,' he said.

'Yes. Of course it does.' Leki paced back and forth, wet ground sucking at her boots. A flock of birds swooped across the lake, competing with the jumping fish for the clouds of insects buzzing above the mirrored water. Something howled in the distance. Songbirds mourned the passing of the day from their perches in a woodland further along the shore. It seemed to Bon that Skythe had returned to itself, which perhaps meant that Aeon was no longer close by.

'What do you need to do?' Bon asked. Something had chilled him.

'Bon.' Leki stopped pacing and stood before him, her back to the sinking sun. She was a silhouette. He found he could read her easier that way. 'Bon, Aeon is something that was never meant to rise. When the Ald put it down so long ago, they thought it was for ever. There has never been doubt about that, although there were those who chose caution over certainty.'

'And that's why you're here.'

'I'm one of the cautious ones. And because I choose not to put my fate in the hands of gods that I know to be false, I volunteered to come here. Investigate. Just . . . keep track of what's happening on Skythe.'

'Don't the Ald have enough agents here to do that?'

'Not ones who know what to look for.'

'And not ones who know the true story, right?'

'Right.' Leki nodded.

'So you acknowledge all that? The magic the Ald drew with the Engines, destroying Aeon, creating the Kolts. Then the Kolt slaughter, and the magic used again to put them down. As an Ald, you admit all that?'

'I'm not much different from you,' Leki said softly. 'We both know a version of the truth. But in mine, Aeon made the Kolts on purpose. *Before* it was put down. It brought them up to fight for it.'

'No,' he said, shaking his head.

'Yes,' Leki said. 'And to leave it running loose once again, ready to do what it did last time—'

'It was your ancestors' twisting of magic that made the Kolts.'

'Are you prepared to take that risk?'

'There's no risk to take!'

'Bon. Look.' Leki shook her head, frustrated. 'Maybe it's ready to create an army of Kolts again, or maybe, as you believe, it can't. Either way, it might want revenge. It has to be put down.'

Bon stared at the amphy's big, fluid eyes. 'You're just as bad as the rest of the Ald,' he said. 'Devout or not, you're still blinded to the truth.'

'*Everything* I do is for the good of Alderia.' He could see that she believed. But her ignorance hurt him.

'And your people set the slayers to kill me. Named me to them as someone to be eliminated.'

'And that's why you followed me. Because of who I am.'

Leki blinked at him, glanced away, looked up again. He could see her agonising over what she had to say next, and suddenly he didn't want to hear it.

'There were rumours of Aeon amongst the Skythians over the past year, and we have our spies. We'd heard whispers of . . . Venden Ugane, and what he was supposed to be doing.'

Bon caught his breath, but could not speak. Leki continued.

'We thought that the best way to find Venden would be to banish his father here, then follow him. I also knew of Juda, and was hoping that he might hear of you. He knows Skythe well, so . . . I just followed. Came to gather intelligence, and see if there was any truth to the rumours. And . . .' She shrugged.

'You knew Venden was alive,' Bon whispered.

267

'No, Bon. We heard whispers of his name, that was all.'

'Whispers amongst the Skythians.'

'Yes.'

'You didn't tell me.'

Leki looked pained, but had nothing to say. She sighed and came closer. Bon backed away. The more they talked, the less he knew her.

'You purposely gave my name to the slayers?'

'A gamble,' Leki said.

'Gambling with my life.'

'And my own!'

Bon shook his head and turned away, wondering how different things would have been if Leki was not there. She had lied so much. He turned back to her and asked, 'What is it you need to do?'

Leki turned and looked out across the lake. It was very beautiful and, with her back to him, he remembered her as beautiful as well. *It doesn't mean she's a bad person*, he thought. But no agent of the Ald could be a friend to him.

'I need to send word that Aeon has risen.'

'So that the Ald can come to put it down again. With magic. With the Engines.'

'New Engines,' she said. 'That thing Juda showed us was . . .'

'A relic?'

'Yes. Dangerous, and unknown. The new Engines are more . . . attuned to magic.'

'They've never stopped playing with it, have they?' Bon asked, and a cool fear settled across his soul. 'Venden always said that. He always suspected.'

'I don't know everything,' Leki said. She still faced away from him. Her voice was harsh, but Bon thought perhaps it was because of tears.

268

Anger rose and fell in waves, and tears came when he was struck with a sudden, unexpected memory of Venden grasping his hand as they walked along the banks of the Gakota River. Older, more innocent times, when history was just that. Now, history had returned.

'You'd bring the Spike here.'

'Can we leave a . . . *thing* like that free, knowing what hate it might harbour?'

'You can't even use the word god.'

'Then I'm more of an unbeliever than you. Can you call it a god when you can touch it? See it?'

Bon lifted a hand and indicated the lake. 'So touch it. See it.'

Leki sighed and came closer to Bon. This time he did not step back, but neither did he react when she placed a tender hand on his face.

'The Spike are *already* coming,' she said, sounding uncertain, perhaps even afraid. 'They set sail days after me. I'm just . . . advance intelligence.'

'You've been in contact with them already?' Bon gasped.

'Several times, when I've been alone.'

'How?'

'That's what I want you to help me with.' She took his hand and lifted it, kissed it. 'Please, Bon.'

Bon did not reply. He thought through what she had said, and wondered how much sense it made. About Aeon, and why it was back, and whether revenge was a part of its aim. The idea of that was terrible, because, much as he hated the Ald and what they stood for, Alderia was his home. He could not bear to see harm visited upon it.

Can you call it a god when you can touch it? Leki had asked. *Yes*, Bon thought.

Leki sighed at his silence. 'At least don't try to stop

me.' If there was threat in her voice it was cool, and camouflaged.

It turned out she did not really need Bon at all. She said she did – told him to stand in a certain place, hold a certain small, metallic valve which she produced from her pocket, and he silently helped – but, in reality, she did everything herself. Asking him to help was asking him to accept, and in observing, he feared he gave tacit approval.

I should be stopping this. I should do *something.*

But Bon's mind was still distant from things, and he could not answer his own silent self-condemnation. Leki was unusual – an atheistic Ald, believing in the good of Alderia. And whatever knowledge she had withheld about Venden, she seemed to care about Bon.

He had heard of racking, and knew that the Ald and Spike used it for keeping their extensive networks in touch across Alderia. Its use was forbidden by civilians or those not involved in government business, and the shoot dust necessary for racking was a rare compound. He had never believed that he would see the act performed himself, but even so his interest was slight. More important was the information that Leki would send, and the result of that communication. He was witnessing Skythe's history changing again.

'There must be another way,' he said, but Leki merely took the valve from his hand and inserted it into the apparatus.

She must have carried a component in each pocket. Set up at four corners of a square, the valves were stuck into the ground three handwidths apart. Leki made a cursory effort to clear some of the grass and loose soil within the square, then she extracted a long, flexible tube from her sleeve.

'The shoot dust,' Bon said.

Leki nodded. 'Not much left.' She popped a stopper on

the tube, then carefully sprinkled two lines of dust along the square's intersecting diagonals.

'I hear rumour it's still living,' Bon said.

'It's the crushed eggs of fleeting lizards,' Leki said. 'About as alive as hair we'll cut off and discard.'

He'd heard talk of fleeting lizards, but had never been interested enough to investigate further. The Ald – and especially its army, the Spike – was surrounded with rumours of arcane knowledge and technology, of which the steam weapons were most visible.

'I went on a hunt, once,' she said. 'I was basic training with the Spike, and the Blader took us down into the caverns beneath New Kotrugam. Deep down.' She worked the square as she spoke, making sure the dust lines were straight and the steam valves properly primed. She was ready to perform a racking now, but Bon realised she wanted to tell him this story. As a matter of trust, perhaps. Or simply an admission. 'There were hints that many had gone deeper, and we'd heard the rumours, of course.'

'The Ald think it's a voiceway to the Fade down there.'

'Well.' Leki paused, kneeling, and looked up at Bon. 'The lizards are a voiceway to something. They flit in and out of existence. I caught one.' She looked at her hands. 'I held it as surely as I've ever held anything before. And then it was no longer there. And then it was there again.' She clasped and unclasped her hands. 'For a while I wasn't sure if it was me travelling, or the lizard.'

Bon shrugged, looked out across the lake. The sun was sinking into the forest beyond the water, setting the trees afire and spilling its colours across the lake's surface. It was beautiful.

'But you're not common Spike,' he said confidently.

She paused only for a moment. 'Arcanum,' she said.

Bon gasped. 'Arcanum,' he echoed. They were the darker side of the Spike, less known, much more mysterious. *I can't allow this. Aeon hasn't risen for war. Venden would have never been helping something that wanted to return for* war*!* He swallowed, then took a step forward.

Leki whipped something from her pocket and aimed it at him. Juda's steam pistol. The valve plugged into its barrel glistened with moisture, heavily primed.

'No, Bon.'

'You won't shoot me.'

'Neither of us wants to find out. Now Bon . . . just listen,' Leki said softly, and she commenced racking.

The valves steamed gently, and the cross of shoot dust glowed a little, faded, glowed again. Between blinks Bon saw it vanish and reappear, and parts of the ground around it grew darker than night, and deeper. A shiver chilled Bon's spine and tingled his balls, but he thought of Venden again and looked away. His son might have loved this. His son, had he remained on Alderia, might well have travelled down beneath the city and touched the fleeting lizards himself. He had never been one to listen to authority, and had always been curious.

Leki, still kneeling, still pointing the pistol unwaveringly, leaned forward until her face was close to the crossed square. She began whispering, and Bon walked quietly away, no longer interested in what message she was sending across the sea.

He sat by the lake and swished his hand through the water. It was music to the falling night. Soon, Leki knelt beside him and put one hand on his shoulder.

'It's done,' she said.

'And now, war,' Bon said.

'They'll come, and it will end quickly.'

'Like last time?'

Leki did not respond.

'You're not certain at all,' he said. 'You're scared.'

'I can only hope,' she said quietly.

They knelt together and watched the last of the sun sink away, then she stood, groaning as her knees clicked.

'We should make camp. And in the morning, we'll try tracking Aeon once more. They'll need to know where it is when they land.'

Bon wanted to flee, to run and leave it all behind. But he felt at the centre of events. Things between him and Leki were far from over.

Chapter 14
blader

Blader Sol Merry had fallen in love with an amphy. For a man who had gained intense respect and trust in New Kotrugam, who had high ambitions in the Spike, and who was a Fade devout, such a pairing was frowned upon, though not entirely forbidden. It was preferred for the Spike to marry into their own. That reduced any chance of conflict within the army, and also lessened the amount of distant blood in the ruling Ald's own defence force. The amphys were of Alderia, but so far south that some considered them as Outers. Such prejudice could be damaging. Such love could distract.

The argument had never sat well with Sol. His family's heritage was Steppe clan through and through, and though he was the third generation to serve in the Spike, his history was plain for all to see. He bore the wide shoulders and narrow hips, the enlarged teeth, the strong fingers and toes of those climbers and canyoners suited to living in Alderia's expansive, remote, central mountainous regions. He was almost as far from a model Spike soldier as an amphy, and that made his love for Lechmy Borle even stronger.

The one time a fellow Spike had questioned Sol's dedic-
ation to the Ald after his affair with Leki had come to light,
Sol had beaten the man unconscious, dragged him from the
barracks where they were based and tied him to an old
execution column in one of New Kotrugam's more exclusive
quarters. He'd been driven with fury, but also restrained by
the Spike training which informed much of his life. The
civilians who had watched the gruesome spectacle had feared
what they might see, but the Spike who had followed knew
that it would not end in murder. The execution column
remained as dry as it had for generations, and the man was
left tied there long enough for humiliation to colour him, and
for shame to lower his eyes.

Sol was now his Blader, commanding him and forty-nine
other soldiers. The man, Gallan Park, was Sol's Side. In or
out of battle, it was Gallan's responsibilty to be Sol's ears
and eyes, and to take his place should he fall. It was the
closest of relationships in the Spike's structure, and the two
men had a brotherly trust for each other. Such was often the
way with soldiers.

And Lechmy Borle had become his wife.

Sol stood at the ship's rail and looked ahead of them across
the sea. The waters were wild and high, spray stinging, waves
undulating like the Forsaken Sea's angry, flexing muscles.
This was not Sol's first time on a ship, but it was his first
time on these waters. They were even more violent than he
had expected, and a third of his men were laid up below
decks, vomiting and groaning as they prayed that Venthia
would return to take them away. Reports from other ships in
the fleet told of similar scenes.

He focused on the horizon, though it was lost in mist. Then
he closed his eyes. His own sickness rose, but it was willpower
alone that drove it down. It would not be proper to be seen

275

puking his dinner up across the deck in front of his men. Their Blader, he must always be stronger than them all.

Please let this storm abate, he thought. *Venthia, touch these waters and calm them, just for me. Or I might just curl up and fucking die.* But Venthia had forsaken this ocean. Sol felt far from the Fade here, and that made him naked.

He leaned against the railing and groaned softly, and it was Leki who gave him comfort. He looked down at the sea crashing explosively against the hull and smiled, because Leki would love this. She would revel in the saltwater smell and its stinging touch, and soon he would see her again.

Someone approached him from behind. He did not hear or smell them, but he knew they were there. He squinted slightly and sensed their mood – queasy, but calm. No ill intent. A shadow flickered against the railing beside him, cast by the hesitant sun, and he recognised his Side.

'Gallan,' he said, turning.

'Blader Merry.' Gallan raised a fist to his brow.

'You can drop the formalities,' Sol said. 'They're for the training grounds and ceremonial marches, not the battlefield.'

'I wasn't aware we were at war.' Gallan's voice was light with humour.

'A third of the men on every ship are incapacitated and you think this isn't a fight?'

Gallan rolled his eyes. 'It stinks down there.'

'You're not feeling sick yourself?'

'No,' Gallan said, but his gaze flickered past Sol to the sea beyond.

'I am,' Sol said. 'If this cursed ship had a private corner I'd puke up my insides three times over.'

'By the Fade, me too,' Gallan said, somewhat relieved. 'My legs and guts aren't built for the sea.'

'Only another day,' Sol said.

'That's why I came. To let you know a racking has been received.'

'Leki?'

Gallan nodded. His embarrassment was always evident when her name came up. 'They're transcribing now; should be ready by midnight.'

'Thank you,' Sol said. 'Will you watch over the transcribing and bring it to me as soon as it's ready?'

'Of course.' Gallan touched his forehead again, smiled, turned and walked back across the deck. Sol knew how unsettled Gallan was by the two rackers they had on board – blind women, young and beautiful and mad, who were sometimes almost not there when the air of their cabin was awash with shoot dust. Sol knew that to see them one always had to look from the corner of the eye. He knew also that their talent was a science, though one unknown by most. But Gallan was a simple soul. To him the rackers stank of the unknown, were part of Arcanum, and were best left alone.

Sol enjoyed his Side's discomfort. They were good friends, but the history between them kept a level of subtle tension alive, and their friendship constantly alert.

The Blader decided to take another tour of the warship. He would not be able to sleep now that he knew a racking message had been received, and he had to find a way to kill time until the racker had transcribed. Leki had been gone from him for over twenty days, and to see words muttered by her own sweet mouth, racked by her smooth, webbed hand, would calm his stormy seas.

He paused outside the ship's rear hold wherein the Fader priests waited and offered a brief prayer to the seven gods of the Fade. They were on a mission for those gods, and Sol felt their influence as he prayed. Though absent from the seas they sailed, Venthia sought to calm his tumultuous waters, those angry tides inside. Shore breathed with him. Flaze stoked the fires of his soul, whose heat and flames would burn bright as this journey moved on. Astradus promised solid land beneath him soon, Lillium gave his life meaning with the shadow of his death, and Fresilia waited for him deeper in the ship, in those weapons of war he would inspect once more after this brief visit. Heuthen, god of consciousness, oversaw his perceptions of the world and informed his faith. It was Heuthen who stole away most whenever Sol dispatched an enemy, and his weapon belt held over a hundred notches.

Sol took a deep breath to silence his whispered prayers, then knocked on the door.

It opened almost immediately, as if the priests had been expecting his visit. He entered, the door was closed behind him, and for a while he was the centre of attention. His skin crawled with their gazes. He bowed his head slightly, then noticed the three Spike generals at the far side of the hold.

They didn't tell me, Sol thought. A brief flush of anger increased his heartbeat and throbbed in his ears, but he did his best not to show it. Blader he might be, but he had always been trained to know his place.

'Blader Merry,' one of the priests said. She wore the heavy woollen garments favoured by most younger Fader priests, eschewing the more ceremonial robes worn by older members of the order. Her jacket was well cut, her trousers tucked into fine boots, and a bound leather belt held her jacket closed around her narrow waist. She might have once been attractive, but frequent fasting had given her young face an aged hue, and her eyes were sunken, cheeks drawn. 'Another honour this stormy night. We've just welcomed a visit from the generals.'

'So I see,' Sol said, wincing inwardly. Petulance was even worse than anger.

'Forgive us,' General Cove said, standing and walking around the hold's perimeter. There were three covered objects at its centre, each the size of a recumbent shire. Three Fade priests sat around these objects, heads bowed, praying, paying no attention to the exchange. 'We came to visit briefly with the Engines, and I . . .' He waved a hand, as if dismissing his own apology. 'I saw no point in troubling you with our movements.'

Sol was in charge of the warship. Its captain sailed it and governed the crew, but it was a military charge, an attack ship, and bearing Sol and the forty-nine men of his Blade – as well as the Engines and their attendant priests and Arcanum technicians – was its purpose. It was not the general's flagship. Sol should have been informed of all visitors.

'It's a pleasure to see you,' Sol said, saluting.

'The Engines are safe, as you see,' the priest said. She stood close to Sol's right side, her hand held out and almost holding his arm. 'Secured to the floor, protected, and given homage.'

'All as it should be,' Sol said, smiling and nodding. His gaze was drawn again and again to the covered Engines. He now knew the history of these things' predecessors, deployed to destroy Skythe's insane and false god. He had felt honoured being told the true story only days before, and shocked that the history he had always believed – that the Skythians had destroyed themselves with diseases plucked from Outer lands and weaponised – was to camouflage the awful truth. But such new knowledge also unsettled him. If such a truth could be withheld, and imparted to him only when necessary . . . then what value did that truth hold? Some nights since, he had lain awake, his mind wandering, outlandish tales now possibly holding their own sheen of accuracy. He'd heard the tavern rumours, just like everyone – that the Alderians were the aggressors in the ancient war, not the Skythians and their false god. And many times in the past it had been his job to put down these rumours when they had started to spread. More than one man or woman had died beneath his blade, their version of history truer than his own, yet more forbidden.

But his was not to question why.

'There's been a racking message received,' Sol said, and he saw in the general's eyes that he already knew.

'Yes, from Lechmy Borle,' General Cove said. 'You must be as keen to hear it as us.'

'Yes, General.' His relationship with Leki was frowned upon, even with her being part of Arcanum. Sol sometimes wondered how closely they were both watched.

'Let's pray it's the news we are hoping for.'

'General?'

'Landing points. And perhaps news of their false god.'

'Aeon,' Sol said, noticing the priest's eyes flicker with distaste. That pleased him. His beliefs were solid, but he had always found Fade priests so righteous and superior.

General Cove was two decades older than Sol, his face scarred from battle, experienced in putting down Outer insurrections on the south of Alderia and something of a legend among young Spike soldiers. But to Sol he had become more of a politician than a soldier when he became a general. A trained and proficient fighter, his battles were conducted now behind closed doors, lies their tactics, hidden purposes their aims. Sol fervently hoped that he would never crave such a position when his years wore on, or be faced with accepting the same.

'You have a purpose here, Blader Merry?' One of the other generals had spoken, but Sol was not sure which. It was dark in their corner, air hazed with spiced smoke.

'Simply the Engines,' he said.

'Yours to place, and to consider no more,' General Cove said. His smile remained, but his voice was harder now.

'Of course.'

The general clapped his hands and looked around the room, gathering attention that was already upon him. The three priests around the covered Engines did not move. Sol so craved to see the Engines, but that would come when they landed. Until then, there was time to pass and, when Leki's message was transcribed, a landing to plan.

'Then let's pass the rest of the night usefully. You and your men should sleep. And we have a battle to muse upon.'

One of the priests muttered a prayer so quickly that his words escaped Sol. The priest who had welcomed him in, touched his arm at last, but it was to urge him back out of the room.

The door closed gently behind him, and firmly. Sol did not wait to hear what might be said. He knew his place, and he continued along the gangway until he reached the ladder leading down into the deeper, main hold area.

While the priests prayed over the mysterious devices and his generals plotted, he would inspect the other cargo on this ship. The Engines might be the bearers of magic, but Sol's trust and confidence would always lie in his Blades' most fearsome weapons of war.

There were four handlers awake, all of them busy feeding, watering, stoking, calming, coaxing and priming the Blade's live weapons. The hold echoed with noise – the creaks of the ship and the crash of waves against the hull, counterpointed by the noises from within. Some breathed heavily as they slept. Others groaned. A few growled.

The smell of the weapons hold always reminded Sol of the stench of battle. There was shit and piss, the rankness of old blood, and the constant animal smells that seemed to accompany him everywhere now he was a Blader. Wet fur, rough hide, knotted feathers. He breathed in and felt at home, and one of the handlers glanced up and saw him. She touched her brow, but Sol waved a hand, dismissing her formality.

'Everything well?' he asked.

'The lyons are both sick, but it's only made them more feisty.'

Sol nodded and smiled. The lyons were always feisty, whether sick or well, fat or thin, good-natured or grumpy. Mood rarely altered the heat of the flames they emitted from their heavily toothed mouths.

'And everything else?'

'Sleeping the sleep of the innocent, mostly.' The handler smiled. She was one of his youngest soldiers, Tamma, and her enthusiasm for the weaponry had quickly marked her as a handler. He had once seen her leading a trio of rawpanzies into a house in the south of New Kotrugam harbouring four escaped murderers. Tamma had stood just inside the door issuing orders, and after a few moments the rawpanzies emerged. They were bloodied. Inside, little was recognisable as once belonging to a human being.

'Good,' Sol said. 'They'll need their rest. You, too.'

'I have more food to prepare,' Tamma said. 'I slept yesterday.'

Sol nodded, then walked past her to inspect the hold.

The lyons grumbled in a pen in the corner, metal clamps pulling lips back from their teeth, ivory plugs impeding their fire-glands. They could be trained to restrain their fire breathing, but on board ship it could be deadly to rely on such training. They both watched him pass by with wet, intelligent eyes.

A flight of sparrs was perched in a large mesh cage. Normal birds, trained to home by distance and direction so that they could be directed against enemy emplacements, they would be given disease pellets just before being sent to fly. The pellets were graded so as to release disease into the birds' guts over a certain time. By the time they landed, they would be crawling with eyemelt or coughing death, or Arcanum-engineered afflictions like bad luck, or rampancy. Sol's Blade had used sparrs to deliver a disease to melt the victim's lungs, and an infection to make an enemy fuck the closest thing to him or her, human or animal. Both were as debilitating, but the latter was less deadly.

Disease delivery might aid a protracted campaign, but the next enclosure housed creatures more suited to a short, sharp attack. Six large sparkhawks sat on their perches, hooded and asleep. Sol admired their heavy feet, shining metallic talons, graceful bodies, and was amazed once again at the perfection that the Fade could bestow on some of its creations. These hawks were the fastest creatures in the world, able to approach an enemy from so high in the air that they were out of sight, and then dive so quickly that they were little more than a blur against the blue sky of day, or the starry night. They merited their name from the results of their attacks – sometimes the impact of claws upon body armour or metal helmet was so great, the heat produced by the speed so intense, that the victim's skull was shattered in a shower of sparks.

The birds shifted on their perches with the movement of the ship, leaning in concert so that they remained upright. Even as they slept, Sol could not help thinking that there was more going on in their minds than even the handlers knew.

Scorch ant bombs, termites to undermine enemy defences, gull rats to sneak into enemy emplacements and vomit plague . . . each creature was carefully nurtured by the handlers, trained, cared for and pampered. And it was only because of Arcanum that the Spike were able to use these creatures at all.

The animals drove fear into the most determined of enemies, and Sol knew that fear was perhaps one of the greatest weapons. The story of Dank Ridge was still recounted, by Spike soldiers to family and friends when they were on leave, and by the Ald when another Spike victory was being celebrated. Over the years it had taken on the feel of a fable, and yet Sol had met one or two very old soldiers who claimed that their grandfathers had been there.

One Blade – forty-nine men and their commanding Blader – defending Dank Ridge against over twenty thousand Outer rebels. This was in the time of the Outer Rebellion, when the southern extremes of Alderia were ablaze with revolution, and Outers took advantage of the confusion to try and forge their own autonomous state. The Ald stamped down hard, and as the Outer army swelled, so did their confidence. One state after another fell before them, and then they marched north towards the Harcrassyan Mountains across the centre of Alderia. Caught unawares by such blatant aggression, three Spike Blades posted in that region fell beneath the onslaught. The story went that the Outers marched on, wearing the decapitated heads of their Spike victims on spears protruding above their own heads. Until, that was, they reached Dank Ridge. A narrow shoulder spanning one peak and the next, it was a vital route through the mountains and into the plains to the north . . . and, from there, New Kotrugam itself.

Blader Sugg and his Blade had heard of the massacres to the south, and had two days to prepare.

The battle was fierce, unrelenting, brutal, merciless. The Outers sent in wave upon wave, and Blader Sugg and his soldiers fought back with every means at their disposal. And in those two days, they had prepared more than weapon stacks and defensive structures.

Each telling of the story elaborated more and more on the types of animals they used, and how. But it was certain that this was the first battle during which Spike soldiers employed nature to aid their fight, and the effect was staggering. By the time reinforcements arrived three days later, ten thousand Outers lay dead across the ridge and scattered down the sheer slopes into the valleys on both sides. Their blood painted the landscape red. Their bloated corpses were still bursting with poisons and gases as the new Spike soldiers arrived, and in the face of fresh troops the traumatised Outers fled. They would be pursued, caught and slaughtered, but not before the stunning victory was celebrated.

Blader Sugg had died in the battle, along with most of his Blade. But six women and four men remained alive, standing true behind mountains of dead Outers. Their eyes wide, their weapons dripping blood and gore. And they saluted Fade and the Ald as they jeered their fleeing enemies.

Sol enjoyed the story and celebrated it, knowing at the same time that it had doubtless been exaggerated with each telling. But Dank Ridge was undeniably the source of the Spike's increasing reliance on such living weapons and, from that point on, fear of the Spike had been so rich that rebellion had been unknown, and more minor skirmishes brief, and decisive.

This war they were sailing for now might be the truest test, the real thing. He shivered slightly, watching the hawks lean into the ship's sway. He was unsure whether it was fear or excitement, because sometimes to a Spike soldier – and

285

especially a Blader – in the face of a fight they both felt the same.

Dank Ridge had also been the birthplace of Arcanum. The several soldiers from Sugg's Blade who had mastered control of the wildlife had first been exposed as dabblers in arcane arts, and then feted for what they had achieved. Both feared and revered, their hidden talents had been nurtured by the Spike, and this had inspired many more soldiers to reveal their interests. Arcanum was created, soldiers were seconded. The Ald, grudgingly approving such a move, could hardly deny its efficacy.

Forbidden magic was never touched, but its fringes were stroked, and sometimes lifted.

This was how Sol had met Lechmy Borle.

He walked around the hold one more time, nodding to the handlers, and then left them to their ministrations. He was an intelligent man, but did not pretend to understand much of what Arcanum and those associated with it could do. It was now its own branch of the Spike, though these handlers were Arcanum trained.

It's like lifting the veil, Leki had told him once, soon after they first met. *The world you know is an oil painting. The most beautiful, incredible, detailed and complex oil painting you've ever seen. At Arcanum we lift the surface and observe how the brush strokes work, analyse the composition of the paint. Decide how a dozen colours and a thousand touches make up one effect.*

And the canvas? Sol had asked.

Oh no, Leki had said, shaking her head, smiling, but deadly serious. *We never go that deep.*

Back on deck, Sol relished the elements' assault. Rain lashed across the deck, blown by a gale, and stung the exposed skin of his face. The ship rocked from wave to wave, its sharpened and strengthened bow cutting a path through the ocean that was doing its best to kill them all. The oil painting of the stormy night sea was vicious, but Sol could not see below the surface.

You have to look a certain way, Leki had said. *See with different eyes. And you, my lover, are a fighter, not an artist.*

He had not taken that as a rebuke. She had scratched at his chest, then submerged below the bath's surface, where she had remained for some time until all thoughts of paintings and canvases were brushed aside. Falling in love with an amphy definitely had its advantages.

Don't the Engines touch the canvas? he had asked Leki a few days before her departure for Skythe. She had been preparing her equipment, a meagre collection of valves, gears and other small devices that could be concealed about her person. Arcanum had instructed her in racking. She'd said that it would help them stay in touch, but he could already feel a distance growing between them.

The Engines are *the canvas*, she'd said. She paused, and when Sol went to her and pressed his hands against her shoulders, he could feel the tension in her knotted muscles. That was when he knew that everything had changed. Arcanum had gone deep.

He staggered slightly as he made his way towards the stern, leaning into the tilting deck like the sparkhawks below. The sea thrust them up at the sky, the sky forced them down into the sea and the ship rode out the storm.

Three Spike worked at priming steam valves for the rifles and pistols that some soldiers would carry into battle. The fire pit was contained in a heavy iron pot, insulated from the deck by layers of gravel between sheets of charred wood, propped, and surrounded with a dozen water-filled buckets ready for any accidental spillage. The ship's crew hated any hint of open fire on board, but they also understood the need. Water boiled, steam was captured, empty valves were loaded and sealed – their spirals bound, ventings barred – and the primed valves were collected in a wooden chest. It was hot, exhausting work, and the three Spike soldiers had stripped to their underwear.

Sol hefted a rifle leaning against a bulkhead and examined its workings. It was cleaned and oiled as if new, metal and wooden parts melded and merged perfectly. A work of art. It was also heavy and cumbersome, and the need to reload both shot and valve between each use made it effective only for long-distance assault. There were pistols for close use, but they too were only one-shot weapons. Sol had always viewed the steam arms as shock weapons, used for surprise and initial assault. Anything after that was crossbow and arrow, and, close in, sword and dagger. Other Bladers called him old-fashioned, but his Blade's kill rate for various campaigns proved his wisdom.

Nodding to the three sweating soldiers, he passed them by and leaned against the stern railing. He could see some of the other ships, keeping a good distance apart in case of collisions. The closest was to starboard, the generals' flagship keeping pace with Sol's warship, ready for the generals to make the journey back across in the boat still tied to his ship's deck. A guide rope connected the two vessels. It sliced through waves, flapping up, straightening in a haze of spray. Beyond the flagship were two more, barely shadows in the stormy night. They were only visible because of the lamps burning at the tips of each mast, lit on the ships' captains' insistence to help avoid catastrophic accidents.

In the night behind them, braving seas already sailed, came more ships. Nineteen in total, each carrying one Blade and its associated weaponry. The largest military force to set sail from the shores of Alderia in a generation.

Suddenly the sea was not so furious, and the angry sky not so threatening. Sol expanded with pride. He gripped the railing and started into the storm, daring it to take him. But it did not dare.

'Blader Merry,' a voice said. It shook. 'Sol. They've transcribed.'

'Gallan,' Sol said without turning around.

'Shall I read it, or . . .?' Sol turned and leaned casually against the railing. Gallan was wrapped in a heavy coat, soaking wet already, wide-eyed at Sol's obvious defiance of the storm.

'Please,' Sol said. *Words whispered by my Leki*, he thought, watching Gallan opening a small notebook and trying to shield it against the weather.

'*Aeon risen*,' Gallan read, his voice slow and measured. He swallowed before continuing. '*This was always its scheme. Trying to track. Watching for Kolts. Will send racking again when enemy located. Fade help us all.*'

Aeon risen, Sol thought, and he closed his eyes, trying to remove himself and shut out the storm. The Engines suddenly seemed so much more important.

'Fade help us all,' Gallan repeated. 'Sol . . . what will we find there?'

'It doesn't matter!' Sol said sharply. 'It's not our job to second-guess. Whatever we find, we triumph over. Aeon, Kolts, *whatever*. With the gods of the Fade behind us, how can we not?'

'How can we not?' Gallan echoed. But he looked more scared than comforted.

'Tell the generals.'

'They already know.'

'Good,' Sol said. *We defeated Aeon last time*, he thought. But that was hundreds of years before. And, impostor god though it was, if this second coming had always been its scheme, what might Aeon have planned over such a long time?

But a Blader could not be defeatist, even to himself.

'Fuck Aeon,' Sol said. 'If we fear its name, what about when we confront it? Gallan?'

Gallan nodded. 'Fuck Aeon,' he said.

'And that is our mantra when we land,' Sol said. 'Spread the word.'

'Yes, Sol.' He turned and rushed below deck again, leaving Sol standing alone against the storm.

Another day and they would be on dry land again. Despite what he had just heard – and, being a soldier, perhaps because of it – Sol was looking forward to setting foot on Skythe for the very first time.

Chapter 15

frozen

Time was nebulous. Venden was unsure whether a day had passed since Aeon's rising, or a year. His perception flitted from the violent seas in the south, to frozen wastes in the north that he had never suspected existed. All the while Aeon observed, and the six-century gap in its knowledge was being filled. It saw the lessening of Skythe that had so obsessed Venden. It understood the disruption in evolution, the way that nature had been corrupted beyond and around suitable forms, following random paths that seemed to bear no relevance to environment.

What is your intention? Venden wondered. He had felt, briefly, his own body coming apart to clothe Aeon's strange bones, and now the fate of what was left – mind, soul, consciousness – was uncertain. Before, there had been life and death. Now there seemed to be something more.

Over time – moments, or months – Venden came to realise that Aeon was acting like a child. It moved across the landscape from here to there, observing, examining, absorbing information as it went and seeking more each and every moment. There was a restrained excitement to it, and also a deep sadness that Venden thought might well have been his own.

Only once did a sudden reaction shock him with its extremes. They approached one of the old Engines – Venden knew of three on Skythe, and suspected there were the remains of more buried or hidden away from view – and Aeon recoiled. He felt its disgust, and something deeper that he had no wish to sense.

Fear. Aeon had passed the Engine and been afraid.

Time and distance drifted by . . .

And, at last, Venden began to sense something forming in the risen god's mind that could only have been purpose. It went down into the land, past a lake of fading fire and into the frozen heart of Skythe. There it settled for a while.

As yet, Venden could not tell what this purpose might be.

Juda spent some time scouring the Engine's surface before finding his way inside. The entrance was not where he had found it a day before. He was certain of this, just as he was certain that everything had changed since then. The skies were darker, and the stars seemed less willing to shine their way through. The land was quieter as everything waited for what would come next. It had begun to snow. And the arrow pinning him to the here and now was feeling more like a guide than ever before. It pointed the way, and Juda followed.

Inside, the Engine welcomed his presence. It should have been dark as the void, but smears of light were seeping from somewhere deeper in the Engine where he could not go, skeins of illumination drifting like exotic sea creatures in an ocean of calm. The bodies of those old dead Fade priests spun like memories stirred by his presence. Amongst them, the few dregs he had not managed to collect on his last visit.

'And this is where I belong,' Juda said again. Not even echoes answered him back; the Engine swallowed all. Perhaps his voice would become an echo in a thousand years, or ten thousand, surprising some other seeker of magic who might venture in here and find . . .

What? His bones? No, not that, because he had no intention of dying. Not here, and not elsewhere. The slayer's arrow could not kill him, nor its poison, and so he would embrace the miracle of his survival. He had so much left to do.

The Engine seemed larger on the inside than the outside. He drifted, feet sometimes touching the floor or walls, sometimes not. The light broke against him like waves, fragmenting and crawling around his body and across his clothes to collect again beyond him, and continue on its way. His mind was awash with thoughts of how to work the Engine. Perhaps deeper down there was a power source, but he could not edge himself deeper. Maybe it was buried in the land itself, probing metallic fingers through soil and rock as it sought the magic it had been brought here to fire.

Or it could have been that magic was always free, and the Engine was a prison.

As he drifted, he became aware of how little he actually knew. About the source of magic, how it had been nurtured, brought here, implemented, controlled, harnessed. He would have cried if he had not already wasted his tears on pain, so he brought his hand to his wound and pressed, welcoming fresh agonies.

'How?' he asked, and there was no answer. 'Crex Wry, whatever you are . . . If you want me to set you aflame, then tell me where to find the ember!'

Nothing.

Delayed tiredness suddenly washed over him. He had been running for a long time, and although the dreg had salved his wound and absorbed the effects of the slayer's poison, his left side was soaked with blood. Juda floated against a solid wall that felt smooth as metal, but warmer. He rested against it, assumed it must be the floor, and rolled onto his right side so that the protruding arrow was not touching anything.

I'll only rest a while, he thought. *I'll sleep away the last of the poison, and then when I next wake—*

But he did not sleep.

The shapes came for him through the darkness. Twisting, questing shapes, glinting metallic and yet flexing like the lithest of limbs. They glided, and even though they seemed to touch nothing, he could still hear the whisper of their movement through the air. *Talking to me*, Juda thought, and the first shape arced around as if inspecting him.

He struggled to sit up, but one of the shapes came in and pressed against his bad shoulder. Its touch was shocking – warm, hard, yet seemingly moulded to the place it had touched so that he felt complete contact. It pushed gently, and Juda could offer no resistance.

He smelled magic on these things. His heart stuttered with shock, and the limbs – four of them now, each independent yet acting together – drew back slightly. He gasped, started breathing more easily. The limbs came close again.

One of them clasped the arrowhead and snapped it off.

Juda screamed. Even though the pain had been muffled by the magical dreg, it came in from the distance and smashed home. His skull rang with it. He flung his head back and screamed again, and then the arrow was grasped from behind and tugged back through his body. Its splintered shaft ripped skin and flesh and scraped bone, and the inside of the Engine suddenly lit up. Juda saw his parents standing there, enacting a familiar argument from his youth before his father's hand lashed out across his mother's face; he saw Rhelli Saal, sitting at a table in a tavern and picking up another jug of beer; Bon and Leki watched him, leaning over his bound body as the sun went down behind them. Something in Leki's eyes made him look twice, but even then he did not see.

Light faded to darkness. True unconsciousness carried Juda away. As he fell, he could feel those limbs tending and fixing him, and the dregs of magic they applied had a touch he had never, ever felt before.

Saving me, he thought. He wondered why.

Venden saw what the once-beating heart of Skythe had become. Where fires had roared and molten rock had flowed, there now lay a frozen landscape of stilled movement. Trapped in a moment, Skythe's foundations were a creaking, ice-encrusted remnant of what they had once been. Aeon moved slowly through these caverns to memory. And as it did so, it remembered.

Like a human's final heartbeat, Skythe's history flipped backward to a time before humanity in an instant. Mountains rose, fought and fell. Seas eroded, volcanoes erupted and built new lands around them, the world turned and became unrecognisable from the world Venden knew, or knew of. Alderia and Skythe were joined as one mass. Rivers were the huge continent's arteries, and there was no difference to the water if it flowed north or south of where future seas would rise. No distinction between lands, no borders, no false gods.

No gods at all.

Aeon walked the land, and remembered its movement like an adult might recall his or her first steps in the world on their own. Brave and confident, facing fresh possibilities as if they would only ever result in a good outcome, not bad. It passed across ocean floors, stepped through mountain ranges, and here and there were vistas that Venden almost recognised. Forests stretching as far as the eye could see, though these trees were larger than any he had ever witnessed. Mountain ranges shifting beneath colossal, timeless forces, rising and falling like ocean waves slowed a trillion times. Strange creatures the likes of which he had never seen, though in some of them he could perceive features that he might recognise in a million years.

A larger shape, a shadow, passing across a gap between two huge trees. Wings, heavy legs, and what could only have been a face turned his way.

There were lakes of molten rock, coughing frequent geysers that threw fire bombs across the desolate landscape. The land was in flux, birthing the future with every gaseous gasp. Aeon passed across the upheaval on long legs that barely touched, and at the other side stood scores of monoliths of cooling rock that touched the sky, smoking, a couple still glowing. Rain beat down and rose again as steam. Between them, a shape moved back and forth like a snake. This shape was as large as Aeon, its skin scaled and fine. It moved with grace and purpose. Aeon paused before it.

The two ancient creatures conversed. Living Aeon's timeless memories with it, Venden could understand the importance of the conversation, and the urgency.

The snake-creature went one way, Aeon the other.

Through tumultuous landscapes, close to where a sea was crashing down mile-high cliffs, Aeon paused to touch a rock. The rock was larger than Aeon, and it moved with a fluid grace that belied its solid appearance. Its eyes were golden fires in its rough-cast face. They grew paler as Aeon and it conversed, and then it flowed into the ocean.

Aeon moved on, and its memory followed the journey.

More creatures came and went, as inexplicable as Aeon.

What we cannot understand, we call gods, Venden thought. They all had a part in some tumultuous place, and Venden understood that these beings were present at the beginning of history. They observed the shaping of the world, and yet he could not glean whether the world was here because of them, or they were here because of the world. Perhaps that was something no one could never know.

Down in Skythe's frozen depths, Aeon shivered at these memories, and Venden did not know why. Sadness, or fear?

He remembered with Aeon, wondering what their purpose together might be.

And then Aeon asked him to speak.

Bon woke from nightmares to sparks, and the gentle shushing of water on a lake's shore.

Beyond the fire Leki sat staring at him. Her contemplative expression did not change, as if she had not even noticed him waking. In her hands she nursed Juda's pistol.

'When did you steal that?' he asked.

'He dropped it.' Still her face did not shift. She was neither benevolent nor threatening, just cold. Empty.

'Thinking about shooting me?'

'Yes.'

Bon blinked, frowning away that final image of what had been his wife. *She fell and died, that's all*, he thought, but of course that was not all. Milian was more than she seemed, he was sure of that now. As was Venden. And as was Leki.

'But I can't,' she continued. 'Shoot you. I can't.' She looked down at the pistol in her hands as if surprised at its presence, then slipped it into her jacket pocket.

'If you wanted to kill me—'

'I don't want to kill you, Bon.'

'But you'd have shot me yesterday.'

'If you'd interrupted the racking. But . . .'

'What?' Bon stood, knees clicking. He did not take his eyes from Leki. *She's so beautiful*, he thought, an idea about another woman that had not touched him since Milian's fall.

'Now we need to move.' She stood and started kicking soil and dust over the failing fire.

'Tracking Aeon?'

'Yes. What else is there to do?'

What else, Bon thought, because he did not know. They had banished him to Skythe with the sense that his aimless life was not moving on, but ending. No hope of progress, no thought to better himself or make good out of bad. Too weak even to consider killing himself, his future had stretched out as an unknown land that he had no desire to explore. Then Leki, and Juda saving him from the slayers, and whispers of Venden, and suddenly he was a new man.

Now, everything had changed once more. Venden was dead. That confused Bon, because his son had been dead to him for years. Their brief reunion had yielded nothing to sate the grief, and Bon was waiting for the mourning to strike in once more, as hard as it had been picking at him since Venden's disappearance. He'd had no opportunity to know his son.

'What else?' Bon said. He turned his back on Leki and walked into the bushes to piss. This morning she was not the woman she had been to him yesterday. Perhaps today he would meet her anew.

And Aeon was abroad, striding somewhere across the Skythian landscape with its aims obscure, its intentions unknown. That terrified him, but excited him as well. Like a ghost from the past, Aeon had returned to haunt the Ald and every lie they had ever told against it.

As he pissed, Bon thought of Leki's comment that she

would have shot him yesterday. If he'd interrupted her strange racking, she would have pulled Juda's pistol and fired at him. He could not picture her face as she performed that terrible act. But he reminded himself that she was a stranger to him once again.

'I'm ready to leave,' Leki said behind him, and Bon thought perhaps he sensed a pleading to her tone. *She wants me to go with her*, he thought.

Buttoning his trousers, he realised that there really was nothing more for him to do. But his aim in travelling with Leki was suddenly very clear – he would do his best to protect Aeon from the forces Leki was marshalling against it. And not only because of what he believed about it, and magic, and the Kolts. That was a surface reason, but his emotional drive was closer, and deeper.

Venden had become a part of Aeon, and perhaps there was a glimmer of his son still there.

'I'm ready too,' he said, returning and smiling at Leki. She smiled back. *I could have loved her*, he thought. But she had become too much of a stranger to love.

'I hope you're feeling energetic.' Leki started running.

They skirted the lake, and on the other side Leki picked up Aeon's trail. She jogged into a thick woodland, scarred here and there with cracked and tumbled trees. The fresh flesh of broken trunks glimmered with morning dew, and small mammals and birds congregated around these areas of destruction. They sniffed and sang.

A new day seemed to have imbued Leki with fresh confidence, and she followed Aeon's trail unerringly through the extensive woodland, never taking the wrong direction even if some footprints were large distances apart. Bon wondered whether she was using any other arcane means to track, but he did not want to know. He followed, and for the whole morning neither of them spoke.

When the midday sun was high overhead and its heat filtered down through the heavy tree canopy, Leki stopped at a stream and filled her water bottles. Bon did the same upstream from her, glancing sidelong at her distorted reflection.

'We're being followed,' she whispered.

Bon resisted the temptation to jump up and turn around.

'Skythians. Since mid-morning.'

'How do you know?' he said.

'I just do. I hear them, but I only know one word in three. Their language isn't as I've been taught. It's regressed more than we believed.'

'Or it's advanced,' Bon said, believing that much more likely. 'More than you Ald bastards know.'

'They're no threat,' Leki said, but her doubt was obvious.

'We're following their risen god that our ancestors murdered,' Bon said. 'Of course they're no threat.'

Leki did not respond, but she sat beside the stream and leaned forward, feet and hands in the flow of water. It parted and splashed around her limbs, and Bon could see the webbing between her fingers catching water as she stretched her digits. She closed her eyes.

Bon stood and stretched, casually looking back the way they had come. He could see no signs of pursuit, but he did not doubt Leki's observation. He tried to put himself in those Skythians' place – their murdered god risen, perhaps a surprise to them, or perhaps the manifestation of a prophecy; and two strangers following in the god's footsteps.

'The word is out,' Leki said softly. Bon turned, and she was pulling herself from the stream, dragging herself through the short grass as if dreadfully weakened by her efforts. She sat up and stared at him, eyes wide. 'They know of Aeon. All of them. All of Skythe.'

'How can you know that?'

'The waters are rich with the rumour.' She stood unsteadily, wiping her hands on her coat as if they'd been dipped in something unpleasant. 'How can word have spread so quickly?'

'You have your methods,' Bon said.

'But not the Skythians. They're regressed, less capable than the most distant Outers.'

'Or more capable than the Ald knows. And able to hide it.'

'No,' she said, shaking her head. 'Not after all this time. They're scratching an existence, almost animals. There's no *intelligence* there any more. We'd have known.'

'You've studied Skythe?'

She blinked at him softly, and he could see her thoughts turning. 'A little.'

'A little,' he echoed. 'Your Ald arrogance is . . .' He shook his head, unable to verbalise his frustration, his growing hatred. 'Can't you admit for a moment that you might be wrong about these people?'

'But they were all but wiped out.'

'By *you*!' Bon said. 'But there are always survivors. Even from what you did to them. Survivors with a whole history behind them. Wise enough to keep low. Keep out of view.'

'We should go.' She looked past him, back the way they had come. 'We should be careful.'

Bon followed her across the stream and deeper into the forest. He soon stopped looking behind him, because the Skythians would only be seen if they wanted to be seen. He wondered if they knew what was coming, with the Spike and Leki's Arcanum.

He wondered if he should tell them.

*   *   *

301

It grew colder throughout that afternoon; then, when they stopped to hunt and eat, it started to snow.

They had been following Aeon's tracks all day, but a sense of hopelessness had settled over Bon. He could see the prints, acknowledge that they were going in the right direction, but still he became convinced that Aeon would not be found unless it desired to be found. There seemed to be no direction to the routes they were following. They left the forest and climbed a steep hillside, emerging onto a ridge between two hills. Before them, a slope of shale led down into a deep, dark valley, and they followed the great slicks of fresh shale movement that Leki said marked Aeon's progress. In the valley there were squat trees, home to angry monkeys that threw spiked nuts at the invaders, and crawling plants that seemed attracted by their body heat. After some time searching, Bon followed Leki back up another slope of shale to the ridge they had only just left. There seemed to be no purpose to the valley visit.

And that set Bon wondering as to Aeon's purpose, and whether something so removed from humankind would even have one. Leki and the Ald feared revenge, but perhaps that was because that would be exactly what *they* would seek were they Aeon. Bon found contemplation of its godhood difficult; it was a physical presence, he had seen it, he could have touched it, and so it had a biology and a build that made it a creature. Yet it was so far removed from everything he had ever known that its intentions must surely be obscure to mere human consideration.

They should simply leave it alone. But it was not in humanity's nature to do so. Anything wonderful would be subject to scrutiny. And something wonderful to one person would be horrible to another.

They crossed the ridge and made camp on a hillside

sheltered from the strengthening wind, and while Leki hunted for their supper, Bon built a fire.

In the crackle of flames, he heard the voice of his son.

North and down into the cold.

Bon gasped, leaning forward and scorching his hand on the sparking embers. He jumped back. The voice had carried such weight and had come from so far that he had no doubt, from that first moment, that it had been his son communicating with him. This was no hallucination brought on by the exertions of his journey.

North and down into the cold.

Leki returned with a rabbit, throwing Bon a curious glance as he splashed water onto his hand. The burn was mild, hairs scorched into blackened nubs.

'Knot in the wood popped,' he said, and she started skinning and gutting her kill. She had snow settled on her eyebrows.

They ate, then Bon sat back against a tree and tried to shelter. The snow was heavier now, dulling sound and turning the night ghostly still. It settled almost immediately, the ground already cold, and soon there was a good covering. The fire spat and sizzled as heavy flakes died above it.

Bon and Leki did not speak. He could sense Leki's frustration as she sat away from the fire on a large boulder, watching for their Skythian pursuers. There had been no sign of them all day.

I know where to go, he thought. And with that came another realisation – that Venden was of Aeon now, and Aeon was directing him. He shivered, and it was nothing to do with the weather.

'I think we should go north,' Bon said early the next morning. The snow continued, and it was now up to their ankles. It was colder than he had ever known it. Wrapped up in all the clothes he had, still Bon wished for more.

Leki seemed unconcerned about the weather; though she wore fewer layers than him she did not shiver, and neither did her face appear chilled. Bon almost asked whether it was due to her Arcanum training. But there was something in her eyes he did not like.

'Why do you say that?' she asked.

'Just a thought. It seems somewhere it might go, and—'

'But the trail was leading west, generally. Diversions here and there, like the shale valley. But west.' She grew cold, suspicious. Maybe she could smell the lie on him. *More Arcanum training*, he thought, smiling softly.

'What's funny?'

'Nothing,' Bon said. 'Everything's sad, and sometimes the only reaction to that is to smile. I thought perhaps we . . . you and I . . .' He shrugged. 'And now you seem ready to kill me at a moment's notice.'

'I don't want to kill you, Bon. I just want everything to work out well. Everything. So why do you want to go north?'

'It's just a feeling,' he said. 'Just an idea that . . . Aeon has been down for six hundred years. Now it's back, and it might know that south is the sea, and those communities. It'll want peace. Solitude. North is unknown to us, but perhaps not to Aeon.' It did not sound convincing, and he could see that she did not believe him.

But she did not appear eager to torture out the truth.

'Perhaps you're right,' she said. 'Maybe with something like this, following a hunch is better than following trails that might lead nowhere.'

'The trails feel cold to me already.'

Leki stared at him for a moment, and Bon guessed she

had felt the same. 'Worth a try,' she said. 'Perhaps we'll pick up a fresher trail. But first, breakfast.'

Bon nodded and smiled. 'I'm going for some privacy.' He turned and stomped away through the snow. The heavy flakes floated like bird down in the motionless air. They were fat and wet, and clung to his clothes, hair and eyelashes. He was swimming through snow. Even though the sun was a smudge above the eastern horizon, visibility was low, and just out of sight there could have been anything. *They could be watching me even now*, he thought. Though he had not been scared of Skythians up to now, he found the idea disconcerting. Their god had returned. What that might do to a people, he could not know.

He retraced his footprints back to their camp, even though they were already half obliterated, and paused to watch Leki. He liked the way she moved. He found grace in her, and certainty, and even behind her Arcanum training she was still her own person.

Now she was on her knees, and Bon could see the steam valves planted in a square in the snow.

He was across the clearing in four bounds, and he kicked the shoot dust tube from her hands. It scattered dust in lazy spirals as it flipped into the snow, disappearing when it struck the ground. The dust confused the air for a moment – full of snow, open to sunlight. Then the blanket of flakes obscured where it had ever been.

Bon turned to Leki, but she was not there. *Splashed with shoot dust?* he thought, and then he was shoved in the centre of his back, head snapping back, falling forward onto his chest beside the square of steam valves. He grunted and rolled, kicking up and back blindly and feeling his right foot connect with something soft.

Leki grunted. He looked for her, trying to distinguish

movement behind the waves of snow. A shadow shifted to his right, and then Leki darted in from the left, so fast that he could barely track her movements.

Got to twist and roll and stand up before one of us—

Leki sat astride his chest and pushed him down, pressing something cold and sharp against his throat. She stared down at him, lips tight. She did not even seem to be breathing hard. The knife at his throat shifted, and he felt a trickle of warmth down his neck.

'So kill me,' Bon said. Leki's hair hung around her face, and snow fell past her head, into his eyes. She looked like some daemon out of a child's story book.

For a moment, Bon thought she would do just that. And why not? For all the claims that she had no wish to harm him, she was Arcanum, and loyal to the Ald. Whatever her personal beliefs – and she claimed atheism, though he had his doubts – she had her masters to think of, and obey. And he was obstructing her purpose. Preventing her from sending her message, in which she would have told the approaching Spike army to head north.

But Leki leaned back and sheathed her knife in one smooth motion. Then she stood and hauled Bon up beside her, one-handed, thumping him back down into a sitting position in the snow. She pointed at his face, tilting her head in a warning gesture. No words.

Bon sat still and watched her gather the steam valves. Then she kicked through the snow until she found the shoot dust tube, examined it, tucked it back into her jacket seam.

'So what now?' he asked.

'Now I leave you,' she said. 'I have to go south, to meet the Spike as they come inland.'

'Come with me,' Bon said. He could sense her surprise at the emotion in his voice. And, in truth, it had surprised him.

Not quite pleading, it had been an exhortation to stay with him, because the idea of being parted from Leki sent him into a spin. To watch her leave would tug at his heart. He was convinced that he could never love a servant of the Ald, but she was not like anyone he had ever met.

'Anywhere near that thing will be dangerous,' she said.

'Not if it doesn't mean harm.'

'I mean from what will happen when the Engines fire up.'

The idea heavily between them. Snow almost obscured Leki for a moment, then he saw her again. Nothing had changed.

'Wouldn't you serve Alderia more by coming to see what it wants?' he asked. 'The Ald see only fear and hatred and danger, and they answer with the same. So, run to them with nothing, or come with me and see.'

'See what?'

'Perhaps wonders,' Bon said.

'I don't believe in gods. *Any* gods.'

'Nor do I. But I believe in things that none of us can understand, and for many that is what makes a god.'

'Your dead son has blinded you to what's happening, Bon.'

'No. My son died years ago, and that is the single thing that opened my eyes.

'I have to tell them,' Leki said, but her hesitation was clear.

'Come with me,' Bon said again. 'Not far. I don't think it's far.'

'How do you know?'

He ignored the question. 'Come with me.'

'How do you know?'

'Come, and I'll tell you.' And he would.

Leki brushed snow from her jacket, a futile gesture. She retied her hair into a gentle braid, sighing heavily.

'My husband sails with the Spike,' she said.

'Husband.' Bon's heart sank.

Leki did not name him, and did not elaborate. But she nodded, and said she would go with him.

They left camp. Bon knew Leki less, and was more fascinated with her, with every moment that passed. The bond between them had changed, but remained unbroken. He was glad they faced this adventure together.

Chapter 16
deep

Sol Merry's hopes for an easy landing on Skythe were dashed several miles from shore.

In their preparations to sail they had made a point of placing a sailor from the prison ships on board each attack vessel. They'd hoped that such knowledge might enable them to avoid troublesome areas of ocean, where the deep pirates were known to operate and decapuses stalked. And, so far, that idea had worked well. They had sailed a curving route from Alderia, heading in towards Skythe to the east of the main islands of the Duntang Archipelago. Amongst those islands was where the largest, oldest of the deep pirates dwelled, surrounded by evidence of their plunder and the displayed bodies of their many victims. But in the open ocean, spinebacks were the greater danger.

Their navigators had ploughed a careful path through violent seas. The Spike were always at the ready, but as they drew closer to Skythe, Sol could sense the relaxing of guards. *We're not there yet!* he'd screamed at his Blade over dinner, and they armed up and went on deck for drills. The deck guns needed easing and greasing, gears and actions being constantly assaulted by the aggressive saltwater, and they unpacked and rewrapped their various hardweaponry. Sol walked amongst them. He commanded respect and loyalty, and he also treated his soldiers as friends while maintaining the distance of command. That afforded him the greatest respect of all.

And then the first shout from the skynest, and the attack began.

Sol had already agreed that should a spineback get amongst the fleet he would cede command of his Blade to the big prison ship sailor Drake for the duration of the assault. As soon as the alert was sounded, Sol nodded to Drake and watched as the man sprang into action.

Shouting orders, dashing back and forth across deck, signalling to the wheelman and the lookout up in the skynest, rushing from one harpoon gun to the next, Drake was a revelation. For the bulk of the journey he had remained a surly drunk, slouching on the steps leading up to the wheelhouse and abusing anyone who came near. He'd instigated several scuffles with Spike soldiers that had left him bloodied and battered. Now, he was a sailor again.

Soldiers strained to see the spineback, a creature of legend to many who had never even seen the sea before this expedition. A little fear, but mostly excitement, thrummed across the ship. But then Drake froze close to the railing, and ran for the mast. As he scrambled quickly up to the skynest, Sol searched for what he had seen.

There was a shape to the west, a wave amongst waves that was cutting the wrong way. Though distant, Sol could already hear the impact of the shape upon the surging sea, and great showers of foamy spray erupted at regular intervals.

'Spineback,' he muttered. 'It is. Must be.'

Gallan arrived by his side, shielding his eyes. 'What's happening?'

Sol did not reply. Instead he looked up for Drake, and saw the sailor busy signalling with other ships using a rig of coloured flags. His hands moved quickly, flags rose and flapped, fell again, furling and unfurling as if in defiance of the direction and strength of breeze. Then Drake swung over the side of the skynest and slid down a rigging rope, hands moving too fast to see as they went from grip to grip.

'Something worse than a spineback,' Sol said. Drake leaped from the rope and slid to a halt a few feet from Sol, a harpoon setting receiving his attention. He was sweating. He looked scared.

'Drake!' Sol called.

'Deep pirate. One of the old ones.'

'Deep pirate?' Gallan said. 'I thought they only hunted in the Archipelago.'

'In and around,' Drake said. He dashed to another harpoon mounting and started switching gears, working mechanisms.

'But you took us this far east to—' Gallan protested.

'It doesn't matter,' Sol cut in, and Drake glanced at him, one eyebrow raised. 'What do we do?' Sol asked.

'Hope it's alone,' Drake said.

'But you've fought them before,' Sol said. 'Seen them away. You know what to do.'

Drake stood back from the harpoon and nodded to the sailor manning it. He placed his hands on his hips and looked out to sea, where spray clouds threw up smears of rainbow light as the deep pirate made its way towards them.

'We can inconvenience it,' he said. 'A force this size, this many ships, this many harpoons . . .' He shrugged, rugged face haunted by fear. 'We can hope it's not too determined.'

He looked from Sol to Gallan and back again. 'Now, will you let me do my job?'

Sol nodded, and Drake darted away across the deck to the next gun.

'Sparkhawks,' Gallan said. 'And if it comes close enough, perhaps we can get some dart worms into it.'

'I think this is Drake's fight,' Sol said. 'Him and those like him.'

Across the fleet, flag signals were passed back and forth, and then the Spike attack ships turned towards the west, bow-on to the imminent assault. The sound of the sea striking hulls changed, booms swung, sails emptied and billowed again.

The deep pirate's trail vanished.

'It'll come up from deep down!' Drake called. 'This bastard's already carrying a few broken harpoons, I'll bet.' He walked back and forth beside the ship's wooden railing, then froze and pointed across the waves. 'There.'

Sol could see nothing at first that distinguished one area of ocean from another. Drake was pointing at a ship a quarter of a mile south of them, its strong hull carving at an angle across the waves and booming, booming with each impact. Then he saw that the waves just before it were already breaking, and he could not hold back a gasp as the deep pirate emerged.

Rising straight up from the depths, the shape powered from the sea and seemed to hang for impossible moments in the air, a sculpture of nightmares made real. What Sol had heard about these monsters, and the few images he had seen, meant that he could distinguish the pirate from its mount, though where one began and the other ended was not so clear. The deep pirates rode a range of sea creatures, from red dolphins to much larger animals. This one attacking the Spike fleet rode a decapus. That in itself displayed the pirate's age, size and standing. And it was almost as large as the decapus, which only added to the surreal horror of the sight.

The pirate had human qualities merged with the worst aspects of the sea. Bare, thick torso spotted with shellfish, a large head with shockingly human features, long flowing hair which was said to consist of poisonous fronds, long limbs that ended in claws ten times larger than the most monstrous crab's, and thick legs that parted into powerful tentacles, each of them suckered and spiked. Its scale made it even more awful – ten times the size of a human, it was a blight on reality.

The decapus beneath it was a vivid red, its tentacles longer and more deadly, its beak clacking, and its huge eyes reflecting sunlight with an alien regard.

Even from this far away, Sol and everyone else on his ship could hear the monster's screech.

'By all the gods, how does something like that come to be?' Gallan said at Sol's side. 'A creature from the Pit, for sure.'

'It's no Pit creature,' Sol said. 'Just another challenge from the gods.'

Several gusts of steam drifted up from the pirate's target as harpoons were fired. Their impacts went unseen. The vessel lurched across a wavetop and the decapus curled its tentacles up around the bow, the pirate climbing its back and clamping around its head with its own limbs. The deep pirate screeched again, and then lurched sideward with surprising grace as another weapon was discharged, dodging the harpoon.

The pirate lashed with its arms, and something on the ship's deck came apart in a spray of red. It climbed higher, angling itself so that some of its tentacles could unfurl and reach across the ship. It plucked two struggling shapes away and backed down again.

'Poor bastards,' Gallan muttered at Sol's side.

'They'll fight all the way,' Sol said, because he could make out the pale leather of Spike soldiers. But whatever fight the deep pirate's victims had in them was meaningless. A glistening flap opened on the decapus's flank and the pirate dropped the unfortunate soldiers inside, then slipped back down its mount's back and sank quickly from view.

The ship fired several more harpoons at where the pirate had disappeared, but already the sea's surface had returned to normal.

'Drake?' Sol asked.

'Easy pickings,' Drake said. He scanned the sea's surface, eyes sharp, concentrating. 'It won't be leaving too soon.'

Sol looked from one ship to another, wondering which would be next. Perhaps it would be them. He closed his eyes, imagining the fate of the two soldiers plucked from the vessel and dropped into the decapus's insides. But they were beyond anyone's help now. They would be remembered, and their families honoured.

'I want it killed,' Sol said.

Drake snorted, still watching the sea.

'*Everything* can be killed,' Sol said, angry. 'And this is why you came.'

'It's old,' Drake said. 'That one, maybe four hundred years. It will have started young, maybe the size of me. Amphibious. Perhaps with a bit of humanity left over from its ancestors, perhaps not, but that will have quickly been erased by the waters of the Forsaken Sea. It probably hunted close to the Duntang islands to begin with, keeping to the shallows. As time went on, the deeper sea became its domain. It'll make its nest where it always has, and that island will be its own. Skeletons, there. Skulls. Thousands.' Drake glanced back at Sol, but only briefly. 'It'll add some more today.'

'It's a living, breathing thing,' Sol said.

'A travesty against the gods,' Gallan said.

'And yet allowed by them,' Drake said, smiling humourlessly.

Sol glared at Drake, but the fear he saw in the sailor's eyes was not for him. 'I want it killed.'

Drake's expression changed, the grim smile dropping. 'Here's your chance.'

Closing on Sol's ship, a trail across the waves quickly became a grey shape breaking water, riding something red, with trailing tentacles and wet hair flicking poison at the sky.

The decapus struck amidships, the pirate screeched, and the fight began.

Throughout the battle, Sol could not help dwelling on what Gallan had said – that this was a creature of the Pit. While the decapus gnawed at the hull and flailed with tentacles not used to clamp it to the ship, the grotesquely huge pirate reared up to deck level and screamed its terrible, blood-freezing roar of fury. Its face was barnacled ugliness. Its large eyes were horribly human, pupils a deep black, surrounds a piercing green, and it blinked a leathery film across its eyes each time a harpoon was fired at it or a Spike soldier dashed in with a spear or fired an arrow. Its hide must have been incredibly thick to withstand such attacks – it twisted to deflect harpoons, and arrows ricocheted from its body – and Sol spied several old wounds that had turned to knotted scar tissue. Some of them still held the broken ends of harpoons, worn smooth over time. Rifles were fired, steam drifted, shot impacted and puckered its hide, or bounced off to embed itself in mast or sail.

The pirate dribbled and slavered, long teeth scoring across the deck as it took a bite from a sailor it had snapped almost in half with one of its huge claws. The man screamed as the pirate chewed at his exposed stomach, and Sol pulled his pistol and shot the man in the top of his head.

More harpoons, and two penetrated close to the pirate's neck. It roared and shook its head, long hair flailing across the deck. Another sailor screamed, hands pressed to his bubbling face. The beast's trailing hair scorched intricate patterns in wood and flesh alike.

As the pirate retreated at last, one of its flailing tentacles clasped Drake around the hips. He cried out and threw himself to the deck, grabbing onto a wooden hatchway, nails scoring the deck, timber and nails splintering as the pirate dropped towards the sea. The tentacle squeezed until Drake's scream of terror was crushed to a soundless gasp.

Sol and the others tried to save him. *A creature of the Pit, for sure*, Gallan had said, and as Sol slashed into a decapus tentacle, ducked closer to attack, and locked eyes with the pirate, he did have to wonder as he almost shrivelled beneath the thing's glare.

Then the terrible pair were gone, disappearing over the side and beneath the waves with an enormous splash. The last Sol saw of Drake, he had a knife in his hand and was struggling against the monster's grasp to open his own throat.

Sol hoped that, inside the belly of the beast, he might succeed.

Three more ships were attacked before the pirate disappeared beneath the waves for the last time. No one pretended that they had killed it, but the bloodstains upon the ocean were plain to see.

'We saw it off,' Gallan said. 'Drove it away.'

'It's gone,' Sol said. 'I'm not sure we factored at all in its decision to dive for the last time.'

'We saw it off,' Gallan said again. He was shaking. Sol let him.

They sailed through the afternoon, and Sol put his Blade to work effecting repairs on the ship. They were not taking in water, but whole swathes of the deck boards had been crushed and splintered, railings had been ripped away and one of the sails hung in tatters, marked with the hand-sized imprints of decapus suckers. It was good to keep the troops occupied.

Through a need to keep himself occupied and distracted also, Sol Merry helped.

By late afternoon Skythe was in view. Sol paced the ship's deck, while his Blade made preparations for landing. The holding pens below were a riot of noise and activity as the beasts were woken from their slumbers. Weapon racks were assembled on deck and loaded, ready for a rapid deployment onto the beaches. The ship's lookout was joined in the crow's nest by one of Sol's best soldiers. It was Gallan who approached, and Sol silently blessed his Side for preventing him having to ask.

'Nothing from Skythe,' Gallan said.

'Thank you, Gallan.'

Gallan nodded. They stood at the bow and watched the land come closer. It looked unremarkable. They had both been to Outer lands on various expeditions, but before them stood a place of legend.

'I'm sure Leki is fine.'

'We can't know that. Let's prepare for landing.' Sol saw the flurry of Gallan's salute from the corner of his eye, then heard the man's footsteps retreating across the deck. *Thank the Fade for solid land beneath my feet*, he thought. And despite his concern at Leki's lack of communication, he felt a deep excitement at the potential conflict to come.

Sol had never before been sent to fight a god, false or not.

*   *   *

317

The landing was taking place along a five-mile stretch of coastline. The rough community of Vandemon was ten miles to the west, and navigators had assured the Spike that the beaches chosen were usually deserted and barren, home to nothing but Skythian wildlife. If anyone did happen to be there, they would be fair game.

Sol's beach – and the landing place for the Engines – would be shared with one other ship's company. They anchored and rode the waves far enough out and apart so as not to offer a combined target, but close enough to stay in contact via flags and glow lamps. Then they sent in the sparkhawks.

The birds, instructed in their purpose by their handlers, spiralled high above the ships until they were lost in the grey sky. A while passed, and then their handlers pointed silently to show the routes of their rapid descents. Sol could not make them out – as ever, they were plummeting too fast for the eye to follow – but on the beach he saw several sparking impacts as the hawks found targets.

The landing craft went next, disgorging an Alderian army onto Skythian soil for the first time in six centuries. The thought crossed Sol's mind, but he paid it no heed. He was a soldier, not a politician.

He left the ship with his soldiers, shoving his concerns over Leki deep down, lest they distract him from his mission. He stood upright in the bow of the first landing boat, Gallan by his side. His blood surged and sang with his life's purpose.

Their first task was to establish a bridgehead, unload the ships, secure the perimeter, send scouts inland and along the coast to investigate any possible resistance to the landing, and then wait for further orders. The rackers, and the Engines and their attendant priests, would be brought onto land. And after that he might express official concern over Leki's lack of communication. Any comment now might be perceived as a weakness by the generals.

They landed unchallenged, assault sloops being hauled up the beach and used as a command post. Spike soldiers moved left and right along the beach, and a troop of eight probed inland, investigating their surroundings and watching for trouble. Seeing-doves flitted back and forth along the coast, bringing news of sporadic resistance to the east from a community of criminals banished there over the years. They were quickly killed, and their motley camp of huts burned down.

The Engines were landed. They remained covered, and each had a troop of Spike to guard it.

Live weapons enclosures were established using native resources – trees for sparkhawk and merrow roosts, moulded sandbanks for termite and rat. The lyons were tethered to rocks further up the beach, a freshwater stream giving them a source of water to cool their simmering fire-glands.

Finally, the two beautiful, mad rackers were brought over. They were concealed within a tented structure on their landing craft, presumably still surrounded by a haze of shoot dust. The tent was quickly transferred and erected close to the command post, and the rackers walked across the foreign beach, pausing every few steps to squeeze sand between their naked toes and communicate with each other in subdued tones.

Many Spike turned away from them, looking inland or along the coast.

'No more racks,' Gallan said. He'd approached Sol from behind, startling him. Sol cursed silently and shook his head. The rackers spooked him as well – their manner and their madness, not what they did – and he knew he should present a stronger front than this to his Blade.

'Fine,' he said. 'Tell me when there is.'

'Of course.' Gallan was alert, eyes wide. Though they had not had a fight, three bodies had been found further along the beach, their skulls shattered by the sparkhawks. From their build, they could only have been Skythian. 'So what now?'

'Now we consolidate for the night,' Sol said. 'The other Bladers and I will meet with the generals. And then tomorrow we establish the first Engine here. While we're doing that, the other two will be taken inland, one north-east, one north-west. If Leki contacts us . . . *if* she does, then we should be able to position them so that the false Skythian god is within their triangle.'

'And if she doesn't?'

'Then what happens with the Engines is dependent upon their technicians and priests. I don't pretend to understand them.'

'Or even like them,' Gallan said. 'Magic is . . .'

'Not our concern,' Sol said.

'It's wrong,' Gallan said. He lowered his voice. 'And what we were always told is wrong.'

'Not our concern,' Sol said again, louder, more slowly. Gallan saluted and walked away, and Sol looked inland. Somewhere out there, Leki, alive or dead.

That *was* his concern.

He closed his eyes briefly and thought of the amazing woman who had honoured him by becoming his wife.

Venden had always struggled with the word 'god', because it implied so much – fealty, homage, rules and fear, and a degree of faith that he had never felt able to give. But these beings in Aeon's memories were so far removed from what he knew that god seemed as good a word as any.

320

The endless journey led from one being to another, and eventually to an alliance against a common enemy. *Crex Wry*, they called this foe, its name a dark whisper. It was the very earliest days of the world, when landscapes were being forged and the chaotic forms of rock and water, fire and air, were observable as a malleable, ever-shifting soup of possibilities. There were vast distances between these interactions, and Venden sensed that they were both geographical and temporal. A quest that might have taken a million years, across an ever-changing and forming landscape, ended finally when the alliance was true and strong, and there was but one abstainer. Venden felt the strength of determination in those old creatures. Their power was staggering, their intention solid.

That single abstainer, Crex Wry, had sought dominion over the world. Venden had no concept of its appearance, but he sensed a heavy dread surroundings its name. It bore powers absent from the other beings. Its ambitions were darker.

The others had formed together to drive it down. Venden caught only a brief sense of the conflict that ensued – perhaps it was too traumatic to recall, too awful for Aeon to see and remember, again and again. That it was tumultuous and almost apocalyptic he *did* know, because much that had been made was unmade. The land as it was, changed once again, fractured and shattered, boiled and frozen. The world that emerged from the other side was more similar to the one he recognised. It had been the first war, and Venden was sad that even these beings of such power sought to fight. Perhaps that was simply the nature of existence.

The errant being Crex Wry was put down beneath reality's veneer, and its sickened soul bled into the world as magic. This final, dangerous evidence of its existence was also drawn from the world, and sealed away within a fold of potential. The act of doing so ruined some of these grand, primeval beings, and the bones of those dead and gone were buried in the foundations of the world Venden recognised as his own.

But, like any sickness, magic had been difficult to eradicate completely. Some of Crex Wry's influence had escaped and remained as dregs of magic, floating in empty places, echoes of that dead thing's dark soul and darker intentions.

The idea of what would happen if Crex Wry was raised existed as a deep, dark pit of utter dread in Aeon's mind, and that was why Aeon persisted. Why it had lived on, while all those other beings had succumbed to time and progress, and lain down, and let history bury them in the past: to guard against these dregs being found and used to raise Crex Wry from its ancient resting place.

But magic had a gravity. And the Ald had felt its pull.

As he explored these grim memories, Venden felt the urging sent out from Aeon, and understood by minds believing its godhood. It invited its followers to listen, and Venden understood that its resurrection had been acknowledged all across Skythe. Those surviving Skythians whom he had met, who had followed him, and whom he had occasionally communed with, would all hear Aeon's words because they were for ever attuned to its voice.

Gather and go south against the forces who would undo what little you have left, Aeon urged. *I am returned, but weak. I am whole, but still lacking. Given time, I can help you rebuild. But the old enemy of truth would seek to deny me that time.*

And for the first time, Venden heard something in Aeon's voice that might have been emotion.

I did nothing to call this down upon myself. I am a wanderer, and would wander again, given the chance. So go south. And when the time comes, I will aid the fight.

Aeon retreated. For the first time since becoming a part

of it, Venden was left totally alone, his mind a speck of ice in an eternity of freezing space.

If I was alive, this would drive me mad . . .

When the emptiness ended after an unknown time, Aeon brought its full regard down upon him. *Just once*, Aeon said. And Venden knew from its tone – sad, and already weighted with guilt – that this was going to hurt.

They walked through snowstorms that day and night, and several times Leki guided them to a hiding place: a cave in a hillside, a hollow tree, a fold in the land shielded by creepers and tumbled boulders. Hidden away, they watched groups of Skythians walking south.

Bon had only ever seen those few Skythians at the ruined village. Animalistic, wild, they had exhibited everything he had come to believe about them.

Now, the people he saw were moving in groups of twenty or thirty, sometimes more. Men, women and children marched in silence. And there was something else different about them. Everyone believed that the Skythians had been reduced by the effects of the long-ago war, regressing along with their corrupted land until they were considered less than, and lower than, the most savage Outers. They were believed to be illiterate and barely able to communicate through language, and there were rumours of widespread tribal skirmishes and cannibalism.

But these people were different. Though still stooped and twisted by hereditary malformations, they were organised and determined. They moved with purpose, and wore thick furs against the cold. They carried weapons – basic spears, rough bows and arrows, and Bon spotted the glinting of newly sharpened blades on some of them. Most of all, they no longer appeared wild.

It's as if they were hiding everything from us, he thought with shame. Bon had always considered himself a fair man, but he had regarded them as below him.

'Where are they going?' Bon asked after their fifth encounter.

'Into chaos,' Leki said. But she looked troubled. She had also seen her perception of the Skythians shattered. Which meant that the Ald, her employers, had vastly underestimated them.

'It doesn't have to come to war,' Bon said. He felt hopeless and helpless. He knew of some of the weapons available to the Spike, and suspected there were many more he had never seen or heard of. The Skythians were carrying sticks and stones.

Leki did not answer. They walked on.

Close, Venden said, his voice so strong that it sent Bon staggering against a tree. *Edge along the next valley . . . then down into cold . . .* Strong, but not the son he had known.

Leki was watching him from a few steps away, head tilted quizzically.

'Almost there,' Bon said.

It was midday. They had walked through the night, and now the snow was halfway to their knees. Still it fell. It muffled their footsteps, obscured their view of the landscapes they crossed. They went west along the next valley, and then the landscape began to change.

The snowfields were pure and untouched, but across the wide valley were what looked like giant white boulders, hundreds of them, a chaotic array of tumbled rocks so frequent and large that even the snow could not camouflage them.

It was only as they approached close to the first rock that it became clear what they were.

'Ice boulders,' Bon said.

'But from where?' Leki asked. She sounded unsettled, and

324

Bon could not blame her. Scattered with the huge objects, the landscape was distinctly alien.

'Below,' Bon said. 'The frozen heart of Skythe.'

'There's been an eruption.' Leki walked to the nearest boulder and touched it, scraping snow from its surface until the solid ice was revealed. It was green, deep with age.

'That's where we're going,' Bon said. Leki turned to look at him, her hand still on the boulder.

'Venden whispers to you,' she said, her voice barely louder than falling snow.

Bon nodded because he could not speak. They stared at each other, and he saw fear and fascination in her eyes. Perhaps it was a reflection of his own.

'Everything I've ever learned from Arcanum, and you're leading us in,' she said.

'Perhaps Arcanum doesn't know as much as it thinks.'

'No, it knows more. But it doesn't matter. I'll know where Aeon is, and then . . .' Leki touched the hem of the jacket where she had hidden the shoot dust tube.

I will never let her, Bon thought, and it felt cool and final. He said, 'We're not finding Aeon to harm it.'

'Then why?'

'Because it's telling me to in my son's voice.'

They walked on, with nothing else to say.

Just as they reached the ragged wound in the land from which the massive ice boulders had been blasted, the snowfall began to ease.

In the utter silence they both heard, from the dark rent in the world that looked bottomless and timeless, a breeze that might have been a breath.

They went down. Bon led, working his way carefully across the rugged, broken ground leading to the fissure. The thick snow camouflaged the sharp edges of rock and ice, and when he fell it buffered him from injury. Leki grabbed his arm and helped him up, and he thought once again of her husband. He knew that the affection between them was not in his eyes only, but the idea that it had been a part of her ploy – a way for her to remain close to him, and so grow potentially closer to magic and the rumoured rising god – made him feel sick. Not because she had taken advantage of him – he was coming to accept that had happened before, in some way, with Milian – but because his feelings for Leki had been growing. Even before finding Venden, she had given him a reason to look forward to the next day.

The caverns caught light in chaotic ice sculptures, filtering down from above and sucked inward as if those deep, dark places drew it down. Soon there was no snow covering, but ice still covered the ground.

If it erupts again . . . Bon thought, but there was no benefit in thinking that way. If the same powers rose once more, he and Leki would be crushed and merged with the eruptions, red smears on ice that had existed at these depths for so long. They were climbing past evidence of Skythe's tragic history. Before the war, these caverns might have been warm with the fires of Skythe's contented heart. Now they resounded with the chill of death. It was as if magic's corruption had made a cadaver of the land.

'How deep?' Leki asked from behind Bon.

'We'll know when we get there,' he said. 'Why? Afraid?'

Leki did not answer. When Bon glanced back at her she was glaring at him as if about to speak. But she remained silent.

'*I* am,' he said. A great ice wall stood to their left, and it seemed to glow with an inner light. Shapes and shadows existed deep within. Perhaps this had once been a wall of fire. He placed his hand against the ice. As if the contact was a signal, a waft of warmer air came from below, deeper down. It carried no scent, but was heavy with moisture.

'Just listen to your voices and move along,' Leki said. 'The time's long gone for standing still.'

Time seemed to distort – frozen, shattered, and melded back together by the ice. They went deeper, along ice tunnels and into crevasses that would have been deadly if another ground-shifting event took place. No water flowed or dripped. This was a completely frozen environment, and though warmer air occasionally wafted up from below, there was no indication of thaw.

Deeper, Venden whispered in his ear, and Bon looked around, startled. Leki had heard nothing. There was no echo. *Not far now . . . not far.*

'And what does Aeon want of us?' Bon asked aloud. There was no reply, other than Leki's troubled look. 'Will you know the way out?' Bon asked her. She was Arcanum, after all.

Leki nodded, but he saw doubt cloud her expression.

They moved deeper, deeper. A solid waterfall threw off a haze as though its spray had also been frozen. Jagged razors of ice promised pain if they slipped. Deep fissures offered dark oblivion. They kept to the easiest routes, and it was almost as if their path was being illuminated for them. The air carried light tainted with the hues of deep time – heavy greens, blues, the solidity of ice formed from the ruins of Skythe's dreams.

Bon listened for Venden. But his dead son only spoke to him again when they stood before the fallen thing, risen once more.

And *Venden* stood before *them*.

After Aeon's words came the pain.

Venden's physical passing had been brief but awful. He had felt his body coming apart, aware of the terrible damage

327

being wrought upon the shell he had always known, the vessel that had been him. The realisation had been worse than the pain – that this was the end, and that the ripping, rending, splashing finality could never be reversed. Then had come the strange continuation as part of Aeon, not apart from it. His mind persisting, not entirely as it had been and yet still an independent glimmer in the ferocious blaze of Aeon's new existence.

This was different. The agony of being brought together was a whole new order of pain, because it was not simply a fleeting moment in time. He felt flesh and bone and blood assembling, and every newfound nerve knew it to be wrong. His mind received each signalled agony and held onto it. Bones melded, blood liquefied and flowed, flesh knitted, skin and veins formed, and the most complex form in the world – a living, breathing thing – came into being from the body of Aeon. Venden screamed in his mind, and then realised that he could hear that scream as well, feel it itching his throat and vibrating through his chest, and taste the spray of blood that hazed the air before him. He took in a deep, juddering breath and screamed again, and he felt a wash of pity swilling around him as Aeon shifted position.

It was in his mind, as he had been in its own. It was a connection both physical and ephemeral. He was still a facet of Aeon, a Venden-shaped projection like a limb giving itself to another use, with thin fleshy constructs connecting them. He had his own face, his own hair, and looking down across his naked body he was struck with a startling familiarity. *It's been so long since I have seen myself*, he thought, although perhaps it had only been a day. Being a solid thing felt so wrong.

Venden opened his mouth to cry out again, but then the pain began to subside. His naked and bloodied body swaying in that freezing cavern. The mass of Aeon was behind him, and before him were great ice walls glimmering with their own inner light. He shivered. A mist of warm air drifted across him from Aeon to swill the blood from his skin.

Aeon wants me as myself for when my father comes, Venden thought.

'Venden Ugane,' he said, his voice barely a croak. He said his name again, more evenly. And again. By the time he heard scrambling footsteps descending towards the cavern, he could almost believe he was himself again.

'There have been rumours of Aeon,' the figure said, and Leki caught Bon beneath the arms as his knees weakened.

It was not *quite* his son. The body was there, and the shape, and Bon even recognised the casual, slightly arrogant stance that had always made him believe his son viewed all others around him as fools. But this was not *only* Venden, because there was something stretching away behind him. Veils of skin, veins, and streaks of something that did not belong in or on a person's body.

These fragments connected him to Aeon.

'There it is,' Leki whispered in Bon's ear, as if he could not see.

In the half-light, Aeon's true shape and size were ambiguous at best. It was huge – much larger than the shape they had seen in that clearing further to the east. Long, low, with heavy limbs that seemed to anchor it to the cavern floor, its body performing a gradual change into ice where it touched, it had blended itself with the frozen heart of the land.

'Rumours,' Venden said again. His mouth moved, but did not quite match the words. His eyes shifted left and right, alighting finally on Bon. They did not change. They did not smile.

'There have always been rumours of Aeon,' Bon said. 'I was one who believed.'

'Belief is immaterial,' Venden said. 'Faith is meaningless. Human things, and humans . . .' He blinked, frowned, then continued. 'What matters is that magic cannot be allowed. Crex Wry must not rise.'

'Venden—' Bon began.

'I am Aeon.'

'Son,' Bon whispered. Leki leaned into him, her contact welcome, fresh.

'They will raise magic against me,' Venden said, 'as they did before. Before, they caught me by surprise. This time I will be more able to withstand it. But also, magic itself will be more ready.'

'Ready for what?' Bon said.

'To hold on, and not be put back down by their . . . Engines. Ready to gain a foothold, so that Crex Wry can claw its way back. And if it does . . .' Venden's face creased as if in sudden pain, and Aeon shivered.

'We'll do anything to stop you raising your Kolts again,' Leki said. Bon flinched at her aggression, but he could not help admiring her as well. In the face of this thing, she still spoke what she thought.

'More rumours of Aeon,' Venden said.

'Your *death* brought the Kolts,' Bon said, appealing for the whole truth. 'Didn't it? The magic destroyed you, and polluted the whole of Skythe, and created those things that wiped out everything they touched?'

'It can say whatever it wants,' Leki said.

'Rumours,' Venden said, and the smile in his voice was chilling. 'The truth matters little to those who can only lie.'

'And you can't?' Leki scoffed.

'Aeon has no need of lies.' Venden shimmered before them,

seeming to blur as if the ground moved. Bon had felt nothing. His legs were firm. He blinked, and Venden was still again.

'You *do* lie,' Leki said. 'It's revenge you want, and—'

'Magic *must not* be touched,' Venden said, harsher. 'It is the dark soul of a fallen thing.'

'Like you?' Bon asked.

'*Nothing* like me,' Venden said. 'Crex Wry is . . .' He raised his arms slowly, and veils of thin skin connected them to the sides of his body. 'I can show you.'

Bon stepped forward without hesitation.

'Bon, no!' Leki said.

He didn't answer, but walked across the frozen cavern floor to the simulacrum of his son. One more chance to touch, however strange the touch might be. One more chance to let Venden know that his father loved him.

'Bon!' Leki said again.

'Don't you want to know?' he asked without turning around. As he reached for Venden's right hand, he heard Leki's cautious footsteps behind him, and saw her reaching for Venden's other hand.

'Oh!' Leki gasped. Bon glanced sidelong at her – her eyes were wide, jaw slack, and she was looking past Venden at the massive shape beyond. Her fingers were splayed around Venden's, the thin webbing enveloping his hand. Bon thought perhaps she might be reading his blood, and then—

A lurch. Dislocation, confusion, and he is amongst a landscape in turmoil. Mountains shaking, valleys folding, rivers boiling, lakes erupting. The sky is on fire and the land flows, malleable and not yet set, and a figure stands solid within the upheaval. A terrible, powerful sentience oversees everything. It has intelligence of an order and type that Bon cannot understand. It has intentions beyond the scope of mere human ken. But he knows its ambition is not pure, and the sense of wrongness exuding from the vision sets his skin on fire. It is shattering and mind-blowing, like the worst nightmare that can never be explained, but which comes again and again. A personal horror, but one which Bon knows will be personal to everyone who touches it. He vomits, but has only a distant awareness of the acid tang spewing from his mouth. The image is everything – timeless, terrible, violent, merciless. The shape stands tall and strong. Its personality sets the world aflame.

The vision was snatched back as quickly as it had been granted, and Bon fell to his knees before Venden. The stink of vomit, the chill of ice, he wiped his hand across his mouth and tried to catch his breath.

'By all the gods,' Leki whispered beside him, but she was using a curse that had no meaning.

'No,' Bon gasped. 'No, only one of them.'

'There stands Crex Wry,' Venden breathed. 'And magic is its lifeblood, its blackened soul. Take the message to leave magic where it belongs – down, in knots that must not be unpicked. Aeon will go its own way, in peace, as ever it did. It wanders the world, from the brightest day of creation to the darkest of end times. Quash rumours of Aeon. Speak the truth.'

'If we believe you—' Leki began, but Aeon spoke over her again.

'Aeon has no need of lies.' Venden's hand holding Bon's changed, skin and bone melding and deforming into some-thing else, leaving an object resting in Bon's palm. It had no weight, and was faultless. 'A gift from Aeon's heart. This is all I can give, for now.' And suddenly Venden cried out and tugged Bon close to him, cheeks touching, his voice his own.

'Father, Crex Wry seeded the Fade to aid its own

332

resurrection. It—' His voice was cut off, snatched back with a deep groan, and replaced once again by that almost-Venden voice which was all Aeon. 'Now close your eyes.'

Bon's heart leaped. Confusion reigned, and he obeyed as Venden began to disintegrate. He heard the sound of something splashing, and then Leki's gasp.

'Bon,' Leki said, nudging him. 'Look.' Bon looked, and when Leki squeezed his hand he squeezed back.

Venden was gone, subsumed once again. Only ten steps away from them, Aeon was moving. Its incredible bulk shifted with endless grace, flowing like smoke made solid, making no sound as it lifted from the floor of the frozen cavern and moved away from them. Bon was certain there was no tunnel before it, yet it disappeared into the ice wall, pulling itself through with slow, gentle movements from its strange limbs.

In its wake, it left a perfect tunnel leading upwards.

'Our way out,' Bon said.

'So we can deliver its message quicker?' Leki asked, doubt still staining her voice.

Bon held his hand out to show her what he had been given. The object was a smooth, round bone, imperfect in shape, yet not apparently removed from any other body part. There were no joints or knuckles, no broken connections, no way in. It was the size of his fist, and still warm.

'What is that?' Leki whispered.

'Perhaps something to help,' Bon said. 'Leki, you heard it. You *saw*. Didn't you feel how dreadful that was? Didn't it . . . make your skin crawl?'

Leki was pale, eyes flitting left and right as if trying to find reality.

'If your people raise magic—'

'Then why doesn't it stop them itself?'

'It's trying,' Bon said. 'Maybe it's weak, or unable, or

knows that Crex Wry will defeat it. So it's trying, by asking us to help.'

They stood silently for a while, and for the first time Bon heard water dripping somewhere in the darkness. A sign of change.

'What did your son whisper to you?'

'That Crex Wry seeded the Fade to aid its own resurrection.'

Leki was contemplative, silent.

'I'm taking the message,' Bon said, slipping the object into his pocket. 'South, to your Ald.' He knew how useless such a gesture would be. If they didn't kill him on sight, what chance did he have of making them believe him? A madman, a criminal who had escaped a death sentence, rushing from the wilds to plead with them to keep their Engines down.

Unless . . .

'And you'll come with me,' he said.

'Me.' Leki was looking into the darkness after Aeon, frowning, yet her eyes were wide with wonder.

'You'll come and tell them what Aeon showed you and told you. Tell your *husband*.'

Leki blinked a few times, bringing herself back to the present. She knelt and touched the ground, ice shards sparkling like rare gems, splaying her hand so that Bon could see faint light reflected through her webbing. She breathed deeply for a moment, then seemed to slump down to the ground.

'Leki?'

'I can't read it,' she said. 'It's . . . unattainable. But, yes, Bon. I'll tell Sol what happened here.'

'Then we should go now,' Bon said.

'They'll have landed, formed a bridgehead, started advancing inland. And they'll have the Engines. When they don't hear back from me they'll ground them anyway. Two along the coast, one far inland to give a triangle. Then they'll fire them up, and direct magic against Aeon.'

'Then there's no time to waste.' Bon turned and started away from her, glad for her fear. It would help them both.

They moved quickly, following the route Aeon had forged. When they emerged from the fresh wound in the land, there were three Skythians waiting. Between them, two large shires stomped their hooves against the icy ground. It was still snowing.

The Skythians watched them in awe. All three stared at Bon's jacket pocket.

'Aeon wants us to hurry,' Bon said. They walked forward together, kicking through fresh snow.

In the east, sunrise set the snow-covered horizon aflame.

Chapter 17
inland

Juda was aware of being watched even before he opened his eyes.

It took a while to place himself. As he rose from the deepest sleep he had ever known, crawling up out of the solid darkness, a shocking memory from childhood presented itself – he is a child, holding a knife to his wrist, ready to vent the Regerran blood that marks him as different in the eyes of other children.

I'm more different than that, Juda thought, and he opened his eyes at last.

The darkness was heavy and slick. The sort of darkness he might imagine inside a decapus's stomach, or the innards of one of the bigger spinebacks that patrolled the sea beyond the Duntang Archipelago. He took in a deep, shuddering breath and gasped it back out, and his hand went to his left armpit. As memory of the wound returned, so he found that he could see more.

Inside the Engine, he thought. His heart stuttered, his eyes fluttered as if sprinkled with dust, and he pressed his hand to the wound. It ached, but there was no harsh pang of agony as he'd been expecting. His bloodied shirt was torn around his shoulder, and he worked his hand inside the tear to feel the knotted flesh beneath. The injury was obvious. Scar tissue marred an area from beneath his armpit halfway across his chest, a swathe of hardened skin where the poison-tipped arrow had sliced and bruised.

It should hurt more. He examined his senses from an objective distance. He could taste staleness, hear his own pulse throbbing at his ears, and when he lifted his hand and scratched at his cheek, pinched his skin, he could feel it.

He remembered those weird limbs that had attended him. They were nowhere in sight now, retreated back to the shadows whence they had come. Perhaps they had been the shadows themselves. Inside an Engine that sang with memories of magic, anything might be possible.

'I have more dregs,' he whispered. He sat up slowly and reached for his shoulder bag. Dragging it closer, he disturbed the broken arrow that lay across it. Juda paused and leaned across, closing his eyes as a faint threatened. He bit the inside of his lip hard enough to taste blood, then picked up the arrow.

It had been inside him. It was the front part, the head a viciously barbed triangle of shaped iron, rough holes punched through its two wings to help it grip inside a flesh wound, or bite into bone. There were also depressions in the metal where poison paste would be applied before combat. The wood of the shaft was much heavier than it appeared, darkened with his blood, and where it had been snapped off the splayed splinters promised more pain.

Juda slipped the arrowhead and short length of shaft into his pocket. He had never been one for totems or charms, but he felt that he should keep this. One day he would show it to someone and tell his story.

He started hauling himself upright, holding onto a network of smooth pipes that lined the wall by his side. The wall was metal, warm, and uneven like a living thing's body. The pipes flexed.

'You're what I've wanted for ever, and I have to start you,' he said. The Engine did not reply. Nothing moved. It had saved him when he had submitted himself to the safety of its womb, fixing his wound and supplementing the dreg he had pressed to his open flesh, the poison negated, pain less-ened. Now he felt its awareness around him. It carried weight.

He moved through the Engine. There was no sign of those old priests' bodies, floating as they had been before like hesitant bats. He thought perhaps they had gone down into the guts of the Engine. Swallowed. The idea was unsettling. But the confusion he had felt on arrival seemed to have flit-tered away with the pain, and now he knew where to go, and what to do. He was being guided, and observed from the shadows. It was a sense of calm contemplation, not something insidious, but he could not see what it was.

The insides of the Engine were mysterious to him, its workings unknown. He could not shift the idea that it had been built to be entered, and that the route he was following was designed for someone to maintain the Engine, or to initiate it from the inside. But how to do so was a mystery, and he wondered why he had ever believed he could figure that mystery out.

Juda was being urged up, and out.

He climbed over metallic structures, felt the flexible give in other parts that seemed like soft, stretchable wood, and he could not shake the idea that the Engine smelled of . . . something once alive. *But not dead*, he thought. *Just sleeping.* He turned a smooth corner and came across the first areas of frozen snow. It had been snowing when he entered the

338

Engine, and it must have blown in behind him, flitting down through the entrance and settling on the innards. Freezing, layer upon layer of new snow falling on top, freezing again, it formed a solid mass across the Engine's insides that provided a slippery, dangerous climb towards the top.

How long was I unconscious? Juda wondered. His limbs were stiff, his wound now a dull ache. He was thirsty, and hunger hollowed his stomach.

Another dizzy spell forced him to sit, one hand splayed across a surface of smooth ice. Ahead of him, up where he believed the entrance to the Engine lay, a solid wall of ice refracted moonlight from outside. So near, yet so far.

His shoulder bag banged against his hip as he shifted, and he smiled. He delved inside and brought out one of his last remaining dregs.

It was a cold, shrivelled thing. He muttered invocations and moulded the dreg to his desires, applying it to the icy barrier. As he leaned back and closed his eyes to rest, water began to flow.

Sol Merry woke in his tent and listened to a foreign wind blowing against the canvas.

He sat up on his sleeping roll and offered his customary prayer to the Fade. Then he dressed, and his thoughts went to Leki, his love, his wife. The lack of any more racks from her at this most crucial of times was troubling, but he was a professional soldier and he could only let the fact trouble him so far as it affected their mission. Personal feelings were not the province of the battlefield. He should have left his love at home.

Instead, he carried it deep inside where only he could see.

There was a tap at the tent post.

'Enter,' Sol said. Gallan slipped through the flap and offered a lazy salute. He looked tired, his eyes heavy, but excited as well.

'Snow's stopped, it's a bright morning,' Gallan said. 'But the scouts have returned, and it's snowing even heavier to the north.'

'How far to the north?'

'Twenty miles.'

'Huh.' Sol continued strapping on his weapon belt and leather harnesses – primed pistol, knife, sword, throwing stars, a hand-sized folded crossbow and a rack of bolts – automatically checking his insignia as he went. 'It doesn't feel cold enough.'

'It isn't, here.' Gallan picked up Sol's boots and nodded at the upended equipment box. Sol sat, and his Side helped strap on his boots. It was purely an act of friendship. He had known Gallan for a long time, they had their tensions, but there was nothing of superiority in private. Outside in the sight of others, the barrier of rank would be between them again.

'And nothing from Leki,' Sol said.

'No. Sol . . . it doesn't mean anything's happened.'

'Any word from the generals?'

'Not this morning.'

Sol nodded, then flexed his toes inside the boots. They were a perfect fit. He'd had them specially manufactured in New Kotrugam by a shoemaker, each boot cut very particularly around the knotted wounds he'd received as a young boy on his ankles. The spit snake had clung on hard, and it had taken his father and brother half a day to cut it away.

'And no contact with any hostiles?'

'Nothing. You'd have been woken, you know that.'

Sol nodded his thanks, smiled. But he was still far away. *Leki . . . what might have happened to you in this forsaken land?*

'Then let's get things moving,' Sol said. Gallan exited the tent first, and Sol followed him out onto the Skythian beach, ready to give his Blade their orders for the day.

But the orders for that day would come from elsewhere.

Even this early, the beach was already quietly bustling. Many soldiers were still asleep in their tents, and other troops had ventured inland to form a protective front curving around the entire stretch of the landing zone. But those who had been assigned to dig in and protect the Engines were alert in their boarded trenches, weapons caches within easy reach, heavy rifles resting on wooden blocks. Others moved to and fro, unloading supplies from small boats that ferried them from the fleet, and there was a kitchen set up further along the beach, three huge cooking fires already ablaze to prepare breakfast. The activity had trodden most of the settled snow into the sand.

If everything went well today, two out of three Engines would be packed and moving by noon.

Sol received several salutes as he and Gallan walked along the beach. They passed the rackers' tent to their left, glancing nervously that way but seeing no sign of the two women. The guards there had set themselves as far away from the tent as possible. They looked glum with their assignment, but did nothing to complain.

'A long time since the troops had foreign sand between their toes,' Gallan said, and Sol smiled. It had been years, the last time an assault on a troublesome Outer stronghold a thousand miles across the Western Sea. That had been a bloody success. As would this be.

He did his best to assure himself of that. A success! But Leki's disappearance did not allow him to be completely convinced.

'And long enough since their blades were bloodied,' Sol said. 'So, fill me in on troop deployment while we walk.'

'Er . . .' Gallan said. 'Sol. General Cove.' Cove was striding along the beach towards them, his long beard rubbing against his chest. Long beards were not allowed on the common soldier, and Sol did not wear one either. The general's was an affectation. Sol didn't like it, and had decided long ago that, though he respected the man, he did not like him. There was too much ego at play for him to be a proper general to his men. He was what Sol had always thought: a politician.

'Blader Merry!' Cove said, and Sol and Gallan saluted. Cove looked at Gallan. 'You may leave us. Fetch . . . breakfast. Your Blader and I have words to cross.'

'I have no cross words with you, General,' Sol said.

'Perhaps I have with you.' Cove stared at Sol, and Sol heard Gallan retreat quietly towards the kitchens. *I've done nothing*, Sol thought, convinced, quickly going over in his mind his method of landing and the dispersion of his troops and equipment. The rackers sat quiet and mysterious within their tent. The Fader priests squatted beside the covered Engines. Guards were posted. All was well.

'General,' Sol said, 'I'm not sure I understand.'

'Your fucking floater wife,' Cove said. He smiled slightly when he saw Sol's reaction, but it did not touch his eyes. 'You choose to take a floater bitch into your bed, and now that Arcanum witch is letting us down.'

Sol had a sudden, shocking image of pulling his short sword and plunging it through the general's breastplate, just at the point where he knew the leather armour to be hinged, and slicing it back and forth between his ribs.

'General . . . I must object to—'

'You must do as you're fucking ordered,' Cove said. He

paused then, falling quiet. Silence was Cove's favoured tactic for disarming his underlings.

'I *have* done as ordered, General. This beach is secure, the Engines and rackers are well guarded. My soldiers have made contact with other Blades, and we're well protected. It's a successful landing. Perfect.'

The general simply stared at him.

'And your language when referring to our Arcanum spy is inappropriate. General.'

'You think so?'

'Yes. She has sent us several rackings over the past few days, keeping us informed of progress. She told us that Aeon—'

'And nothing since.'

'Perhaps something prevented her from doing so. Perhaps she was injured, taken prisoner, or killed.'

'If she was killed, she should have told us.'

Sol sighed, and immediately Cove bristled. 'Am I boring you, Blader Merry?'

'No, General. Frustration with your attitude to what our Arcanum contact has already achieved. She's no witch. And—'

'And, Blader?' Cove took a step closer, almost inviting Sol's imagined sword attack.

'And my marriage to Lechmy Borle is nothing to do with this operation or this landing. And is nothing to do with you.'

The general raised an eyebrow, seemed about to counter, and then stepped back, stroking his beard. He glanced away from the sea and inland, as if seeing further than the first hillside.

'We have no idea what awaits us!' he said sharply. 'If only she had told us more.'

'If she's alive, she will find a way,' Sol said.

The general nodded. It was his turn to sigh. 'I . . . apologise for calling her a floater. That was unfair of me, Blader. My great-grandmother was an amphy.' He smiled softly. 'And my relationship with that old bitch should be no reflection on your wife.'

'General,' Sol said, noncommittal.

'We're blind here, Merry. We have the seeing-doves flying sorties, but there's nothing like a soldier's view on things. These Skythians are lower than Outers, but that doesn't mean they might not be gathering against us. Therefore, myself and the other generals have decided to send a reconnaissance Blade deep inland to see how the land lies, and we think it should be yours.'

'Yes, General,' Sol said. He was frowning, and Cove tilted his head, inviting comment. 'Is it because she's my wife?' Sol asked.

'Partly,' Cove said. 'But also because you've spent the sea journey with the Engines on your ship, and with those . . .' He nodded along the beach behind Sol at the rackers' tent. 'I think your troops could use something more constructive to do, don't you?'

'As a matter of fact, yes, General,' Sol said. 'If only you'd been more constructive in how you gave the order.' It was a daring rebuke, but once spoken it could not be taken back. Sol did not avert his eyes as the general's gentle smile fell.

'Well,' the general said. 'Well.' His smile returned, still not touching his eyes. 'My apology stands. Ready yourselves, Blader. Take what weapons and handlers you see fit, and I'll be bringing troops from the next beach along to guard your charges. Report back by sundown.'

'Yes, General.' Sol saluted, but the general was already turning away.

'While you're away, the first Engine will be established

where you stand,' the general said over his shoulder. 'Time to get on with things.'

Easier just to shoot him in the back of the head, Sol thought. His pistol was heavy on his belt. Dreaming of violence and blood, he watched his bastard general stride along the beach. 'Fuck you, General,' Sol whispered. When he turned around, Gallan was already approaching.

'That looked fun,' Gallan said.

'Delightful,' Sol said. 'Get the Blade together. Briefing at breakfast, then we're moving out.'

Gallan raised his eyebrows, but Sol turned away. He looked at the covered Engines and the rackers' tent. Weird things, both. Much as he hated to agree with what General Cove had said, he'd be glad to leave them behind.

Sol and the forty-nine Spike soldiers of his Blade ate breakfast together, and it was an animated affair. Not raucous, because they were in enemy territory, and any trained soldiers knew to keep their noise low. But there was an excitement bubbling through them all now that they were aware of what the day would bring. The landing had been achieved successfully and without any casualties, but now the Spike were itching to move on. And, perhaps, for a fight.

Half a Blade had already been drafted in from the next beach to take over their positions, and as they gathered after breakfast Sol saw the displeasure on some of the other soldiers' faces. Eight of them settled around the Engines, leaving a comfortable distance between them, the devices and their priests. Several more stationed themselves around the rackers' tent. Its canvas flapped, and sometimes Sol saw a waft of something rising from the tent's vents. Once, walking past, he had heard chuckling inside.

His Blade checked each other's weapons, ensured their

equipment was tied and packed properly around their bodies to avoid noise, shouldered packs containing food, water, sleeping and cooking supplies, and ammunition, and the four handlers they were taking with them ensured their charges were properly prepared for movement. They were taking two sparkhawks, a nest of ving wasps and one of the lyons, its fire-glands still plugged but calming drugs obviously fading from its system. Each time it exhaled it growled, glaring left and right. Its handler, Tamma, kept a prod stick in her hand at all times – any misbehaving from the lyon and she would poke it with the stick, firing a steam-fuelled pellet into its stomach that would incapacitate it until she could bring it back under control. Sol had once seen the prod stick used on a person when two Spike fought to settle a long-term quarrel, and the woman had been blown almost in half. Such an effect showed how fearsome the lyons were.

He was as glad as any to leave the beach. Betraying his unconventional approach to leadership, he led his own Blade from the sands and over the dunes, Gallan by his side. He knew that General Cove would be frowning upon such a brazen display of rule-breaking – Bladers were instructed to remain close to the centre of their Blade in case of attack, not near the front where the danger was greatest – but Sol was a leader, not a politician. Since the moment he had been promoted nine years before, he had vowed that he would never expect his soldiers to undertake something he was not prepared to do himself. Him leading improved morale, and maintained respect amongst his soldiers.

It was their eyes he felt upon him as they pushed inland, not the weakened gaze of the ageing general.

The sand dunes quickly gave way to rocky, hazardous terrain. Sol ordered his troops to spread out and advance in three lines, and Gallan took the line to his left. They communicated via hand signals, never drifting far apart enough to lose touch. Moving silently, cautiously, Sol issued the command that they should ready their weapons.

A rustling, and a few subtle clicks as weapons were unclipped, unsheathed or hefted.

Perhaps three miles inland, Gallan whistled once. They halted. On a rocky slope above Gallan's line a shape stared down upon them.

Tamma was close behind Sol, the lyon calm by her side. 'Slayer,' she said.

'By the gods,' Sol said. 'Heard about them. Never thought I'd see one.' He signalled to the lines to his left and right to hold back.

'Ugly bastard,' Tamma said, and Sol chuckled.

The slayer stood and watched, offering no indication as to its intention. Sol considered ordering it taken down – his archers could undoubtedly strike it from this distance. But he'd heard the rumours about where these things were birthed, and how, and he feared that a chestful of arrows would simply piss it off.

'Lyon?' Tamma suggested.

'I think subtlety is the better move,' Sol said. 'It's under the Ald's employ, after all.'

'Yes, but they're . . .'

'I know,' Sol said. 'Not quite alive. Not quite dead.' He considered for a moment, then signalled for Gallan to take several Spike to confront the slayer.

The Blade spread out slightly where they waited, and Sol watched nervously as Gallan and five others worked their way around the foot of the rocky outcropping. They parted into two teams and climbed in different areas, presenting separate targets should the slayer choose to attack. But it barely seemed to notice their approach.

'If it even moves the wrong way, riflemen and archers,' Sol commanded. 'And then the lyon.' The slayer's stillness was troubling him, and, as Gallan drew closer, Sol's sense of doom increased.

Tamma attended the lyon, removing the plugs from its fire-vents and loosening the collar with which she controlled it. It growled deep within its chest, and Sol was convinced he felt the growl through his feet, rather than heard it.

'It must know they're there now,' Tamma said.

'It knows.'

Gallan approached and halted a few steps from the slayer, hand on his sword, knees slightly bent. A fighting stance. From this far away Sol could not hear what was said, but the slayer's head dropped and it went to its knees. It seemed to slump down, like a candle melting under intense heat, until it was little more than a low mound on the rock's upper surface.

Gallan turned and waved at Sol, one single hand signal that conveyed that all was well.

'Move on,' Sol said, waving forward. As one, the soldiers moved out.

It took a while for Gallan and the others to descend the crag and catch up. When they did, Sol slipped from his line and trotted through high bracken to where Gallan had rejoined the head of his own troop.

'What happened?' Sol asked.

Gallan looked troubled. It did not suit him. 'I've never been in the presence of anything like it,' he said. 'Have you ever . . .?'

Sol shook his head.

'It was in mourning,' Gallan said. 'I could smell the sadness coming from it.'

'Sadness over what?'

'It said its mate was killed by a god.' Gallan shrugged as they walked on, and Sol moved back to his line without another word.

It began to snow again. The terrain rose steadily inland, and they could see the hillsides before them glistening white. The dividing line between clear skies and snow-laden passed without them noticing, and soon they were trudging through an ever-deepening layer. They were equipped for such weather, and most soldiers in Sol's Blade had spent at least a year training in the Harcrassyan Mountains.

The snowfall remained relatively light, so that although the going was tougher, visibility was still good. As they climbed to the top of one gentle slope, they could see across a wide valley to another, though the valley floor itself was obscured by a low mist.

'Almost noon,' Gallan said. 'How long do we head inland?'

'Until we make contact,' Sol said. They shared Gallan's water canteen. Sol wished for something warm.

'I thought the General suggested we return today?'

'And if we return with news of nothing but snow?' Sol asked. *Leki is out there somewhere*, he thought, hating the idea of her corpse cooled enough to allow snow to settle in her open eyes.

There was an awkward silence, broken only by Gallan screwing the top back on his bottle. 'The chance of just running into her is remote,' he said at last. 'Even if she's heading south to meet us, it's a long coast and the landscape is wild.'

'I know that,' Sol said. 'I know.'

They descended into the valley, sending four soldiers ahead to probe the mist shielding the valley floor from view. They returned at intervals to report the way across safe, and when the Blade reached the shallow river and saw what surrounded

349

it, the source of the mist became apparent. The rents in the land seemed new – fresh rocks lay shattered across the landscape, some of them so recent that they were not yet covered with snow – and ice-cold mist rose from within. Several Spike ventured too close and fell back, their skin and flesh frozen by contact with gushing mist-geysers. They were treated and patched, and Sol led his soldiers towards the river.

There was a single stone bridge, in a bad state of repair and with its span holed in several places.

'The water will be too cold to touch,' Sol said.

'We could send scouts along the river,' Gallan suggested. 'We might find somewhere safer to cross.'

Sol examined the bridge, and ventured out onto the first of its three spans. Gallan and several others followed.

'The surface is gone,' Sol said. 'But the sub-surface . . .' He stamped his foot against one of the heavy blocks set into the bridge's arch and, though it vibrated, it held firm. 'The old Skythians built well,' he said, surprised.

'I still don't like it,' Gallan said. 'We should try fording the river.'

'No. You saw what just happened at the ice vents. I don't want half my Blade freezing to death.'

'Fine,' Gallan said. 'Just as long as you—'

'I'm going first.' Sol turned back and indicated his intent. They were all watching – the creatures as well as the soldiers – and he did his best to exude confidence.

'If I fall, send in the lyon to fetch me,' he muttered to Tamma as she came close to watch. She nodded, her hand loosening the lyon's leash.

Sol began his crossing. Tamma followed close behind, then other soldiers, following in Sol's footsteps. Gallan remained behind, and would only begin crossing when Sol had reached the opposite bank. If the Blade was to lose its Blader, it would need its Side to take command.

As he reached the bridge's central point, and its highest span, Sol felt an unaccountable rush of enthusiasm and excitement. A breeze seemed to follow the course of the river, blowing snowflakes against his right side. The sound of the water rushing by below him was a thrill, an alien sound taking news of his presence from nowhere to somewhere else. He was here in the wilds of Skythe, looking for his love, commanding one of the finest Blades in the Spike, and at that moment everything felt fine, and his joy at existence was, briefly, as intense as it had ever been.

Life was good.

A rock shifted beneath him and he took a gentle, rapid step forward, not even looking back as he heard the sound of stone grinding against stone. There was no splash, so the block had not fallen. He knew that those following on behind would mark the loose stone and avoid it.

He heard another sound, more familiar, from ahead of him. He looked up and peered through the snow at the opposite end of the bridge.

A shire stood there, larger than any he had ever seen back on Alderia. It stomped its front hoof again, and sparks faded quickly in the snow covering the bridge stonework.

Sol paused and looked around. The shire was unharnessed, with no sign of a saddle. *Wild?* he thought. Then he saw another shire away from the bridge, standing side-on like a phantom in the freezing, flowing mists. He raised his hand into a fist.

'Tamma,' he said softly.

'Yes,' she said. She would have the lyon on a loose leash, now. Ready to send it, with the special touch she and it had between them, developed over years of being in each other's company.

Sol's heart raced, but his thoughts were calm and decisive. *Halfway across the bridge. Any sign of movement and we go back, defend that side.*

The mist came alive. Shapes rose from the snow on the other side of the river, twenty crouching silhouettes dark against the light background. The clear edges and points of the weapons they bore were obvious.

'Stand ready!' Sol shouted. The lyon behind him growled, and he felt the comforting heat of its breath against the backs of his legs.

More shapes moved against the bridge's sides, swinging over the crumbled parapets, clambering up from where they had been waiting slung beneath the old structure. Something cut the air past Sol's ear. Someone grunted behind him, and a body slithered across stone and splashed into the water.

Tamma let out an ear-splitting battle cry, and the lyon leaped past Sol as it dashed for the attacking shapes, wisps of flame sizzling falling snow around its head.

'Ambush!' Gallan shouted. 'Defensive positions!'

Sol drew his sword and crouched down, readying to back across the bridge so that they could fight on firmer ground. *They look pained, deformed*, he thought. But he had been a soldier far too long to judge the opposition by its appearance.

It was only as he glanced over his shoulder, and saw Gallan and the rest of the Blade forming defensive positions around the end of the bridge, that he realised the ambush had come from both directions.

Trapped above the river, Sol and his Blade prepared to face the attacking Skythians.

Once landed on Skythe, each flanked by Spike escorts, the priests part company. None of them are sad.

They have been together for many years in the deepest

basements beneath the Fade Cathedral in New Kotrugam. The building is almost as old as the Skythian War, constructed soon after that triumph and added to countless times ever since, its deep parts all but forgotten by those who build, patrol and inhabit the newer structures above. Home to the three newest Engines, it was also a place where the Engines' inspirations were gathered – carvings, ancient writings, broken parts of what might have been older, less effective Engines from thousands of years before, all brought to New Kotrugam from across Alderia. They were found in caves or old ruins, and they all provided information that went to make these the finest, most effective Engines to date.

It was also home to the priests. They lived, ate and slept together, but their hearts and souls always belonged to the Fade, and to the Engines. The Engines are an addiction, and leaving each other now is no hardship at all.

They take one Engine to the east, its priest riding alongside it in the wagon, praying to the gods of the Fade that its purpose will be fulfilled, its use is pure, and that she will be able to accompany the Engine until its initiation. *Magic will flow*, the priest thinks, and a tingle of anticipation flows through her, feeding her craving. She allows it, though she is meant to be devoid of physical desire. This is deeper than anything she has ever felt before. No one will know.

She reaches out and touches the Engine. It seems to throb beneath her hand, though it has not yet been started. Perhaps it is the vibration travelling up from the wheels through the body of the wagon and into the Engine. Or maybe it is potential, an almost sentient delight in this thing's ancient purpose almost being served.

She knows this thing better than she knows herself. Its smooth carapace, connectors circling its round base, the

353

skylines protruding from its top, all are familiar to her through sight and touch, smell and taste. She has rarely been more than a hundred steps from the Engine for the past decade of her life, and it feels like a part of her soul.

The thrumming continues. The priest fidgets in her seat, glancing around at the Spike soldiers protecting her journey along the coast. It will be miles before they are ready to establish the Engine and prepare the rituals that will lead, eventually, to its purpose being fulfilled at last. She has a long time sitting up here.

Still touching the Engine with her right hand, she slips her left hand beneath her robes and feels the growing warmth between her legs.

Moving away from the beach in a north-westerly direction, the second Engine is accompanied by a priest who has spoken nothing but hymns to the Fade for almost forty years. He whispers the hymns when he sits beside his Engine, and mutters them in his sleep. The gods of the Fade are his companions, and more real to him than any of the soldiers trailing alongside the wagon, or the Arcanum engineer following on behind. The Fade are more known to him than the fellow priests with whom he has spent his life, kinder to him than the years, and more willing to listen to the constant, almost unending prayers he offers.

The priest knows that they will travel west, and then north, before establishing the Engine. He is the Engine's companion and Fade conduit, not its designer or engineer, and he only has a vague understanding of how and why the three Engines must be spaced such a distance apart. He has listened to talks of triangulation, deep-core vibration, transmission, resonance, prashdial wavelength . . . he has listened, but smothered his confusion at such terms with more prayer, and more devotion to the gods that both he and this Engine device serve.

He is honoured, and touched by greatness.

One Blade has been dispatched north to locate the risen Aeon – the pretender god, the intruder, the bastard monster of heathen Skythe and unbelief – and the wagon he and the Engine ride upon is guarded by another complete Blade. The sound and smell of their animals of war have always troubled the priest, but right now he is glad of them. Skythe exudes wrongness, and has the stench of a dead land that should have ceased moving centuries before. The fact that it is dead, yet still exists, makes it all the more revolting in his eyes.

He prays to the Fade, and feels the Engine vibrating through the heavy wagon's wood. It seems to shiver in delight at what it is about to do. Its excitement is contagious. The priest's erection shoves against his robes, and he makes no attempt to hide it. Sometimes he strokes himself in time with the Engine's delight.

The priest has heard chuckles from some of the Spike soldiers walking close to the wagon. He does not care. They do not understand. He prays to the Fade.

Back on the beach, as the other two Engines are being moved away from the landings, the third Engine is being established.

'Be gentle with it,' the priest commands. His name is Hanx, and he has not moved from beside the Engine since landing. He has not lost contact with it, either, because it is already speaking to him. Beneath the hourly prayers he offers to the Fade gods, and the conversations he has with those who choose to come close – of all three priests Hanx is the most approachable, and the least affected – he can sense the Engine's desire to free itself from inactivity.

'I always have been,' the engineer says. Hanx does not know the man's name, and has no desire to discover it now. Though he has been close to the Engines for as many years as Hanx, his ministrations seem like abuse. There is nothing holy about this man. His is a harsh touch.

'Don't hurt it,' Hanx says. 'Treasure it. Honour it.'

'I'm honoured,' the man says dismissively. He is walking around the Engine, inspecting its outsides and adjusting certain spiral dials that might have collected sand or saltwater on their journey. 'Please, Revered, leave me to—'

'The Engine is ready,' Hanx says. 'It is eager. Excited. Don't harm it.'

The engineer stops on his next circuit of the machine and stands before the seated priest. Hanx senses his antagonism, and does not care. But the man knows how to treat a man of the Fade.

'Revered, I've worked around the Engines since I was a boy, from the day I joined Arcanum. I know more about them than . . .' *Than you*, Hanx knows he wants to say. 'Than anyone,' the man continues. 'When the time soon comes, my touch will honour the Engine. It's the Fades' duty the Engine carries out.' He speaks with little conviction.

He's just an engineer, Hanx thinks. He closes his eyes. 'The Engine is already alive.'

'No, Revered,' the man says. 'It's just a machine. A device. When the time comes, I will give it the semblance of life.'

'No,' Hanx says, and he opens his eyes and smiles. 'The Engines have always been more than that.' He holds out his hand and touches the metal casing, feels the thrill that this engineer cannot, and promises the Engine that all will be well.

A pulse, like an invisible nod, is his reply.

Chapter 18

north

Venden had expected Aeon to head south towards the coming conflict, but instead it turned north, forging through the snow, over mountain ranges and across a frozen ocean before entering a land of volcanic eruptions and cascading glaciers. Steam and smoke filled the air.

This is no memory, Venden thought, and Aeon went further, skimming across lakes of lava and passing by screaming geysers of steam and fire. Beyond, in a land untrodden by human feet, Aeon came to rest before a fallen tree, in the roots of which was entangled something that might once have been alive.

Venden's perception of the thing was confused. Aeon saw it as it was then, and as it had been before; a dead, skeletal thing, and a being that had once run and flown and burrowed. Its limbs had merged with the still-thriving wood of the fallen tree, and crawling things made homes within the spaces between bones.

Crex Wry will rise, Aeon said. This was the language of mind, and Venden was a part of Aeon's. *The humans have* new devices to conjure its sickened soul – what they call magic – refined and improved from before. But they have even less knowledge, and no belief. Crex Wry will rise, and this time it will not be put down again.

We put it down before, a terrible voice said. It came from something not used to talking. Something dead.

Venden drew back, terrified at what he had heard.

Yes, Aeon said. *Very long ago. And again six hundred years ago, it was confused, and the humans and their Engines put it back down before it was fully risen. But this time . . .*

The humans' devices may not suffice, the voice said.

Crex Wry is ready. This time, it will take the Engines quickly into itself. Make them its own.

Once freed, it will not be beaten again, the voice intoned. *There is only you left to fight back.* The shape twisted into the tree roots seemed to move, and then the tree itself flexed and stretched, great cracking impacts echoing across the thunderous landscape.

I came here to ask— Aeon began.

Permission.

I don't require your permission, Aeon said. There was a note of anger in its voice, even superiority. But there was also respect.

No, the voice said. The tree settled. The skeleton reflected fire. *You need my advice.*

The two old beings – resurrected, and long dead – fell silent. The landscape spoke around them, uttering its own eternal monologue. It might have been moments or decades before Aeon spoke again.

The fools might be stopped. There are humans.

There are always humans. Or if not humans, then those that came before, and those creatures that came long before

358

them. We have always known them, and they us. But none of them has ever made a difference.

And did we? Aeon asked.

The dead thing pondered, and the tree seemed to breathe with its eventual sigh. *Given a chance, we would have.*

I have to give them *a chance*, Aeon said. *They choose to call me a god, but it's their own actions that will define them.*

How much of a chance? the old thing asked. *How long can you give? Crex Wry* cannot *rise again. It* must *not. Last time it froze the heart of a thriving land; next time . . .*

It will not rise again, Aeon assured. *But if I did stop them this time, they would have more reason to see me as an enemy. And they would try again, and again. Better I give the humans time to halt their own folly.* A silent nod, as Aeon agreed with its own thinking. *And imagine the results should they triumph?*

And you're weak, the dead thing said. *Even the tools of magic, the Engines, repel you.*

Yes, Aeon admitted. *But the humans are stronger than you think.*

The dead thing mocked without speaking.

You never did admire them, Aeon said.

They've had their time.

Perhaps, Aeon said. *But should they make all the right decisions, they will move on. The advance will be huge. And I will be able . . .* It trailed off, and Venden sensed the things that made it not quite a god. There was selfishness there, in its desire not to be involved. And there was a dreadful weariness.

You have existed for so long, the old thing said.

Alone, Aeon said.

Something changed about the dead thing's appearance tangled in the roots of that ancient fallen tree. The skeleton yellowed and crumbled in places, the tree fell to rot, and a distant volcanic explosion splashed it with reflected red light, like flowing blood. Venden saw it as it really was – dead, and long, long gone.

Aeon fell silent.

Father will triumph, Venden said, every sense determined.

Far to the south, his father's burden increased a thousandfold.

Bon was having trouble keeping up with Leki. He suspected it was her Arcanum training. They probably told her how to ride shires. Showed her how to send a racking. Revealed to her every cursed secret of every inner working of the Alderian empire and every creed, state and people. She galloped her mount ahead, and had not once looked back to make sure Bon was following. Maybe she knew. Maybe she was inside his head right now.

I thought I might love you. He wondered if she heard that, or knew it. Still she did not turn around.

Bon had ridden much smaller shires on Alderia. There had been a route that led from their village of Sefton Breaks and along the Ton River, heading towards Gakota but then veering across a shallow part of the river and snaking out towards a huge spread of farmland beyond. It had been a favoured walking and riding path for many villagers, and for the space of two or three years he and Milian had taken Venden with them. They'd borrowed shires from a neighbour's farm, setting out early morning, lunching by the river, then exploring the farm-land into the afternoon and evening. They'd watched crop gathering, and sometimes helped. Venden had caught insects on the wing and told his parents about them. Once, their son had gone swimming in a tributary of the Ton, and Milian and Bon had made surreptitious love beneath a blanket.

Those shires had been small and tame, used to being ridden. These, he was certain, were wild.

The beast beneath him bucked and snorted, spraying foam across its head and back as it ran. Bon held onto its mane, legs tight against its sides, his pack hugged around his stomach and pressed between him and the shire. His jacket was tied, the pocket containing Venden's gift securely closed. Bon had not looked at it since, but it was the centre of his attention.

Leki rode with ease, sitting up on her shire and steering it, urging it on. Bon suspected that his mount was simply following Leki's, and he did not attempt to interfere.

He could feel the great power of the beast beneath him, and could not sense any lessening of speed or energy. But several smears of foam spattered across his hands and against his cheeks, and when he wiped them off he saw specks of blood, thick and heavy in the mess.

He thought of calling to Leki to stop, but she was too far ahead to hear. And if he somehow managed to slow or halt his own shire, he would be lost.

Skythe was white, and growing whiter. Snow fell heavier. Their race south was almost silent, but for the muffled impacts of the shires' hooves through thick snow and the creatures' grunting and snorting.

They carried Aeon's message with them.

For a people supposedly denuded of civilisation and existing as savages, the Skythians launched a staggeringly effective attack.

We are so wrong about them, Sol thought, but he had no time to dwell on the mistake. Every moment, every ounce of his experience and determination and will to survive, was given to his command. His soldier's mind took over completely, and Sol Merry became a machine of war.

361

As the fighting began, he assessed their enemy's numbers. Perhaps a score had risen from the snowscape beyond the other end of the bridge, squat shapes that shrugged off their snowy camouflage and came straight for the bridge. Others had been hiding below, their numbers unknown. They slung spiked grappling hooks on the ends of ropes, the twisted, sharp metal impacting the snow-covered bridge and scraping across the stone surface. And behind them, closing on Gallan and the soldiers defending the bridge's southern end, perhaps twenty more attackers.

Tamma crouched down not far from Sol, screeching her orders at the lyon.

He remembered what they'd been told of the Skythians. Once a proud, advanced, civilised people, they were now little more than savages, less advanced than most of the Outer tribes. The cause of such regression – the lies, the truths – were a moot point right now. There was no industry on Skythe, and society was feudal, consisting of small communities sparsely scattered across the vast southern plains. The northern lands were barren and uninhabited, so they were told. The Skythians lived in caves and basic reed huts, scraped a living from the land and died young. So they were told.

They're very little threat to us, General Cove had announced to a thousand Spike soldiers on their last briefing before the fleet departed. *It's the bastard thing they worship that we sail to destroy once again, and once and for all.*

The familiar coughs of steam weapons discharging sounded all around. Several Skythians on the north bank fell, blood blooming around them as they caught rifle shot. Two more climbing over the bridge's crumbling parapet flipped back into the river. Shot ricocheted from stone, whining and hissing as if upset at missing its intended home of flesh and bone.

A Spike screamed as a grappling hook arced down and

buried itself in her shoulder. She grabbed the rope and tugged, but then whoever had thrown it out from beneath the bridge swung from cover, and the rope thrummed as it tensed. The soldier slipped and slid across the snow, crashing against the parapet. She growled in pain and frustration. Her blood speckled the snow.

Sol stepped forward and swung his sword, slicing through the rope as he felt an arrow flit past his ear, parting his hair. A splash below, and he looked down in time to see the attacker carried away by the river.

'Can you fight?' he asked, and the woman did not even answer. She stood and nodded her thanks, then rushed along the bridge towards the Skythians coming their way. She trailed rope and blood behind her, and the grappling hook clung like an ugly parasite, still stuck in her shoulder.

The lyon was standing its ground towards the northern end of the bridge. It had one enemy already beneath its heavy front claws, and the victim's ruined head still bubbled and spat from the fire the lyon had breathed upon it. Several Skythians stood beyond the range of its flames, firing arrows which the creature ducked and twisted to deflect from its thick hide, or batted from the air with a big paw. Sol had seen lyons in battle many times, and they never ceased to amaze him.

He looked away from the furious, fiery animal.

Spike soldiers had spaced themselves along both sides of the bridge and were hacking at ropes as they appeared. A couple were stabbing at attackers who had managed to gain the bridge parapet, and who soon fell bleeding into the river. One Spike had fallen part-way through a damaged section of the bridge and hung there, trapped. He screamed. Something was happening to him below, out of sight, and he jerked back and forth in the hole as he was attacked, spent pistol clasped in one hand. He spat blood. When the screaming stopped, the movement did not.

'Tamma!' Sol shouted.

She turned to him, wild-eyed and breathless from screeching instructions to the lyon.

'Launch the ving wasps!' Sol called.

Tamma nodded, then signalled with both hands back along the bridge.

Sol looked that way as well, and quickly assessed the attack against their rear. Gallan had pulled the remaining troops on the southern bank back towards the bridge, forming a defensive line which was successfully repelling the assault. The Spike were engaged in hand-to-hand fighting with Skythians, metal clashing on metal, and several of the enemy were already down. Spike weaponry was far superior to the uneven arrows, rusted sword and carved spears Sol had seen thus far.

Gallan glanced back at Sol and nodded once. He had the situation there under control.

A handler ripped open a pack and fell to one side. At that, an uneven, pulsing cloud rose from the pack, hovered for a moment over the handler and then dispersed to the air. Ving wasps. They were vicious creatures, only the size of a thumbnail but packing a sting that could paralyse a limb and drive the victim to distraction from the pain. Sol hoped that each Spike soldier had smeared on his or her repellent gel that morning.

As they quickly spread out, the wasps became difficult to make out individually. But then they started stinging.

Skythians cried out and slapped wildly at the stings. Thus distracted, they were easily put down by Sol's troops, with sword or spear. When the fight turned into a slaughter, the Blader turned back to the situation on the bridge.

Another handler had let loose the sparkhawks, and one of

them plummeted to strike a target on the northern back. The Skythian's neck snapped with a sound audible to everyone, and he fell to the ground with sparks sizzling out in the snow around him.

Sol ducked another grappling hook and squatted by the parapet, waiting until its thrower had climbed and was reaching up onto the bridge before slicing the man's arm across the elbow. The Skythian shrieked, but hauled himself higher onto the bridge, swinging up a stocky leg and lashing at Sol with a sharpened branch in his other hand. Sol side-stepped the blow and buried his sword in the man's throat. He kicked at his face and held tight, the sword withdrawing in a spray of blood, the dying man falling into the freezing water.

Tamma ran past Sol, screeching her orders to the manic lyon. The creature dashed left and right, gasping fire at shapes that barely jumped out of its way in time. One of them cried out, and as she struck at the fire erupting in her clothes, the lyon pounced. It bit, bone crunching. Sometimes it ate.

But while it chewed, the lyon was a motionless target. Three arrows struck home in its side, and Tamma's cry resembled one of pain. The lyon spun around and raced after the bowmen.

Sol moved forward, wary of arrows and scanning the land-scape beyond the immediate area of battle. He moved to the centre of the bridge, feeling forward for loose stones, and looked over the heads of his defending Spike and the Skythians they fought. The enemy had come from out of nowhere, and the fact that they'd laid an ambush meant that the coastal bridgehead might now also be under attack.

But that was not his concern.

He scanned the snowfields on either side of the river. Nothing moved across them. There seemed to be no danger that far out, so he brought his attention back to the battle.

Several soldiers were dealing with the few remaining enemies climbing onto the bridge from below. And so, sword in one hand, knife in the other, Sol ran to join the fight at its northern end.

Tamma was down on one knee, hand clasped around an arrow protruding from her neck. Still she shrieked her orders to the lyon – it had run wild upon being struck itself, but now it moved left and right according to Tamma's calls.

'Tamma?' Sol called, amazed that she could still be functioning. But when she turned slightly towards him, he saw that the arrow had merely pierced a finger's width of her neck. Blood flowed freely, but she would survive.

The woman with the grappling hook buried in her shoulder hacked and stabbed left and right, keeping several Skythians at bay. Other Spike soldiers did the same, forming two curved lines across the bridge and taking it in turns to harry the enemy. Many enemy had fallen, and several Spike were down as well, mostly victims of Skythians archers who hung back from the hand-to-hand fighting.

Sol parried a blow from a long spear, darted into the man's fighting circle and buried his knife in his stomach. The man gasped and spat into Sol's face. The spittle was warm, his breath stank, but this was the real fighting Sol had always trained for. He never concerned himself with the morals of what he was ordered to do. Even now, gutting the man with his sword and then slashing his throat, he did not consider why he was an enemy, where his family were and whether slaughtering him was right or wrong. It was kill or be killed, and in such an instance there were no such things as morals.

He pushed the dead man aside and squatted just as a heavy, rusted sword passed over his head. The Skythians were bent and malformed echoes of their ancestors, but their strength was surprising. Sol took three steps and, as the Skythian backed away to swing again, stabbed at his stomach.

The man tensed back and avoided the blade. Sol drove onward, letting his own weight carry him forward as he stabbed out again and again.

He heard the blade descending and fell to one side, kicking the Skythian's bare leg and hearing a satisfying crunch as his knee bent back at an unnatural angle.

His enemy shouted and fell to his uninjured knee, and then several ving wasps buzzed around Sol's head. He tensed, but the wasps smelled the repulsive gel smeared across his skin. As intended, it drove them away, and they stung the Skythian's hand and shoulder. As his eyes opened in shock, Sol swiped the sword across the bridge of his nose and blinded him.

The enemy dropped his weapon and pressed his hands to his leaking eyes, keening quietly. Sol cut his throat.

The lyon, meanwhile, had been struck by a spear, the weapon piercing its side and emerging behind one back leg.

'It's gone,' Tamma said, standing and falling against Sol. Blood loss had weakened her, but he felt her rage. 'I can't talk to it any more. Pain has deafened it, and death closes.'

'It'll go well,' Sol said, reassuring her. The battle here was almost done, so he backed away with Tamma to help her to safety. His soldiers were driving the enemy from both ends of the bridge. The snow around their feet was a muddy red, a sea of writhing bodies, and Sol made a rapid assessment of how things had gone. At least thirty dead or dying Skythians, and six Spike down.

'I can feel the fire,' Tamma said softly.

Sol watched the lyon close on a group of Skythians. They circled it, taking turns to slash and stab when its back was turned. They were being cautious, working together, but it would do them no good. They had no idea what they were fighting.

367

Sol felt almost sorry for them, and he smiled as he imagined what Leki would say. *A soldier going soft?* He could almost hear her voice.

The lyon slumped to the ground and then erupted in flames. Limbs of fire lashed out from it as it died, catching two of its attackers across the midriff and settling into their clothing, their flesh. They fell to the ground and rolled in the snow, screaming. But this was not any fire that water could so easily extinguish. Its flames burned deep.

Sol left Tamma slumped down and ran back to the centre of the bridge. Several bodies lay in the snow close to the parapet, all of them Skythian. The Spike who had fallen into a hole had been pulled through, his body given to the river. And at the southern end, Gallan and those around him had performed a perfect defence, and were even now patrolling the battlefield and dispatching enemies who had only been injured.

Sol nodded, grunted. He would have a story for General Cole, and before moving on he would send six Spike back to the beaches with a warning. If they were not already under attack, it was likely that attack would come. If only Leki were with him, she would be able to start racking—

He heard a sparkhawk's shriek, then saw the dark streak of the creature disappearing into the trees north of the bridge. There was a thudding impact, and a human scream.

'More,' Sol said softly. He looked back past Tamma. There was movement across the landscape in that direction as well. The ambush sprung and put down, the real attack was about to begin.

Hundreds of Skythians surged towards the bridge from both sides of the river. They said nothing, and the deepening cover of snow swallowed their footsteps. The silence of their attack was disconcerting.

'Stand fast!' Sol shouted. 'Defensive! Reload the rifles only if you've time! Archers, mark your targets!' His Blade quickly regrouped, dragging the injured behind them onto the bridge. They readied their weapons – sword and bow, spear and knife, heavy rifles hot from use. No lyon, now. And the ving wasps were dispersing.

'For Alderia!' a voice shouted, and forty others took up the call, sending a shiver down Sol's spine.

The battle raged on.

Hanx feels the Engine's life becoming something more.

He is sitting beside it, high on the beach. They have moved it away from the high-tide mark so that no waves might touch and damage it, but it is easier to dig in sand, so they have placed it amongst the taller, wider dunes. The prashdial generators have been buried deep. They surge and throb in time with the heartbeat of the world – some cannot feel or hear the beat at all, while Hanx has seen others terrified at what they suddenly know – and they are the heart that drives the soul of the Engine.

His whole life has been a rehearsal for this moment. From the time he was born he was introduced into the influence of the Engines, and from an early age he knew that he wanted to be associated with them. His rise to priesthood was already certain – it ran in his family, and such a vocation followed generations – but he had to strive hard to be attached to the Engines. The posting came early. Now he is sitting beside an Engine that is about to be initiated. Such an act has not occurred for six centuries, and the remnants of those older, larger, less refined Engines must lie somewhere on or beneath this landscape, ruined testaments to Alderia's terrible war with this place, and the monsters it made.

Now, with the bastard, heretical god returned from

wherever it had been driven by Alderia's brief summoning of magic, the danger is greater than ever.

Hanx watches the engineer going about his work. To him, the Engine is a construct to work on, a machine to tend, to lubricate, polish, maintain and marvel over when he meets fellow engineers in taverns and restaurants. Theirs is a job, and the Engines are something their ancestors built.

But Hanx knows the truth. The Engines are far more than machines, and the engineers' ancestors did far more than simply build them. They *created* them.

You have strange dreams? he is fond of asking engineers. They frequently complain about his analysing them, but he is a Fade priest, and thus superior to them. The complaints remain informal and whispered, and Hanx pretends not to hear. Few of them answer, but he knows from the looks they give him that it is the truth.

They have strange dreams.

Preparations continue around him, and Hanx closes his eyes once again in prayer. He exhorts the gods of the Fade to smile upon their endeavours here. He feels their attention, their scrutiny, and in the ground beneath him, the air around him, the snow blowing in again and the heat radiating from the Engine and warming his hands, he senses their approval, and their blessing. It is a sense of the Fade he has always had, since when he was a young child, and he takes even more comfort from it now than ever before. The gods are smiling on them, and the Engine is a machine of the gods.

If he told the engineers that the dreams they had were messages from the gods of the Fade, some would think him mad. Others might be terrified. So he keeps the truth to himself, and feels the Fade's touch even as he touches the Engine.

'Almost ready,' the engineer says.

Hanx opens his eyes. 'I know.' Around them is arrayed a protective guard of Spike soldiers. General Cove is there, representing the three generals who have come on this expedition, and he is busy talking with his commanders, strategising and preparing for war. He glances at the Engine occasionally, but his is a look of ownership. He sees the Engine as a weapon, and that assumption disgusts Hanx. It is as much a weapon as Cove's heart is a dead lump of meat. Both are home to the Fade, and Hanx will have words with Cove about his beliefs. He knows the general is devout, but the business of war must never become something that usurps fear of the Fade.

Cove catches Hanx's eye and smiles, nods towards the Engine. Hanx does not acknowledge the look.

'Almost ready!' the engineer says again, this time directing his words to the general.

'Fire it up when you're done,' the general says.

The engineer glances at Hanx, a wry smile. He steps back from the Engine, hands on hips, and examines his charge.

'Does it feel ready to you?' Hanx says.

'It looks ready. I've checked the capacitors, connected the prashdial generators, made sure the sumps are deep and solid. Other things, too.' He waves a hand, as if the priest might not understand.

'All that is good,' Hanx says. 'It all sounds very . . . thorough, and interesting. You have always been one of the more caring engineers. One who almost knows.' The Engine throbs beneath his hand, and he feels a corresponding sensation in his groin. 'But does it *feel* ready?'

For a moment Hanx sees a flash of understanding in the man's face. He knows this is not simply a construct. It is something more, of this world and another. Magic is the stuff of the gods, from the home of the Fade, and they are honoured indeed to be able to tap into that realm, however slightly.

371

'It does,' the engineer says. 'It feels ready.'

Another pulse beneath Hanx's hand, warm, intimate, and he closes his eyes.

'Then let us touch the gods,' Hanx whispers.

He only hears what happens next, because he cannot open his eyes. The world inside is too precious and wonderful. He sees everything he has ever believed played out across the darkness behind his eyelids, and as the engineer turns levers and pushes one heavy button, the Engine hums to life.

It grumbles, shifts, roars.

It's beautiful, Hanx tries to say, but he is not sure whether his mouth works.

He opens his eyes just as warm wetness bursts against his robes, groaning aloud at the wonderful, terrible intimacy of the touch of his hand against the heating, heating metal.

Away from the Engine, the general and soldiers are watching aghast. They are backing away, and the general seems to be shouting orders. His voice is silent. Everything is silent, and distant, because the Engine suddenly *is* everything.

The Engine is part of a system, and the other two are still being transported east and north, to the points where they will be dug in and initiated when the time comes. But being established is important. This place will be the fulcrum around which the coming battle against Aeon will be fought.

Like the giant heart of every god, the Engine starts to beat.

The engineer comes apart. Hanx registers the brief look of surprise on the man's face before he is shattered across the snowy sand, limbs falling aside as his body erupts blood, innards, bones.

Hanx frowns. He cannot remove his hand from the Engine. It is growing hotter, hotter.

Gods of the Fade, he thinks, *grant us the ability to . . . give us the wisdom to . . .* But his thinking is no longer clear.

His hand is melted to the metal now, flesh flowing and bone searing, and he ejaculates again, the pleasure an agony. The robes at his groin simmer, then catch fire.

The thing in the Engine is no god he has ever known. It is much more real, and dreadful.

Hanx opens his mouth to scream at this terrible blasphemy, but no sound emerges.

Only blood.

They see the priest come apart, a man-shaped cloud of gas that expands quickly around the Engine and hazes its surfaces a dull red. General Cove orders them to withdraw, and the Blade surrounding the Engine pull back in a widening circle from the initiated device. They can feel the heat emanating from the thing, and see the rapidly melting snow expanding around where it is settled between the dunes, a melting line following their retreat.

The mucky ground starts to change. Sand melts and flows. It *glows*. The air shimmers, almost on fire itself. Falling snow sparkles and hisses into steam high above.

Further down the beach, the rackers burst naked from their tent and run across the sands, screaming and tearing at their hair. Shoot dust hazes the atmosphere around them, making their presence doubtful. One of them splashes into the sea and continues running, falling eventually, thrashing, drowning in the surf. The other throws herself at the sand and starts to dig.

There is no eruption. The Engine settles. Heat starts to wane, and over the next few hours until sunset, heat haze above the melted sand will form dancing wraiths to haunt the Spike soldiers.

General Cove watches the Engine where it has come to life, and sends no one closer than he is prepared to go himself.

Can we truly control this? he wonders. He quizzes another engineer, but the man is wide-eyed and terrified, shaking his head as if he does not understand a single word. Cove orders everyone to offer a prayer to the gods of the Fade, and as he himself prays, the Engine looks on. He can almost feel its smile.

Juda awoke to the touch of fresh air against his skin. He was stirred from strange dreams of a man who wandered the land in search of magic. He knew this man was him, but in the dream he had been distant and unknown. Juda had wanted to approach and question his intent, but he had felt frozen in place. The dream had disturbed him. But now he was awake, and reality was returning with a chill.

Water flowed around him within the guts of the ancient Engine. He had fallen asleep leaning against a hard wall of what looked like petrified wood, and as the ice blocking the entrance had melted, it had formed many streams into the Engine's structure. He heard water disappearing into places he might have seen, and those he never would.

The cool breeze came from where his final dreg had rescued him from being trapped in here for ever.

The hole up through the ice was made just for him. It was wide enough to crawl through, and angled so that he would not slip back down into the Engine. Steam or mist hazed the air. He breathed in and it tasted of age.

'Magic has freed me,' Juda said, and he frowned as someone echoed that voice in his mind's eye. It was the stranger from his dreams. The man acknowledged the truth, nodding from a distant hillside. From this far away Juda could just see his own face. He was urging himself to climb, leave the Engine, shed the foolish dreams of starting it again. He would never know how, and there were other ways to magic.

He stood and stretched stiffness from his limbs. His clothes were frozen, but slowly loosening. The wound through his left shoulder was heavy with scar tissue, and a little stiffer than the rest of his body. But it would not trouble him.

He started climbing through the ice tunnel. Its surface was close to him, and as hard as rock. He wedged himself against the sides and pulled with his fingers, making steady, slow progress up towards the light.

The air smelled differently in here, as if the outside was somewhere else.

Juda could not tell when he had left the confines of the Engine. The compressed snow was thick, and by the time he saw a circle of starry night sky, he was almost exhausted.

He pulled himself up out of the hole and rolled into soft snow. Gasping for breath. Tired, hungry, thirsty. And between each blink he saw the man on the hillside of his dreams, watching and urging him on.

It's been snowing for ever, Juda thought. He stood in the deep snow and looked around. The landscape had changed, subsumed beneath a blanket of white. And yet the sky was clear now. Stars winked at him as if sharing a secret.

The Engine no longer mattered. The man on the hill beckoned, and Juda knew he had to follow.

He closed his eyes and shivered from the cold. His wound throbbed, and the faces of Bon and Leki touched his memory. But they were soon washed away.

The other man turned and started walking, and Juda followed.

Chapter 19
ambush

They halted as daylight faded, the shires gasping blood and foam and sweating through their hides, hooves splintered and bleeding, eyes wide. Bon wanted to leave the shires and start running, because the idea of remaining motionless for any length of time – standing still, while somewhere to the south of them madmen sought to raise a monster – made him want to vomit. Venden's words, Aeon's message, demanded movement.

'We have the world in our hands,' he said, catching snow-flakes in his palms. The snow had lessened, and the flakes were smaller now, icier. The landscape barely whispered.

'And that's why we have to rest,' Leki said. She had led their way through that long day, running ahead without looking back to see whether Bon still followed. But now she was urging restraint. Bon trusted her now more than he ever had before, and he understood that she had somehow, at some point, taken charge.

But he could not stay still.

'We can run ten miles through the night,' he said. 'We

might meet someone then. A Spike soldier, or one of your Arcanum. Then we can show them, and and tell them.' He shook his head, trying to clear his vision of the terrible things his mind presented to him – memories of his own, replayed visions, fears for the future. 'We can't just camp!'

'When's the last time you ate?' Leki asked.

'I . . .' Bon could not remember. At the thought of food his stomach echoed hollow.

'The shires will drop dead if we drive them any further. They're almost dead now. Give them until after midnight to eat, drink and recover. We'll do the same. And then we'll cover four times ten miles by dawn.'

Bon considered what she said and knew it was the truth. But while Leki built a fire and led the shires to a bush bearing heavy, rotten-smelling fruit, he walked in circles. To come to a complete standstill would feel like giving in. And he brushed the outside of his pocket, wondering at the promise of what it contained.

He wore a path in the snow around the camp as Leki made a quick, tasty soup.

'Food,' she said. Bon went to her and scooped some soup into his bowl. He ate it standing up, not walking but eager to move.

'You'll have to rest,' she said.

'I don't think I can when—'

'Fuck!' Leki slapped at her forearm, scraping a crushed insect away. '*Fuck!* Oh, Bon.' She stared at her arm, then looked up at him with pleading eyes.

'What?' He dropped his bowl and knelt beside her, and in the failing light he could already see the angry red lump forming where something had bitten or stung her.

'Ving wasp,' Leki said. 'This is really going to hurt.

377

But . . . ving wasp.' She grabbed a burning brand from the fire and pressed it to the sting.

Bon was ready for her when she screamed. He gathered her in his arms and held her tight while she kicked and thrashed. He could hear her teeth grinding in agony, and her skin felt hot beneath his hands. Her body was tight and muscled. All this time, and this was the most intimate he had ever been with her.

He pressed his face against her neck, kissed her, and just for a moment her writhing lessened. He held his breath, and thought she held hers. Then the pain washed in again and, as the sun set, Bon comforted Leki through her agony.

Not long after, with the fire burned down, Leki shrugged him off and struggled to her feet.

'You should rest,' Bon said.

'No. We have to go on. Push the shires as far as we can; then, when they drop, we run.' She glanced at him and smiled. 'You get to keep moving, Bon.'

'The thing that stung you?'

'Spike weapon. There's a fight going on somewhere close by. And if they're deploying the wasps, it's more than just a skirmish.'

He could see that her arm was swollen, gathered to her chest in a sling he had made from a torn blanket. The strain on her face betrayed the pain that still burned. But she had scorched much of the venom from the site of the sting before it had a chance to surge through her veins.

'Do you think Aeon sent the Skythians against them?' Bon asked.

'That's what I'm guessing.'

'I wouldn't blame it. Making sure. If we don't convince

them to halt the Engines, then maybe the Skythians can beat them and—'

'They won't,' Leki said. 'If anything, the fight will convince the generals to employ the Engines sooner.'

A sense of doom settled over Bon as he helped Leki onto her shire. The creature snorted and stomped its foot softly, as if signalling its weakness. Leki leaned forward and vomited a thin fluid onto the ground. Morning seemed a long way off.

They left their fire still simmering in the camp; moving off was like leaving safety behind.

As a site for an ambush, the old bridge had been well chosen. But in not destroying the entire Blade in the first attack, the Skythians had also given Sol's soldiers a perfect place to defend.

After the sun fell, the battle became a different beast. The soldiers had been defending the bridge well against the swarming Skythians, taking advantage of the structure's narrowness and the fact that only so many could attack at any one time. Enemy dead lay piled across both sloping approaches, and at the bridge's central span the Spike soldiers had created a tight, solid defence. One sparkhawk had swooped down into the enemy to the south and not risen again, but the other creature rose, circled and dropped many times, each fall ending with a sickening impact.

The Blade had lost twelve soldiers. Most of the dead had been dragged away and dismembered or flung into the river by the enemy. There were many injured, though all but three of these still fought hard. Those three were dying, lying on their backs listening to the sounds of battle around them. Bleeding onto the bridge. Wishing, by every god of the Fade, that they could somehow join in.

There were perhaps five hundred Skythians now, gathered

on both sides of the river and launching sorties against the bridge's defenders. Sol knew that there was no aim to this attack other than to kill them all, slaughter the invaders of their land and throw their tattered corpses into the rushing waters. Along with the simplicity of their intent came a haphazard fighting strategy. These were not soldiers, and they bore their weapons clumsily. There were spears and swords and a few hunting bows that continued to cause problems for Sol's Blade, no matter how many times the remaining sparkhawk was sent after them. The creature could smash skulls and destroy people, but could not target a weapon.

But although the Skythians were not a proper fighting force, their rage went some way to making up for that.

The darkness brought fire. The enemy lit several huge blazes on both sides of the river to illuminate the battlefield. There was a break in attacks while the Skythians regrouped, and Sol ordered injured enemies to be thrown into the river. As they were hauled to the parapet and dropped, some of them shouted in a language none of the Spike understood, but from the tone Sol took it to be defiant rather than pleading. He could see those on the banks betraying their anger at this display, and that was what he wanted. Angry fighters made mistakes.

Spike riflemen took advantage of the lull in fighting to snipe at the enemy. The night was punctuated with the cough of steam valves venting, and though the distance was at the extreme of the rifles' effective range, shadows fell. The Skythians countered by floating blazing rafts from upriver, the fires licking up at the holes in the bridge as they drifted underneath. But they were an ineffective mode of assault, and Sol's soldiers merely took comfort from the heat.

The enemy cooked and ate, the smells drifting across the river.

'My stomach says to rush them,' Tamma said. The arrow had been ripped from her neck and the open wound dressed, and Sol had seen her fighting with the best of them. The loss of her lyon had enraged her, and if she fell she would go down hard.

'That's what they want,' Gallan said.

'Perhaps it's not a bad idea,' Sol said. 'I'm tired of fighting standing still.' He looked along the bridge, past the piles of dead Skythians which had formed a useful defensive line. Hundreds of them stood around the huge fires eating and drinking. Stooped people, malformed shadows dancing with flickering flames, the dark landscape was inhabited by wraiths.

As they observed the enemy, so Sol watched his Blade. He knew them all so well that he found it easy to assess their condition, both mental and physical. He saw wounds and blood, bindings and clasped weapons, determined stares and eager stances. Their readiness for the fight thrummed in the air. And as the Skythians taunted them with food and warmth, Sol considered their options.

'Gallan,' he said quietly. They moved to the bridge parapet, hands on swords in case anyone climbed up from below. 'We could be here for days at this rate.'

'We're holding them off.'

'We've lost twelve, and three more dying,' Sol said. 'It's attrition. One of us can fight ten of them, but they'll wear us down. We'll grow tired. Hunger is already upon us. And the cold is debilitating.'

'We're already overdue back at the beach,' Gallan said. He had a cut across his face, slashing both cheeks and the bridge of his nose. Sol wondered whether he even knew.

'It'll be dawn before Cove sends anyone, and then it'll only be a scouting party. Ten Spike at best. And it could be

381

they're already under attack, in which case no one will come.'

'How can we have got them so wrong?' Gallan said. 'They were supposed to be little more than animals.'

'Like our lyons, or sparkhawks, or rawpanzies?' Sol asked.

Gallan shrugged. 'They're our weapons, not our soldiers.'

'But effective nonetheless.' The men stood silently, looking back and forth to either side of the river. There seemed to be something of a carnival atmosphere growing amongst the Skythians. They ate, sang and danced. Couples rutted close to the fires. Sol was sure he could see piles of weapons where they had been dropped.

'It's not about us,' Gallan said. 'It's about establishing the Engines.' There was a hitch in his voice, awe and fear of the unknown. 'And if and when we don't return, they'll simply move the others as far apart as they can and initiate them. Whether or not Aeon is caught within the triangle . . .' Gallan shrugged. 'That's Arcanum territory. Not our concern.'

'Our concern is to defeat our enemy, and return to the beach with news of what has happened,' Sol said. 'Staying here fighting them off won't achieve either of those ends.'

Gallan nodded, smiling slightly. 'Then we storm the south end.'

'Soon, while they're still eating and fucking. The handlers will direct the remaining sparkhawk to attack the northern shore, make them believe the breakout will be on that side. And the three mortally wounded, if they can stand and walk for a while, will also assault the north. It'll be brief enough distraction, but it might cause some confusion, at least. And in that confusion, we drive south. Spear handlers first, then swordsmen. Archers hold back and cover the run, then they can join us.'

Gallan nodded grimly. 'It will work,' he said. 'But my one fear is—'

'Pursuit,' Sol said.

'Pursuit. This is their land, and they know it well.'

'And that's why we cannot let them pursue us,' Sol said.

'We kill them all?'

'We kill them all,' Sol confirmed. 'South side first, then those from the north as they cross the bridge. Surprise is our first weapon. And we're Spike.' He gripped Gallan's shoulder. 'Spike!'

'I'll pass the word.' Gallan turned to leave, then glanced back. 'Sol. I'm sorry. I know you were hoping to find Leki out here.'

'She could be anywhere,' Sol said.

Gallan went to spread word of the impending attack. Sol watched as his Blade prepared, quietly checking their weapons, priming pistols, and collecting arrows and throwing stars from the dead. In the darkest midst of any fight, he would always be struck by an intense love for his troops, its impact almost shattering with its depth and intensity. That moment came now, and his heart swelled with pride.

The three mortally wounded soldiers were helped up, holding in their guts, hands clasped to spurting arteries, and they took up arms and readied themselves for their final fight. Sol watched them, ignoring the impulse to look away. They took strength from his respect.

These are my soldiers, he thought, *and this is my Blade.* He knew that stories would be sung about today.

It took moments to prepare, and as soon as Gallan gave Sol a nod, Sol whistled his order. He knew that the results of any battle could swing on the sharpest decisions, and this was a move that hung on surprise.

The sparkhawk handler uttered a series of short, sharp

clicks, and north of the bridge a shadow plummeted through the darkness. Sol heard the crushing impact of claws into skull, and between the big fires sparks flew as the creature cracked the head of another victim. The bird rose and dived again quickly, and an immediate ripple of panic spread through the Skythians on that side of the river.

Sol looked south and saw the enemy still dancing and singing, eating and rutting. The river was wide, and they had not yet noticed.

The three fatally wounded Spike warriors charged to the north, two of them leaning on each other, one hand on wounds, the other bearing a weapon. They roared, making as much noise as they could, and even before they left the bridge the first one went down, an arrow protruding from his face. He picked up his dropped sword and started crawling.

Sol turned his back. The sacrifice was selfless and brave, but he had no time to watch. Their deaths would be honoured with their comrades' success in the fight to come.

The rest of the Spike silently charged the bridge's southern end with Sol in the lead, and Gallan by his side. Tamma was there, too, a sword in each hand and blood soaking through the dressing around her neck. She grimaced, and Sol would not have been surprised to see fire leaking from between her clenched teeth.

They climbed over Skythian dead, leaping from back, to head, to stomach, and the dead belched and groaned beneath them. Soon they would add more to the pile.

Arrows whipped by the soldiers and dropped Skythians. Sol felt them whisper past him, so close that he could feel them. Ten enemy, twenty, and then the spear bearers charged ahead and the archers ceased firing.

Sol marked his target, scanned others, watching for the flexing shadow of a bowman, looked left and right to assess the chances of being flanked and surrounded. Some enemy seemed to be scattering, confused, but enough were picking up their weapons to offer a fight.

He ran headlong at the stocky target he had marked; then, ten steps away, he lobbed a throwing star underarm. It skimmed from the man's nose, slashing a ragged tear across his left eye. As his enemy reached for the wound, Sol ducked in low and opened him across the abdomen.

He darted left and heard the groan as the man fell behind him.

Metal clashed, steam hissed, people grunted and cried out, blood splashed, guts spilled. Enemy arrows licked at the air, but this close in they were just as likely to strike friend as foe. Sol lost himself to the thrill of the fight, and he and his soldiers danced through the battle as if each knew where everyone else was. They had fought so many times before that this battle dance had become instinctive. Individual characters faded and they became Sol's Blade, almost a single being, their pale leather tunics the only identity that mattered.

None fought alone. Where one Spike soldier distracted an enemy, another slipped in and dispatched him. Two soldiers harried a group of Skythians to hold off the attack, while three more knelt and loosed a hail of crossbow bolts that broke the wall. As enemies slumped down dead, the two soldiers closed in to kill those untouched. A call here, a whistle there; a thrown sword, a shared kill; the Spike soldiers knew war as well as they knew eating, drinking and loving, and the fight came as naturally to them.

Sol drifted across the battlefield like a ghost, untouchable and yet dishing out death whenever an enemy came too close, or when he closed on an enemy. Tamma raged to his left, exacting vengeance for her slain lyon. Far to Sol's right, keeping his distance so that Blader and Side might not be killed together, Gallan and several others were attacking a group of Skythians who had centred themselves between two of the huge fires.

The fight went on, and when Sol glanced back at the bridge he saw the Skythians from the northern bank swarming across.

'Ten to me!' he called, and ten soldiers answered his call. There was no pause to count, but an instinctive drawing away from the fight for that small group. Sol led them to face the bridge.

Briefly, like an uninvited memory, a flash of doubt crossed Sol's mind. *This is slaughter*, he thought, though his training welcomed it, and the tacky blood on his hands felt as good as home. *Are they really the enemy? These wretched, tortured souls?* But then he saw them rushing across the bridge waving spears and swords stolen from dead Spike, and any thought of right or wrong was shoved aside. Such contemplation had no place here, and was best left for aged reminiscence, should he reach a good age.

'Before they leave the bridge!' he said, probably needlessly. Those with him knew what they had to do.

Three archers and two riflemen held back and started firing, quickly bringing down the frontrunners and tripping those behind them. Sol and three swordsmen stood before the archers, and before the swordsmen were two spear carriers, stocky women glimmering with blood and with blades tied into their long hair. One whip of their hair might take out an eye or open a throat. In moments, Sol knew, the fight would be close enough for them to try.

More arrows and shot whisked past his ears and flung two Skythians back, screaming as they writhed on the ground. Three more leaped over them, rough blades at the ready. These were weapons manufactured from hammered metal, twisted rope for handles and blades already dulled from combat. They

386

were nothing like the Spike swords – many-folded, much-forged works of art that would take a thousand impacts before any sign of wear.

Yet the Skythians' faces were twisted with anger and hatred, and for the first time it crossed Sol's mind that their mission here had already failed. *Maybe these are the Kolts!* he thought. But he had read accounts of those mad, damned things and what they could do, and heard stories passed through the ranks, both up and down, upon news of their posting. Kolts would fall and rise again, limbs missing and torsos punctured by a dozen arrows. Kolts could wave arrows aside and bend swords with a look. Kolts were Skythians cursed to kill their own. Before him were a people furious about the invasion of their land, but when an arrow or blade hit them they stayed down.

'Legs!' Sol shouted, because he realised the rush of enemy was too much. The spear women knelt and swept their weapons left and right, slashing tendons and muscles, tripping their assailants. Sol and the swordsmen stalked forward and finished the fallen, then raised their blades to face those following on behind. Sol slashed one man across the guts, stabbed another in the groin, ducked a heavy blade. A Spike's arrow killed the blade wielder, and Sol shoved the falling body back to trip up his comrades.

A warm spray of blood splashed across his face and blurred his vision, and as he wiped his eyes he felt something strike his hip. He grunted, twisted violently to the left. His flesh ripped and metal scraped across his hip bone, and he roared in agony as he brought his own sword around in a killing sweep. He felt the resistance as it entered flesh, and as he blinked away the blood he withdrew his blade and stabbed forward.

The dead Skythian still clasped the spear that had pierced

Sol's side. *Poison*, he thought, but if so, there was nothing he could do. He and the other Spike soldiers forced the flow of enemy back onto the bridge, ten against a hundred. They walked over the bodies of those they had dropped, some of them dead, many still writhing beneath their boots. They were invincible.

Sol's vision blurred from the pain, and he bit his lip and screamed in rage. As the rush of enemy seemed to diminish – not only in numbers, but also in confidence – something made him turn around.

He could see Gallan and the others making headway, but beyond the battle, beneath the trees where the firelight barely reached, something was moving.

We won't fight off more of them, he thought. Resignation hovered close by, but he would not allow it to settle. A Spike soldier never gave up, and as their Blader he would fight until he had spilled his blood and shed his limbs.

Away from the bridge by one of the fires, Gallan turned, some finely honed sense telling him that his attention was required. He caught Sol's eye, and Sol pointed out towards the trees. Gallan looked in that direction . . . and paused.

Sol looked again. The shadows had manifested, lit pale by reflected firelight. Such stillness seemed out of place within the sounds and smells of battle. And such stillness he had seen before.

'Lechmy Borle,' he said, speaking the name of his love as blood soaked his bare leg. She sat on a huge shire, a man on a similar beast beside her. From this far away Sol could not make out her expression, but he did not need to. He would love her silhouette. He would love the idea of her, the memory, and all the spaces she had ever filled.

The man beside her held something in his hand. As he lifted it, the fighting ceased.

There was no gradual falling away of the battle. One moment metal clashed and bodies fell; the next Skythians dropped their arms and went to their knees. Spike soldiers killed a few more, and then paused in their assault, confused.

Surrender, Sol thought, and he knew that his Blade must honour such a gesture.

But then he realised that he was wrong. This was nothing like surrender. He turned back to the enemy he had been facing, all of them kneeling on or beside the bodies of their fallen brethren littering the old stone bridge, and they all stared past him with a strange expression in their eyes.

Wonder.

And awe.

They had galloped into the night, the shires pounding at the snow-covered ground, fine snow stinging Bon's face and blurring his vision, Leki gripping her reins in one hand while the other arm was tied tight across her chest, and Bon had followed her without question. She knew where they were going. And he carried what they would need when they arrived.

Now they stood at the edge of the clearing before the river, and Leki seemed transfixed by the scene before them.

Bon had never witnessed anything like this. He could smell blood and smoke on the air. Several large bonfires illuminated the river bridge and the areas at either end with dancing light, and it seemed to make the people there – dead, kneeling and standing – quiver and dance. Snow had been churned into a muddied mess. Weapons glinted. He saw the pale leather of Spike uniforms, and they looked so out of place.

'The Engine?' Bon whispered.

'Not here,' Leki said, still motionless. 'But Sol.'

'Your husband.' The way she spoke his name . . . That should have told him everything. And yet he sensed a tension in her, and as he urged his shire forward to draw level with Leki, she glanced sidelong at him. She looked sad.

But this was beyond both of them, and she looked at the thing in his hand.

'They already sense it,' she said. 'The slaughter has stopped.'

'Let's hope we can keep it that way,' Bon said. 'Leki . . .'

'Bon. Not now.' She seemed terribly pained. He wanted to hold her. But the pressure of events weighed heavy, and there was no time to waste.

'Your arm,' he said.

Leki smiled. 'The pain led us here. Small price to pay if we can stop . . .' She nodded past him at the frozen battle.

'That, and everything else,' Bon said. 'Will you ride with me?'

They moved off together, shires side by side. The animals snorted and sweated, and Bon discovered a new respect for the creature that had carried him so far, so quickly.

They crossed the river's flood plain, and soon the snow turned slushy, and then dirtied with mud and blood. They passed the first dead bodies, and their wounds were shocking, gaping, exposing insides to the fire-lit night. *No one should ever see that*, Bon thought, but as the shires walked closer, he saw so much more.

He held the object handed to him by Venden, his not-quite-son, and knew that it was the focus of attention. That such an object could exude so much power confused him, and he imagined the false gods of the Fade kneeling and trembling before him, as these Skythians did now.

But this was not fear the Skythians were displaying, and perhaps not even homage. They watched him and Leki with respect, and hope. His own hope was that they would not kill the messenger.

A gift from Aeon's heart, Venden had whispered. Bon had not known his son's voice at all, though his imagination had let him place a little boy's voice in that alien mouth.

They paused by the furthest fire from the bridge, and Bon raised the bone object in one hand.

A whisper ran around them, like shadows cavorting just out of sight. The Skythians watched, almost hypnotised, and the whisper came from them. Not their mouths, or the slight movements in their nervous stances. This whisper was the intensity of their regard.

'What are we supposed to do with it?' Leki asked.

'He didn't tell me,' Bon said. The bone seemed suddenly heavy with potential, his arm muscles locking, cramping. He knew that he needed to think of something quickly.

The Spike soldiers were taking their enemy's fascination as an opportunity to regroup. They walked among the kneeling or prone Skythians, stepping over the dead, keeping a wary eye open, and gathered together not far from where Bon and Leki sat on their exhausted shires. The soldiers kept close to one of the large fires, ready to shift behind it should the Skythians attack again. They would not wish themselves silhouetted against the flames.

A man and two women broke from the group and walked towards them.

'Your husband?' Bon asked softly.

'Don't speak,' Leki said. 'Not a word.'

Bon examined the trio. The limping man was tall, strong, handsome, everything he imagined a Spike Blader should be. One woman was short and slight, vicious looking, with a blood-soaked bandage around her throat. Her companion was heavier and pretty. She carried a thick wooden spear, its handle wet and dark.

Blood. They were all covered in it, perhaps theirs, more

391

likely their victims'. Their eyes glared from smeared faces. Firelight glinted.

'I need to tell him about—'

'Let me do the talking, Bon.'

The two women held back slightly, turning their backs on their Blader and watching the shadows. Leki's husband – Sol Merry, she'd told Bon, a name so unsuited to this blood-soaked daemon that he almost laughed – strode directly to their shires and stood between the creatures' heads, glancing back and forth between Leki and Bon.

'Who is this?' Sol asked. His voice was surprisingly soft, yet it commanded attention.

'Bon Ugane,' Leki said. 'He's been helping me.'

Sol nodded, eyes fixed at last on Leki. 'You look different, Leki. Yet it's still so good to see you.'

Leki's laugh was forced. 'You look different also.'

'What's that?' Sol asked. He held out his hand, nodding at Bon's hand.

'No,' Bon said. Sol's eyes flashed with anger. Here was a man not used to being refused.

'Not for the likes of you,' Leki said.

'The likes of me?' Sol asked.

'Or me,' Leki continued. 'Or Bon, or even the Skythians. It's not for the likes of any of us, except as a message.'

'Did you find Aeon?' Sol asked. 'That was your duty, and your mission. Where is it? He can stay here, hold that thing up and keep these bastards down, and you and I will go south with the news.'

'And then the Engines will raise magic to destroy Aeon once again,' Leki said.

'Of course,' Sol said. 'That's what we're here for, isn't it?' Bon could already hear doubt in the soldier's voice, and confusion.

'Everything you know is wrong,' Bon said. He was surprised at the conviction in his voice, the strength. He lowered the bone in his hand – sighing as the discomfort lessened – but kept one eye on the Skythians. The fight seemed to have gone from them all, but it might return without warning. Everything was in the balance.

'You speak when I address you,' Sol said softly. He was looking back and forth between them, his expression dark and unreadable.

'Bon, I told you to let me—' Leki started, but Sol reached up suddenly, grasped her arm and pulled her from the shire. She tried to land on her feet but stumbled, falling onto her side and hitting the ground hard.

Bon stiffened on his mount, but the heavy woman had slipped silently to his side. She rested her spear against his right thigh, ready to shove its tip into his stomach.

Sol paused for an instant, then bent to grab Leki's arm again.

Leki kicked up and out at Sol's hand, knocking it aside. He inhaled sharply. Fisted his hand, examining his fingers. The moment froze as Sol Merry avoided looking at anyone.

'So, Leki,' Sol spoke softly. 'Have you and he . . .?'

'No!' Leki stood, tense and ready. She looked shocked, confused. 'Sol, why are you doing this?'

'I thought you were . . .' He stood away from his wife, and Bon noticed something strange. It was no trick of the light, and no imagination on his part. Leki's blood-spattered husband was shaking. 'I thought you were dead.'

'Things have changed,' Leki said. '*Everything's* changed.'

Bon wondered what she meant.

We don't have very long, he thought, not quite sure where that idea had come from. He glanced across the battlefield, at the blazing fires and the people who had until recently been trying to kill each other. And he was struck by a terrible sense of hopelessness. In his right hand he carried something beyond human comprehension, and humans continued to fight and kill in the name of one god or another.

'There's nothing we can do,' he said.

'You. Quiet, or Deenia will—' Sol began.

'Will what? Kill me?' Bon glared at Sol, holding the bloodied soldier's gaze, and slowly shook his head. He carefully showed him the bone-like object, not wanting it to look at all like a threatening gesture. 'This is incredible, yet you want to destroy it. We live in a time of wonders, and you want to fight, and to kill.' He looked across at the bridge, and the slew of bodies across its span. He felt beyond sad. He felt empty.

'We have orders,' Sol said. He nodded towards Leki. '*Both* of us.' He and Leki stood apart, and their stances said that the distance between them had never been greater.

'Founded on wrong information,' Bon said.

'*So* wrong,' Leki said. 'Aeon is not the enemy here. It's just a thing, a wanderer. *Magic* is the enemy, Sol, because it will raise something *terrible*. You have to know what I've found out, and if you'll only let me tell you—'

Sol drew his sword and pointed it at his wife's face. Bon tensed, and felt the tip of the heavy spear pressing against his jacket and the roll of fat around his stomach. The eyes of the woman holding the weapon had barely changed, and he knew that she would gut him without blinking.

'You *believe* all this?' Sol shouted. 'You're blaspheming. Why? Because you're Arcanum? Because you're a *witch*?'

'Magic came from another god,' Bon said. He tried not to look at Leki, knowing that anger would not serve him well against these killers. 'A being as much a god as Aeon, at least. It was called Crex Wry; it fell long ago, and must never rise again.'

'What?' Sol said, angry. 'So now *you'd* tell me a story?'

'A story is fiction,' Bon said. 'This is the truth. If the Engines work and magic is raised, it might be the end for us all. It will destroy Aeon, magic's Kolts will rise, and this time they won't be so easy to put back down.'

'And if we let that Aeon thing wander the world, what then?' Sol said.

'Then nothing,' Bon said. 'Aeon and its kind wandered the world for ever, and witnessed the creation of the world we know today.' Bon felt the warmth in his hand. 'But one of them went mad.' The warmth seemed to pulse, a living part of Aeon. 'They put it down, because it was set to destroy everything they had made. And they worked hard to keep it down, for so long that the mountains forgot magic, and the valleys and seas had never known its corrupt touch.'

He held the bone tighter.

'I'm not interested in stories,' Sol said. 'Not even if they're the truth. I'm a soldier, and I'm only interested in orders.' He turned away from Leki and raised his sword at Bon. 'Now if you don't hand that thing over—'

'No,' Bon said. 'Not to someone like you.'

'Then I'll *take* it.' Sol came for him.

Bon glanced at Leki. He saw a slight shake of her head, a widening of her eyes. Sol saw it also, tensed—

Bon thrust his hand forward and struck the woman across the nose with the part of Aeon. She grunted and fell back, and Bon winced away from the spear's point as it slipped from his leg and fell with her.

He waited for the bone-thing to grow, or surge, or flow with the power of Aeon, spewing its message across the landscape so that these fools would know the truth. *I have Aeon in my hand!* he thought, feeling the heat, the pulse.

But nothing happened.

Hands grabbed him and pulled him down from the shire. Bon gasped in a breath to shout. Something struck his face, the fires visible between the startled shire's legs faded and true darkness fell.

The priest watches the battle, but is no part of it. Hers is a higher purpose. She keeps close to the Engine, one hand against its warm, shivering surface, the other nestled between her legs. The Engine seems to speak to her of its intentions. She listens, and loves.

They moved twenty miles along the coast before the enemy came. The going was easy, and the three Blades escorting her and the Engine – a hundred and fifty Spike soldiers, armed and ready for a fight – made sure the ground ahead was scouted, and any dangers eliminated or avoided. The priest watched some of their creatures of war move ahead, and sometimes she caught rumour of their implementation. A smell, a smear of blood on the sand, the ruined remains of some unknown enemy.

They said the Skythians were little threat.

And then the attack.

But the battle is almost over now, and the Spike soldiers are close to victory. The glade close to the sea where the ambush took place is covered with dead. Several large fires have been started, and in their deceiving light she can see piles of corpses, all of them Skythian. They are being heaped high and burned, and the Spike dead will be taken to the beach and given proper cremations, their ashes and the heat of their demise given to the gods.

'May the gods of the Fade smile as they accept the sacrifice made today,' the priest says. The Engine throbs in response, the sensations travelling across her shoulders and down her other arm. She closes her eyes and sighs.

'It'll be ready soon,' the engineer says. He is a weedy, rodent-like man, and she has never liked him. She once saw a tattoo on his shoulder that might have been Outer, and when she confronted him and forced him to strip before a jury of Fader priests, it was revealed as a birthmark. He has never trusted her since then. He says she does not believe how devout he is.

But, in truth, she is a little bit afraid of him. In the Engine, the engineer has something that is just beyond her understanding. A gateway to magic, when magic is a forbidden thing. A route aside from the Fade, not alongside it. Yet she calms this fear with the knowledge that this is the Fade's work they are doing – the destruction of a false god, daring to accept the term deity.

'The fight is almost over,' the priest says. 'I have sent word back to the generals that we will establish the Engine here.'

'Good a place as any,' the engineer says. He licks his finger and holds it to the air, looks through spread fingers inland and then back out to sea. He grins. She knows he is toying with her.

'You'll not grin when this is over,' the priest says. 'When your Engine is planted, perhaps you will stay with it.'

The man's face grows grim. 'You think any of us will be allowed to stay?' he asks.

'What do you mean?'

He chuckles. He is twisting wires together, connecting thin, membranous tubes to the Engine's side. He is a few steps away from her, but she can smell his sweat over the scent of roasting flesh. The battle made them closer together than ever; them, and the Engine.

'What it will release,' he says. He pauses, looking at the machine as if it is something he loves, and hates. Then he nods at her hand beneath her robes, buried in the wet warmth between her legs. 'It's already been talking to you.'

'I . . .' the priest says, preparing outrage. But the engineer is right.

'A few moments,' he says. 'The Engine where we made land is already awake.'

'How do you know?'

'Don't *you* know?' All humour has left his voice. He sounds like a man resigned.

'What will happen?' the priest asks softly. It is her first, and last, expression of doubt and concern.

'The Engine comes alive.' The engineer works on in silence, and the priest's fingers dance to the Engine's silent song.

The third Engine moves north. Its journey has been an easier one – no Skythians have yet found it, and the three Blades accompanying it have nothing worse than rough terrain to contend with. The wagon bearing the Engine has already lost two wheels, and repairs take time. But the priest is happy because the gods of the Fade are with him, and the Engine is his friend.

He prays to each god in turn, as he does every day, and has done every day since he can remember. He whispers exhortations, but he also tells them about himself, grasping reality by making himself real to the gods. His thoughts and fears, excitements and yearnings, all are whispered up amongst and behind his prayers. People have long since stopped listening to this priest because they think him mad, but he barely notices that lack of attention. The gods attend him. They welcome his voice. Soon, they will answer.

Because he can sense them waiting within the Engine. This, the construct of their victory over false gods, will soon gush forth the magic that they forbid because it is *so close* to them. The priest is certain of this, just as he is certain that they do not disapprove of him thinking so. They whisper to him, and he is their familiar.

The engineer works around the Engine as they travel. Triangulation, resonance, prashdial wavelength . . . the priest cares nothing for these, and he and the engineer have never spoken. Sometimes he prays for the engineer, but it is a lonely prayer. Their worlds are far apart.

The Engine sings inside, and the priest hears its song as echoes of the Fade.

It was only Leki's presence that prevented Sol from ordering the slaughter of their prisoners. While the remaining Spike soldiers – there were less than thirty out of the forty-nine who had marched this way with him – gathered the Skythians together and disarmed them, Sol sat with his wife. Tamma remained close by, keeping watch on the man Sol had punched unconscious. He was tied up. The thing with which he had killed Deenia was on the ground between Sol and Leki.

Everything was changing, and so much going wrong.

'I don't know who you are any more,' Sol said.

'You can say that? You're the one who attacked *me*!'

'I only pulled you from the horse.' Leki did not reply. 'I thought you were dead, Leki. Then I saw you, with him, and you started saying things that made no sense—'

'I'm the person I always was,' she said. 'But I'm aware of so much more.'

'The person you were served the Ald, and the gods of the Fade.'

'No,' Leki said softly. 'I was always Arcanum first. And . . .' She glanced away from him, eyes dancing with fire.

'Maybe Cove was right about you.'

'The General?' Leki asked.

'He called you an amphy witch.' Leki did not reply. Sol went on, 'So maybe it *is* your arcane arts you place before everyone, and everything else.'

'Can't you speak to me as your wife?'

'I feel like I'm married to lies.'

'No,' Leki said sadly. 'No lies, Sol, I promise. The truth has power and weight.'

Sol stood and kicked the bone-thing before him. It did not roll as far as it should have, as if it were much heavier than it actually felt.

'You have to believe me,' Leki said.

'Why? A threat, Leki?'

'You forget. I've seen it.'

'And you forget we're here to kill it.' Sol was conflicted, confused, and both emotions fed his anger. He had killed so many so recently, yet he wanted now to kill more. His blood was up. That unconscious bastard would be first, as revenge for Deenia, her face smashed back into her brain by the bone-thing. And then some of the prisoners.

And then Leki? His wife, for her betrayal of their cause? If he took her back with him, she would doubtless face banishment from Alderia anyway. Banishment back here. Perhaps he should leave her here, killed by his loving hand. If he acted quickly, maybe the memory of the woman he had loved might still survive.

'You still love me too much to kill me,' Leki said. She was smiling, one hand splayed in the blood-slushed snow, finger pressed into the muddy ground.

'You'd dare read me, floater?' As he spoke the word, a pang of shame made him turn away. There was silence for a precious heartbeat, and then Leki spoke.

'You're such a fine soldier,' she said to his back. The words were so loaded they hurt.

'I'm a *loyal* soldier!' Sol snapped. The distance between them was growing. He wished she had never found them, even if that meant the battle would still be raging. *He held up that thing and the Skythians fell to their knees.* Sol glanced back at Leki and the fist-sized object, pale in the reflected firelight. *I should kick it into the fire.*

His wife was lost to him. He loved her so much, and yet a stranger sat before him now, loaded with lies and corrupted by the land she had come here only to visit, not to be absorbed by. Its false god had made a disease of her mind. She shunned the Fade, and the mere idea of that sent a shiver down his spine – Sol was never an obsessive, but he was a devout Fader because that was how he had been brought up, the life he had lived.

His skin was stiff with dried blood, his hip burned and raged where he had taken an injury, his fingers were open to the bone where a sword had slipped across them. Yet the greatest pain nestled deep within his chest.

'There are no gods but the Fade,' Sol said. He drew his pistol and walked past Tamma, kneeling beside the bound man and pressing the barrel against his chest.

'Sol!' Leki cried out, and in that one word Sol heard so many admissions that it made the pain in his own chest heavier, and deeper than he thought he could carry.

'Oh by all the fucking gods of the Fade . . .' Tamma said. Her voice dripped awe and terror, and when Sol looked up past the fire he dropped his pistol, fell onto his rump, pushing himself back across the wet, cold ground.

Beyond the fires, where snow still lay relatively untouched outside the battlefield, something emerged from the shadows of the trees. Something huge, and pale, and impossible.

'There, Sol,' Leki whispered tenderly. 'Aeon arrives.'

Chapter 20

witness

Aeon gave them a chance, Venden thought. Before Aeon lay evidence of humanity's squandering of that chance – bloodied snow, bodies, flaming pyres, and at the battle's centre another act of violence about to take place. The message it had sent with his father and the woman had been cast aside.

Now, Aeon was gathering itself, its aura of sadness pushed aside as something began to rise. Venden sensed a shadow deep within the ancient being's mind, forming inside and ballooning outward, and at its heart was such violence, turmoil and hatred that he had never imagined.

What is *that?* Venden thought, but Aeon did not respond, and he quickly realised why. *That's . . . they're . . .* Recoiling in horror, Venden could not turn away.

Soon, they would soon be released.

Sol kicked his pistol aside and drew his bloodied sword, angry at himself for dropping his weapon, shocked, staggered by what he saw, but already he was struggling to gather his senses. Tamma was behind him, standing and shaking. Gallan was to his right, edging sideways closer to his Blader and showing no external signs of his shock. Sol knew that it must all be inside.

He had seen one of his Blade press a knife to his eye and fall on it. Suicide was a mortal sin amongst Alderians, and even more so for a soldier during the height of battle. Each Spike soldier bore the weight of the brothers and sisters within his or her Blade, and to remove one's own life – in whatever circumstance – was to put the rest of the Blade in danger. Sol wanted to rush across and stab at the soldier's corpse, slash and ruin his body as punishment for what he had done. But his soul had already filtered to the Fade, and any punishment was now in the hands of the gods.

'Sol, what *is* that?' Gallan said. Tamma answered from behind them.

'Aeon,' she said. 'The Skythian god, Aeon.'

'It's what we all came here to kill,' Sol said. Such a statement seemed so foolish in the presence of this thing.

'You can never kill it,' Leki said. She had regained her feet and stood almost within Sol's reach. Almost. She was not afraid.

As the huge shape drifted closer to them, ambiguous, difficult to discern fully in the shifting shadows and dancing firelight, Sol was overcome with awe at the history it implied. It was a manifestation of the purest blasphemy a devout Fader could imagine – a player at being a god, in denial of the Fade. He could understand why the Skythians believed it a deity, but in the same thought he hated the very idea of such beliefs, and hated Aeon for attracting them.

Around him, captured Skythians had dropped to the ground and lay prone, faces averted.

'This is why we brought the Engines,' Gallan said.

'We can't run away,' Sol said.

Gallan turned to him. 'I wasn't suggesting we should.' His tone betrayed the lie in his statement. Fighting this was the last thing he wished to do, and Sol could not blame him.

But Spike *never* ran. There were countless stories about the Ald's soldiers holding out against all hope, succeeding against all expectation, triumphing against overriding odds. Stories, too, about heroic defeats.

'Blade, re-form!' Sol shouted. Gallan blinked, afraid. But he pressed his lips tight together, and nodded once at Sol.

'Alderia,' Gallan said, the fighting call barely a whisper.

'Sol!' Leki said. She moved closer, holding his arm as she used to. But her touch had changed. 'Sol, listen instead of fighting, and perhaps you can learn something.'

'Don't condescend to me!' Sol hissed, shoving her away. She tripped over a discarded spear and fell close to the man Sol should have killed. But there was something larger to kill now. She was welcome to him.

'Sol . . . you're so wrong.'

Traitor, he thought, but he did not respond. His wife was lost to him, and Sol turned his back on her.

The remaining soldiers had formed into three groups, each placing itself between two of the Skythians' large fires. Aeon paused at the edge of the battlefield, its pale body reflecting blood-tinged flames in streaks of red and orange.

'Alderia!' Sol shouted. Without another glance at Leki he hefted his sword, charged Aeon, and knew with complete faith that the remainder of his Blade followed.

Bon surfaced, blinking away pain, and wondered if he was the only person to notice the sky.

It was smeared with dawn in the east, and the snow had stopped, yet the sky was ominously heavy with something ready to fall. He noticed Leki close by, looking up and frowning.

'Something wrong,' he said.

She turned, surprised at his voice. 'Yes,' she said. 'Laden with doom.'

Bon sat up and Leki helped him, and her words struck home. *Laden with doom.* His whole time here on Skythe had felt like that, and now it gathered towards a climax. Doom watched him, and he looked around to see what else it saw.

Fires burned, piled bodies cast spiky skeletal shadows, and Aeon was here. They were attacking it, but ineffectually. Spears ricocheted from its body, some snapping in two. Swords wielded by experienced hands seemed not to touch its legs, nor its stomach where it dipped low enough for them to reach. Its huge head turned lazily, knocking two soldiers to the ground almost by accident. *It's not fighting back*, Bon thought. *It's almost as if . . .*

'Waiting for something,' Leki said.

'I think so too,' he said.

'What about . . .?' Leki nodded at the Skythians, scores of them still lying on the ground.

'Waiting as well.' *Aeon doesn't need them to protect it*, he thought. A pile of Skythian corpses burned close to the bridge, grotesque shapes of bone and simmering flesh thrown out by the flames, and he felt so sad. Tears blurred his vision. *It sent those as well as us, and . . .*

'What if we've both failed?' he asked.

'What do you mean?'

'Look at the sky,' he said. Dawn was brightening, but the sky was still rank with something terrible.

'Oh, by all the gods,' Leki said, and she slumped against him. 'Bon, I see it now. I *smell* it. I think maybe one of the Engines is working already.'

'Already?'

'Magic draws close,' Leki breathed.

'And this is growing warm.' Bon had pulled the bone-thing Aeon had given them closer with his foot. Wet mud steamed around it, slushy snow melted. He was about to kick it away again when Venden spoke in his mind. The voice was his son's when he was very young, barely able to talk. But the words carried great weight.

Hold this part of Aeon's heart, and close your eyes again, father. Whatever you hear, whatever you sense . . . close your eyes.

Sol Merry had fought Outer rebellions, dissenters in western Alderia, a plague of rabid Ban Chock tribesmen in the east, and a rash of rawpanzie attacks on the Chasm Cliffs. But he had never faced an enemy like this. Aeon was beyond imagining, because it was blasphemy to imagine a false god. To even consider them capable of being imagined was heresy, and as he drove a spear towards the monster's underbelly, and darted between its legs to hack at the heavy swinging parts either side of its head – tentacles, or other appendages – he felt the gods of the Fade moving with him. He was fighting for them and every honest, devout Alderian who paid them the homage they deserved. He was fighting for his dead father's warrior heritage, his politician mother who strove to better her town's outlook and future, and his sister and her burgeoning family.

But he was no longer fighting for his wife, and that left a knot of scar tissue at the centre of his soldier's bloody heart.

Aeon did not seem concerned at the attack. It moved towards the river, kicking apart one of the Skythian's fires, and the Spike followed. It swung its huge head from left to right, knocking two soldiers aside. But their fall was an accident, not a deliberate attack.

'We're not touching it!' Tamma yelled.

'The Engines will touch it,' Sol said, lunging with his sword, blade skittering from the thing's hard foot. He felt hollow, bereft. Empty of every good thing. Even the memory of his family seemed to be fading, replaced with an all-consuming understanding that nothing he did, and nothing he had ever done, held any significance.

Who am I what am I why am I? It should have been a scream, but when he opened his mouth, he only gasped.

His friend was staring at him. Gallan had dropped his sword and mace and stood wide-eyed, as if a profound realisation had struck. His face looked calm and uncreased by the stress of war. *Hollow man*, Sol thought, and as he and Gallan locked eyes, something filled them both.

The world exploded and blew Sol backwards, sprawling in muck and blood, conscious only of the shattering violence erupting around and within him. There was no refuge from its fury, no islands in this convulsive turmoil. Something entered and wrestled with his consciousness, a twisting mad thing, ancient and abhorrent and yet suddenly rejoicing in this strange freedom.

Kolt! Sol thought as his mind was shattered, shredded, ripped apart by the invader. Sol's scream of agony was silent, because his body was paralysed by the extent and shock of the pain. Everything he was – every dream and love, habit and history – shrivelled to nothing, and witnessing the loss was awful. Sol's last full, conscious experience was seeing his whole life and self erased and replaced with something monstrous.

Sol Merry ceased to exist at that moment, leaving a travesty of what he had once been. His new present – his here and now, where existence was as interesting to him as a bug's existence to the bug – was filled with one impetus.

407

He picked up his dropped sword and spear and examined his surroundings. There were more who looked like him, but they were of no interest. There were other shapes prone on the ground, not like him, but these also held no interest. And there were two more shapes huddled together around something that burned and shone like the sun.

Sol flinched from the glow and started running, raging, as an instinct he did not understand took him south.

Bon kept his eyes squeezed tightly shut against the rage. He could feel Leki pressed against him, the fragment of the heart of Aeon blazing between them, her breath warm against his cheek, her heartbeat welcome against his chest, and he so hoped that she was keeping her eyes closed as well. Whatever was happening, neither of them should see it.

The explosion had been incredibly violent, and all but silent. Bon had felt himself compressed and then pushed across the ground, sliding through mud and blood with Leki clasped against him. They had come to rest against a pile of Skythian bodies.

I smell blood and fear and something unknown, Bon had thought, and the storm raged. He heard the subtle rustle and clink of other bodies striking the ground, clothing and weapons knocking together. The air seemed to writhe and flex around them, whipping back and forth as if indecisive about which way to blow, scouring his skin.

He kept his eyes closed and felt Leki's hand squeeze his shoulder, and the pressure remained as she found comfort in the contact. *Was that the end of Aeon?* he thought, and he could almost not bear to look. But the thing between them kept them warm and safe, and Venden's words rang with him, spoken in the voice of his beautiful young son before he had grown up and away. *Whatever you hear, whatever you sense . . . close your eyes.*

Bon almost opened his eyes. Leki seemed to sense his inclination, because she pulled him tighter, closer, and pressed her mouth against his ear.

'No,' she said. 'I want to see as much as you, but no. We do what Aeon told us.' She kissed him below the ear, a desperate, hard kiss. 'A few more moments of ignorance might be all we have.'

So they hugged close, and though the object Venden had handed Bon was pressed between their stomachs, it did not come between them. Bon kissed Leki on the side of the face, the eye, and then a full kiss against her lips, sharing passion and need and pleased to feel them both returned.

'I should have helped you,' he said, meaning what he had seen between her and her husband.

'I could have helped myself, if I'd needed to. Besides, Sol would have killed you, and I would have never forgiven myself.'

'I should have *helped* you.'

'You have helped me.' Leki's tears touched his cheek.

The sense of the world being turned upside down and inside out settled, and in its place was a dreadful, foreboding silence. *Something is watching us*, Bon thought, and the skin on his arms and the back of his neck prickled.

'It's horrible,' Leki whispered, because she felt it as well.

The fragment of Aeon's heart was cooling between them. Bon shifted slightly to touch it, and Leki clasped his arms as if he were moving away.

'I think now,' he said. His voice quivered. The fear was terrible. What would he find remaining of Aeon? And what was staring at them?

Bon opened his eyes.

409

They had come to rest against several dead Skythians, whose sightless eyes watched what happened. Perhaps they were the more fortunate ones.

He looked around the dawn-lit battlefield. It was taking on colour with the sun, and the predominant hue was red. The ground was sucking in the blood, the snow wet with it. Fires were still crackling, and beyond them he saw the body of Aeon.

It moved, casual and slow as ever. Alive!

But then, to his right, between where they lay and the river bridge still piled with bodies, he saw what had become of everyone else.

'Bon,' Leki whispered, because she had seen as well. 'Are they . . .? Can they really be . . .?'

'I've been so wrong,' Bon said. 'It wasn't Aeon's demise that made them, but Aeon itself. Aeon made the Kolts.'

The Kolts were standing, grabbing weapons, and all of them had changed, Spike and Skythian alike. They wore the same clothes and were the same shape, but were no longer the same people. They did not fight. Faces filled with hate, eyes with fury, skin glowing with red rage, mouths grimacing and teeth begging the feel of weak skin and wet flesh, the Kolts scanned the battlefield once, and then ran away towards the south. There was no organisation here, and no orders being called. These things had been born, and would live and die, alone.

One purpose. One aim.

'They're going to kill everything,' Bon said.

'What about us?'

Bon touched the object between them, cooling now. And he watched Leki, ready to hold her again should she crumple and descend into grief. He had seen her husband, changed from the soldier he had been to the mindless, driven killer

410

Aeon had made him. Walking dead, Sol was gone from a man to a monster.

'Why?' Leki asked. But already Bon was trying to see what might happen next.

Father, Venden said in his mind. Bon gasped, and Leki looked at him.

'He's talking to me,' Bon whispered.

One last request of you both.

Bon looked past the battlefield and beyond the fires at Aeon, virtually motionless in the pristine snow. 'It's not over,' he said.

Leki clasped his hand. 'Then whatever comes, we do it together.'

Sol Merry ran, seeking something to kill. Others ran around him, but not with him. A woman with a bandage around her neck, a tall man. Some looked alike, others were shorter and wilder, different. But only on the outside. On the inside they were all the same, and the proof of that was not long in coming.

They came across the group hiding on the leeward side of a small hill. Twenty adults and thirty children, they quickly fell beneath sword and spear. Sol slashed and stabbed, the daemon within relishing the blood that bathed him and the gore that splashed in the snow at his feet. He felt the sting of weapons striking him and merely brushed others away, not even blinking as his arm snapped the arrow shafts, his roar bent swords – his fury exerted a terrible weight, but the ability was no surprise. He turned and went after the attacker, but she had already been taken down by two others like him.

Sol heard the screaming, the pleading. He mimicked the sound, his voice surprisingly high, and it rose into a bloodthirsty scream as he thrust his sword deep into a woman's chest. He ducked a sword and fisted the swordsman in the face, then turned to gut him. Kneeling, hacking through the hot remains, Sol picked out the choicest morsel and pressed it to his mouth. His eyes rolled as he bit the slippery liver in half.

The rage was hot, the daemon on fire. It thrummed through him, pulsing in his toes and fingers, head and knees, stomach and back, and he painted it across the landscape in blood.

The slaughter was soon over, and Sol and the others ran on. *Kolts!* he heard some of their victims shouting. He knew the word and felt its comfortable fit. He nurtured the killing and the rage, along with the daemon settled within him. Running south, he soon lost sight of anyone else like him. But sometimes, from left or right, he heard an occasional shout of surprise, and a scream, and then silence as another Kolt made a kill.

His mind was red, and nothing else. A blind purpose drove him on.

Chapter 21
following

Juda walked across the frozen landscape and felt watched every step of the way. Sometimes he thought he caught sight of the man he followed – the man he knew was him – but other times he thought perhaps it was only a shadow. Never close, always half hidden from view, the wraith drew him south.

Deep, thunderous sounds echoed in from the north. They were so much a part of the landscape that they did not register with him for some time. There were snow and ice, trees and rocks, small birds and an occasional larger creature. There was a grey sky and high crags, a smudge of sun in the east, and that momentous cracking sound, like giant rocks being crushed together many miles away. Juda paused until the noise rumbled in again, and he thought he felt a slight shock through his feet. He could not be certain. It was very cold. He wondered at the size of the impact to be felt through the ground. Glaciers cracking, perhaps. Ice cliffs falling.

How far away? he wondered. He glanced back at the mountains in the hazy distance. They looked like a memory.

Juda walked on, disconcerted rather than afraid. It was hard going, because his feet sank into the deep snow, and soon he had to rest. He was already exhausted. The shadow he followed rested as well, leaning against a tree and not moving at all while Juda stared at it. He closed his eyes and leaned his head back, welcoming the weak sunlight on his face. When he looked again, the shadow had moved position.

I'm following, he thought, talking to the shadow from his dreams.

And then he remembered his dreams, and for the first time in years they were a long way from nightmares. There was repetition in following the man up hills and down, as if he were remembering the same walk again and again. There was constant cold, ice caves containing unknown things, and the ground opening and giving birth to huge glaciers. But his half-Regerran blood must have frozen in Skythe's sudden winter, because the dreadful nightmares that had haunted him for so long seemed to have withered away.

Something was driving, and luring, him south. A compulsion he could not quite identify, and a sense that everything important was happening there, not here.

As the sun painted the eastern horizon a gorgeous array of reds and oranges, there was also the shadow following him. It was more obvious than the shape he pursued, though further away. He recognised his own gait, and his own shape. He saw himself.

Wondering if the man before and the man behind were thinking the same things, Juda hurried on towards something momentous.

'Oh Venden, my sweet son,' Bon said, and he could not tear his eyes away from the terrible sight. He had seen this once before, but now his son's agony was plain to witness as he manifested from Aeon's hide, squirming and writhing against the god's embrace. As his mouth formed his scream came, a gargled, distant thing at first, then something that roared to life across the silent battlefield. It brought sound to the grisly scene.

'Be strong,' Leki said, holding Bon's hand. 'Be brave. He's come to tell us something important.'

'Why can't Aeon tell us itself?' Bon asked, and just for that moment he hated Aeon. 'It spoke to me before. Why can't it just let us *know*?'

'I think it's tired,' Leki said. 'It's barely moving. You heard Venden in your mind, but perhaps that takes great effort. This way must be easier.'

Easier to torture and mutilate what is left of my son, Bon thought, but he did not speak what was on his mind. Torture and mutilation was often the way of humankind. He only had to look around at the scene revealed by the dawn to acknowledge that. Perhaps it was the same for a being like Aeon.

Venden drew out and formed, rising up from a squat to the tall boy he had once been. 'Nothing is won,' he rasped. 'Aeon has raised daemon-shadows from the depths, and tasked them, and they will surge southward to take away the Alderians' means of controlling the Engines.'

'You mean to kill them all,' Leki said.

Venden's eyes did not change. His expression was empty.

'And will the Kolts go back down?' Bon asked.

'That is no concern,' Venden said. 'Halting the rise of Crex Wry is everything.'

'You're not only here to tell us that, son,' Bon whispered. Venden's head turned, just slightly.

'The Kolts will not end the Engines. They will kill the . Alderians. But two of the Engines are alight. One more, and the magic will come through, and Crex Wry will rise to claim its wretched soul. The land will grow *dark*. The world will *shudder*. Time itself will fall.'

There was urgency in Venden's voice, now. And perhaps fear.

'What do you want us to do?' Leki asked.

'Three Engines are needed. Destroy the one not yet alight, and the others will die.'

'How can we destroy an Engine?' Bon asked. 'Leki?' He turned to her, hoping for an answer, or support, or some sign that she understood.

She stared at Aeon, seeming to witness something else.

'Leki?' he prompted.

'You allow us to retain Aeon's heart?' she asked.

'You must,' Venden said.

'Then we'll follow the path of the Kolts, and find the Engine,' Leki said. She turned to Bon. 'We might not have much time.'

Aeon groaned. It was a terrible sound, like a huge edifice crumbling and collapsing, and the thing the Skythians called a god slumped to the ground. It touched so gently, yet an impact wave washed out from its bulk and kicked Bon's feet from under him. He stumbled and fell, catching sight of Venden's dissolution as he did so. A scream hung in Bon's mind. But he was not sure whether he had truly heard it, or imagined it.

'It *is* exhausted,' Leki said, picking herself up. 'Whatever it did to raise the Kolts . . .' There was something strange about her voice now; heavier, lower. She carried a weight.

'What is it?' Bon asked.

'We have to go. It's all coming together for me, Bon. It's all . . . I may know how to destroy the Engine. But time is short, so I'll tell you on the way.'

'Do you know where it is?'

416

'We can follow the trail of the dead.'

One of the shires had collapsed and died from exhaustion, the other had fled. So Bon and Leki started running through the snow, following the footprints of Kolts. Murderers, monsters, daemons, and things not of the world.

It started snowing again. Sol ran alone now, others having drifted apart from him as they raged southward. Occasionally he heard distant sounds of brief battle, and once or twice he caught the faint whiff of blood. His mind processed these sounds and smells, and little else. Personality was a nebulous thing, and he was all but absent from his own mind. Only the driving need to kill remained.

He came across a group of soldiers, all dressed the same and bearing weapons and sigils that he recognised. There were six of them. Surprised, they formed into defensive postures, then seemed to relax when he emerged from the swirling snow. He killed them all, a fury-filled daemon slashing and stabbing and spitting blood, screaming aside arrows and avoiding serious injury. The brief fight over, he started hacking at one of the female corpses. Armour and clothing discarded, skin and flesh and ribcage rent, he plucked the prize from its still-warm resting place.

The liver was rich and healthy, and Sol sucked it dry before chewing it into soft chunks.

Waving flies from the pouting lips of a wound across his chest, he ran on shirtless. Snow stuck to his chest hairs, ice formed across his cheeks and eyebrows. He saw others like him, and though they did not acknowledge each other, some-where deep in his ruined soldier's mind Sol recognised a confluence of routes, and a single aim that must be drawing them.

For the first time since being blasted into something new,

Sol slowed down. His senses still raced, a frantic sprint that set him twitching as he stalked beneath low-hanging trees towards something hidden within the confines of the next valley. His mind raced ahead too, but some need, and a comprehension his lessened mind could not understand, urged caution.

Like hive ants closing on prey, Sol and the other Kolts drew closer together.

Still wet with the blood of slain soldiers, Sol crested a rise and saw many more. They were arrayed protectively around a wagon, on which sat a strange construct. It was metallic, spiked with protruding parts, asleep yet sickly aware. A man in a grey robe sat close to it. *Engine*, Sol thought, and he was repulsed. But he would not turn and run when so many victims stood before him.

Someone screeched to his right, and the Kolt with a bandaged neck pounded downhill towards the soldiers. Arrows and crossbow bolts whistled at her, but she waved most of them aside. A rifle hissed and shot shattered her shoulder, but her pace did not slacken. She dodged a thrown spear, tripped, rolled, and then she was amongst them, slashing and furious as they fought back.

Sol uttered his own scream as he charged the small army. He could smell their livers, and he had only to open bodies to find them.

The bandaged woman lost her head to a sword's swing, but as Sol launched into bloody battle once more, he saw her headless body still swinging blades and spinning in murderous, blood-splashed circles.

Then the hunger consumed his attention entirely, and his daemon revelled in the slaughter.

The priest watches a massacre and prays to the Fade. White snow turns red, and falling flakes are sprayed with blood-mist.

Bodies fall, whole or in parts. He sits on the wagon with one hand pressed against the vibrating Engine, the other clasped around his spent cock, and he feels his gods' excitement at what is happening here.

It confuses him. Excitement?

'Out of the way!' the engineer shouts, shoving past the priest and almost tumbling from the wagon. He attends the Engine and leaps to the ground, thrusting two pronged spikes into the snow and leaning on them as they sink down. They are attached to snaking pipes, which in turn trail up onto the wagon and into the Engine. The pipes move, as if alive.

'Gods of Fade, aid the Spike in their need,' the priest says, but already he is afraid. Almost a hundred Spike soldiers are fighting, but their enemy seems, at first, invisible. The priest sees the results of combat, but where violence occurs there are only Spike uniforms.

The Engine thumps against his hand, one heavy, hard impact that cracks bones and bursts the flesh of his fingers like cooked sausages. He cries out and holds the mutilated limb to his chest, and the Fade gods soothe him in his own voice. It is always his own voice they speak in, in his own mind. *Everything will be well*, they tell him, and it is exactly what he wishes to hear.

But looking around, biting his lip against the pain of his shattered hand, he begins to realise that everything is far from well.

Another shattering thud from the Engine, and the wagon beneath it disintegrates. The Engine drops through the mess of broken boards and split axles, impacting the ground and sending a shockwave that ripples the snow all around. Some soldiers fall, and others fall on them as they go down, blades flashing.

The engineer is back at the ruined wagon, and the priest

realises that he has swallowed his surprise at what the Engine has done. *It was always more than we thought*, the priest thinks. *The engineer knows that perhaps better than me.*

'Gods of the Fade, aid us in our tasks, and give your holy warriors—' the priest intones.

'Oh for fuck's sake, pick up a fucking spear, or something!' the engineer shouts. He is attaching cables and twisting sprung dials, clearing snow from the ground with one foot and then drawing a pattern in the exposed soil, plunging ivory-clamped connectors into the pattern's centre. He glances over his shoulder at the fighting, his shock and urgency self-evident.

The priest realises at last what is happening when he sees Sol Merry, the Blader who had travelled across from Alderia on the same ship as the Engines. Except he is no longer Blader Merry. His face is the same, his body a similar shape, but everything about Merry has left him. He is a daemon alive with blood, spiked with broken arrows, slashed with gushing wounds, and raging at his former comrades. He kills with a furious precision and hunger that the priest has never seen nor heard of before, and many fall before him.

As the priest sees several other Spike killing their own – and squatter, wilder shapes that must be Skythians – one word plays across his mind.

'Kolts! The Kolts are among us!'

The engineer glances up at the priest. 'Oh. So you do talk.'

The priest shuffles away from the Engine, his shattered hand held to his chest. But the engineer grabs his robes and pulls him back. It is a violation, but even the priest does not acknowledge the travesty of the man's touch.

'Too late now, priest,' the engineer says. 'We've all come too far to do anything but carry on. Here.' He hands the priest a small, flexible bulb. It is black, and warm. 'If anything happens to me, that goes in the port in the Engine's upper surface. Understand?'

'The gods of the Fade will smile on us, and see away the calamity that we are—'

'*Do you understand?*' the engineer shouts. He is scared but excited, and the priest knows why. He has known such excitement since they landed on this island. The Engine is alive, a throbbing potential, and it craves the opportunity for release.

'Yes,' the priest says.

But neither the priest, nor the engineer, finds an end to their excitement. The engineer moves around the Engine, connecting other ivory clamps into the ground, and takes a spear through the chest. He tugs a pistol from his belt and blasts the Kolt in the face. It merely shakes its head, then lifts him high and smacks him back against the Engine. Blood stains the construct's metal surface, and the engineer is dead before he drops to the ground.

And the priest, the Engine's bulb growing warmer in his hand, can only watch in wide-eyed terror as Sol Merry runs at him. The Blader's mouth is open, bloodied, his teeth clotted with fresh meat, eyes black pits into shadows that the priest has prayed against his whole life.

As he is broken open and his insides spilled out, the priest's head tilts back and snowflakes caress his face. His last thought is a prayer to the gods of the Fade, but his only answer is endless, silent emptiness.

With almost everyone around the Engine dead or dying, Sol took a heavy mace across the backs of his legs. He dropped the dead robed figure he had been delving into, tried to turn, and his legs crumpled beneath him.

Two young soldiers faced him, and he roared and lashed

out. He tried standing, but his legs failed. One soldier came close with a spear, and Sol twisted slightly, allowing the weapon to pierce his hip instead of repulsing it. It was more the way of a warrior. The soldier grinned, then Sol grabbed the spear and pulled sharply. It slid through his body and the soldier, gripping tightly, came with it. Sol sliced the smile from his face.

The second man cringed, and fell beneath another Kolt's blade.

Sol snapped the spear and tugged the shaft from his body. His wound gushed, but the pain was a remote thing, the curse of something far away. He tried to stand, leaning on the dead man for leverage, but his legs folded. They were slashed deeply, bones scored, and the thigh bone in his right leg was shattered.

With the massacre ended and feeding done, the Kolts continued their rampage towards the south. The thing that had been Sol Merry crawled in a wide circle around the Engine. He growled and screeched, picking up discarded weapons and digging deep for sustenance. The food gave him strength. But knitting broken bones and pulling broken arrows was beyond any powers he might have.

Through bloodied snow, his crawled path continued.

At its centre, the Engine exuded a terrible readiness that troubled even Sol's daemon consciousness.

The Kolts' trail became harder to follow. Their paths diverted the further south Bon and Leki went, and fresh snow was burying the signs. But Leki paused frequently and splayed her hands in the snow, face creased in concentration, her amphy eyes glimmering as she read the frozen water.

'South,' she said. 'Always south.'

They found the bodies of slaughtered Skythians. A single

man, then a small family group, and then, heading down into a wide valley, the expansive stain of blood was evident across the southern slopes. They paused only to gather weapons, and Bon fell to his knees and vomited. It was a thin, pathetic stream, and he could not remember the last time he had eaten.

'Aeon did this,' Leki said. 'To its own people. It knew they'd die before the Kolts, yet it set them raging.'

'The Skythians *aren't* its people,' Bon said. 'You still don't understand that. Still in the Ald mindset. Aeon is a god only to those who choose to see it as one.'

They hurried on, bearing the weapons they had gathered from the dead. Bon carried a spear, Leki a short sword. Bon also carried the fragment of heart, and he thought it was growing warm again.

They reached a ridge and looked south. In the distance a plume of smoke turned the swirling blizzard grey. Leki knelt and read the snow. The act seemed to cause her some hurt, but she braved the pain. Amphys preferred running water. Perhaps reading snow chilled her to the core.

'More dead bodies,' she said. 'Maybe three miles?'

'Three or four,' Bon said. He hefted the spear. 'So, Leki. What do you know?'

She looked at him as if dreading the question. He saw uncertainty, and fear, but he stepped in close and touched her face. She closed her eyes and did not pull away, but he saw her pain.

'In Arcanum we learned so much,' she said. And as they set off towards the grey stain on the landscape's whiteness, Leki laid bare her heart, and her secrets.

'Arcanum was never about magic. There were always the whispers, from those who might disapprove politically, or sometimes from Faders who believed what we did went against the Fade. They were designed to cast a slur on Arcanum and make it something it wasn't. These people wanted to promote a climate of fear about a group that was . . . well, just interested in deeper things. We aren't magicians, but we do have imaginations. We're critical of knowledge, because that's how it progresses. We interrogate beliefs, because that's how new discoveries are made. And every truth that Arcanum holds dear is interrogated as well. We're open enough to call a truth a lie, if there's proof of the fact. It's how *we* move on. Can you imagine Alderia as it was a thousand years ago?'

'I'm not sure I can,' Bon said. 'So much of what we're taught is lies, and so much of what I believed to be the truth turns out to be . . . untrue.'

'Arcanum could imagine,' Leki went on. 'If it weren't for us, that's where we would still be. We have been steering from behind the scenes for centuries – advising the Ald, conversing with the Fader priests, being open when we were welcomed, manipulating when we were not. And in all that time, our understanding of magic has increased.

'Six hundred years ago we believed it was a force to be conjured and controlled. More recently, we began to suspect that it had a sentience we could barely comprehend. But all our suspicions were based on supposition, and analysis of the few dregs we managed to procure.'

'Aeon told us the truth?'

'It told me more in one breath than Arcanum has learned in centuries. If only it would come with us.'

'I don't believe Aeon has any intention of doing anything it doesn't desire,' Bon said. They were negotiating a steep slope, heading down from a ridge and into a deep valley, at the end of which the smoke trail rose. Either of them could slip at any moment and perhaps alter the course of the world. The fragility of existence struck Bon then, and that interweaving of every person, every thing.

'The Engines are Arcanum's,' Leki said.

'You told me you knew nothing of the Engines!'

'I'm sorry, Bon. Truth and lies . . . we all trade in both. Arcanum had more input into the Engines' construction than the priests, and the Ald, and the engineers they both hired for the task. I've seen carvings gathered from the western deserts that provided the early Ald with schematics for Engines, and I have met those whose sole work is to refine the designs. Incorporate all the Fade sigils and elements, but—'

'Fade?'

Leki did not seem eager to continue, but Bon pushed.

'Fade, Leki? You started this. Don't tell me half and then walk away.'

'The schematics . . . no one can age them, or place their origins. They were carvings in a cave, that's all I know. And there are sketches on weathered parchment, found in other places. And they contained aspects of every Fade god, built into the Engines in a very active way. Not just aesthetically. These are the guts of what seem to make them work.'

'But the Fade gods—'

'Don't exist? What about what Venden said to you?' She shook her head, trying to make sense. 'About Crex Wry seeding the Fade to aid its own resurrection. Don't you see? What if those seven gods of the Fade that the Ald insist their people follow, believe in, worship and fear, were all made up by Crex Wry, so that specific aspects of them were incorporated into the Engines to give Crex Wry its route back? If that's true, then for millennia most of Alderia has been following a false religion initiated by the one thing that *might* be close to a god.' She laughed out loud.

'But the Fade began . . .' Bon thought of all those origin stories, told to youngsters by their teachers at school, and by

425

parents as darkness drew in and fear made their children more receptive.

'The Fade made the world,' Leki said. 'So the story goes. There have been rumours of the Fade for as long as there has been language, and writing.'

'And carvings on cave walls,' Bon said.

'Divine or not, those Engines we build work at raising magic.'

'And you built without understanding them,' Bon said, both awed and horrified.

'Early Arcanum did their very best to understand,' Leki said. 'We continue to do so. There are those who can't handle such proximity to magic, and I've seen many grown mad like Juda. But we're trying to learn more. To *become* wise.'

'What matters now is that we need to stop them,' Bon said. The true impact of what Venden had hinted at was staggering, but it was also meaningless to them. And even if they survived the next day and made it back to Alderia, theirs would be just another rumour. Another story against the Fade, ready to be put down by the Ald's agents, prosecuted, expunged. In the Ald's blind and blinkered faith, Crex Wry had built itself the perfect defence.

'I've spent years studying the Engines, and I know as much about them as anyone,' Leki said. 'If one has been initiated, it will be drawing magic from the fold where it lies. If two are fired up, the prashdial generators will be forging a circuit around which magic can travel. Once its flow is established, its energy and power will build.'

'And the third Engine will release it.'

'The third completes the circuit,' Leki said. 'Magic draws up at the centre of the triangle.' She hurried on ahead, the silence between them loaded. Neither could forget what Aeon, through Venden, had shown them of Crex Wry, that fallen magical being.

'Leki?' Bon prompted, because he sensed that she had more to say.

'The thing your son handed you must have a purpose,' she said. 'It's part of the enemy of Crex Wry. Part of *Aeon's heart*! It's the exact opposite of everything the Engines are, and are created for. It's *anti*-Engine. We must have been given it for a reason, and because of that I believe it holds power.' She paused with her back to him. 'And so I have two things to ask of you. The first is that I take that part of Aeon's heart from you.'

'Yes,' Bon said. She turned, he handed it to her. An act of total trust. It had felt alive in his hand, and Leki's eyebrows rose when she touched it.

'What's the second thing?' Bon asked.

'That you run. Leave now, head south, reach the coast. Flee Skythe with everyone you can find. Take them far away. Just . . . go.'

Bon gasped in the cold, and it chilled him to the heart. He shook his head and saw Leki's pain.

'No,' he said. 'Not a chance.'

'You *can't* help me, Bon! I'm certain that Aeon gave us a weapon, and I think perhaps I know how to use it.' She looked down at the object now resting in her hand. 'Inside the Engines there was always a core where the powers converged. Energies from all those aspects of the Fade gods that were built into them met with source energy from the ground, drawn up by the deep-set prashdial generators. I think if those energies meet this . . .' She hefted the shape, holding it up between them.

'What?' he asked.

'Repulsion,' she said. 'Two opposing energies fighting. An eruption. An explosion.'

427

'I'm coming with you.'

'No, Bon! I have to find my way into the Engine. Get
. . . *inside* it, and find the energy core. And these newer
Engines are smaller.' She shook her head, frowning. 'More
refined.'

'I'm not going to run,' Bon said. 'Not after all this. After
everything, I'm going to help you, and—'

'You *have* helped! If it weren't for you, and Venden, Aeon
might never have spoken to us. You've helped more than you
can imagine. Now, please, for me. Go.'

'I came here with nothing, I'm not leaving with nothing
as well.'

'Oh, Bon . . .' Leki said, and it was frustration as well as
gratitude. *She really wants me to leave*, he thought, which
meant only one thing.

And he would not allow her to kill herself.

Bon pushed past her and hurried on, keeping the smoke
trail in sight as he descended to the valley floor and traced
the small stream that ran there. Leki followed behind, and
Bon's grip on the spear was tight, determined. She might
know how to stop the Engine, but it would not be an easy
route there.

He thought of those Kolts, their fury . . .

They smelled the fire before they saw it. And then they
saw the Engine, and the blood-patterned snow surrounding it.

The two beasts of burden that had pulled the wagon were
dead, the wagon shattered. Spike soldiers lay strewn around
– gutted, beheaded, ripped open. Several Skythians lay there
as well, and Bon could see even in their dead expressions
the fury of the Kolt.

The Engine seemed to hum without making a noise, to
throb without moving. It was rooted to the land. Bon stood
beside Leki for a moment, both of them catching their breath.

'It's horrible,' Bon said. He felt sick and wretched, and knew the source to be the Engine.

'It's yearning initiation,' Leki said. 'The other two . . . they've fired up. We're so close, Bon.'

'If the Kolts hadn't come through, it might have happened already.'

'I think it might happen anyway. Magic is forcing forward. I can *smell* it.'

'I'll be close by,' Bon said softly. Leki held his hand gently and leaned towards him, brushing his lips with hers.

'Another time, another place,' Leki said, full of regret. She let go and walked towards the Engine.

Bon saw movement from the corner of his eye.

A dark metallic shape flashed through falling snowflakes and struck Leki on the side of the head. She dropped like a felled tree, tall and straight, and the splinter of Aeon's heart rolled into the mud.

The Engine roared.

Sol's crawling fuelled his rage, provoked frustration, drove his daemon mind madder, and after the third circuit of the Engine and his dragging left leg getting tangled in bushes, he sat up and hacked it off. His right leg was not so badly damaged, but he hacked that one off, too. Then he sheathed his sword and started grabbing handfuls of ground, hauling himself south past the machine and in the direction the other Kolts had taken. Their victims would be his victims. Bloodlust drove him and the daemon within screamed, *More! More!*

He passed the Engine on his left, repulsed by its power and potential. He could not look at it, and the skin on that side of his face seemed to stretch and burn. Pain did not matter, but he closed his left eye to retain his sight.

The snow he crawled through changed from red and muddy,

to pure white, trodden only by the heavy boots of stampeding Kolts.

He left his own trail of blood, but a Kolt did not look back, not unless—

Sol heard the voices and shuffled around, half hidden by the deep snow. If he'd had feet, he would have stood and run at the voices. Something emerged from his mouth that might have been a chuckle. But he felt no mirth.

He saw them emerge from the snow shower to his right. They carried something bright, an object that might burn, but he would not turn away. Somewhere deep down he recognised the woman's face. It was a kill that he must make.

The pair paused close to the slew of dead people, and Sol seethed at the disgust on their faces. His daemon urged him to crawl at them, take them down, slash them apart. But something of his human nature remained as well, and that told him that he would never reach them as he was.

So he slumped down amongst the torn bodies and waited until one of them drew closer. Then he lifted himself on his left arm, plucked a throwing knife from his belt with his right hand, and flung it. His aim was true, and the woman fell with the handle protruding from the side of her head.

Sol screeched in delight and started crawling, hand over hand, ignoring what his hands sank into, and dragged his body across. Some of it was still warm. But he was focused on the woman he had dropped and the man running to her aid, because they were still fresh and alive. The thing she had been carrying had fallen into the mud. Its brightness forced against him, but his determination blinded and numbed him to its pain, his daemon madder and hungrier than ever.

The running man reached her first, glancing nervously at Sol as he went. But Sol did not pause to analyse threat or intent. He dragged what was left of himself forwards, and as he reached them he brought his sword around in a killing stroke.

The man stepped in front of the woman and lashed out with his spear. It connected with the sword and knocked it aside, but Sol's grip was solid. He struck the ground and rolled, then he threw himself at the man again. Sword and hardwood clashed, then the man's foot followed through, aimed at Sol's chin.

Sol dipped his head and felt the boot shatter one of his front teeth as it entered his mouth. Then he bit down hard, tasting mud and blood and snow in the boot's grip. He thrust up with the sword and heard a grunt, then started slashing left and right, his view blocked by the man's foreleg before his face.

Something hit his arm and drove it down against the ground. Sol bit harder, and the man screamed. Glancing to the left, Sol saw the spear through his hand, his arm pinned like a collector's insect.

He let go and rolled, hoping that the momentum would pull the spear free. But he felt and heard the crackle of breaking bones in his hand.

Lying on his back, Sol reached for the short knife he kept in his belt.

Gasping, foot and thigh wet with blood and hot with pain, Bon staggered against Leki and tripped backwards over her prone body. He fell hard and heard her grunt, relieved at least that she was still alive.

But the knife is in her head!

He had little time, no time, because the legless monster that had been her husband was even now trying to rip himself free from the spear, mutilating his hand even more as he lunged towards Leki.

431

'Bastard!' Bon shouted. He was shaking from the pain and fear, and now anger added to the rush that heightened his senses, pulsed through his muscles. He stood and looked around for a weapon, seeing a wide-bladed pike covered in blood and muck. Leaping for it, Bon was already swinging it as he turned back, bringing it around in a wide arc just above Leki's body.

The blade whispered through flesh and growled across bone as it opened Sol's throat to the elements.

His mouth fell open as he slumped down, but no sound emerged. Blood spurted from Sol's wound. He dropped the knife and tugged at the spear pinning his hand again, but his strength seemed to be leaving him. Each gout of blood made him weaker. He writhed, kicking with the ragged stumps of his legs, and Bon smashed the pike once more across his face.

Leki groaned, started shaking, hands and feet kicking against the snow-covered ground. Her groan went on and on, and Bon knew he needed to tend to her. But Sol was still alive, and still struggling.

Bon stepped past Leki and kicked Sol down. As he lifted the pike he felt a warm touch against his knee. Sol, weakened, was gripping him there, pulling himself upright and trying to bite his way into Bon's thigh.

He lifted the pike with both hands and brought it down hard onto Sol's shoulder. It entered at the base of his neck and Bon leaned with all his weight, driving the point down through the Kolt's chest and out of his stomach. Bon let go and stepped back, and Sol tipped onto his face in the snow.

His twitching decreased, and eventually he grew still.

Bon stepped around Leki and knelt by her side so that he could keep Sol in view. Then he saw for the first time the extent of what had happened to her, and all the breath went from him. Winded by confusion and grief, Bon cried out loud when Leki's hand found his, and squeezed.

'Bon!' she said. 'Get me to the Engine!'

The knife had entered her head just above her left ear. Only the handle and a finger's width of blade protruded. She still shook, and her left eye was filled with blood. But she was talking to him.

'Leki . . .' he said.

'Engine.'

'I'll help you,' he said, and he could not hold back the blurring of his vision.

'Bon . . . *Engine*.' She squeezed harder, insistent. 'Help me up. Guide me. And the heart . . .'

Bon picked it up from where it had melted a pool of snow, wincing at the heat against his hand.

'Tell me what to do,' he said. He eased her up and Leki stood, holding onto his shoulder but supporting her own weight. She raised her hand towards her head, and Bon held it, forced it gently back down.

'I can't feel.'

'Don't touch,' he said. 'We can't touch. We mustn't.'

Leki turned to look at the Engine, and the movement made her unsteady.

'There's a way in,' Leki said. 'Help me find it.'

You should be dead, Bon thought. *Your brains should be ruined, your skull shattered, your eye is full of blood.* But to say any of this might invite the inevitable, so he helped her walk cautiously across to the machine.

It sang and growled, its voice almost too deep to hear. If it weren't for Leki's courage, Bon would have turned and fled, running from this place until he dropped. Everything wrong with the world was here, and here stood the woman he loved with a knife in her head. He knew that Leki could drop at any moment.

Close to the Engine, she let go of Bon's hand. She stumbled only a little as she went forward, leaning against the metal construct for support. She nursed Aeon's element against her breast like a baby, then turned slowly to look back at Bon, her left eyelid drooping to hide her blindness.

'A way . . . in,' she said.

Bon nodded and circled the Engine. He stepped over bodies, picking up another spear in case some of them were still alive and ready to fight. But they were motionless and dead. Twenty steps later he had circled the Engine, and Leki looked even worse.

She leaned against the construct with her head tilted to one side by the weight of the knife. Her left eye was swollen with blood pressure, the lid almost completely closed, and her mouth hung open at an angle. She was shaking. But she was still alive.

'I can't find anything,' Bon said. The Engine had contours and seams and attachments and sockets, but nothing that resembled any sort of access. Each step he took, he'd felt that it was watching him. 'Is it initiated?'

Leki started to shake her head, then swayed. 'No . . . but . . .'

'But?' Bon prompted. *How long until she can't talk? How long until she falls?*

'Crex Wry . . . is pushing.' Leki leaned her forehead against the Engine. 'I think magic might . . . come through . . . soon . . .'

Bon stared at the Engine. *It sees me*, he thought, and compared to Aeon's glare this thing's scrutiny felt deep and dark.

'Top,' Leki breathed.

Bon climbed up, hating the feel of the thing – the metal was warm, and gave the impression of *giving*, like a fleshy body – yet fighting against it. With each handhold or foothold he cursed what it might contain. Muttering old Fade curses under his breath felt good, and in a strange way invoking the names of gods he did not believe in gave him comfort. Perhaps it took him back to his childhood, when there were no dangers and he always felt safe.

On top of the Engine he had to crawl carefully, avoiding short spikes and longer antennae that seemed to thrum as if recently struck with something metallic. At the Engine's curved apex he found what he was looking for. Snow melted the moment it landed there, and the metal was slippery and warm, like something just born. The hatch bubbled at the edges.

Something escaping from inside, Bon thought. He tried not to breathe in. Edged back. Looked for a handle on the hatch.

'Bon?' Leki called.

'Yes,' he said. 'Wait.' He turned to slide back down, but Leki was not waiting. She was climbing without care, head still tilted and left eye bleeding bloody tears. He wanted to hold her and care for her wounds, but there was no time for that. He knew there never would be again.

He reached out and grabbed her offered hand, helping her up onto the Engine's top and relishing her warmth. It was natural and sweet compared to the construct's heat. That was the warmth of something diseased.

'If we open the hatch and drop that inside—' Bon said, almost touching the thing Leki held against her chest. But he knew he was clutching, trying to grasp something that could keep him here, with her, for longer. What she said next settled things, and moved everything on towards a future neither of them could know.

'You need to open the hatch and then leave me,' Leki said.

Her voice was soft, unhindered by the hard blade buried in her skull. Head on one side, still she managed to give him a smile. Her last.

'I don't want to leave you,' Bon said. 'I've only just found you.'

'But I don't want you to die,' she said.

Bon turned away and attacked the hatch, biting back tears. Still they fell, splashing in the melted snow and merging with the water bubbling gently around the hatch's edges. The handle turned easily, and he lifted the metal cover open on soft hinges.

A warm breath wafted out, carrying the smell of something unknown. Bon closed his eyes, but none of the complex scents were familiar. The mystery of it was terrible.

He looked inside but it was dark.

Leki was shifting past him, gently but firmly shouldering him out of the way.

'Wait,' Bon said.

'No time.' Her voice broke, growing weaker. She sat on the edge of the hole, legs dangling inside. Then she looked at Bon one last time, left hand coming up and almost touching the knife's shaft. 'No time,' she whispered.

Bon was about to say something more, but Leki shuffled herself from the edge and dropped into darkness.

'Leki!' he gasped. He did not hear her strike the bottom. Neither did he hear her voice, crying out in pain, or surprise, or horror. He heard nothing. It was as if Lechmy Borle had been plucked from the world, and the only evidence that remained of her was the confusion of Bon's heart.

As he sat there bereft, and alone, something changed.

The Engine ceased its subtle vibrations. The scrutiny he had felt before faded, abandoning Bon to this blood- and body-strewn landscape. A moment of utter loneliness followed, in which the losses he had felt hit home afresh – Milian, tumbling from the tower with the truth still close to her heart; Venden, an awkward boy fleeing and becoming something else; and now Leki.

He sighed and it turned into a cry. It seemed a fitting theme to the scene before him.

But this moment of Bon alone was brief, because then the Engine began to assert its presence again. Rage gushed from it, so deep and profound that Bon tumbled from the Engine and struck the wet ground in his efforts to escape it. He was on his feet and running, leaping between the dead to begin with, then tramping through trodden snow, and finally sprinting across a glade of virgin snow, running, running, from the horrible thing behind him and knowing that he had only a short time before Leki's actions struck home.

Whatever she knew about the Engines, and whatever use Aeon had intended for that part of its heart, it seemed she had already made her move.

Bon had never known he could run so fast, and the thought of what he was leaving behind ironically sent him faster. He mourned Leki, the lover he had never made love with. And his good son Venden, lost to him years ago, and lost again to Aeon. Both were behind him, and his need to survive in their honour drove him on.

Snow fell more heavily. The ground began to shake, as though something huge chased him. Bon did not look back. Creatures were fleeing with him; flying, running, crawling, squirming. Most were small, but he heard larger animals thundering through the undergrowth and, once, a huge shadow passed overhead, a winged thing the likes of which he had never seen made ambiguous by the snow. A tadcat sprang past him, hissing and growling and swinging its spined tail, but not pausing to attack. Bon watched it go and ran on, not knowing what else to do.

Each time he thought of slowing, Leki's image appeared in his mind's eye – head tilted, knife protruding, the truth of her demise sparkling in her one good eye. She knew that to die now was her fate, but there were greater fates at work here. If he let himself die also, he would be failing her.

Something was building behind him. He felt its terrible weight and repulsion, shoving him onward through the snow, beyond the limits of his stamina, through the barriers erected by his doubts and fears. He ran and ran and then, way behind him, the Engine exploded.

A great hand lifted him and shoved him forward, up through the leaning and shivering tree canopy, and this time when he fell he was accompanied by other falling things, both living and dead.

The snow will deaden my fall, he thought, and then he struck the ground.

Bon Ugane felt nothing else but blackness.

Chapter 22

wise

Wake, Venden thought. *Wake . . . wake . . . wake . . .* And then he realised that Aeon *was* awake, and that its inactivity was due to something else.

Aeon was remembering those old things with which it had once wandered the land. Its memories were vague and diluted through unimaginable time, yet there was a pride and content-ment that felt shockingly human. There were also aspirations and fears, most of them old but some still relevant, and strong. There was sadness. And there was hope.

Hope that what it had done would suffice.

And then, behind this staggering mass of history and memory, Venden sensed the brutal power of Aeon's heart in sudden turmoil. Disgust flooded his mind, a sickening sensa-tion that he was surrounded by all that might be bad or rotten in the world, and Aeon's consciousness writhed where it lay. Its body and mind were both repulsed by what it sensed and felt. Far away, that part it had given became a loaded point of rapidly growing energy, its power shocking, and it sat at the centre of Crex Wry's burgeoning, pitch-black soul.

Ready to explode, and cleanse.

With a sigh, Aeon calmed and settled, and somewhere south of them a massive detonation rocked the land. Two more followed soon after, further away but even more impactful. The three blasts plunged seismic fingers deep down to the icy core of Skythe's heart and stirred it, rupturing connections, erupting pressured ice and giving violence, for once, to the land itself.

A distance grew around Venden, as if everything that Aeon had once been was expanding to fill an endless void.

What's happening? Venden asked. The distance threatened to consume.

Fading, Aeon said.

Dying? Venden wondered. But he was not afraid.

Only as much as we can ever die.

As Aeon drifted away, so did Venden, swallowed by the void and settled into nothing. But he knew that sometime – soon, or far into the future – they might wake again.

Following initiation, the Engine pushes them further and further along the beach. General Cove does not call it a retreat, but there is no other way to view the Spike's progress along the shore, then inland away from the Engine's spreading influence. The priest is dead, the rackers are dead, sand is melting, and to the north a snowstorm rages like a beast waiting to strike.

Cove sent scouts along the coast to contact the other Blades, and more scouts north, and north-west, to make contact with the other Engine and Sol Merry's Blade. None of them have returned. The Spike do not dig in, because they always have to be ready to move again.

There have been skirmishes with Skythians all along the coast. The forces are not large, and they are disorganised and easily fought off. But the small combats mean that no one can rest. The soldiers are tired, and the expanding influence of the Engines has started to inspire rumblings of discontent among the ranks. *Magic rises for us*, the voices protest, *so why must we retreat before it?*

Cove has many of the same concerns, but he is their general and cannot voice his worries. *All is going to plan*, he says. *This was all anticipated, and soon magic will be our tool in destroying Aeon, and returning the world to the rightful hands of the Fade.* He speaks these words with confidence, but his stomach does turns and jumps as he watches the Engine's influence scorch its way along the shoreline. He can only assume that the Engine further along the coast is doing the same, and the one to the north . . .

But when his scouts do not return, and his suspicions grow, and the discontent amongst his troops turns in some cases to outright questioning of their cause and method, Cove makes a stand. He calls an audience of the Bladers, and as they wait before him the ground begins to shake.

They look to the north.

A pillar of fire burns through the hazy atmosphere inland, illuminating snow clouds and sending colourful swirls of flame dancing through the air. Clouds boil, steam billows, and then the sound of the staggering explosion reaches them.

'Back to your Blades!' Cove commands. It is the last order he issues, and they are the last words the Bladers will hear.

Along the beach, out of sight around a headland where it stands amidst a sea of molten glass and drifting gas, the Engine erupts. Cove lives long enough to see the land itself rising, and the sea rising with it, as though the world is punching a fist from beneath to destroy some travesty.

Then all is fire as, in the majestic beat of Aeon's heart, Alderia's offensive force is wiped from the face of Skythe.

*   *   *

Venden as he might have been, tall and smiling in his Guild of Inventors graduation robes. At his side stood his Guild invention, a mechanism whose use was hidden, but which impressed Bon nonetheless. There was craftsmanship in its construction, and a gentle pride in the way Venden stood close to it, not quite touching. Perhaps it would win him a scholarship, perhaps not, but Bon was as proud as could be. Venden opened his mouth but could not speak, because this was not real.

Milian Mu as might have been, a smiling woman with love in her eye and a carefree demeanour. She sat beside Venden at the ceremony and had tears on her cheeks, thankful tears at what they had in their son, and in each other. There were no doubts here, and no shield between her dark secrets and the long, happy life ahead of them. Bon reached out to hold her hand, but she was not there.

Leki appeared across the Guild parade ground, a thin, fleeting shadow peering between the upright graduates and their many and varied inventions. Bon saw her and raised a hand to wave but Leki showed no sign of seeing him. She was motionless and not breathing – a statue, raised in honour of something none of those present knew – and the shadow of something protruding from her head chilled Bon's heart.

He looked to Venden and tried to catch his son's eye, but the boy was looking elsewhere.

He turned to Milian, but she was subsumed in sadness once more, and already falling away from him.

Bon closed his eyes on the vision, slowly, so that he retained a final glimpse of the young man and the two women he had loved.

And he opened his eyes onto a world in ruin.

Fire and ice. The two did not belong together, but as Bon staggered across the clearing to a pile of fallen trees at its edge, he struggled against them both. Fire stretched the skin on the back of his neck and probed his clothing, seeking flesh to seed itself in. It rose behind him like a solid wall at the end of the world, and though he guessed it to be several miles distant, it almost scorched the life from him with every breath he took.

Through the heat fell chunks of ice. Green and opaque with age, he had seen its like before. Deep in the land, where Aeon had lured them, Skythe's frozen depths had been an illustration of the hurt it had suffered centuries before.

Now the land was erupting and the ice raining down, and another hurt ensued.

Snow had ceased falling. Warm rain came down in its place. Trees had tumbled, some snapped off high up, others seemingly shoved by the same heavy hand that had flung Bon through the air. Reaching the shelter of the pile of fallen trees, he hunkered down behind them to assess his wounds.

There were many, but none appeared life-threatening. Lacerations, grazes, bruises, some cuts were filthy with mud, others seeping surprising amounts of blood. But now was not the time to tend himself. Chaos had taken Skythe, and the coast lured him.

Leki had told him to go that way.

Leki. She was gone. Whatever she had done inside that Engine, the resulting explosion had punched a hole in the land and set the air aflame. There was no sign of Aeon, and no indication that magic – that obscure force, blackened soul of an evil thing – had succeeded in manifesting. She had done Aeon's bidding, but at such a price.

Bon headed south through the fire-lit night, across a landscape that had been shattered and reshaped by the Engine's explosion. The further he went, the less he felt the effects of the huge fire. Ice still rained down around him, but in smaller chunks and quantities. He scooped melted snow to drink, and picked fruit from tumbled trees to eat. He had no way of telling whether what he ate was poisonous or not, but he did not care. If Skythe deigned to kill him after all this, there was little he could do to protect himself.

As morning dawned and the sun smudged itself against the smoke-filled sky, Bon collapsed in a heap to rest. He found a small cave in a rugged hillside, and though he sat warm and sheltered from the outside, he could not sleep. From the north came the sounds of thunderous impact, transmitted through the ground to kick up at him, as if the world itself was ripping open and spewing out its frozen guts. And to the south-east blazed another incomprehensible fire where another Engine had exploded. Miles across, miles high, there seemed to be an unnatural life to the blaze that Bon knew he must evade.

Stunned, numbed, he leaned against the cave wall and watched the colours of destruction dancing at the entrance.

After a small rest he set off again.

He walked through that day, and found the first dead Kolt just before nightfall. It wore a Spike uniform and was pricked in several places with heavy arrows, but these were not the cause of its demise. It was a thin, wasted thing, limbs and torso shrivelled, face drawn, eyes sunken and picked out by birds or insects. Its mouth hung open in an endless exhalation of rage, and Bon would not draw too close. It was dead, but still exuded malevolence. He passed it by and moved on quickly, glancing back several times while the body was still in view to make sure it had not moved.

He discovered several more dead Kolts, all in a similar state. Each was on its own, all had fallen in their drive southward, and many still clasped the weapons with which they had done so much killing. It was not the explosions that had ended these corrupted things, nor the many wounds they carried. They had simply burned out and withered away.

From the land of the dead, as he came close to the coast he began to meet the living. They were always Skythian, cowed and shy and terrified. He tried not to bother them, but he was hungry and thirsty, and they seemed adept at surviving in this changing land. He humbly accepted help from one small family, but felt no compulsion to remain with them. He was Alderian, however his heart might speak otherwise. Alderia was this land's great abuser, and when they did not kill him, he shed a tear of shame.

This land, so abused six centuries before, had been subjected to another calamity that must surely mean its end. A disaster initiated once again by the people of Alderia. When Bon's tears had dried, the shame remained, a constant presence inside. He knew he would never be able to reach in and tear it out, and he was glad for that. Someone had to take responsibility.

At the coast, little remained of the scattered communities. A tsunami had swept in from the sea and reclaimed the beaches and much of the low-lying ground inland. Everything was changed. Countless people were dead. He met few survivors, and those he did meet – all Skythian – were heading west, away from the great cataclysm that was still visible as a boiling tower of flame along the shore. Massive clouds of steam glowed from the chaos within.

From the north, the thunder of ice and the fading heat of another great explosion.

Bon followed the survivors.

Three days later he found a cave. It was a mile inland, sheltered from the sea breeze by a lip of rock, and it had once been home to others. There was a fire pit close to the entrance, and inside he discovered blankets and a sleeping roll, a blunted sword, some clothing and a few basic cooking implements. They were of Alderian origin, and Bon wondered who had lived here, and what perceived crime they had committed to deserve expulsion to Skythe.

Maybe they were alive; perhaps they were dead. Either way, all that remained of them here were a few roughly painted scenes on the walls deeper in the cave. They were of a man and a woman and two small children. Bon thought they were a girl and a boy, and the images made him sad. They gave evidence of an adult desperate to record his family, lest it fade from memory.

He wandered the area, gathering wood for a fire and considering what he might eat. He was not a hunter – not yet anyway – and he could find no fruit trees, so that evening he would likely go hungry. But by the time the fire was roaring, deeper in the cave he found fat grubs emerging as the heat filtered through to them, and he cooked them wrapped in heavy leaves. They were bland but filling.

From the north came the constant thunder of change. A grinding, cracking sound, as ice rose and then flowed. *It'll erase everything*, Bon thought. And he decided, as he bedded down, that might be no bad thing.

Dawn broke, Bon rose; during the night he had decided to stay. He was alone again, cast adrift with memories of extraordinary people, and the incredible things they had done.

Venturing back into the cave to view those old images afresh, he thought perhaps he might begin to paint. He hoped that if anyone ever discovered his images painted onto a cave wall, they might become wise.

Pursuing, pursued, as Juda worked his way south he began to understand.

He was guided by something inside that was not wholly him. This presence sat deep and quiet, yet asserted its influence. It was larger than him, and Juda fled and followed because he had no choice. To contradict was not permitted. This presence had calmed his dreams and given him proper sleep for the first time in his life, and for that he owed it a measure of loyalty.

There was little to the landscape here that he recognised, and he was several miles out to sea before he realised he had even passed the coast. The ice he walked over was thick and jagged, and when he came across a deep ice ravine and heard water surging and withdrawing deep down, he knew that he travelled over the ocean. He had left Skythe behind.

'What will I find on Alderia?' he asked the leaden sky. It had ceased snowing, but the threat of more snow was still heavy.

The presence inside did not reply, but he could sense something of its mood. Here was patience, an ancient contemplation of time as a means to an end. Here was fury at actions that had been taken against it, and pride in the way it had escaped that intended fate. Here was madness.

Juda shivered, but the shadow inside warmed him. It came forward, brief and powerful, to give him a glimpse of what it was, and what he had become . . . and he was awash with more magic than he had ever dreamed of. *I am everything I always sought, and all that I wanted to be.* Yet he had never felt so wretched. The immense and dreadful half-formed mind hid within his own, and he found hints of the truth. Perhaps it was letting him see this, perhaps not. But once seen he could not unknow.

His time in that old broken Engine had been centuries beyond counting, not days. Hidden away and protected, he had been a vessel for the hiding thing after its full re-emergence into the world had been sabotaged and halted. And now that ages had passed, and Alderia had moved on to whatever fraught future its false gods might have inspired, he was walking across the frozen sea to visit.

Juda carried the seed of Crex Wry. He would find someone, or something, in which to plant it. And then the people of the world would cower in fear of new rumours of old gods.

extras

www.orbitbooks.net

about the author

Tim Lebbon is a critically acclaimed, award-winning author of fantasy and horror novels and also writes screenplays. He has won the British Fantasy Society Award four times for his novellas and novel-length works and the Bram Stoker Award for his short fiction. His *New York Times* bestselling novelisation of the movie *30 Days of Night* also won him a Scribe Award. Tim writes full-time and lives in Monmouthshire.

Find out more about Tim Lebbon and other Orbit authors by registering for the free monthly newsletter at www.orbitbooks. net

interview

Have you always known that you wanted to be a writer?
I've always known that I wanted to write. But it wasn't until my late teens that I even entertained the idea of being a *writer*.

I've written stories since I could hold a pencil, and before that I probably told them. Analysing why that's the case is something I no longer do . . . not because I'm afraid of questioning the urge to tell stories, but because there's no easy answer. My grandmother always had a saying about why people are like they are: 'It's the way their parents put their hat on.' That might partly be the case here, because my folks always encouraged me to read from a very early age, and one of the first TV programmes I ever remember watching was *Doctor Who*. I always loved using my imagination, and stretching it, and that meant that I naturally loved telling stories. I did so all through my teens, starting dozens of novels, finishing a few. And then it struck me that because I loved doing this so much, maybe it's what I could do for a living. That took some time to achieve, but the efforts to get there are a large part of the reward.

But I also believe that people are wired a certain way notwithstanding any outside influences. Some people are born sports-people, or scientists, and some are born with a driving urge to tell stories.

You've now written two fantasy novels for Orbit. How does *Echo City* compare to *The Heretic Land*, and do they address similar themes?
The theme that runs through both novels is how religions and beliefs affect society, sometimes for good, sometimes bad. Both involve societies in decline. Both follow groups of people who might be able to save the day. But there are also big differences . . .

In *Echo City*, most of the action takes place in or below the city of the title. It's a very, very big place, but still I wanted the sense of confinement to be claustrophobic and unsettling. The idea that a civilisation could believe that their city was the whole world I found fascinating – similar to flat-earthers, or even people who believe we are a unique, inhabited island in a dead universe (I don't believe that at all . . .). Of course, most of my characters suspected that there was more beyond the toxic desert surrounding the city, even though recorded history denied this. And it is these people who confront the unknown with courage and open-mindedness. Oh, and there's also a big monster approaching the city from way, way down, where its oldest histories lie . . .

In *The Heretic Land*, it's a very big world in which events unfold, with wide tracts of virtually uninhabited land, all of it ringing with a sad history. There's not that sense of physical enclosure, although there are still blinkered beliefs and unwillingness to entertain wider, more startling possibilities . . . but not within my heroes, of course. They're the ones who see the light, and who struggle to keep it shining.

Although I'm perhaps better known as a horror writer, *The Heretic Land* is actually my sixth fantasy novel. They're all dark and grim, and I think my fantasy writing will always be informed by my horror-writing background. Fairies? Unicorns? If I *do* ever use them, they'll definitely have their dark sides.

Did the idea for *The Heretic Land* come to you fully realised or did you have one particular starting point from which it grew?
Very few of my books come to me fully realised. That's a huge part of the enjoyment of writing for me – if I knew the whole story before I'd even written the first sentence, I wouldn't get nearly as much enjoyment out of writing. Often at the end of the book my writing speeds up, because I'm keen to get to the end to see what happens! That was the case with *The Heretic Land* as much as anything I'd written. I've always been interested in the idea of sleeping and/or fallen gods (an idea I explored before in my novel *Fallen*). And I'm fascinated with the perception of gods, and the idea – so beautifully articulated by Arthur C. Clarke – that a being sufficiently advanced might be viewed as a god. I wanted to explore that idea, and the world of *The Heretic Land* built up around that. But it's as much about humanity's use and misuse of religion, as it is about the subjects of such beliefs.

What advantages and disadvantages do you see in using fantasy as the vehicle for your stories?

The main reason I love fantasy could be viewed as both – because I get to create whole new worlds! Some might find this daunting, and often it is. But it's also one of the most enjoyable elements of writing a fantasy novel for me. I have, quite literally, a blank canvas. And although I also know that my novel is going to feature very human characters, and landscapes that are at least partially recognisable, I also know that I'll be able to create whole new races, flora, fauna, societies, religions, politics . . . while at the same time commenting on our own.

And the thing is, I think the fantasy world is always so integral to the story I'm trying to tell that it would be impossible to tell it in any other way.

Do you have any particular favourite authors who have influenced your work?

There are many, and I'm sure any writer would tell you the same. But when asked this question, I always mention three particular writers from different parts of my life.

When I was pre-teen I read all the Adventure books by Willard Price, and I guess these gave me my love of adventure stories.

In my teens (and still to a large extent now), Stephen King was the main man. I sometimes go through difficult phases with my reading (maybe it's a middle-age thing), where I find it very hard to get into a book. But with King, I always know that once I pick up one of his novels, I'll be hooked.

In my mid-twenties I started reading Arthur Machen. Machen was a turn-of-the-century writer of esoteric, supernatural fiction who told some wonderful, chilling tales of wonder and terror.

Do you have a set writing routine and, if so, what is it?
My writing is built around my busy family life. My wife and I have two young children, so there's school, football, hockey, rugby, scouts, cubs, ballet. I tend to follow a normal working day – when my wife's in work and the kids are in school – but I do often work in the evenings, or sometimes at weekends if the deadlines are pressing. I'm also currently in training for a marathon and, more distant, triathlons, so there's all that to squeeze in. Anyway . . . a writer's *always* working.

Do you have a favourite character in *The Heretic Land*? If so, why?
I really like Lechmy Borle (Leki to her friends). She's strong, determined, complex, and she has dark depths which only become apparent as the book progresses. It's strange that I'd choose her because she's not actually a POV character . . . maybe that makes her that much more mysterious.

Some authors talk of their characters 'surprising' them by their actions; is this something that has happened to you?
I think for me it's usually the story surprising me more than the characters. My characters are carried along by the story, and as story isn't something I plot out to the nth degree, I think often they're as surprised as I am by a particular turn of events. I think that's a really good sign that the story has taken over, and it's important to give ideas their full range of scope and possibilities. Otherwise it's easy to hamper

yourself – or blinker your creativity, if you like – if you try to restrain a growing, living, breathing story to previously conceived ideas. A few pages of notes cannot amount to the three-dimensional, complex world you create when the actual writing begins. I listen to the story, and sometimes it takes me in directions I hadn't anticipated. And I love it, because, as I've said before, I'm often keen to get to the end of writing a book to see what happens.

Do you chat about your books with other authors as you're writing them, or do you prefer to keep the story in your own head until the first draft is complete?

I suffer what many close writing friends of mine suffer from – insecurity about my work. So if someone asks me what my new book is about and I throw a couple of sentences their way ('It's about a sleeping god who wakes, and the people who have an interest in why it's woken up'), I instantly go into panic mode. Is that it? What else is it about? Where's the story in that? Is it original enough? Haven't I read that novel before? What if it's rubbish? For this reason, I tend not to talk much about work in progress. There's partly that insecurity thing . . . and also the fact that I hate telling a story verbally before I've written and told it on the page. For the same reason, writing synopses doesn't fill me with glee, though I understand the need for them in business terms.

If you have to live for one month as a character in a novel, which novel and which character would you choose?

Well, as it would all be made up . . . I think I'd have to go for someone really, really bad. Randall Flagg from Stephen

King's *The Stand*. That's one novel that really fed my desire to be a writer, and Flagg has always been one of my favourite bad guys, both charismatic and brutal. And let's face it, he's pretty cool too. Cowboy boots, denims . . . the bad guys are always the cool ones. And I've never been cool. So yes, just for one month I'd be the Walkin' Dude.

What would you do if you weren't a writer?
I did have a day job for twenty years, but that feels like the hazy past now . . . almost another life. I think because writing has always been a part of me, I really can't think far beyond it. There's nothing I'd rather be doing, and nothing else I'd really want to do. But if realities shifted and I found myself in another version of my world, maybe I'd have learned an instrument when I was younger and I'd be in a band. A rock band, of course. Although the lack of hair might be a problem. Can't head bang when you're a baldy, see.

if you enjoyed
THE HERETIC LAND

look out for

VENGEANCE

book one of the Tainted Realm series

by

Ian Irvine

He's coming for me. There's no way out. He's going to take me to the cellar and they're going to hack my head open like Mama's and *there's no way out.* He's coming for me.

Round and round it cycled, as it had ever since Tali had read her father's horrifying letter this morning. To survive, she had to escape, though in a thousand years no Pale slave ever had. There was only one way to gain your freedom here – the way Tali's mother had been given hers.

'Your eyes are really red,' said Mia, arms folded over her pregnant belly. 'Something the matter?'

They were in the sweltering toadstool grottoes where they worked twelve hours a day, every day of the month, every month of the year. At times the drifting spore clouds were thick enough to clog the eyes.

'Stupid spores,' Tali lied. 'They gunk everything up.'

'You look terrible. Have a break; I'll do this row for you.'

'Thanks, Mia.'

Tali had woken in the middle of the night feeling as if a stone heart was grinding against her skull with every beat. And with each beat, brilliant reds and yellows swirled madly in her inner eye, like beams trying to find the way out of a sealed lighthouse until, with a spike of pain, they burst forth and she collapsed into sleep.

When the work gong had dragged her into wakefulness this morning, the inside of her skull felt bruised. She desperately needed to think, to plan, but now the colours were back, spinning like clay on a potter's wheel, and fits of irrational anger kept flaring. She had to restrain herself from smashing the toadstool trays against the bench.

He's coming for me and there's no way out. They're going to cut a hole in my head, just like Mama. No way out, *no way out!*

Tali pressed her cheek against the wet wall and after a minute the colours faded, the headache died to a dull throb. Take deep breaths and stay calm. Don't do anything silly. You've got time. He might not come for months, even years. Mama had been twenty-six, after all.

Her racing heartbeat steadied and Tali wiped her face. 'I'm all right now.'

'Be careful. The Cythonians are really agitated today.'

'Why?'

'I don't know. Keep your head down and don't attract attention.'

Tali managed a smile. 'When did *I* ever do that?'

'I'm always getting you out of trouble.' Shaking her head fondly, Mia turned away to her work.

The grottoes were a series of broad, low-ceilinged tunnels linked by arched doorways. Cages filled with fat-bellied fire-flies provided a bluish light that barely illuminated the walls, which were sculpted to resemble a forest by moonlight – a humid glen whose every surface was covered in fungi, like the grottoes themselves. The air was so heavy with their mixed earthy, fishy, foetid and garlicky odours that it made Tali heave.

The floor shook, grinding the stone trays against the benches. It had been shaking all day. What was the enemy up to in the secret lower levels? Was that why they were so touchy?

'Tali, *try* to look like you're working.'

'Sorry.'

Today's job, one of the worst of her slave duties, was de-grubbing the harvest. Tiered stone benches running the length of each grotto were stacked with trays of edible toad-stools and mushrooms, dozens of kinds, plus leathery cloud ear fungi and giant red puffballs as big as Tali's head. The puffballs had to be cut and bagged carefully lest they gush clouds of stinging flame-spores everywhere. In the darkest corners, tiny toadstools sprouted in clusters like luminous white velvet, though Tali wasn't fool enough to stroke them. They were delicious when properly cooked, but deadly to touch in their natural state.

Reaching between the brown toadstools in front of her, she found a red-and-yellow girr-grub by feel and crushed it, wincing as the sharp bristles pricked her fingers. After dropping the muck into her compost bucket she rinsed her hands under a wall spring. Last year she had sucked a sore finger covered in girr slime and spent the next three days throwing up the lining of her stomach.

Mia was humming as she worked. At least she could still dream. Tali's vow to hunt down her mother's killers had never faltered, but in ten years she had learned nothing more about them and this morning's revelation had extinguished all hope. This morning, her eighteenth birthday and coming-of-age day, Little Nan had given Tali the letter her father had written her mother only days before his own tragic death. The letter that made it clear Tali would be next to die.

Her hand clenched on the stone tray. 'It's not right!' she hissed.

'What?' said Mia.

'Our servitude! Living in terror every day of our lives. Sleeping on stone beds. Being flogged for a scowl or a side-ways look. Torn apart from our loved ones—'

'Don't say such things,' Mia whispered. 'What if the guards hear?'

Tali's voice rose. 'Worked to death in the heatstone mines, killed for no reason at all.' The blood was pounding in her head. 'We've got to throw off our chains and cast the enemy down.'

'Shh!' Mia slapped her hand over Tali's mouth. 'They'll condemn you to the acidulators.'

Tali yanked the hand away. 'If they try,' she said recklessly, 'I'll smash—'

Mia shook her head and backed away, her eyes wide and frightened.

A ululating whistle sounded behind Tali and she sprang aside, too late. The chymical chuck-lash wrapped around her left shoulder and went off, *crack-crack-crack*.

She staggered several steps, clutching her blistered, bloody shoulder, and through a drift of brown smoke saw Orlyk, the bandy-legged guard, scowling at her. A fringe of chuck-lashes swung from Orlyk's belt like red bootlaces and she was raising another, ready to throw. Most of the guards were decent enough, but Orlyk was an embittered brute and she had been in a foul temper all day. And if she'd actually heard what Tali had said—

'Lazy, Pale swine,' Orlyk grunted, her blue-tattooed throat rising and falling like a calling toad. 'Come the day when Khirrikai leads us to take back our land and we don't need your kind any more. Oh, soon come the day!'

Tali's head gave another throb. She fantasised about tearing the chuck-lashes from Orlyk's belt, driving her to the nearest effluxor with them and dumping her head-first into the filth.

'Tali!' Mia hissed.

Lower your eyes and say, 'Yes. Master.'

Tali shivered at the hatred in Orlyk's bulging eyes, then managed to regain control and forced out the sickening words, 'Thank you for correcting me, Master.'

She bowed lower than necessary. One day, Orlyk, one day! Tali knew how to defend herself, for she had practised the bare-handed art with Nurse Bet every week since her mother's murder, but raising a hand against a guard was fatal.

Orlyk snapped the tip of a chuck-lash at Tali's left ear, *crack-crack*, grunted, 'Work, slave,' and headed after another victim.

The pain was like a chisel hammered through Tali's ear. She lost sight for a few seconds, the colours in her head swirled and danced, then her returning sight revealed Orlyk's broad back as she approached the archway. Scalding blood was dripping from Tali's ear onto her bare shoulder, and blood-drenched memory roused such fury that she snatched up a chunk of rock.

'Tali, no!' Mia hissed.

As the guard passed the puffball trays, Tali hurled her rock twenty yards and struck a giant puffball at its base. It disgorged an orange torrent of flame-spores, but then the shockwave set off a hundred other puffballs and she watched in horror as the guard disappeared behind churning spore clouds. When they settled, Orlyk was convulsing on the floor, choking, her face and throat swelling monstrously.

'Are you insane?' hissed Mia. 'If she dies . . .'

'I didn't mean that to happen,' Tali whispered.

'You never do.'

'Sorry, Mia. I'm really sorry.'

Mia ran down the far side of the bench, picked the rock out of the puffball tray and tossed it out of sight. Reaching up to the clangours beside the archway, she struck the square healer's bell with the ring-rod. The bell's chime was picked up by trumpet-mouthed bell-pipes running across the ceiling, and shortly Tali made out an echo from outside. Mia came back, glaring at her.

'I'm not taking it any longer,' Tali said defensively. 'If I have to die, I'm not going quietly.'

'Leave me out of it,' Mia snapped.

Shortly a lean, austere Cythonian, the red, linked-oval cheek tattoos of a healer standing out on his grey skin, ran in. 'What happened?'

'Puffballs went off spontaneously,' Mia lied.

He inspected the tray of burst puffballs and the thick layer of orange spores surrounding Orlyk, then stared at Tali. She kept working, watching him from the corner of an eye. Her cheeks grew hot.

'I tried really hard,' Tali said under her breath once he had turned to Orlyk. 'But when she hit me with the second chucklash—'

'I told you not to draw attention to yourself.'

'Mama died because I didn't act quickly enough, and I'm never—'

'Shh!' said Mia.

Several slaves appeared on the other side of the archway, pretending to work while looking in sideways.

'You!' called the healer to the nearest slave, a thin girl with stringy yellow hair and eyes that must have seen a nightmare. 'Run to the spagyrium. Get a sachet of blast-balm and a large head bag, quick!' He handed her a rectangular healer's token made from shiny tin.

'B-blast-balm and head bag, Master,' she said, head dutifully lowered.

'*Large* head bag.'

'Master!' She ran out, sweaty feet slap-slapping on the stone floor.

The healer dragged Orlyk away from the spore-covered area, dampened a cloth and began to clean the spores out of her eyes, mouth, ears and nose. Orlyk's face was scarlet, the swollen skin shiny and balloon-taut. Clotted sounds emerged from her throat as her lungs struggled to draw air.

'Pray she's all right,' Mia said from the corner of her mouth. 'If she dies—'

Tali could not meet her eyes. Why had she been so stupid?

The slave reappeared, panting, and handed the healer a clear bag made from the intestines of an elephant eel. The healer pulled it over Orlyk's head, inflated it with a small bellows, pulled the string on a pillow-like sachet of blast-balm, inserted it inside the bag and held the bag closed around Orlyk's tattooed neck while he counted to five.

A loud, wet *flupp* sounded, like gas bubbles bursting at

the top of the squattery pits. Mustard-yellow vapour swirled inside the head bag, then it shrank tightly against Orlyk's head. After a minute the healer peeled the bag off, thumped Orlyk in the chest and she took a gurgling breath. Red blisters protruded through the coating of yellow balm but the swelling was already going down.

As the healer and the slave girl carried Orlyk out to the Healery, her black eyes fixed on Tali and, with a convulsive snap of the wrist, Orlyk hurled another chuck-lash. Tali ducked, it soared over her head and struck Mia on her swollen belly, *crack-crack-crack*.

Stifling a cry, Mia pressed both hands to her wildly quivering belly.

Tali ran to her. 'Are you all right?'

Mia nodded and took her hands away to reveal a red and white welt as long as a finger. 'Only the tip caught me. Lucky.'

'Lucky,' said Tali, guilt churning in her. 'Let me heal—'

'Someone's coming.' Mia began to squash girr-grubs as though it was her sole delight.

Tali did the same. A replacement guard came in, stared at her for several minutes, then went into the next grotto. Through the archway, a toothless slave was scattering compost onto trays of mauve, curly-tipped Sprite Caps. One cap could cure the worst toothache within minutes; three caps would cure life almost as quickly. It was not unknown for desperate slaves to take that way out.

'We got away with it.'

Mia touched the welt on her belly and winced. She was paler than usual, and in evident pain. Her belly was churning, the muscles clenching and unclenching.

Any other slave would have sworn at Tali, or slapped her. Tali wished Mia would do the same. Anything would be better than this sickening shame. But Mia was too nice, too gentle. She reminded Tali of her mother.

'I'm really sorry, Mia. I just snapped.'

'What is it with you? You've been acting strangely all day.'

'You know what happened to Mama?'

'You've told me at least fifty times,' said Mia. 'You never stop talking about it.'

Tali hadn't realised. 'Well, according to Father's letter, Mama's mother, grandmother and great-grandmother were also killed the same way, and now I've come of age I'm marked to be next. Every time someone looks at me, every time I see a stranger pass by, I think they're the one. I can't take it any more. I've got to—'

'Shh!' Mia jerked her head towards the archway.

Tali glanced at the old slave. 'Suba's no harm. She's simple.'

'I think she's a *kwissler*.' An informer.

Tali moved out of Suba's sight and pressed her hand against the welt on Mia's belly, beginning the charm Nurse Bet had taught her when she was little. Most Cythonians turned a blind eye to healing charms, since they weren't real magery, though a vengeful guard might still chuck-lash you for using one.

Healing charms were all Tali could do. She had practised her mother's gentle magery every night since her death, but it never worked. Tali's own gift had only come a handful of times, always when she was furious, though it was neither gentle nor controllable. It exploded out of her, wreaking unintended ruin, then vanished for years. Was that because she was so afraid of it?

To save herself and beat the enemy her mama had spoken of, the one that had fluttered in her nightmares like a wrythen, Tali had to find her buried magery and learn to control it. She had to find it fast, but who could she ask?

Trust no one.

Death is Only the Beginning

COLDBROOK

TIM LEBBON

**THE WORLD AS WE KNOW IT HAS CHANGED
THE REASON IS COLDBROOK**

The facility lay deep in the Appalachian Mountains, a secret laboratory called Coldbrook. Theirs was to be the greatest discovery in the history of mankind, but they had no idea what they were unleashing.

Now the disease is out and ravaging the human population. The only hope is a cure and the only cure is genetic resistance, an uninfected person amongst the billions dead. In the chaos of global destruction there is only one that can save the human race.

But will they find her in time?

11/10/12

http://coldbrook.rhgd.co.uk/

HAMMER